THE REACH

For Dan & Linda,
Now remember; the only
way to tell a true
Hemmingway 1st Edition is
by the mistakes!
[illegible]

THE REACH

By

Sprague J. Theobald

ISBN 1-58500-566-5

1stBooks – Rev. 1/26/00

For Kimberly Ann
… and Sefton

ABOUT THE BOOK

The Reach 3,000 feet below them, hiding in the black night of underwater caverns, the Dead Ones followed the small boat as she sailed on towards England.

The year is 1860, the town is Chester, Rhode Island and a young English girl has done the unspeakable; after ten brutal years of scullery duty, she has turned her back on the Mansion Elmwood and has gained passage back to her family in England. 160 years later, in the fall of 1990, two men prepare to deliver a forty foot sailboat from Chester to Plymouth, England.

Three sets of lives hang in delicate balance as the wandering soul's who inhabit the Atlantic's black depths play cat and mouse with those who dare to cross over their realm.

Katherine Worthington is desperate to get back to the love and spirit of the family she left as a young girl in England. Risking the wrath of her employer and fellow house servants, she leaves her position at one of Chester's more ducal mansions and with what money she has managed to salt away, strikes off to purchase passage back home. Entrusting her future into the callused and impersonal hands of a working New England seaport she soon finds herself aboard the 110 foot packet *Galatea*, where from the depths of the Atlantic, forces unholy seek to cut her return short and keep her as one their own.

Over one hundred and fifty years later, Chris Barlow and Paul Dwyer, two drop-outs from the nine-to-five workings of the corporate world, are trying to give their fledgling boat delivery business a jump start. They agree to deliver *Curlew*, a forty foot sloop 3,500 miles across the dangerous North Atlantic to England. It is a risk proposition as dwindling bank accounts, an absent owner with hidden agendas, seasonal hurricanes and forces inhuman conspire to block the way.

Built from a foundation of strong characters portraying a historical depiction of maritime life then and now, tying three lives together over a 160 year gap, examining life at sea and life ashore, from the sublime to the surreal, The Reach is a novel which address the hidden terrors which inhabit the depths of the Atlantic as well as the limitless love to be found in the human soul.

CHAPTER 1

1990: Fall Something was missing.

Some very basic part of my morning was clearly missing and I knew that if I didn't come to grips with it soon, there was not much point in getting out of bed.

Try as I may I couldn't put my finger on it. If I was still a smoker, it would be about now that I'd reach over to my bedside table, a shipping crate, and light up a butt. Sitting up a tad I took a quick visual inventory and judged by the usual scattering of dirty clothes, sailing magazines, marine hardware and foul weather gear which lay about my bedroom that the answer to my dilemma was going to have to be found in either my small living room or smaller kitchen.

There was no point in checking my day calendar, just as there was no point in my tuning into the weather broadcast and listening to the marine forecast for the day. Clearly something was missing and until I figured out just what was nagging at me so, nothing of much worth was going to get accomplished today.

Hoping to find a clue outside, I propped myself up on my side and pushed a water stained linen curtain out of the way. I gazed out of my window onto a still and flat New England harbor which I had the good fortune to call home. Everything out there seemed just as it should be, nothing amiss, yet some missing element of my usual morning waking held my full attention and I was damned if I knew what it was.

Sitting up fully in bed I took a longer and more appreciative look out onto the new day. The harbor was where it had always been and the boats that were still out there were resting comfortably at their moorings slowly circling the compass, decks and teak glistening with morning dew, waiting for the land to heat up and draw in the new southwest breezes of the day. Focusing my attention back inside I looked about at my immediate surroundings; as comforting as the faded rose-patterned wallpaper and well worn wide plank flooring of my bedroom were, they offered up no answer to my quandary.

I live on the second floor above what was at one time a very active ship's chandlery for what was then known as The Township of Chester Rhode Island. Where Dunbar's Chandlery once provided Chester with mast hoops, pine pitch, hemp and lamp oil, Skinner's Chandlery now offers global position satellite receivers, radio direction finders, personal flotation devices and emergency position indicating radio beacons, all state-of-the-art navigation gear. My apartment is unique for this small seaside community in that it has always been an apartment, and wasn't simply a storeroom which was converted years later in order to try and pull in a few extra dollars for an absent landlord.

I really hated to start a morning like this, clearly feeling as though I were somebody's punch line. If I owned a car, right about now I'd be trying to remember if I parked it in a tow zone last night. I didn't, so, I knew that I hadn't. If I had a nine to five job, I'd be feeling the effects of the adrenal rush from sleeping through my alarm, but nine to five and I had a falling out sometime back. Yet the feeling persisted. I had paid the rent, I had put off the dentist for yet another two months, I didn't have to stretch far to know that I was predictably alone in bed once again. I had met with my chiropractor the day before and I had long since given up breakfast meetings. List B: alimony had been paid, no dog to take to the vet, -- she got him too-- and as far as I could remember I hadn't made any promises to be somewhere I obviously wasn't.

As I lay there I tried to figure out just what it was that was determined to push me out of the wrong side of my bed. It felt as though the new day was daring me to join it, but clearly it was going to call the tune. From my perch in bed, I could see down my narrow hall, past the single- burner kitchen and out into my living room. No answer there. I did notice that the wood stove in the kitchen was in need of a good dusting.

I decided to get out of bed and investigate this mystery further, but not before the clickings from the phone/answering machine on my shipping crate announced that some un-invited voice wanted to speak to me. Bar none, the most valuable invention of modern man has been not the answering machine itself but the small button on the side which kills the ringer and keeps it from making a person drop what they were doing and jumping to its Pavlovian demand. I had an absolute phobia about ringing telephones and I found that the road to peace of mind started with that miraculous button. I would usually hang around just long enough to hear who was leaving the message and then decide if it was worth dealing with. By this method I could successfully put off my ex-wife looking for her check, my ex-wife's lawyers looking for her check and banks calling to tell me that checks written in the name of the aforementioned ex-wife had a wee bit of trouble clearing. Breathing room was all that I was after and man's greatest invention of the twentieth century afforded me just that. This time I hung around just long enough to hear that it wasn't anything to do with matters marital or financial. Those things I could have handled.

"Chris, pick up. Chris, it's me, pick up. Fine. Look, I know you're there so you're going to have to listen anyway."

I sank back into my bed and pulled the sheets up over my head. It was my sister. We never quite figured out just where my sister Ellie came from. As best as I could see it, she was a changeling at the hospital. For generations the Barlow family boasted tall, fair haired children with the classic chiseled Yankee features. Ellie boasted the stoic features, but lacked the height and the fair hair. When she was born she was substantially underweight. She was healthy, but barely tipped the scales at three pounds. My parents felt that this dark-haired wonder might be at a disadvantage as she belonged to a family whose average height was 5'8". Their compassion and concern lasted almost through the third week of her life, for once she managed to get the general lay of the land, our home was never the same. Locked firmly in the bosom of a household which was publicly steeped in discretion and loaded with New England after-you-isms was a child who should have been bartering rugs in a Mideastern bizarre. Ellie was an exhausting, bottomless source of energy. As a child, if she didn't rearrange my bedroom on a bi-weekly basis, I knew that real trouble was brewing elsewhere. I was three years her senior but that edge failed to give me any sort of advantage.

"Chris, I ran into Ed Brecker at one of the Law Review functions last night," she said, "and he said that you should give him a call. His brother's production company is beginning to take off. Weddings and Bar Mitzvahs for now, but they have a shot at some sort of cable contract and he thinks that there might be some room for you," she said referring to my past life as a worker bee in the broadcast industry. "If I don't hear from you on this by the end of the working day I'll assume that you got this message and will set up a meeting."

Ellie was fully aware that at one point in my life I worked as a television producer but for reasons of personal pride never fully recognized my abilities. The morning after I won my first Emmy Award, I did what I promised myself I wouldn't do and called her with the good news. Without missing a beat she asked if there was a cash award with it. I should have seen that one coming. I didn't call her after winning my second Emmy Award and by the time my bleeding ulcer announced itself, the only call I made was to my immediate superior to announce my early retirement. Ellie never understood the logic behind that one.

"Hey, kiddo," I said as I picked up the phone, "I was in the other room and thought I heard your voice on the speaker. What's up?"

"You're screening your calls again. Look, I'm not going to go through it for a second time. It's a chance at some real work for you and you'd be crazy not to follow it up. Play the tape back and listen to it. This Wednesday is Mom's birthday and it wouldn't kill you to send her a card. Check your schedule and tell me if you can give me a ride to the airport day after tomorrow."

"No need to check," I stammered, "I can tell you now that I won't be around, I have to take a boat down for the Annapolis used boat show." After the first lie, they rest start to flow so easily. The truth was that in years past I had made the trek down to the Chesapeake Bay to either drop off or pick up a boat which was going to be featured in this floating used car lot. This year however, I was to remain in Chester, a decision which I was starting to regret.

My sister knew how to give pause on the phone better than anyone I had ever dealt with. Several times I tried to wait out her waiting and came close to screaming out anything she wanted to hear. No one could live through her silences. In the past five years things between Ellie and I had been a bit more pointed than usual. My decision to start sailing again was not a popular one with what was left of my family. As much as I missed my father, when it came to this I was glad that he was dead. He would not have been amused at my new attack on life. My mother took it, as usual, in stride: "I'm sure you know what you're doing." But the real fireworks came from Ellie. She gave freely of her opinion that for one, I had walked out on a brand new career, failing yet again to acknowledge the fact that I was with the station for ten years, nine years past "brand new," and two, it was I who had mentally walked away from my ex-wife Carolyn months before she physically walked away from me. The pit bull lawyer side of Ellie prided itself on calling them as she saw them, the clutter of family loyalties and sisterly pride simply falling by the wayside. Finally punching in at number three, in her words mind you, I was fooling no one by wanting to spend my life at sea sailing around in ever widening circles, determined to avoid responsibility and reality.

"Look, Ellie, let me see if I can get a ride for you."

Pause.

"Ah, I'll check my calendar, maybe I've got the dates screwed up."

Longer pause.

"Look, I don't really think I can actually get out of the delivery but I'm pretty sure that I can get you a ride."

Her longest yet.

My nervous laughter. "Hello?"

Silence.

"It's really quite a boat, you'd love it."

More silence.

I was on the verge of disgracing myself. "You know, maybe someday you'd like to come along for one of the shorter trips. It'd be great to have you along." Total disgrace.

Every once in a while my faith in God is given a real boost and at that moment an epiphany couldn't have stood me better. The click of the phone company's call waiting brought me nearer my God to thee.

"Hold tight, kiddo, let me get rid of this call."

Somebody wanted the optical department.

"Ellie, I've got to take this, let me get back to you."

"I'm sure you will. I'll be here, bye."

As I put the sweaty hot phone back into its cradle, I could feel the familiar bead of sweat starting its long cowardly trip down the middle of my back. My hands were wet and my ears were starting to ring. Ellie had done it to me again. One of these days she was going to make a hell of a judge.

Ellie's call reminded me that no matter how far away from family I felt I was, their presence is always felt. Take the dilemma to which I awoke this morning. Our mother used to refer to this feeling as waiting for the other shoe to drop and would easily dismiss it as that, nothing more. She was tough, stoic and practical to more than one fault. The woman had the ability to let injustices roll off her back like so much water. Her core was wrapped with New England pragmatism, which at times made her seem to me more demanding than unreasonable. This was a woman who would have to be pushed to great lengths in order to show emotion, any emotion. My mother was not what you'd call a tactile woman, she bordered on cold. Her power was swift and sure. Her trademark was her eyebrows. When one of these was raised in your direction, no pleading, whimpering or groveling could successfully plead your case. If you were ever in the death seat, receiving a double barreled raised eyebrow assault, well, as the old sea shanty goes, "You'd wish to God you'd never been born."

I could have used my mother's eyebrow power this morning as things were clearly not falling into place. Life needed a good zap. Getting out of bed I went into the dark bathroom, raised the shade on the white sunlight of yet another New England day, put toothpaste to brush and started my morning rituals.

Looking out the multi paned bathroom window as I brushed my teeth, the street traffic below my second floor apartment assured me that my day had already started without me. My town of Chester was awake and running.

Chester's harbor has always been one of her better modern day assets as its natural oval shape keeps her well protected from Atlantic storms. The downside of this is a shallow granite shelf which runs along the bottom at harbor's entrance. During the eighteenth and nineteenth centuries, this shelf kept out her fair share of larger ship traffic, a fact that was nearly Chester's undoing.

It was the trade from the smaller coastal shipping packets which the town courted so aggressively. Never being able to compete with the larger ports up and down the coast, Chester lived a hand to mouth existence.

When steam sounded the death knell of trade under sail, Chester found herself slowly crawling away from the edge of the void of obscurity, a void from which one of the more valuable resources of the twentieth century was born: the seasonal invasion of day-tripping tourists who come to get a glimpse of how the simple life must have been before they spent weekends going off in the car to invade towns that showed how simple life must have been before all the above.

As Chester eased into the twentieth century she started to come into her own, the powerful and distinguished money crowd from cities as far away as New York started to discover her. As Chester started to bring in money, her profile began to reflect this change. Over the years the area which stood the most commanding view of both the Atlantic and Chester's protected harbor, Knowles Hill, was to be the home of as lavish and decadent lifestyle as any had witnessed up until that time. It was a lifestyle of sheer decadence only to be muted by the First World War, and the stock market crash. As with the great agricultural Dust Bowl of the West, the inhabitants of Knowles

Hill were driven to their financial knees and were forced to sell what they could and simply walk away, leaving their palaces and places of business silent shells. Those buildings that could be neither pizza parlors nor T-shirt emporiums were either torn down and tarmaced over for parking lots, or now boast several fresh coats of paint and a plaque attached to the front allowing as to how something or someone knee-high in our country's adolescence either took place there, built it, was born there, slept there or died there.

And herein lay the answer to this morning's mysterious angst. Funny how in the space of a second the human mind can run through a seemingly random series of thoughts that would otherwise take ten minutes to explain to anyone polite enough to sit and listen, but that was exactly what happened. As I stumbled down the short hall from bathroom to kitchen, I remembered that I had no more of my loose-leaf Earl Gray tea, without which no morning could start. The day before I knew full well that I had run out of my tea and that I was going to be looking for some this morning, but seeing as yesterday was Labor Day, all the stores in Chester would be jammed with people all vying for quickly dwindeling goods. I opted to lay low until today, the day after Labor Day, the day when the stores would once again be approachable, the crowds would be gone and the streets of Chester would gratefully be back in the hands of those who loved her. That was exactly what was missing from my morning; the din of traffic from the street below my bedroom window. No tour bus passed under my window at 7:30 AM announcing the ever changing facts about Chester's rich if not decadent legacy, a legacy which grew richer with every bored bus driver's telling. Silent were the horns from the out-of-town cars followed by the loud, intrusive demands couched as questions from the out-of-town drivers of these out-of-town cars. But lest I bite the proverbial hand, I'd best explain why it was that this particular day after had such special meaning for me.

I am what you would call an anachronism. Actually that's what I'd call myself. Others have called me everything from an escapist to a man who simply refuses to grow up. After many pointless years of banging my head against the ungiving walls of television broadcasting I now try to make my living on sailboats, yachts, anything which floats. More to the point, I try to make my living off of those who would like to make their daily lives a bit richer, and perhaps their social standing a tad higher by owning very expensive boats. I try to help these R.O.s, rich owners, achieve their daydreams -- spending sun drenched, leisure filled days drifting away at sea.

It's for this reason that I was now stepping around and sorting through a myriad of spare boat parts which lay scattered about the green linoleum of my sloping kitchen floor. Having the money to own a sailboat in excess of forty feet doesn't necessarily mean that you know anything about that sailboat or just how to keep that sailboat in proper nick. I'm sort of an alter ego. I am also half owner of a small but growing yacht management and delivery service which had its birth in the summer days of my childhood not a day's sail down the coast. As a child I was always the happiest when wandering and working in boat yards. So much so that it was what I wanted to do as an adult, own my own yard. But, after many so-called aimless summers, my family, common sense and college had their way with me and my dreams and I slowly slipped away from the challenges of the Gulf Stream, took a wife and landed in the mainstream of corporate television broadcasting. Slowly I found that I was inexorably becoming the sort of person I always held in great disdain.

In the 1850s, Melville wrote,

> Whenever I find myself growing grim about the mouth; whenever it is a damp, drizzly November in my soul . . . whenever my hypos get such an upper hand of me, that it requires a strong moral principle to prevent me from deliberately stepping into the street, and methodically knocking people's hats off -- then, I account it high time to get to sea as soon as I can.

Against all corporate, not to mention marital convention, I

took the man at his word. After great deliberation with a six-pack of beer on a seawall, I came to the realization that if I was to mind my future financial Ps and Qs, I could perhaps move into something that was totally different, offered totally less pay, but was totally me. Looking back on it, perhaps it was the beer talking.

It's been said that a man who would go to sea for a pastime would go to Hell for pleasure. I knew Hell, I was missing pleasure. I gathered up my forces, said my good-byes, handed in my three weeks notice, fell fifteen years short of my twenty-five year retirement, took leave of my department, reclaimed the sensibilities that I had left at the door some ten years earlier and started my journey to find the love I left over a decade ago, if she would have me back. I wanted to be back working on the water with boats. I once again started to haunt boat-yards looking for part time work.

For reasons still unclear to me, my now ex-wife found that she could no longer be associated with a man who wasn't locked in servitude to catching the 7:10 each morning. After splitting the proceeds on Barlow Manor and practically anything else that wasn't nailed down, I traveled up the road from Coopersville and landed here in Chester where my fledgling yacht management and delivery business of five years is hoping to someday come into its own, a state in which rich customers beat a path to my doorstep instead of my having to go in search of them. But until the arrival of that day, I had to get out and start pounding the wharves once again in search of new ways to get me offshore and more importantly, to get my bank balance breathing on its own again.

Truth be known, what I was desperately in search of at this particular moment was a cup of tea.

It was time to hit the docks.

As I started my way down toward the yards the sense of relief was nothing short of immediate. For the first time since Memorial Day I didn't have to slide between opposing baby strollers, dazed families in search of more ice cream, paramours tucked behind seemingly full scale maps of Chester and the usual aimless wanderings of the other dregs from other towns who had nothing better to do than add to the congestion and confusion of my town while drinking a beer out of a Big Slurp mug.

Another autumn was blowing in off the harbor and how smug I felt not having to share it with anyone. Shopkeepers had that well fed glaze in their eyes as they opened shop for the day and started to tally just what their products and patience had put into their coffers after yet another summer season in hell. This was the time of year for which we all waited, for which we all suffered through the tourist season. No traffic, no congestion, no lines. Old friends once again began coming out of their forced summer hibernation's. The die-hard and truly dedicated sailors were starting to plan their fall cruising schedules: Tarpaulin Cove, Woods Hole, Hadley's Harbor, canal transit, Cape Elizabeth, Boothbay Harbor, Monhegan, all within a two-day sail and now starting to experience their own thinning summer crowds as well.

Heading down Aubery Street, past the trinket shops, past the time-sharing condo units and on toward Chester's few remaining boatyards, I could hear a familiar rhythmic song coming from a distance off. It drew my attention to the right, down through the narrow alley which ran between the brick buildings and out on to the harbor. Here the ringing of halyards slapping against their masts were no longer in competition with the summer's traffic. What my intuitions had been trying to tell me since 7:00 a.m. this morning, my eyes now confirmed; the sight of empty moorings in the harbor was the final proof that it truly was The Day After. At the peak of the summer season one could almost walk across Chester Harbor by hopping from deck to deck. Many of these boats were now headed back to their own home ports, soon to be hauled and readied to spend the next seven months in yards of their own, out of their element.

During Chester's heyday, one had a choice of fifteen shipyards that could tend to anything marine. Now there were three. The press of developer's cold hard cash brought an end to the others. The three remaining yard owners who didn't buckle under to fast money were actually experiencing better times.

Beckman's, who was in Chester since the beginning, was in the catbird seat with the only 40-ton travel lift for twenty miles up or down the coast. Gufstason's Yard still handled its share of the commercial fishing fleet and was clinging firmly to the principal that once Chester lost all her commercial contracts, the last nail would be put into her coffin. Which left Pachico's Yard. Barely boasting a bathroom for his clients but with plenty of Portuguese determination and strong business savvy, Fee Pachico was not only managing to keep his head above water, he was actually pulling ahead in the race. Fee also offered two things which neither of the other two yards could and these were his ace in the hole: Madeline, his bookkeeper, and, across the street, Eagle's Lunch. With one you were guaranteed a warm reception and a good meal, the other was as sobering and belittling experience as they came but oddly enough had you coming back for more.

"Chris, Paul's been looking for you all morning" Quint, the owner, cook, waitperson of Eagle's said as the hot mug of tea landed on the counter in front of me. "If you guys are still planning on heading out in a few weeks, I can order some extra canned stuff for you."

Having Eagle's across the street from Fee's yard was a godsend for reasons not only practical, as Quint would order food for our trips through his supplier, but for reasons social as well. As with any small community, news which spreads fastest spreads by word of mouth and Eagle's was more times than not the best place to get things off and running.

"Got tied up on the phone with Ellie again." Though no one had actually had the chance to meet her, the usual crowd at Eagle's was well versed with my sister's weekly edicts.

"Sorry."

"Say where he was headed?" I said as I started to sip my tea.

"Just ordered some coffee and then bolted out of here talking about going to Dutton's to buy some return trip flights. Said you were to sit tight 'til he called."

"Shit, Jasperson's going to take care of the tickets. His boat, he buys."

Paul Dwyer was my delivery partner. We had first met in

Cooperville at the ripe ages of nine and ten, I being the senior of the group. We had been childhood friends, sailing partners, comrades in arms. Four years ago we had the great fortune to cross paths on the streets of Chester some twenty-five years after his family moved away from New England. I don't know why I didn't recognize him immediately. Even as a boy the man sported a set of eyebrows which were more one than two. A "monobrow" I used to call it and it was from under this furry roof that the familiar deep brown eyes studied me. I came to the remarkable realization that contrary to the man's statement of not being able to go home again, I found that that was just exactly what I was slowly beginning to do. Many hours and several beers later Paul and I discovered with great joy that we still shared the same philosophy on life -- non-philosophy was actually a more apt description. We both agreed that life would have at you as she wanted and no matter what you said or did, she was most assuredly going to have the final word. We found that the best way to get along with her on a daily basis was to offer no resistance and get by as best one could. A posture which made for great drawn-out fireplace conversations, but in practice was hard to stick to. I learned that Paul had given up a mediocre career in real estate in our nation's capital a few years back after he realized that all the financial rewards of a particularly tricky sale were being doled out to the nonparticipants. Rather than fight and claw his way through a system which had been around long before him and was quite capable of continuing on after him, he took his cue, pulled in his shingle and headed north, bound for a better life in Camden, Maine. He stopped off to see some friends in Chester for the weekend. That was four years ago, and like most of us who came to Chester to lick our wounds, he stayed. He and I picked up exactly where we left off those many years ago. Soon we were getting together on a regular basis reminiscing about races never won and summer loves never consummated, a fact only secure in the telling some twenty-five years later.

We had been managing and delivering boats together now for the past four seasons and oddly found ourselves to possess the right strengths to match the other's weakness. He hated to wash dishes, I hated to cook. He loved to navigate, I had an ongoing love affair with the foredeck. We both felt that if indeed there was a God, he lived off-shore and that the green flash was something which only occurred when your back was turned, proving once and for all that Mother Nature did have a sense of humor.

Barlow & Dwyer was now at a pretty heady crossroads, for we were now two weeks away from the big one. We had been hired to deliver a forty foot sloop, 3,000 miles across the Atlantic, to Plymouth, England. I can't put my finger on the exact hour it actually started, but we were slowly starting to feel the pressures of a late start and quirks of a new client.

Paul's buying our return trip airline tickets from England himself was going to insure that we had to try and get more money out of the owner, Jasperson, a wee wrinkle we didn't need. Collecting cash owed from rich owners was my least favorite part of the job and for that reason we kept our contracts very basic. We charged one dollar per mile, expected return airfare and supplied our own food. Anything which suffered storm damage along the way was chalked up to normal wear and tear and the owner picked up the tab for the repair of equipment which we found faulty at the dock. If for any reason a boat had to be hauled while in our care, the owner had to wire funds up front before she was pulled out. We had been over all of this with Colin Jasperson and two weeks prior to departure was no time for our usual crossed wires. If Paul laid out the cash for the tickets now, God only knows when we'd be reimbursed. I stood up and reached over the counter for the phone. Chester had only one travel agent which actually tried to find cheap fares. The rest catered to the tourists, and if this summer proved anything like the past ones, they all had done a land rush business flying sightseers in and out, arranging for water tours and booking bed and breakfasts because the hotels had long since filled up.

"Dutton's Travel," the weary voice answered.

"Hi, Jean, it's Chris, happy Day After. Been up all night counting your money?"

“Might be the day after for you guys, but the leaves are going to be changing soon. We’re going to be up to our ears in geriatrics any day now,” she said, clearly lacking humor. “Chester’s been added to the foliage tour this year and I really don’t know if I can take it, I really don’t. Any idea how many hotel rooms seven busses a day represents? Jesus, Chris, something goes wrong in your work and what, you get wet? Worse comes to worse maybe you drown. I screw up and I’ve got 140 leaf gawkers sleeping in my living room. You want to try that?”

“Nope” I said. “You seen Paul?”

“Sitting right in front of me. Want to speak to him?”

“Sure do,” I said, hoping that she’d hear my best Chamber of Commerce smile.

“What’s up?” my partner asked.

“Listen, Jasperson said that he was going to buy the return tickets from England, don’t do anything right now ‘cause I don’t want to have to try and collect the cash from him.”

“Sounds good, Chris, I’ll try to stop off on my way back.”

This was not good. “You’ve bought them already haven’t you?”

“Yes indeedy, just like we discussed. Jean’s just finishing the paperwork now. We’re all set. She’s done a hell of a job.”

“God damn it, Paul, we’re not all set. What if we have to wait out some weather? We’re not exactly sure when we’ll get into Plymouth and if we miss our target date I don’t want to be out the price of the tickets. Get her to cancel them. When did we discuss this?”

“That’s great, Chris. By the way, Jasperson’ll be happy with the price. Got great deals.”

“Great as in no refund.”

“You bet, that’s the one. I’ll meet you at the yard shortly.” Paul hung up.

A nonconversation is a way of making a noncommitment around what you hope to be a nonevent. Paul was usually a bit more forthcoming about life and trying to be evasive or cryptic was not his strong suit. I can only imagine what he must have landed in with Jean.

I should explain that the object of our panic was haplessly floating not 100 yards from where I now sat as I rested my forehead on crossed arms. Colin Jasperson's boat, *Curlew*, was a ten-year-old forty foot, fibergalss sloop. Her original owner sailed her across the Atlantic via the Azores and Bermuda four years ago. The then owner was planning on taking her to Newport for the Onion Patch series, five days of buoy racing before the whole fleet headed off for a 600-mile race to Bermuda. When money problems arose with his business he was called back to England before he could start campaigning. Lacking the funds to race her, what was left of the crew spent the rest of the summer cruising New England's waters and ended up tucking her away for the winter in South East Harbor, Maine. For the past few years she had been sailing down East and was just recently bought by Jasperson, a land developer from New Hampshire whose specialty was stripping virgin acreage and putting up housing tracts. As proficient as he was with bulldozers and potential buyers, he knew next to nothing about sailing but had always wanted to play the part. He did know enough to want *Curlew* in England for next year's Round Britain Race and was of the opinion that what he didn't know, he could learn at any one of several sailing schools in the Caribbean over the winter. Word of mouth came from Eagle's that she was lying in Maine and was in need of a delivery crew. I immediately called him in Nashua, NH with my sales pitch. It wasn't audience shares and demographics, but it was my prime bull-shit nonetheless and a very low-ball bid at that. After ten years out of the show it was comforting to know that if need be, I could still pour it on with the best of them. A month ago Jasperson left the message on my machine that Paul and I were the ones to be taking her "across the pond," Jasperson's words not mine.

The more I thought about sailing an unknown ten-year-old boat across 3,000 open miles of the Atlantic in early fall, the more my gut shook its prudent little head. Yet when I looked at my schedule and bank balance, my brain overruled the determined efforts of my gut and closed the discussion. It was a simple case of the benefits outweighing the drawbacks; the delivery would help the business' reputation beyond measure. To date Paul and I had built up a fair following for the shorter coastal hops and occasional yearly trips to or from any one of several Virgin Islands. A successful transatlantic of our own would be a welcome entry on our resumes. Three thousand dollars split two ways wouldn't hurt matters either, in fact it would be just the shot my anemic financial situation needed. By no means was the wolf at the door but he knew where I lived. It was also very hard to argue with the chance to be at sea for thirty days. Our joint decision to pitch for the job stemmed from two basic facts; the money and the fact that despite all of Paul's worldly travels, he had never been to England before.

That was then, and now was running out. I paid for my tea and headed out to meet Paul and get some sort of damage assessment.

Crossing the street from Eagle's to Pachico's this cloudless fall morning was a real pleasure, definitely one worth waiting for. Instead of the usual dash through bumper-to-bumper traffic, tour busses, baby prams and bicycles, it was accomplished in my normal, long stride. Nor did I have to stop and give directions, answer any questions or receive any lost-and-confused-tourist glares. I had always wanted to sell bumper stickers that read "Have A Good Day Somewhere Else," but the Chamber of Commerce never warmed to the idea.

Not knowing when I'd feel this cocky again, I simply had to stick my head in the door and check in with Attila the Hen. At that moment, my slate with the yard couldn't have been cleaner. In Fee Pachico's books, there were simply no outstanding accounts, not since Madeline started tending to them five years ago. There was no fluff, no frills to this lady. You either owed the yard for supplies, work done, slip space or storage, or you didn't. If you didn't you had no cause to be her office and don't let the door hit you on the way out. If you did, you had no cause to invite friends sailing for the day as Madeline kept the key and as long as the books said your account was outstanding, due to a fairly substantial chain between boat and dock, the vessel in question was as good as hers. For an industry that thrives on false promises of work being done on time and checks in the mail, Madeline was a renegade. Either you had the money or didn't, and if your category was "didn't," don't even think of offering up any excuses. It also didn't hurt matters that Madeline was Chester's answer to Dolly Parton, though no one ever remembered hearing her sing. The woman was blonde, exceedingly self-assured, bright and built. Truth be known, I looked forward to going in to see Madeline, there was something about her, try as I may, that I couldn't overlook.

"Morning, Madeline, ruin anyone's weekend plans yet?"

Without looking up or missing a key, Madeline kept at her typing. "Fee's looking for you and shut the door on your way out." She really was a master at a typewriter, her fingers were an amazing blur across the gray keys, made all the more amazing by one-inch green nails which for some reason today were blue. Watching the blue blur for a moment I found that I simply had to know.

"Madeline, are those nails real?"

She stopped her typing, took a slow, deep breath and in a steamy fashion turned towards the general direction of the door that I was now supposed to be on the other side of, expanding her sweater to its very limits.

"Chris," she said, smoldering, "everything about me is real."

I don't care how sophisticated, how worldly a man thinks he is or how clever his sexual innuendoes, when an attractive blond, buxom woman comes forth with a direct come-on, completely out of the blue, this once proud and self-proclaimed sexual sage will in a matter of seconds be reduced to that of a blushing schoolboy and end up making a complete fool of himself.

"Ah, yeah." Jesus it was getting warm. "I'll, ah, just shut the door for you."

I relaxed my death grip on the door as my voice cracked like it hadn't since I was thirteen. Whatever dignity I had managed to salt away with Madeline in the past was now being filed somewhere between buffoon and moron.

As I took what pride I had left, Madeline took one last lunge.

"If you think you can find your way down there, a present was left for you on B dock last night. Four guys from Maine said she was to be turned over to you this morning."

It appeared as though *Curlew* had been delivered to us as promised, if not a day early. So far so good, at least with *Curlew*.

As I walked through the yard and on down toward the docks I smiled knowing that Aubery Street wasn't alone in putting on her new fall face. Happily the seasonal changes in Chester were occurring along the waterfront as well. Seemingly overnight the whine and whirl of electric sanders, forklifts and mast-tugging cranes had all fallen silent. The constant hum of workers and crew massing around boats either in the ways or alongside had now been reduced to small jobs here and there, isolated conversations were being held without having to duck into a shed in order to get your point across, without having to shout. No lines at the supply shack, no constant chatter from the P.A. system, one radio station playing instead of the offerings from the entire dial.

Looking out across the harbor, the air seemed a little cleaner, the ocean lived a little brighter and I was not totally convinced that this was simply due to the fresh northwest breeze filling in. Clouds of sawdust were no longer being stirred into the air filling the senses with their sweet and gritty offerings. Only the slightest suggestions of fiberglass resin and varnish lingered in the breeze, gone was the rustle and snap of sails flying free on headstays, trying to dry out before the southwesterlies filled in. Rigs which were once dollied past you at seemingly breakneck speeds by college bound kids were now being cradled quietly in their winter racks for yet another long, dark, seven-month wait. The two remaining yard hands were now free to go about their autumn ritual of buttoning up Pacchio's without having to make small talk with men in new and shining deck shoes, accompanied by women toting matching canvas bags which proudly boasted the name of their latest boat.

Now the unburdened slips were free to float with the slight harbor swell as they saw fit and were no longer constrained by lines to or from restraining deck cleats. It appeared as though the few boats which were left were taking the time to finally slip off their shoes and at long last catch their breath. Shortly the docks to which they were secured were going to be pulled and stacked like so much firewood for the New England winter.

The distraction of frenetic yard life no longer held one's attention to the harbor. For the first time in months one's eye could travel out with the morning's fishing fleet, past the breakwater, up the tide-swept channel and across the sound and as far as one's experiences or dreams extended. Beyond the continental shelf where the coastal swells are matched and bettered by the North Atlantic surge, where the meaning and intent of that ever changing and demanding mass is no longer just a distant abstract, but a living entity that must be recognized and respected on an hourly basis and dealt with on her own terms. Beyond the banks where a seldom seen navy of men stand with one foot firmly in the 20th century while the other stretches back through past generations, hauling in its nets and setting its traps around a clock that knows no shifts. Over plateaus and mountains thousands of feet deep that once offered up timber for hulls and shelter for long gone tribes. Out where man is the tolerated visitor, the uninvited guest who is greeted at the threshold but not encouraged to linger. For this is where your eye stops and can follow no further, this is where the rules change, where the Atlantic gains her voice, where she begins to speak and starts to guard her answers with the power of her largest and most brilliant creatures. Her leviathans from the black, pressure laden depths, which lumber along with distinct purpose while dodging deadly harpoons. They and all like them watch the uninvited guest as he tries to convince her that here too man is dominant, that man will cut through and clear, that man will open new ways of coming to terms with that which he'll never understand.

"The ultimate arrogance," she answers. "You can be sunk with the blink of an eye, yet you push on and refuse to acknowledge that what hangs in balance is as fragile as the world you travel through."

Here, where the constant blizzard of barely perceptible sea

life is strained through baleen and sent back on its way down to where the dead and discarded, spent of all hope, fall into the silence of decay and despair. For here, in a blind world, where cold and time are the only witnesses to the futile and hopeless wanderings of souls undelivered, for those who die at sea remain, only to rot and wait. Here is where her Dead Ones serve their time in purgatory awaiting their deliverance. They are ruled by her great knowledge. Any sailor who has ever passed across her depths knows that she will not only find your weaknesses but exploit them with the same brutality and swiftness that she has been displaying for countless centuries.

She speaks with direct purpose. She talks and entreats those who have been too tired and spent to explain away the voices they heard while on a lone and troublesome watch. The wind is her posthorse and is conveniently credited with the delivery, but never the content. Every sailor has heard her voice, yet none are bold enough to acknowledge it, to speak out and answer it. Every sailor has been haunted by dreams from these great depths, these timeless vaults of cold and darkness where spirits stir, not quite alive, never quite allowed to die and be released from their endless drifting through silt, thousands of feet deep, holding firm to her secrets and bearing witness to surface weakness gone by.

For once a man falls to her grips, no amount of conscience thinking could comprehend the Atlantic's unconscious horrors and terrors which refuse to give up her numbers. How long does it take for the screaming of the dead to stop? How long will it take for the white horses to rip apart and suffocate the fallen intruder? How long does the brittle cold of the North Atlantic trenches keep the aimless wanderers and their futile tears suffocating in her grips?

Deeper than her brilliant creature's needs would ever take them, deeper than man's arrogance would ever lead him into betrayal, where traps are crushed and lost nets lie while invisible ice chokes their every movement, the North Atlantic watches patiently while those who lost her horrific game of dare drift between decay and deliverance. These are a sailor's nightmares, the voices that linger for a lifetime. More reality than fantasy, but never discussed, just relived silently over and over again. These are the dreams from which superstitions are born. This is the very terror which awakens you from complacency.

"Out in the Reach?" Paul said from behind me.

"Among other places," I said from somewhere other than dock B. We'd better check the calendar, I don't want to start this one on a Friday."

The breeze was slowly clocking to the northwest and as I felt it turn slightly more to Autumn, colder and sharper, I started to realize that in a few weeks time I would be the uninvited guest who pushes east with the hopes and determination of not overstaying my welcome, trying not to be outguessed as to what weakness I've overlooked, trusting that dreams will stay where they belong and that her strengths and powers will cradle the intruder and not crush him.

CHAPTER 2

1850: Fall

"Mr. Dunbar? Mr. Dunbar," the young Englishwoman called out toward the cobbled courtyard below. Hearing no immediate answer Katherine leaned her small frame a little bit further out of the second story window of her modest flat above. "Mr. Dunbar? Are you there?"

Beneath her, the slow steady shuffle of the old shopkeeper's salt-encrusted boots made their way across the wooden floor and announced his arrival outside in the courtyard as they scraped to a stop on the fog dampened bricks beneath them. The courtyard below was bordered with the thick offerings of rose hips which had been feasting on the moisture laden air of the summer. Dunbar sighed as he realized that once again they were in need of being cut back. Perhaps Miss Worthington would like to turn her hand to the task, he thought to himself. The persistent mist had been rolling in off the ocean and limply pushing along the waterfront of Chester Township for several weeks now and the long anticipated northwesterly breezes seemed to have all but overlooked the small sailing community that summer. Nothing in Chester had been dry since the rains of early July and now the heavy blanket of fog was successfully keeping the autumnal sun out. The thick, damp air was refusing the deep muddy ruts along Aubery Street a chance to dry. At times it seemed easier to try and negotiate the six-inch mud base on foot than be stuck in a carriage going absolutely nowhere, but better the horse lost his shoe than you lose yours.

Katherine's leaning out of her window and talking to the various workers below in the back courtyard was a daily ritual, and the sound of her English lilt coming through the chandlery's back door had become something the various stockboys and suppliers were becoming quite accustomed to themselves. Although this was far from the proper manner in which she had been trained, it did save the long walk down the back staircase, across the courtyard, out onto Aubery Street and in the front door of Dunbar's Chandlery where one wasn't sure that those arranging stock in the back could always hear the bell. Besides, who was going to reprimand her now that she was on her own and no longer simply just staff? Wasn't this the very reason she was determined to get back to family where a person was free to be as she wanted and could raise her voice if she had an inkling to do so?

"Ah, Mr. Dunbar." She relaxed as she heard the familiar sound of the boots below her. "You are there. Have you heard anything yet?"

Standing just outside of the delivery door to his chandlery, the patient shopkeeper stood looking up to the young girl above, a posture which by this time the old man's neck was slowly beginning to tire of. For now, he found it far easier to look straight ahead and simply let his voice rise out and up.

"Yes, Miss Worthington," he sighed with great tolerance, "I am here." For months now Dunbar had been hearing Katherine's daily pacings upstairs above his chandlery and had actually started to look forward to day's end when he would close up shop and stand out on Aubery Street exchanging evening pleasantries with this English girl, he out on the dirt street, she sitting quietly on her stone stoop. "Mr. Dunbar, I'm so sorry to bother you again," she said leaning further out, "but have you heard anything from the docks yet?"

"Nothing new today" he said, the usual response, but this time he added a new twist. "But I did hear that one of them managed to get her sails drawing last night though, last I heard she was slowly pulling east. The *Liverpool* I think, can't say just how far she'll get but maybe something's filling in out there after all. At least she's with the tide for now."

It wasn't only the horse rigs and pull carts along Aubery Street which were being trapped by the mud; for all intents and purposes nothing was moving near Chester. The fog had been holding all of Chester's scheduled sailing at a complete standstill for days. Those few coastal packets that were light enough to actually drift out of the passage were the lucky ones. Most sat to their anchors at the exact spot where they were three days ago when the fickle New England breeze died. Conditions such as these had seen ships sit off of New York Harbor for weeks at a time before they could get their impatient cargo heading east. For now cargo would simply have to sit by the wharves and wait for the winds of autumn to put life back into limp canvas and lift the fog.

"Indeed, Mr. Dunbar, indeed," she said more to herself than him. "Do let me know as soon as you hear any news. Have you seen anything of the agent's cart?"

"No, but if he's stuck with the rest down Aubery Street, you'd be better off carrying your own trunks down yourself." He smirked in reference to the ongoing bog the town fathers called a street. "Have to get back inside now, Miss Worthington, but if I hear anything you will most certainly be the first to know. Good day, Miss Worthington."

"Good day, Mr. Dunbar."

As she continued to lean on the chipped and damp sill of her window, her eyes ran up over the rooftops toward the hill where she had spent nearly half her life. How she had suffered the anger of the housekeeper, Jillian, when she announced that she would not be staying on at Elmwood past her tenth year. Some of the other girls voiced their opinions as well, but for the most part those voices came from the older ones who viewed her decision to leave as a reminder of their own locked-in positions, positions which would see the most of them no further than underhousemaid regardless how many years they gave to Elmwood. Only one of them could rise to lady's maid and God knows few were even remotely clever or resourceful enough to become considered for the position of housekeeper.

It was only three months ago that she had turned her back on her "family" of ten years and taken the unpopular road. Her decision to leave her post in America as a servant and go back home, back to England, was not received well. There really was no life in Chester for her. The people were kind enough but a girl with her background usually had a tough time making the transition, her days as housemaid on the Hill would see to that. The promise of meeting a nice future in her house or any other house on the Hill was as hollow as her future in a town that itself was starting to look for rescue. She only took the room on Aubery Street to wait out a ship bound for England. One, two weeks at the most. Truth be told, because of Chester's reputation for being off the major sea lanes she would have to wait for whatever could be arranged, for whatever captain felt it worth his while to sail up the sound and anchor off the harbor, after he himself had waited in Boston for proper cargo. One thing was guaranteed though; her passage to England was not going to be a quick one as no ship of any consequence was going to veer off for a town barely on the chart.

"It won't be the luxurious accommodations that I'm sure a young lady of your position is used to," the shipping agent had said smirking, "but you'll be havin' your own bunk." The agent on the wharf promised her passage with a packet from the Sefton Lines, a small, rarely used shipping concern out of Boston, sometime this fall.

"They make a habit of having their smaller ones haul in from time to time, I should think by May. You just sit tight now, we'll send a rig around in due time." It seemed the more she would travel down to the docks to find out about her passage the vaguer and vaguer her man became, offering nothing more than to recommend that she continue sitting tight. The truth, which usually took a back seat to dollars in the pocket, was that the man forgot to tell Katherine that there really was no set schedule, sailings were solely dependent upon if and when a shipping company could find enough cargo to fill the holds of its ships. Freight was what these owners relied upon to realize a handsome return on their investment, not the comfort or time schedules of the few paying passengers available. For several days now Katherine had begun thinking that perhaps it never would happen, that maybe she had been sold something that was useless. Perhaps no ship was coming for her, no captain was willing to sail into Chester. She did have her paperwork saying that her one-way passage was assured, but on whose word? No one could say just when the Sefton Fleet of Boston had last sailed into Chester. They had passed along the coast a lot, but never really sailed in. Yet she was told over and over again that it was simply a matter of time and that some ship would be hauling in soon. No strict sailing schedule, no guaranteed transit times. The one thing that was assured was that she would be leaving and to keep her trunks at the ready.

"At the ready," she had remained through a hot and muggy New England summer that was now heading into fall. Weatherwise, time was running out. She was no mariner, but it wasn't easy to forget the great storms of autumn for the past ten years which seemed to thrive on this hot and heavy weather. Once the fog started to move and blow out to the south again, Katherine just might breath a bit easier, but that still wouldn't bring her ship in any quicker. Somebody downstairs might know of something. Until then one had to simply sit and be patient and keep herself busy.

Pouring herself some hot water for a cup of tea, Katherine moved into her street facing front room and once again set about to organizing and re-packing her small trunk. Not surprisingly, the usual flood of memories filled the small room. As others before her, Katherine was elated to get the opportunity to come to America and work for a sponsoring family, sponsors who paid for her fare west, sponsors who in return asked that she work a certain number of hours, during a certain number of weeks, over a certain amount of years and tolerate a certain amount of abuse, all for a less than certain amount of a yearly stipend. Some of the girls actually made a career of it in these mansions, which were more small communities than actually homes. Vast rolling estates that sat just above the rest of Chester, looking down on the small shipping town with just the right amount of distance and disdain. All backed up, contained by their communal seawall which pitted mortal power against eternal might. These homeowners could be considered neighbors but with almost as much acreage as attitude, it was unlikely that any of these neighbors would deign to visit.

Sipping at her tea, Katherine remembered the discomfort she

felt when announcing she was leaving Knowles Hill for England. A house on the Hill which had trouble holding staff was targeted for sharp and decisive criticisms. No matter the method, one was never to lose girls, but instead insure their stay by any means. Frequent turnover of staff belied internal struggles, which invited external questioning. From the start Jillian let her displeasure with Katherine's decision felt. To have one of her girls be unhappy was customary -- they were always the younger, weaker lot -- but to have one simply announce that she was leaving with the lack of respect with which she would announce a trip across the lane was simply unheard of. Jillian didn't demonstrate her displeasure by the usual methods, such as assigning Katherine to black the first floor fire grates right up until the time she was needed to stand by Richards as he served lunch, which would all but guarantee a dirty uniform. She did not order Katherine to wax all the good wood in the drawing room prior to the footman's hauling of the fireplace ashes so that a fine layer of dust would settle and negate her work. Nor did she fail to tell her when she had been summoned by cook. These were all the standard fare which, if a girl was worth her salt, she would see coming and easily maneuver around. These Katherine could easily have handled, but the road that the vengeful Jillian took was far crueler and more painful. For all intents and purposes, Katherine simply ceased to exist at Elmwood. She wasn't spoken to unless she had made a glaring error, the frequency of which was becoming less and less, nor was she referred to. It had been made painfully clear that her leaving was a deterrent to a content working staff and any girl that was caught talking to her about anything other than house-related matters would most probably suffer the same silent treatment as well. But that was then and now she was her own person with her life back.

Satisfied that her trunk was once again organized and secure for her upcoming Atlantic passage, she closed and locked the leather lid and dutifully went back to her kitchen's iron stained sink. Rinsing out her fragile tea cup she remembered the day she rescued the small and chipped china object from her lady's trash bins in back of the house's kitchen complex. The simplest of things, she thought to herself, why do people refuse to see the simplest of thing? Katherine's logic for wanting to leave Elmwood and America flew in the face of household thinking; nothing but hard times were guaranteed back in England. Yet here it was said that not only did you have a family that cared for you but one that was willing to provide as well. By turning your back on them you were only showing your contempt and disregard for all that they had provided for you: meals, room, clothing, pay, perhaps the chance to work your way up through the ranks into a better position and life. It was all possible but not necessarily probable. Some of the others who couldn't or wouldn't take it left their lives of servitude behind and ran out to live in various Irish and English hovels harboring other wayward emigrants seeking their futures while wedged in between Boston and New York.

Glancing out her kitchen window, taking a long sweeping look up towards the Hill once again, she felt a recommitment to her efforts to leave that dubious security behind. For all the things that Plymouth, England couldn't offer her, it had something which Katherine had been longing for the past ten years, since the very day she sailed from there: the rest of the Worthington family. Her future back home wouldn't necessarily hold any more potential than what she was facing in America, but her spirit was telling her it was worth the gamble.

Katherine continued to stare out over Chester's roofs as a lazy summer sun cut through scattered layers of fog with warm rays of yellow and orange. In spite of all, she thought to herself, I have grown. She had to laugh at the memory of the young girl who was so terrified to leave house and home those many years ago. Looking down at the withered and useless source of her concern she recalled that long ago fear which began to well up inside of young Katherine dockside which arose not so much from the sadness of having to leave her family but from the fact that perhaps a servant with only one good hand wouldn't be welcomed. Farm accidents were common in and around Plymouth and she was lucky to have use of her left arm at all, but in the light of the fact that she was soon to be a servant on display, this one concern began to weigh on her heavily. She had long since forgotten the pain of the horse's grinding hoof, but never would she forget the fear she set sail with. She knew that light objects could be held within her the partial grasp of the hooked fingers and yes she could use the left hand to balance what the good right one was carrying, but never would she be able to securely hold and move the heavier objects which she would most certainly be called upon to do.

So young, so fragile, she remembered as she thought back through the haze of her new American life. She remembered standing on the bustling docks looking out across the harbor toward the green country hills which ran down to Plymouth's crowded commercial port, a port which clearly would wait upon no girl's tears and protests. With total indifference ships would sail out of the congestion and confusion and into the uncertainty of the Atlantic's squalls. If she missed her berth, it would be sold out quickly to the nearest passenger willing to risk lice, rats, rotting food and sailor's strengths. Many in the small town actually voiced their envy that Katherine was being given the opportunity to travel to the country where troubles were as scarce as lice. But hollow was the encouragement compared to the fact that she was leaving all she knew.

Almost immediately upon arrival at Elmwood, Katherine's education began in earnest. As foreign as the opulence and splendor of Elmwood was, she would have to tolerate the obvious social distinctions between the haves and have-nots and learn well the different ways each member of the family wished to be addressed. Never making direct eye contact, always backing aside to let them pass, she went about her rounds of hauling ashes, emptying slop pots, washing and waxing. She grew accustomed to the older girls' vile and sudden tempers and even managed to take solace in her horsehair mattress. Yet through all of the new and foreign ways, Katherine was happy to find that, among the other lower girls, there was a modicum of acceptance; the object of her shame became nothing more than an ongoing idle curiosity. Often she would catch them stealing glances at her twisted hand, and of course the more curious would ask their questions and occasionally the friendlier would even try to help her out when their own hands weren't busy. But these initial curiosities were eventually quelled and they soon came to realize that new girl's abilities were no different than any of theirs. However, it was among the family and the head staff, that Katherine's new-found shame of her deformity began to grow. No sooner had she started to unpack her small case of belongings in the upstairs dorm then word was sent up to her that Holliwell, the house steward, wished to see her in the kitchen immediately. As she found her way through the unfamiliar maze of halls, rooms and open chambers to the kitchen far below, she felt as though the cause of her embarrassment was slowly choking her. She had been quickly introduced to Holliwell, an older man, when she first arrived but hadn't thought that her arrival would cause so much of a stir as to have him stop his day and personally send for her. After a cursory examination of her useless hand Holliwell dismissed her, yet not before he drove home the point that that if this deformity interfered with her work in any manner she would be seeing the back door in quick time.

Getting up and closing the window to the damp breeze Katherine smiled. Look at me now, she laughed, aren't I the free one? If the past ten years on the Hill had taught Katherine anything it was that money only gave a person a freedom to come and go as they pleased, to do as they wanted. If you had enough money you had to answer to no one. What it did not buy was what her mother used to refer to as "spirit," the joy of being with others, the joy of helping others, the simple joy of being. Looking about at her tiny apartment she found herself laughing aloud. Three tiny rooms, she said to herself, but three rooms of joy. What had been missing from the start of her new life in America for these past few years was so very simple but no life could endure without it. From the beginning days at Elmwood she had felt isolated and inside slowly began to feel numb. Spiritually she had been dying. Katherine had been tough and determined enough to handle the work and injustices, but her concern and care for others had started to flicker, and perhaps more importantly, her concern and care for herself.

Katherine's continued determination to leave grew from a most curious of places. During her brief free time from her duties at Elmwood she would walk down to the great house's seawall. Slowly she would place one foot in front of the other, as on an invisible tightrope. Sitting down and closing her eyes, she would shut out her immediate world as her hands felt the coarse sharp edges of the seashells imbedded in the cement beneath her. Soon her mind's eye would float up and off the cement wall, soaring far out above the continuous surging of the gray Atlantic and look down as the great ocean swells rolled past. Slowly over time Katherine began to notice a change. No longer did she feel that she was free, but instead, she was starting to be pulled out into her fantasy. It was as though she were being pulled by the sounds of the great undulating mass below her.

A loud crash from Dunbar's chandlery below brought the girl back to the present. This was a dark side of her memory at Elmwood which she seldom wanted to look back on but was with her ever present.

Too much time alone is good for no one, she thought, time to stretch the legs and ask about the shipping. Arriving on the street below, Katherine started to head up Aubery Street, glancing in the windows of the other shop keepers. She wished that she could buy even the smallest of keepsakes to bring back for her family but the extended stay in Dunbar's second floor apartment was quickly eating through what money she had left. Still, window shopping never costs a penny, she thought. It wasn't long before the fog swirling down Aubery street brought Katherine's thoughts back to a very specific day at Elmwood's seawall. She remembered the first day that she sat on the course cement wall and watched the ragged death of a spring storm passing over the horizon. It was then that she began to realize that she could now feel the sensation of being pulled out to sea without having to summon it. It seemed that all she had to do was make contact with the ocean itself. Surfacing from deep beneath the waters, it spoke to her. All along she had known this strangely familiar feeling as a voice she once heard as a child in

Plymouth. After market days she and her father would stroll slowly back to the farm, talking about nothing in particular and everything in general. Religiously they would stop to sit on a fieldstone wall and look at the sliver of ocean which peered from behind furrowed green hills off in the distance. It was here James Worthington taught his daughter to listen for the soft distant voice from the sea.

"If you're still and listen for it," he would say, "it will take you any place you have your mind set on. Look to it when you're lonely, girl."

It was from Elmwood's seawall that this voice began to take hold of Katherine and build to levels which she had never dared to feel before. She would find herself exhilarated if not a bit scared, and with the same cunning and stealth with which the voice first came to her consciousness, it now slowly began to take control. The tides started to turn as host became guest. Having found a home in the girl, the sea's voice grew in strength and volume. Lulled by song, she failed to notice the change in intent. Unwittingly Katherine had begun to acquiesce to it. No longer being her vehicle of deliverance, it began to serve its own agenda and exploit her vulnerabilities as it coerced, dared, haunted her with promises of a timely deliverance back to that spirit of love which she had left behind, all hollow promises. Soon every wave which broke against Elmwood's seawall teased her to follow as it ran back out to the waiting depths. Wherever the girl was she could feel it inside of her. Every wave which ran in from the reach and thrust against the wall was now doing so within her, and the power and intensity of the rhythm made her flush with excitement as her eyes searched inwardly as far as they dared to go. Finally she would be lifted out past the horizon, out where storms wreak their havoc with unseen force and terror, and there it would abandon her. For the voice wasn't lifting her home as promised, but instead was serving its own ends. In her mind's eye, Katherine was swept out into the great depths of the ocean where for the briefest of moments she was allowed to witness eternity. Behind closed eyes she heard the voices and saw those dead souls who wandered aimlessly thousands of feet deep and through the black ice of perpetual night.

Shaking herself back into the present she continued to walk down the mud caked Aubery Street. Stopping to gaze into the baker's window she failed to take notice of the freshly baked offerings, but instead was pulled towards distant raised sounds. Trying to move a bogged-down cart through the mud, raised men's voices could be heard shouting orders at one another. These voices transported Katherine's mind once again back to the far off muffled cries she used to hear from far out in the Atlantic. The tormented voices drifted about her as her mind's eye witnessed the icy cold blackness where wasted and spent life forms stack up and decay, never finding rest nor home. Plucked from wet decks, taken by the raw strength of the surf, old men, young children, all like Katherine had heard the voice of the sea. What became of centuries of rotten flesh and diluted blood? Only raw evil could paint an image so horrific as what was passing before Katherine's closed eyes. The screams of childhood nightmares now rose within her to a breaking crescendo shattering into a fading echo of pain. Opening her eyes, she stood transfixed, as she found herself staring down the length of the street. Her frenzied thoughts of the torturous North Atlantic and what lay below rushed out of her as she tried to replace them with thoughts of home and Plymouth.

"Still waiting on that ship are you?"

Katherine quickly landed back in reality. "I'm sorry?" she said.

"Your deliverance back from whence you came."

Katherine had always been amused at the baker's use of the language and actually began to look forward to her brief encounters with him on her daily walks. "Oh, indeed, yes. No word yet I'm afraid." She said

"Well, here's something for the inner woman." He handed Katherine a small paper bag. This wasn't the first time she had been the benefactor of such a gift from him. Lord knows old breads and donuts were welcome indeed.

"I promise, as soon as I get settled back home, I will be the one sending you something special."

A quick smile and the man disappeared back into his shop. I will write to him, she told herself. A promised thought which was quickly replaced by a more pressing one, Bridie's letter, she thought, I haven't even started Bridie's letter. Katherine told herself that before she left Chester she would manage to take pen to paper and let her one confident at Elmwood know how much she meant to her, how special their time was together. She turned to walk back to her apartment to finally start her writing, at this point more a needed distraction than fulfilled promise. It was during her first month at Elmwood that she had met Bridie while on one of her seawall walks. Never having enough time or privacy to exchange words with her fellow worker, the seawall provided a needed refuge. Katherine felt safe with Bridie and it wasn't long before she began to pour out her plans and hopes. At first she could only muster enough courage for intimations about her plans, but soon she was actually pressing Bridie with her decision.

"What you're saying is true, Katherine, but things back home are the devil's own," Bridie would argue, referring to the chances one would face in an England wrought with poverty and unbending class distinctions. "It's a good life here, she cares for us and sees that we're never without."

"You're sounding more and more like her every day," Katherine would warn.

As they walked along the wall, along the lawn of the great house, around the well kept parameter of the expansive gardens filled with vegetables, herbs and exotic flowers, the presence of the Atlantic was clearly everywhere and in everything. The trees which they now walked under were twisted and stunted from past winter gales, having long since lost their strength to fight her relentless winds. The same winds had made the bordering roses grow thick with thorns and knots of vines and drew patterns along the grass, which gardeners pampered and preened daily. The patterns ran with no particular order but showed how teasing and capricious her gentler winds can be. The Atlantic was calm, resting, allowing the men in their boats to work her and try to gain another day's wages.

"Yes, we're never without, but just what is it that we have?" She stopped walking. "A bed, a bureau and two uniforms which have to remain spotless at all times. If we're lucky, that's *if* mind you, we might get a third one by our fifth year. Yes, we're fed, and yes, we have rooms, but you see the food that chef sends upstairs every day, you clean her bedrooms. Bridie, in your wildest dreams do you think even for a minute we'd ever see the likes of that?" Katherine's words failed to deliver her true unhappiness. It wasn't the tangible things, it wasn't the blatant inequities between the haves and have-nots. Once again it came down to spirit, or more precisely, lack of it.

Bridie's concern for her friend was sweet and caring, but she was locked in the system and couldn't or wouldn't see the way in which Elmwood smothered the very spirit Katherine was so in need of.

"If you go home now," Bridie said, "you'll be living in one room with the rest of your family. You'd have no privacy there, now would you?"

"What sort of privacy do we have here? Eight girls to a room? One bath for the twelve of us?" Katherine stopped the younger girl by the arm. "Why just look at the two of us now. If we want to talk about anything other than her and her house we have to walk down here to water's edge. What makes you think that it would ever be any different?

"I got a letter from Flora yesterday and she says that working in the mills is terrible but she's doing it for herself, she takes home her own money and has only one boss to answer to and has only one job to worry about. No serving twenty different masters. She's living with some other girls in a boardinghouse. Bridie, they're free to come and go as they please." She paused. "Can you imagine such a thing? One person to answer to and only one job to do. Sometimes I don't know if I'm gardener or scullery maid. Besides, you saw what happened to Colleen. Twenty years she's been with her and that's the treatment she gets? I might not have the money they do and Lord knows I haven't the airs and delicacy some of them claim to have, but I do know that people are not meant to be treated in such a manner. She sees us as disposable animals. Each day I serve under her I feel like I can take less and less breath. I have to leave before I find myself looking at her the way she looks at us."

Perhaps it was the strength of Katherine's words and not the actual content that won Bridie over, but the Irish girl's arguments fell far short of their mark when matched with Katherine's resolve. Slowly the walks along the wall began to take on the note of a farewell rather than protest.

"You'll have to promise me this, Katherine Worthington" Bridie whispered as she gripped her friend's hands firmly in her own. "If it means that much to you that you'd risk losing this, you're never to go back on what you've decided here today."

That was all several months and a lifetime ago. As Katherine now climbed the two cement steps which led to the narrow winding staircase to her apartment she realized that it had been far too long since she had been able to have a good chat with Bridie. With Bridie having alternate Sundays off, their paths didn't cross as often. The occasional meeting at church and notes passed between them were all they had now.

Taking one final moment before she entered her new home, Katherine turned toward the harbor and drew in a deep expanse of sea air and smiled. The haunting voices which used to scare her so were for the most part silent now, and without the intrusions and suppressing energies of Elmwood she could once again breathe and feel the spirit in her heart. She felt a mixture of excitement and apprehension knowing that any day she would be starting the final leg of her journey back to the spirit of love, which was patiently waiting to wrap its arms around the girl and embrace her. The spirit waited for her across a vast and powerful ocean several thousand miles wide and several thousand souls deep.

CHAPTER 3

"You've always been the superstitious one, haven't you?" Paul said as we walked thorough the chain link entrance gate into Fee's yard.

Paul and I had caught up with each other just outside Fee's. With hope of trying to take a little steam out our earlier problem I headed away from this subject by mentioning that whatever else happened, I didn't want to start our crossing on a Friday. Paul didn't share my concern. I can't say that I had had problems every time I sailed at the end of a work week, but I do know that it seemed that every trip which had problems departed on a Friday. Leaving on a Friday and re-naming a boat were the only two superstitions to which I subscribed. Whichever way I looked at it, both were guaranteed to bring bad luck with the usual disastrous results.

"*Southern Lights*", I said. "Remember *Southern Lights*? We left on a Friday then. Remember how you spent your midnight watch? And your following off-watch?" Thinking about it for a moment, the look which began to come to Paul's angular face boosted my confidence that we would be leaving on any day of the week other than a Friday. Several years ago, we were hired to take *Southern Lights*, a Preston 34', to Bermuda, meet the owner there and proceed along to her winter berth in Antigua. The trip was relatively straightforward, the usual Gulf Stream squalls, beautiful nights with wall to wall stars, flying fish on deck and the floor of the boat five inches deep in the evil which brews and gurgles in holding tanks, right up until the point of bursting hoses and spraying seams. The reason five inches is burned into my memory is because that particular Contessa's bilge was only three inches deep and the ungodly mess which was sloshing across the cabin sole crested just above Paul's shoes. Simply put, we were up to his ankles in it. Neither of us had checked to see whether the Y valves which routed all waste from the head into the Atlantic were turned in such a manner as to do just that. Instead the elusive valves made sure that whatever Paul and I had to eat the day before and the day before that was being pumped directly into an already too full holding tank. The Coast Guard regulations insisted simply that you have one aboard, and any problem you had with these tanks were yours and yours alone. Paul had used the head around 0030 and shortly thereafter I was awoken by a muffled thud and a smell second to none. There followed six hours of mopping and scrubbing. Paul, who pulled the short straw, was on his knees, while I ran with the buckets of sea water.

"Hell, I've even read somewhere that after Ulysses fought the battle of Troy, he left to go home on a Friday. Looked what happened to him."

"You're right, screw Friday," he said. "I guess we should go over the boat and find out what this guy has aboard and how much of it actually works."

Many was the time that we had been assured that a boat had all the safety equipment she needed and the electronics were all up to snuff and in working order. Just as often we found out the hard way that there lay a world of difference between what an absent owner considered "working order" and what we needed to safely get her to point Z without unscheduled side trips to points B, C, D, and E.

"We've got the ticket mess to straighten out," he added.

"So what the hell was that all about?" I asked as we made our way toward dock B. "Since when have we started paying our own way? We build it into the cost and don't have to fight for reimbursements down the line. You sounded like a half-wit on the phone."

"I thought that it was all part of the up front money and that we should take it right off the top and buy our own," he mumbled.

Our practice was to look over a client's boat, see what we had to add to the boats inventory for our assured safety, figure out mileage, and then calculate return trip expenses, and then present the owner with an estimate which we expected to have whittled down by one quarter. Having done that, we would counter his comeback with a nice rounded up number, which was usually accepted, shake hands and hope for the best. In *Curlew*'s case we were dealing with 3,000 miles of open ocean and not a coastal hop, so the numbers were bound to confuse any off the cuff calculations. One of the many charms which Paul and I offer is that we occasionally cross wires, and just about now these wires were beginning to arc -- several hundred dollars worth of arc.

"No, the up front money is completely separate and he was to buy the tickets for the flight back himself. Look, if for some reason or another we don't make Plymouth on or around our target date, we're not out the cost of two one-way seats. Hell, man, you're always the anal one. We've been over this all before, did you forget?"

"Shit," he mumbled, giving me my answer. Getting the credit card account credited was one thing, asking Jean at Dutton's was yet another.

As we walked down the ramp to dock B, I noticed for the seemingly thousandth time how everything about Paul was neat and orderly; his rigger's knife was neatly tucked away in his jeans pocket at the end of a well spliced lanyard, his shoes were well oiled and proudly betrayed the many seasons through which they had seen him. How his wrinkle-free, clean T-shirts always managed to stay tucked in was an ongoing mystery to me. I didn't remember him being this way years ago when we were paddling around Cooperville. There he was as loose and worn as any of the rest of the water rats in our crowd, but the man who now walked in front of me was wearing matched socks and carrying waterproof matches. I imagine that the time he spent in and around the egos and pressures the real estate business in the Washington area had had its effect on him. At times his compulsive fastidiousness was almost the death of him, with me being the one who was left holding the smoking gun. Regardless the aggravation which straightening out the ticket mess with Dutton's would cause, it was comforting to know that Paul had the ability to screw things up.

Curlew sat to her lines patiently as a slight chop in the

Chester harbor lifted her lightly up and down against the fendered sides of dock B. Her dark blue hull was picking up the sun's rays reflected off of the small fry waves slapping around her water line. It appeared as though the deep shine of her hull was nothing more than a beautifully curved dark blue tinted mirror reflecting the oceans energies right back toward her. *Curlew* was the only boat at Pacchio's yard that appeared to be outward bound. The others were all either awaiting the travel lift to tuck them away in their various iron sheds for another long New England winter, or they were scheduled to be trucked into their owner's backyards, where they would sit out eight months of winter's winds and snows, resting securely under their canvas covers, while owners with numbed fingers chipped away at various winter projects. It appeared as though *Curlew* knew her fate was neither shed nor heavy canvas as she rested there, pointing out to the bay which would soon usher her toward her second Atlantic crossing. This was the first time that Paul and I were able to get a look at our home for the upcoming 3,000 miles and what we saw before us was pleasing. She was everything Jasperson allowed her to be and from what first glance told us, apparently more. She had been brought in by her delivery crew from Maine the night before and, in typical Down East tradition, she was left to our charge in what appeared to be immaculate condition. If regional traditions were to be relied upon, she was probably now in better shape than when she departed Maine.

Curlew's overall length was forty feet. She boasted silver bleached teak decks, deeply varnished rails, a low profile cabin house supporting state of the art multi-speed winches, each with its own canvas cover, tightly furled sails with matching sail covers sporting her name and official sail numbers, roller furling, a six-man life raft, a bulletproof dodger protecting a smoked Lexan companionway hatch cover, itself surrounded by several rows of wind, speed and general navigation instruments. Tremendous foresight and deep pockets saw that all of these instruments were repeated by the mast as well. The stainless steel pad eyes which were evident in the deep cockpit and at key locations around her deck told us that at one point someone was more interested in heading her offshore than simply spending afternoons racing around the buoys. Each one of these pad eyes was deep enough to accommodate the snap hooks found at tether's end of a safety harness. As I stood behind the oversized stainless wheel in the cockpit, my eyes followed up the well thought out mast steps of the mast to the top of her rig and once again back down to the teak grating on top of which I was standing. What I saw up top gave me the answer to my question of why Paul, who was by now down below, was muttering, "Holy shit." Not only was there a VHF antenna, but an SSB insulator (for the two-way radio which could give us instant, around-the-world communications), GPS antenna for instant satellite fixes, two LORAN antennas for coastal fixes and one oversized radar Radome. The bite from the north west breeze was barely noticeable as I stood there looking upon a rigging job well done. All was bright and gleaming stainless with the proper amount of faded elkhide leathers to help protect the sails from chafe and rough edges. Even the frame of the dodger was sheathed in elkhide to protect its heavy canvas from potential boom wear. Every color coded line was securely led aft insuring that almost all reefing, rolling, and shortening could be done from the security of the deep cockpit. To keep the cockpit from becoming a maze of spaghetti, someone took the time to see that each one of the eighteen lines had its own jam cleat. When not being pressed into service, each line could be coiled and held neatly in place by its own bungee loop. Canvas pockets were strategically placed to hold the flowing yards of working line, and judging by the six oversized winches which were found along the cockpit combing alone, it appeared as though any line which needed handling was going to be well assisted and very civilized.

"Jesus, Chris, you're not going to believe this," Paul said from below, taking the words right out of my mouth. "Our Mr. Jasperson appears to have some bucks."

As I climbed down the companionway to join Paul, the first thing I saw was the bridge of the Starship *Enterprise*. Immediately to my right Paul sat at the nav station slowly shaking his head at a bank of electronics which covered every sailor's wish list: wind direction, wind speed, close hauled indicator, boat speed, drift and set, two Lorans, two global position systems, Omega, single side band radio, one emergency position indicator radio beacon, one radio direction finder, a chart plotter, a depth sounder with accompanying graph indicator, a digital compass, an autohelm, a sea temperature gauge, and a stereo with CD player. The galley was complete with microwave oven, diesel heat, trash compactor and a refrigeration unit. There were gauges for a propane water heater as well as a water maker, something which would have to be hunted down later. On the starboard side of the nav area was a bank of meters to indicate various states of the engine's health and pressures, as well as tank level monitors for not only the water and fuel but, as God is my witness, we now had in front of us a little monitor which would tell us the state of *Curlew*'s holding tanks, and I was delighted to see that they were now registering empty. Judging by the smile on his face, this item was not wasted on Paul.

"Seems as though if we get really bored with all those bells and whistles," Paul said as he now made his way aft, "we can occupy our time playing with any one of ten different headsails."

"You're kidding me. Paul, this is a forty footer, with roller furling at that."

Colin Jasperson was apparently trying to squeeze the program of a maxi racer into what appeared from the docks to be a docile family cruiser. But what I now saw across the main salon pushed everything else into a distant second, for before eyes was the icing on the cake and the cherry on top to boot. We now had a TV/VCR combination with a library of what had to be fifty tapes from which to choose: documentaries, action adventure, comedy, and what no true ocean racer should ever leave shore without, a sterling collection of pure unadulterated porn. I guess that the waterlogged skin magazines of years past had become victim to the video revolution and today's tired and lonely off-watch crew members could be coddled, comforted and mentally caressed in bold and brash living color.

"My, my, my. Seems we're going to have a mighty interesting crossing ahead of us," Paul mumbled as he gazed at the creature comforts with which *Curlew* was warmly embracing us. "Very interesting indeed."

We continued to pore over all of *Curlew*'s toys and were pleased to find that apart from needing to get various charts of the East Coast of the U.S., a master plotting chart of the Atlantic and charts of the Irish and English coast, the only major things which we were in need of were filters for her two Lorans and some backup handles for the manual bilge pumps. We found that when we fired up the auxiliary engine, the electronic noise from the alternator caused interference with the Loran's reception and its readings were a tad less accurate than when the engine was off. Hopefully most of our time crossing would be spent under sail, but in the unlikely event that we sailed into high pressure systems and ran out of air, we would have to rely on the engine. We needed to be assured that the numbers which the instruments displayed were as accurate as possible. Although we would primarily be relying on satellite fixes from our GPS, we would also be plotting our course by the more traditional means of dead reckoning with the Loran signal as a backup. While the Loran signals were only good for the short time we were around any of the coasts, it was always comforting to have a backup to the backup, and Jasperson had seen to it that we had two. And if all else failed, we could always turn to our sextant, an art at which I have to admit I was more than a tad rusty on and took no great joy in practicing. Each year, during the spring equinox, I would trudge out to the breakwater off of Chester's harbor, take a few sun sights with the old girl, rush home, reduce them via my hopefully up-to-date almanacs, plot them and, if I came out within an acceptable neighborhood, confidently pack all away until the next spring equinox. I have no desire to break with my yearly tradition and actually use the thing to find out where I am, or more precisely, where I am supposed to be.

The rest of the morning was given over to looking underneath floorboards at well maintained through-hulls and sea cocks, poring over the workings of what appeared to be a partially rebuilt marine diesel engine, checking fluid levels and unpacking the myriad sails to check for signs of rot, small bullet holes or wear. Happily, we were pleased on all levels. I wanted to take a quick climb up the rig to check the mast head sheaves and insure that all electrical connections up there were watertight and solid. Figuring that this would take about the same time that it would for him to run up to the chandlery on Aubery Street, Paul set off to gather what charts he could as well as pick up the Loran filters. We arranged to meet at Eagle's in an hour and start checking off the long list which would hold us in port for the next week or so.

I can't say that I've ever become completely comfortable climbing a boat's mast, but as I started the ascent, whatever adrenaline I was starting to pump was countered with the sheer joy and comfort of gaining a higher and higher perspective on a harbor that was up until a few days ago more Coney Island than a tucked away New England refuge. Sitting in my harness eighty feet above a slowly rolling deck I remembered the crowds and noise of yet another summer. As I made a 360 degree survey of my almost forgotten harbor, I felt a smile begin to well up from a place of peace. For the first time in months I could see the wind's cats paws dance and skate their way across the blue water of an open port that seemed to be stretching and expanding in front of me. Those lobster boats which were left in Chester were now free to drop their strings of pots without having to keep one eye peeled for runaway day-sailers and the other for overloaded tour boats. I could see the small, refurbished schooner fleet which many years ago hauled light loads of lumber up and down the New England coast now resting lazily along Chester's main wharf, all given over to day charters for those who wanted a simple taste of the sea without having to give total commitment, all now empty of their cargo. Their skeleton crews were busy offloading modern gear which wasn't necessary for their fall migration down east to Rockport where they and others like them would wait while the sun made its yearly round-trip below the equator. I imagined how Chester's docks must have looked when her harbor was filled with such gracefully rigged work boats as these, when the sought after commodities were cargo and courage, not tourism and T-shirts. As much as I would loved to have seen her in her prime, right then and there I would trade my vantage point with no man, regardless the century. If not for the freshening breeze I could have frittered away any number of hours atop *Curlew*'s rig, watching as the past slowly pushed its way into the present.

It is someone's long ago established theorem that for every foot a deck eighty feet below rolls, the man at the top of the rig which stems from that deck rolls an extra five. By now the morning's north west breeze had filled in with assurance and created a chop in the harbor which made my perch more and more precarious. Turning my attentions from imagined sights of long ago to matters at hand, I found that I had best concentrate on what it was I had climbed up there to do in the first place. Starting with the masthead I checked all electrical connections for any signs of wear or corrosion. As I inspected the masthead tricolor and wind instruments, I found that no detail had been overlooked. Each connection was neatly spliced, wrapped and secured in such a fashion that the Atlantic would be hard pressed to find her way in, unless we were knocked down and had the rig in the water, and in such a case whether our masthead running lights were in working order would not be a pressing priority. As I made my way down the alloy rig, her tangs and fittings all looked clean, the shrouds and stays felt secure and tuned. As on the deck, the chaffing gear here looked intact, and whoever wrapped the spreader ends knew his or her stuff. Here again the exposed blunt ends of these horizontal struts were covered in well weathered elkhide, all tightly secured by a professionally executed lock stitch. Walking my way down the permanent mast steps I found that the sail track was neat, clean and showed no burrs for the slides to hang up on. It was a comfort to see that whoever was in charge of *Curlew* for the past few years clearly had the big picture in mind.

Next to and outboard of the internal track for the mainsail ran another, shorter, external track. This foresight allowed the storm trysail to have her own means of being raised. When the conditions called for the delivery main to be struck and a trysail to be raised, the last thing I wanted to have to worry about was handling yards and yards of canvas on a wildly pitching deck in fifty knots of wind. Hauling up a handkerchief-sized main on its own track and not having to mess about taking off another can mean the difference between relative safety and sheer terror, the latter being something I promised myself I had left far behind in the world of broadcasting.

It had been an hour since Paul left. Having assured myself that *Curlew*'s rig looked about as good as it could, if not better, I went below to grab the folder marked "Ship's Papers" from the nav table and headed up the dock toward Eagle's to discuss Quint's prior offer of canned goods at cost. Somehow canned beans and chili seemed a bit of a dead fish compared to the luxury in which I had just spent my morning, but unless I was willing to literally eat what profit I had hoped to realize from this trip, the old man's generosity couldn't be turned down.

"Captain Ahab, just the man I wanted to see."

How rare and unsettling it was to see the lovely Madeline out from behind her typewriter and walking down the ramp toward me. I was amazed and dismayed to find that now that she was on my turf, my territorial rights did nothing to boost my courage and confidence with her.

"What brings you down here, Madeline?" I hated to ask. "Going to lock one up for the weekend?"

"Only you have the answer to that one, skipper." She pressed an envelope into my hand. "All bills due at the end of the month." Awkwardly we held the contact between our hands perhaps a second longer than normal. Just as a small smile crossed her lips she took a small step to the side and turned to walk back. "Fee wants to see you." she said over her shoulder as she and various parts of her pleasing anatomy which I'd never had the opportunity to admire before headed back toward her lair. As a child I was forced to take piano lessons. My mother thought it would be the just the rounding out I needed. I hadn't thought about those lessons in years, but the sight of Madeline walking away from me took me right back to the days of watching that old metronome swing from side to side. I truly wished that things had been different, for there was a basic attraction I had to Madeline and I would like to have gotten to know her a bit better. Under different circumstances. We had an energy between us that I felt should not have been dismissed as readily as it was. But it was the same old story, since the divorce I hadn't been too trustful of women and viewed almost all of them as a threat. I never pursued anything with Madeline for fear of hurting the friendship, albeit strained, that we shared.

Present distractions not-withstanding, I felt confident that the envelope couldn't possibly be a bill. I didn't own a boat and any dealings I had had in the past with Pacchio's yard had all been cash up front. Whatever it was that I was now stuffing into my pocket would have to wait until Eagle's. I didn't want to distract myself from enjoying what was left of the view.

The usual crowd filled the stools and booths at Eagle's. The general consensus was that it was damn good to have our town back. Quint was starting to get busy in front of his grill so all conversation with him was aimed at and returned from the searing hot surface in front of him, which now held hamburger patties, hash browns, shaved steak and frying onions. The ex-Navy man was clever enough to have placed a small mirror on the wall, eye level and just to the side of the grill. This way he could keep whatever free eye he had on the front door and greeted every incoming customer with the same welcome: "The galley's starting to fill, folks, let's double up." The purpose of the greeting was twofold; first it cheerfully acknowledged your presence as you made your way into his steamy luncheonette and second, and perhaps more importantly, it notified those who were thinking of paying up and leaving that they should, as Quint now had the chance to seat and sell another meal

All levels of Chester's thriving industry were represented in Eagle's this morning. The crew of the fishing trawler *Rainbow* was tucked into a far booth and judging by the animation of their conversation they were discussing things other than setting nets or yields of recent hauls, probably dock prices or near misses they had survived out on the bay this summer. Tommy

McFarland, Chester's Third District councilman, was holding court at the counter blatantly trying to assure all that could hear him through the din that his office doors were always open to rich and poor, young and old, long-time resident or carpetbagger, and that Chester's concerns were indeed his. When not holding forth at Eagle's, Tommy could be found in his office, a strictly one-man work space which was packed into the side of his garage where his snowblower used to be. I've yet to meet anyone who actually had matters pressing enough to go and squeeze in beside his Chevy Nova and aluminum canoe. Yet we all slept well knowing that Councilman McFarland was a man of, for and by the good people of Chester. Where Tommy really came into his own was his seemingly limitless knowledge of Chester's waterfront. Since he was a small boy, this small, pug-nosed rock of a man spent all of his free time wandering along Chester's wharves taking mental stock of who had sailed in the night before, how long they were to stay and where it was they were soon to be headed for. In those days, if you were in need of a spare, hard to find, expensive part ASAP, Tommy was your man. He prided himself on getting it for you for bottom dollar -- no questions asked, no answers given. These traits made him a natural politician. I took great comfort in the fact that the demands of office were never so pressing as to keep Tommy from his appointed rounds. On any given day Tommy could still be found wandering through what yards were left. "Drumming up support," he called it. Listening to Chester's music was how I saw it.

Looking down the row of stools at the counter hoping to find Paul, my eyes rested on the man sitting in front of Quint reading Chester's daily newspaper from a few days back. I recognized Fee Pachico's full, hunched back, which was clothed in the same faded blue and white flannel he has worn as long as I knew him. Fee had gotten a jump on the rest of the lunch crowd and was patiently awaiting his chourico and mashed potatoes. Of all the wonderful cultural riches which the Portuguese brought with them from the Azores, surely this spicy native sausage was one of the most appreciated. Chourico was a main staple of Fee's and knowing him for as long as I had I couldn't remember a day when he didn't have one of these in one form or another. Today's offering seemed to be suffering needlessly on Quint's grill.

"Rumor has it you're looking for me," I said as I sat down, clearing the newspaper off the stool next to Fee. "What's up?"

"Just want to make sure that you know your ship came in last night." The double entendre being an old favorite of Fee's, I wasn't sure if I was expected to still find it funny after all this time.

"Yeah, I just came from her," I said "Somebody's got some bucks."

"As long there's enough bucks to pay for the slip. Who's signing the checks?" he asked staring forward.

"Jasperson asked that you bill him directly," I said. We had been over all of this many times before, but Fee was looking for his usual reassurance. "I left his address with Madeline, he said that he was going to call you directly about it himself." As with the airline tickets, experience had taught me that it was far easier to have the client handle the slip rentals himself. It was cleaner to charge him for miles sailed, not time at the dock.

"Just see that he does, Captain. Don't want to upend Madeline's books."

Since I had recently had the pleasure of watching her walk away from me earlier on the docks, I had been occupied by thoughts of upending old Madeline herself.

"How long you going to need the space?" Fee asked with his nose still buried in the paper.

"Another week?" I said. "Maybe less"

"Have this guy call me, I want to start pulling those slips next week," he said as Quint placed Fee's lunch in front of him. Conversation over.

"The galley's starting to fill, folks, let's double up," Quint said as Paul walked through the door. Under his right arm was a stack of charts rolled tightly in a tube. In his left hand he carried a box of what most probably were the filters for the Loran. The crew of *Rainbow* was slowly getting up from their booth as Paul and I headed over to the area, hoping to slide in right behind them and start on our first of many lists.

"You guys really going to head out soon?" her captain asked. "It can be a handful out there this time of year. Hate to see you get yourself in over your heads."

"They know what they're doing, Mark," one of his deck-hands said, "Besides, Chris told me yesterday that he was gonna buy him a brand new pair of yachting shoes for the trip. Them and racing gloves to keep him nice and comfy."

Knowing my disdain for the armchair ocean racer who wouldn't be found anywhere near the water without his official, miracle-fabric, guaranteed-to-make-you-look-the-part-but-leave-you-soaking-wet foul weather gear and gloves, it was their constant joy to lump me in with the recently departed summer crowd.

"What's to worry," I said. "As long as we know that the good ship *Rainbow* is off in the reach chasing fish, we can sleep comfortably all the way across. Hell, if we find ourselves in trouble all we have to do is whistle, right?"

"You do that, mate." One of them said as they headed for the door.

"If you guys need anything let me know," Mark said. "Give me a holler before you head out." And with that, the crew of the good ship *Rainbow* rolled out the door and down towards their ship.

"Jesus, I just about blew the budget on the charts alone," Paul moaned as we slid into our booth. "Got what Skinner's had. We're still short on the coastal approaches to the Irish coast."

I shrugged. "Screw it and hope for the best?" Although we had no intention of landing in Ireland, or Nova Scotia for that matter, it was prudent, that we have cruising charts of both areas. Being on the wrong end of an extreme weather system or crippled by a mechanical breakdown could alter our delivery route in a hurry.

"Fee's over at the counter. Just got through talking about *Curlew*'s dock fees. I guess Jasperson hasn't set this up yet." I lowered my voice, "I'll call and double check all of this, seems to be a bit of a loose end here." I now remembered Madeline's envelope. Pulling it from my back pocket I slid it across the table to Paul. "Madeline gave this to me earlier today. Probably got something to do with it."

As Paul read what looked like an invoice from my side of the table he slowly reached into his pocket and started to dig out some change. "Best call Jasperson now. This is starting to get complicated."

Reading the paperwork myself, I saw that it was more work order than actual bill. Just why *Curlew* was scheduled for work wasn't clear, but I knew that the longer I sat there trying to decipher it, the sooner the heading titled "Estimated Cost" would turn into "Account Now Due."

"Shit, no wonder her crew took off so early. She's scheduled to be pulled out of the water ASAP. God damn it."

The delivery crew from Maine had arranged for *Curlew* to be hauled out of the water for a reason or reasons not spelled out to me or mentioned on the work order, but judging by the now dwindling crowd at Eagle's, most everybody's lunch hour was just about over and this meant that Fee's travel lift operator was probably just starting to slide the lift straps under her hull. I had just enough change for the pay phone.

Jasperson was direct and to the point, "Don't know anything about anyone arranging for her to be hauled out, but if the crew felt it necessary who's to argue."

Jasperson's secretary had patched the call through to his car phone. I knew nothing about *Curlew* being hauled, it appeared as though Jasperson knew nothing about her being hauled, Fee made no mention of her being hauled and the best I could figure it, Madeline was the only one who had any idea of what was going on.

"Hold on a minute," I said. I covered the mouthpiece of the pay phone. "Paul, this is screwed up, get the counter phone from Quint and call Madeline and find out if *Curlew* is being hauled. We gotta stop this until we know what's going on." I turned my attention back to Jasperson and heard a crackle and hiss in place of his voice. "Hello, Mr. Jasperson?" nothing. "Hello?" it was like talking to Ellie. “God damn it, I hate cellulars!” I muttered as I hung up. I had lost him.

I looked back over the counter where Paul had been using the phone and all that I saw now was the empty phone.

“The galley’s starting to fill up, folks, let’s double up,” Quint announced to two empty booths and a handful of hangers-on.

“Quint, where’d Paul go?” I said.

“No idea, just flew out the door. You guys’ve had quite a day of it haven’t you?” The old man laughed. “Morning started out the same way. Paul comes in here, checks a piece of paper and heads out real quick. Chris follows in later, catches up with him on the phone then steams out of here same speed. How do you shipmates get along when you’re on the water?”

Did he really expect me to answer that? I “steamed off same speed” for the yard. Quint was right, though, the day was barely half over and so far Paul and I had potentially spent almost a third of the money we had hoped to make on the delivery. A tired but nonetheless true old adage about sailing suggests that to experience the real thrill of ocean racing, one should simply stand under a shower and tear up $100 bills. I felt as though I had just gotten out of the shower for the second time today.

As I flew down the shortcut toward Fee’s, I ran between what was once Chester’s customs house and her old armory. Both buildings were scheduled to be condo-ized and were starting to fall victim to the wrecker’s ball. More of the same, I guess, but my immediate concern wasn’t as much for Chester’s financial future as my own. Sliding around the corner on loose and broken asphalt my worst fears were confirmed not as much by what I saw, but what I heard. The sound of the slow and methodical beeping coming from the travel lift around the corner told me that the driver had already hauled his load and was now backing up to park and block a boat. Great, I thought as I saw *Curlew* looking every bit the fish out of water that she was. Just great.

Paul shrugged as he came walking up to me. “Madeline said that the Maine crew fouled some pots a couple of miles out and thought it’d be best to haul her out and take a look. They might have bent the shaft."

"Paul, I could have dove on her. We're not going to pay for this," I announced to no one in particular.

We both stood there for a bit, not speaking, just watching as Fee and his man set the braces under her still dripping hull.

"Well hell. Now that she's out we can go over everything from the outside," Paul said, demonstrating his usual optimism and cool head. We could get a real close look at her through-hulls, grounding plates and zincs, but that really was something which should be saved until her final fall haul-out and most certainly should be arranged and, more importantly, paid for by her owner once she was in England. I didn't feel the flood of relief that I should have knowing that Jasperson had assured us that he'd take care of everything. As I stood there feeling the old familiar bead of sweat starting to zig-zag its way down my chest, I realized that at five dollars per foot, and with *Curlew* punching in at forty feet, I was looking at $200 worth of haul out alone. The voices from my stomach told me that we were nowhere close to seeing the end of this thing. As Paul started to poke and prod around under her hull I reckoned it best to go into the lion's den for the second time today.

"Look, they left a note arranging for it first thing this morning." Madeline said from behind her typewriter. "They would have stuck around but they grabbed the first bus up to Boston. Besides, it had to be done now in order to hit the tide right."

"If you'd missed the damn tide, this would have been put off until tomorrow and we probably wouldn't be going through all of this right now." I mumbled as I hinted at the fact that Fee's level of efficiency was known to rise and fall in direct relationship to the cash potential of the job.

I was happy to see that my mumble wasn't wasted on Madeline.

"Chris, their note explaining all of this is in with the ship's papers. Now unless you've got something that's real important, I suggest you go read it."

"Look, just set her off to the side and let her sit until I can get this all back on track. I don't want to get stuck paying for something I didn't authorize. Don't worry about her shaft, we can look into that later."

Through the window next to me, I began to notice an increase in activity under *Curlew*'s hull. What workers were left were slowly being drawn to one of the season's last opportunities for them to make some money. I could see that Fee himself was now under her hull, running his hand along her still glistening bilge. His presence clearly announced that *Curlew* was now on his clock, and the longer we sat there discussing her immediate future, the more expensive it was going to be for either Jasperson or me.

"Let me tell you something, Chris. Right now there are only two people in this room who have any concern for your welfare, and one of them is rapidly losing interest." The woman had a brilliant career waiting for her in television. "The original note and work order are all in with the ship's papers. Read it for yourself. Bye now."

Strange feeling, having to stand in line to take responsibility for a boat which had been left in my care for the next month or so, like one of those dreams where you're trying to deliver news of the utmost importance, but no one is interested in what you have to say. Clearly I was getting nowhere hanging around and trying to hammer it out with Madeline. She was right, I figured, it was best to go back and find out exactly where it was that the wheels started to fall off this whole thing and the file marked "Ship's Papers" would hopefully give me a start. Only problem was that in the quick confusion of the morning, that particular file and I had parted company somewhere along the line, and judging by the way Madeline was now smiling at the blank expression on my face, it would be best if I was on my way to find the missing file before she had a chance to suggest I do just that.

"Will it be a fresh cup of tea, or would you like me to heat up the other two you didn't drink earlier?" Quint asked as he handed me the errant file. You could leave the Crown Jewels in Eagle's and no one would give them a second thought. His honesty made up for what his food lacked; it could always be counted on. Quint kept a box in the back room which contained items that his customers had left behind over the years. Sooner or later they would all be restored to their proper homes, all but a set of false teeth which had been orphaned for so long now that they had worked their way forward to a jar of honor right beside the cash register.

Quint's sarcasm was to be expected. So far I had dashed out his door twice and had successfully worked myself up into a bit of a lather. The real crime in all of this was that this was the Day After and so far I hadn't much of a chance to enjoy it. Perhaps it was time to start the morning all over again. *Curlew* was out of the water and this was probably all for the better. Jasperson hadn't given me any indication of being unreasonable and to date I'd had no reason to doubt his word. Once we cleared up the airline ticket problem and got *Curlew* back in the water, we'd most certainly be reimbursed and in a few days time we'd be heading east and all of this would be filed under the section marked "Learning Curve."

Finally having a chance to let the Earl Grey work into my system, I settled back into a window booth and started to flip through the usual papers found in *Curlew*'s file. Jasperson's Coast Guard documentation showed that all was up to date and proved that he was indeed her one and only owner. His bill of sale from one Mr. Nigel Covely-Ames of South Sussex, England stated that three years ago Colin Jasperson had paid "ten dollars and a considerable sum" for a forty-foot sloop. No easy feat here as buying a vessel of foreign registry usually brings about some pretty high import fees. Yet it appeared as though our absent owner had covered himself and avoided Uncle Sam's deep reaching hands. I reckoned that Jasperson's genius was to be found in the neighborhood of "considerable sum." There were some various yard bills from a Mather's Ship Yard in South Hampton, England, and indeed the note from a Wayne Frazier of East Boothbay, Maine addressed to Fee Pachico stating that while *Curlew* was up the coast aways, she powered over a string of lobster pots causing a line to wrap around her prop with enough force to stall out her engine. It went on to say that they had taken the necessary steps and dove on her to cut the line free but weren't too sure if the force of the wrap had caused any bearing damage or not. He then went on to assure the yard that Jasperson would want her hauled and that he, the undersigned, our Wayne Frazier from East Boothbay, Maine, was now so requesting Pacchio's yard to haul her at their earliest convenience. Seeing it all spelled out in black and white made me feel a tad more secure than I had a few hours ago. The potential damage happened while *Curlew* was under Wayne's watch and here he had clearly assured one and all that Jasperson would foot any and all bills. I was clearly out of the loop.

As I sat there feeling the warmth from the afternoon sun on my back, I finally relaxed enough to enjoy the peace of the Day After. Paul was right, *Curlew*'s being hauled was actually more to our favor than not in that we now could get a complete view of the hull that was going to be our home across 3,000 open miles of the Atlantic. We could address any problem below the water line while we were safe and secure on shore. If the shaft was out of alignment or the bearings were damaged, how much better to find out about it on dry land than becalmed and fighting the currents of the English Channel.

I paid for my cups of tea and headed out to check with Paul back at the yard.

"Nice to have our town back," I said to Tommy McFarland, who was now heading toward me down the sidewalk.

"Very nice," he said as he made his turn into Eagle's. "Very nice indeed. If I don't get a chance to tell you before you leave, Chris, best of breezes to you and Paul for the big one."

"Thanks Tommy" I said as I crossed the street, raising my voice enough to carry over a cool fall blast. "Went over her this morning, she looks great. Should be pretty straightforward. She seems a good strong boat."

"Always has been, that one," he said as he started to turn into the door.

"You know her, do you?" I said as I crossed back toward him. "You must know Jasperson then."

"Don't know any Jasperson, but I do know *Skara Brae* when I see her. She came trans-Atlantic about three years ago for the Onion Patch series, but her owner fell short of cash. Never did race. At first I didn't recognize her with her new transom, but that's her all right. Same profile, same rig, hell, even same bottom and cove stripe.

I was caught flat-footed. "You're thinking of another boat. Originally she was from England, but she's always been called *Curlew*."

"May be *Curlew* now, but I know my boats and that's *Skara Brae*."

I didn't like the direction that this conversation was turning, not one bit, and like the reluctant child, I was tempted to stick my fingers in my ears and start singing the National Anthem very loudly.

"I remember having a long talk with her captain about her name," he said. "Seems she was named after a small coastal town on the western tip of Scotland, he used to summer there or something. She was built in a South Hampton yard. I guess her original owner's eyes were far larger than his wallet. He found out too late."

I don't know if it was due to the lack of breakfast, lack of lunch, two bouts of potentially bad financial news or the fact that I was about to proceed head-first into the open jaws of one of my two superstitions, but I slowly felt reality start to slip from me as I stood there, simply staring at Tommy. "What you're telling me is that *Curlew*, the boat I'm about to sail across the Atlantic, was once known as *Skara Brae*. And that somewhere along the line, someone changed her name."

"That's just what I'm saying my friend. Check your papers," he said, nodding toward the file under my arm. "Must be in there somewhere. As I said, best breezes to you two." With that he flashed his vote insuring smile and walked on through Quint's door.

Now, my father was a brave man, he once pulled a neighborhood German Shepherd off of one of our Deerhounds with total disregard for his own safety. These two dogs were clearly intent on seeing it to the bitter end, yet he waded in between them and with brute force separated them. When all was said and done, his arms were covered in blood yet not a scratch was to be found anywhere on him. Yet put this same brave man in a pool with a small green frog and in the blink of an eye, or the croak of a frog, he would turn into a frightened child, scampering for the safety of the side until the frog was either removed from the pool or jumped along and went about its business. Take Paul Dwyer, the man who had amassed over 10,000 miles sailing singlehanded, scaled the Matterhorn and even took on the Yukon River by himself. Mention the word "rabbit" on or near a boat and he would exhibit a more than a heightened state of anxiety. Something to do with an old French maritime superstition, he was never quite sure where it came from or when it became so permanently wedged under his skin, but suffice it to say that the mere mention of the "R" word, or even worse, "*lapin*", was enough to make Paul literally walk away from any sailing commitment, regardless how exciting or lucrative. The point being here that we all have our foibles, our weak points, our superstitions, our kryptonite. Again, the two that kept me up at nights were leaving on a Fridays and renaming a boat. Tommy would have gotten the same effect had he slugged me in the stomach. Judging by the events of this day, the gears of superstitious retribution had already been set into in motion and they were beginning to grind.

Had there been any questions about it before, there and then I decided that this day had most assuredly come to a close and it would be best for all concerned if I simply retreated to my apartment before any more unexpected news could find its target.

Wandering up Aubery Street in the opposite direction from the one I so optimistically bounded down this morning, I found my mood to have changed as well. This particular Day After had been far less than good. The wind was no longer just cool, but held the strength and bite of the fall season. There was actually some weight to it as I realized that simply rolling down my sleeves or turning up my collar wasn't going to keep the chill out. It had been quite a while since I had last felt the familiar edge of a cold wind.

CHAPTER 4

It was the same dream which Katherine had had so many times before, and the same haunting chill of finality would eventually shake her awake. As she lay in her bed staring at the moon's bright path, illuminating the faded, yellowing paper on the wall of her small bedroom, she was locked in the grasp of that midnight confusion, the state of trying to separate dream from reality, fear from chill. So many times she had found herself on the tall schooner finally heading home. All of the dreams led her to the same outcome. She was leaving Chester behind her. As the unhappy memories of Elmwood drifted further and further off the stern, she was at last allowing herself to relax and allowing the hopes of her awaiting life room to grow. The ship was heading straight and true back toward England, rail down, sheer bow plowing aside the gray and cold waters of the North Atlantic. The warmth of the Gulf Steam had long since passed under the stern of the great ship, and had now turned off to the south to complete its circuitous journey of the Atlantic. Katherine now found herself balancing on the wet decks of this fog-enshrouded greyhound, looking up the wide tapering spars which supported the massive, straining canvas sails. The wind which carried as much spray as power buffeted Katherine as she stood at the weather rail, wondering how and when the coastline of her home would first make itself known.

"She's a hard driving hungry old lady," said someone behind her.

She didn't have to turn to know that Captain Middleton was at his station, his weathered eyes continuously searching for an elusive clue as to when he'd best give the order to shorten sail against the building gale.

"She's homeward bound now, Miss Worthington, she smells the barn all right," he hollered above the wind. "She's been pushing this route for eight years, I reckon she knows her way by now. There's nothing you can do, young lady. Best you tend to yourself." He looked to the scudding clouds. "We're heading for a breeze."

His kind and caring words did not find their mark. As much as Katherine was open to it, the reassurance of being in the captain's wind shadow never would arrive, for here is where Katherine's haunting nightmare would start to claim its power. She would wheel to answer her captain and time after time she faced the sudden terror and void of realizing that these encouraging words from the man were nothing more than the voices in the building winds and that the comfort of the good ship's master never had been offered. Katherine was alone on deck and was slowly being encompassed by the pressing darkness of the storm. The dark and brooding clouds rolled down and started to lash at the ship with driving rain. As the schooner leaned harder into the building wind, the ocean's spray was replaced by sheets of solid water. Great waves were starting to break against and onto her glistening decks. Katherine cowered as the growling wind pressed the canvas above her to its limits. What just a few minutes ago had been a building breeze was now a storm of furious proportions. How long she had been on deck she didn't know. Where her hands had once held a fair grip on the weather rail, her knuckles were now twisted and white. The schooner shook and shuddered with each new burst of wind. Her long awaited journey had turned into a nightmare of fury and rage.

High above her the hundreds of square feet of wet and ragged canvas shrieked as it flailed and whipped out against anything within its reach. The tapering spars whose tops were well hidden in the darkness of approaching night and weather were starting to shake and vibrate where they passed through the deck. The seams between the wood which made up the ship's deck started to work, and some began to open as they tried in vain to keep her doomed rig in place.

Hollering for help, her words were torn out of her mouth by the blazing wind. Katherine could barely hear her own voice and her horror intensified as she now realized that no one from the off-watch would fall out to shorten sail against the building frenzy. As with the phantom captain, Katherine knew that the ship boasted no crew, no cook, no carpenter. Katherine alone was being hurtled east by the furious storm. As every one of these dreams had shown her in the past, she was alone with her building fate.

Fighting against the wind and water which ran the length of the pitching decks, Katherine slowly struggled her way to the forward hatch just aft the twisting and tortured mainmast, to try to seek some shelter from the maelstrom. But by now she was all too familiar with the futility of her efforts. Every time she came close to the hatch, the boat would lurch and throw her back, solid walls of water would tear at her and slam her into the lee scuppers. The best she could do for now was try to crawl across the wildly pitching deck, again try to slide back the hatch cover, climb down the companionway ladder and secure the hatch above her.

Pausing just enough to build up more energy and fury, the Atlantic offered the momentary respite Katherine needed to reach safety at the solid hatch. Sliding back the cover, she threw herself into the dark hole leading below. The guts of the schooner were far too dark for the girl to find her way and for now the solid rails on the ladder offered her only safe grasp. Knowing that it had missed a chance to claim Katherine, a fevered Atlantic once more threw a boiling and determined sea at the ship, slamming into the port side of the struggling ship and raking its fury across the deck just above Katherine's head. The energy of the explosion threw her from her perch on the companionway ladder. The handholds which Katherine was able to find in the dark were intent on shaking loose her grip with every shudder and lurch which the ship took. Landing face down against the ship's cold and dark sole, she heard far below her in the bilges the distant shrieking and splitting as the backbone of the schooner was starting to pull from all which was fastened to it. The great schooner was driving herself too hard into the gale and was dying for her efforts. No one was helping her meet the pressing fury. As the mounting seas towered above her charging bows, no deck-hands were there to shorten sail, veer her away from the eye of the storm, help slow her down and try to meet the storm on its own terms. Laying there, Katherine could hear the sound of water rushing and swirling through the bilges, telling her that the powerful gray Atlantic was slowly beginning to rise up further into the ship, trying to reach up and claim what it could.

Katherine slowly groped her way back toward the ladder, trying not to lose what ground she could gain on the wildly pitching sole. Each time the boat fell off a wave, Katherine's feet would go out from under her as her worn leather shoes failed to gain a grip on the wet and slick wood. There was a massive explosion outside, high above in the crosstrees, as the ship's foremast shattered from the terrible pressure of having too much sail against too much wind. Once again Katherine lost her footing and went face down on the hard wood, raking her face against the ladder as she fell. A sudden and violent lurch of the ship threw her hard across the breadth of the schooner and planted her against the hull, only inches of wood protecting her from what was so desperate to get inside.

"Oh, God, Bridie, what have I done?" Katherine wailed. "Bridie, help me."

As she put her hand up to the side of throbbing face, she knew the warm thick fluid to be blood. She couldn't tell how badly she was hurt. Lying in terror, listening to the rage of the wind and tearing of the seas, Katherine thought back on to the many discussions she and her young friend had while standing on the seawall of Elmwood. She thought back to those feelings of power dwelling from deep inside of her, those pullings which seemed to come from so far out at sea.

"My God, what do you want?" she screamed.

Wedging herself between two of the ship's ribs, Katherine realized her fate. The sides of the schooner shuddered in resignation as the dying ship once again fell from a great distance, slamming onto her beam ends into a trough of the continuously building and limitless seas. The splintering and grating continued from far below in the ship's bilges. Katherine could now feel the drop in temperature telling her that the icy grip of the great Atlantic was getting closer to its prey. Once more and with great effort, she crawled across the heaving and bucking ship's sole as she tried to make her way back to her perch on the ladder, which would provide safe haven between the screaming fury of the elements on deck and the rising, freezing grave below.

And here it would end.

Each time Katherine would awake with a bone-jarring shudder. Her sheets would be soaked and her pillow wrenched beneath her. She would lie motionless, hoping to quell the terror. In a few hours the sun would start its path across her yellowed wall, she lay there listening to her own heart pound. She knew that it was only a dream, yet the cold, angry grip was always so slow in releasing her. She fell back to sleep.

CHAPTER 5

Though the pounding on her door became more and more insistent, it was the urgency in the old man's voice echoing outside in the courtyard which pulled Katherine's attention back into the here and now of Aubery Street. Sitting up in bed she listened desperately hoping that it wasn't a dream.

"Miss Worthington? Miss Worthington!" the old man bellowed, stressing each syllable of her name. "Miss Worthington, it's time!"

Up until a few minutes ago, Dunbar had been transferring pine tar from the supplier's fifty-gallon barrels into his own one-gallon containers, a sloppy affair which more times than not insured that Dunbar's chandlery continued to boast the acrid distinction of having a tarred floor. At first it had taken the busy chandler a few minutes to gather in that the cart driver waiting outside on Aubery Street was actually talking to him. This hopelessly disheveled driver was sitting atop his open delivery cart, which followed behind his equally disheveled horse, which pulled the worn and splintered platform through the streets.

"Here for the girl. Get her," the driver said, more to his horse than anyone else. Rummaging through the pockets of his tattered denim jacket as though he was trying to find something which had been eluding him for the past few years, he continued to stare forward, offering no more than a vacant gaze. He clenched an unlit pipe firmly between what was left of his uppers and lowers. "Get her. If she need a ride, now's it."

Dunbar had seen this man many times before, bringing freshly off-loaded goods through the dirt-choked streets of Chester, but this had to have been the first time the shopkeeper ever heard the man speak. He certainly would have remembered any previous attempts. He had the scruffy look of a man who spent the better part of his time at sea, but as thin and sunken as he was, his body suggested otherwise. Dunbar was always glad to see that the man's horse never showed any signs of being underfed or overworked. A working contrast to be sure.

Finally acknowledging the old shopkeeper's presence, he slowly turned to him. "The one who's waiting on the ship. Get her," he said with great effort and finality. With that both he and his steed slumped, truly worn after the morning's conversational efforts.

Finally understanding the cart driver's mission, Dunbar spun on his heels and hurried back into his shop, instructing anyone within earshot to take a quick turn out to the street, hop up on the stoop and start banging on Miss Worthington's door for all he was worth. He barked the orders on the run as he himself went straight out to the back courtyard and tried rousting her from below.

"Miss Worthington, it's time. Your ship's here. Hurry now."

The words which were now coming through Katherine's back window brought the news she had been waiting to hear for so many months now, and the pounding downstairs on her door confirmed it. She had been living out of her small leather case since the day she took the room, and every day it was at the ready. Yet now that the time had come and she was truly on her way, the shock of realization kept her from attending to the basic things. While she was dressing, she tried ever so neatly to fold and pack her nightclothes into the top layer of her case and attempted to answer both the front door as well as Mr. Dunbar below.

"Yes, yes, I'm ready!" she hollered, trying more to convince herself than those who waited. "I'm ready," she mumbled. "How the Lord knows I'm ready."

"Miss Worthington, the driver's out front and the time is now. I'll tell him you're on your way. Hurry along now." Dunbar raced back into his shop.

The few special things which Katherine had managed to collect these past few months were now unceremoniously shoved into the flimsy and cracked leather case which was already too full. The small leather satchel, which had already seen better days when she first left England with it, was now threatening to betray Katherine's personal life and belongings in one loud tear.

"Well, you fit yesterday," she said as the urgency of the good news was sinking into her. A small single-bladed knife which Dunbar had given her during a midsummer's eve as they had one of their usual visits out on the stoop was slid down between her heavy oiled wool sweater and one of her three worn skirts. The delicate lace tablecloth she had sewn and hemmed out of some remnants she had found behind the linen shop found a home atop the heavy cotton blouses which saw her day in and day out at Elmwood, evidence of Katherine's determination to leave the site of her former employ with more than simply bad memories. The two shells boasting swirls of mother of pearl which she had collected while she and Bridie had walked along the water's edge were frantically shuffled around the case, from top to bottom, side to side, each new home they found quickly given over to a safer one.

Bridie, she thought as she exhaled. My letter for Bridie. Katherine stopped and sat down hard on one of the few chairs which her room boasted. So many were the times that Katherine tried to put pencil to paper and open up her heart to the young girl from Ireland and so many times she sat there knowing that when it came to telling Bridie her concerns and love, words simply failed. Since she had walked away from Elmwood, Katherine had seen Bridie in and around town on rare occasions, yet, knowing the position it would put Bridie in, Katherine never actually spoke with her old friend. It wouldn't do to have one of her girls being seen with one who snubbed the hand that ruled her. They would pass by, exchanging knowing and joyous glances, and in this Katherine rested assured that their friendship and love was still alive and growing, if somewhat muted. Realizing that a missive hastily scrawled out with just as hasty thoughts would fall far from her intended mark, Katherine continued to pack and scurry, promising herself that by hook or crook it would be written and sent.

Trying not to take the stairs two at a time, Katherine, her bag and a wealth of determination all landed at street level with all the excitement and energy as if she were finally setting foot on

English soil. Her mind was in a whirl as she stood there looking at the tired driver. She had forgotten to take a final glance around her room to check for any overlooked possession, she hadn't even checked to see if her gas was off, yet all of that was trivial now. She was on her way home. So many feelings came rushing at her -- one second she was happy, the next scared, and for some strange reason she began to feel some sadness slowly beginning to creep into it all. The driver looked her up and down very deliberately and then gave a nod toward the back of his cart; either the bag or Katherine herself was to find a seat back there among the oil-soaked rags and various scraps of tarred hemp.

Little matter, she thought. Now that her new life was awakening before her, the lack of a comfortable ride down to the water front was of no consequence. Using the grip of her good right hand combined with the upward push of her left one, she worked her bulging leather case over the sideboards and walked around toward the open back of the horse drawn cart, hoisted herself aboard, and tried to get herself situated as best she could for the short trip down to the docks.

"You've got precious cargo here, mister, and I'll not see you sitting idly by while she has to find the way for herself." Dunbar bellowed as he came out of the shop, wiping the morning's work off his hands. "Get your lazy self down off that perch and help out this young lady."

Totally unconcerned the driver hopped down off his seat and sauntered around toward the back of his cart as Katherine slid herself down off the back. She gently raised her skirt up to negotiate the gutter headed toward the man who had been her link with hope and promise for the past few months. More astonished than embarrassed, she realized that she was charging right along without stopping to say goodbye to Mr. Dunbar.

"Miss Worthington," he said gently, "this is your start, this is what you've been waiting for. You'll not begin it by sitting in the back of a cart." He took Katherine by the arm and escorted her up to the passenger's seat. In all the months that Katherine and the old shopkeeper had known one another, this was the first time that he had actually touched her. Katherine was amazed to realize that she knew the feel of his touch, she was so familiar with his concern and strength as they walked those few steps. This knowledge was from so long ago, another life, another country. Dunbar's firm hold on her arm reassured her that her decision to leave Chester was the right one and that she wasn't blindly setting out alone on her trip. The care and concern that she could feel from him was just the tip of what she had been missing. Slowly, barely perceptibly, her long buried feelings of joy and comfort were coming to life.

Katherine began to feel her excitement pressed by a new sensation, one that for the first time had her start to question the efforts which lay ahead of her. She looked down the length of Aubery Street and began to feel a sense of loss for the town which had been home to her for these many years now. Katherine had spent so much energy and time keeping her determination to leave straight and true that she never stopped to think that, as far away as Chester was from her home, imperceptibly it had managed to work its way into her consciousness. She realized for the first time that she was truly scared by what lay ahead of her and sad for that which she was leaving.

Her eyes answered Dunbar's firm grip. In them he saw the doubt and fear which were threatening to betray her excitement.

"It's a long road ahead of you now, girl. You've been down longer."

Katherine was surprised to feel her throat tighten and her senses fill with the moment. "All of a sudden it's here. I'm going home," she whispered. She remembered Bridie and the walks, she remembered the reprimands from the upper staff, she thought back onto those nights curled up in her bed under the eaves of Elmwood, trying to hear her heart over the pounding of the Atlantic's waves. She remembered the power and the voice of the sea which had been able to reach so far down inside of her and grip her soul and fears.

"Oh Mr. Dunbar," she whispered "Am I doing the right thing? I feel as though my insides are frozen. I can't see ahead of me anymore." She started to cry.

The shopkeeper drew out his handkerchief and offered it to the girl. “Girl, none can truly see ahead. It’s only the heart that can. You must trust yours now more than ever.”

“The wind won’t wait,” said the anxious driver. “Go or stay, all the same with me.” He started to gather up the reigns in hand.

“All of our good hopes and wishes travel with you girl,” Dunbar said as he swung her up beside the driver. “Don’t you be damaging any of these goods now, driver. She’s a long journey ahead and I’ll not see her getting off to a rough start.”

The driver clucked at his horse, snapped his reigns and started off toward the harbor. Katherine turned to give her old friend one final wave. Waving back, Dunbar’s hand started to slow as he noticed that apart from the rags and cans on the back of the rig, Katherine’s leather bag was the only other cargo to be seen.

The rutted street shook and twisted the wooden frame of the old cart, it was all Katherine could do to hold on with her withered hand while she watched Dunbar’s Chandlery slowly disappear behind the bend as Aubery Street meandered toward the waterfront. As Katherine watched the familiar buildings and faces fall past the cart she had the sudden sensation that she had only just arrived in Chester. In the face of what lay ahead of her, the long lonely days at Elmwood were quickly compressing into one block of disjointed gray memory and with the flush of her journey and new life coursing through her, she was hard pressed to stop and separate the good from the bad, the orders from the helpful instruction, the friends from the distant staff.

The mixture of fear and excitement was an intoxicating combination. What Katherine now saw ahead of her was not a harbor bustling with trade but more a pocket of energy and promise which was waiting to launch her out into the reach and then home. All the sights were the same and yet different. The wharves which bordered Chester’s harbor were no longer simple bleached gray wooden platforms which pushed out from Aubery Street. They contained life in all different sizes, forms and colors.

“You jump out here now. Haven’t got all day.”

"Jump out where?" Katherine asked.

"Right here girl, this is where I'm to leave you," he said over his shoulder as he walked toward the back of the old cart to get at Katherine's trunk.

Katherine looked around slowly, blinking her eyes against the raised dust and the occasional explosion of voices. What she saw in front of her was not very promising. Surely the driver had failed to take her to the right wharf. Between stacks of lumber, barrels of tar and countless piles of coiled hemp, Katherine could see evidence of only one ship resting along the bulkheads, a two-masted affair which was nothing like what she had prayed would be her passage home. The weathered old schooner which seemed to be the center of the day's activities gently rose and fell with the harbor's surge as she waited patiently for her crew and dockhands to clear her topsides of well lashed piles of cargo. The old ship seemed to be taking deep, slow breaths as she waited, leaning to her dock lines. What were one time surely straight and true spars now sat out of column, almost promising to tumble to deck at a moment's notice. What paint the old ship boasted was for the most part ringed with a green beard of growth around her water line.

"Good Lord," Katherine mumbled as she continued to look up and down the quayside searching for any sign of a ship in better nick. The old sagging ship in front of her looked no more capable of crossing the Atlantic than Draper Sound.

While she stood there in disbelief, an autumn breeze off the harbor raised a cloud of dust and grit up and around her, forcing Katherine to shield her eyes from the swirling dirt. As the air cleared and the small storm rolled its way down the wharf, Katherine was surprised to see that her trunk had been deposited directly in front of her. The driver and cart pulled away and were now long gone.

"Move your cargo, these horses don't stop for nothing, no matter how pretty," someone shouted from a fully laden cart which rumbled by just a few feet in front of her. A loud report from a rack of lumber which had been released from its boom sling made Katherine jump as it crashed to the wharf not five feet behind her. Katherine whirled around in time to see that another rack was being offloaded from the gray decks of the old schooner. The cargo boom seemed intent on dropping its charge at the exact spot to which, up until now, Katherine seemed glued.

"Move, you damn fool!" shouted a sailor from high in the rigging of the old ship. "Damn you, move! Now!"

Katherine quickly did just that and was able to get herself to safety on the other side of her trunk just seconds before the new load of lumber crashed to the wharf beside her.

"To one side!" someone said as Katherine found herself being pushed back once again to the other side of her trunk. "Keep it clear for the carts now."

She knew that if she wasn't able to find some answers in a hurry, she was going to be spending what was left of the afternoon jumping back and forth between her two temporary islands of safety.

Noticing the only man who stayed still in all the frenetic comings and goings, she called out to him. The sailor was working far above the silvered decks of the tired old schooner. He was shouting orders to another man, who in turn was coaxing all the available strength from a horse not ten feet from where Katherine was standing. A stout line ran from the working harness of the horse up to where the sailor stood, through a block and back down to the wooden dock again, where it was fastened to any number of large crated shipping boxes. Such was the swirl of confusion around her that up until now she never saw the large brown animal as it stood patiently, oblivious to the chaos which had Katherine spinning on her heels.

"Lift her now!" the sailor in the rigging hollered down toward the dock. The horse slowly began to lean its great weight against the line, which in turn slowly slid the cargo up a ramp, over the wooden rail and onto the deck of the old ship. And there it sat, no bother to the horse; once the pulling was done and the cargo was on deck, he got his feed bag regardless.

"Danforth. Danforth!" the sailor in the rig bellowed down to the open hatch on deck. "Damn it, Danforth, where the hell are you, man?"

A somewhat beleaguered face poked out from the dark hold below decks.

"It's not going to load itself, man, now is it?" the sailor snapped as he quickly climbed down the weathered ratlines of the tired schooner.

"Excuse me," Katherine said.

Not hearing Katherine's voice above the dockside din, the man landed firmly on deck and started to head for an aft hatch into which the cargo boom's sling was slowly snaking.

Again she tried, mustering up all the volume and energy which she had been trained against for so many years now. "Hello!" she shouted.

This try seemed to work, for the man now slowly turned looking for the source of the small, shrill call.

"Can you help me?" Katherine shouted.

The man turned back toward the cargo hatch, leaned in for a few seconds, proceeded across the deck, hopped over the old schooner's rail and started to make his way toward Katherine. As he came closer to her, Katherine held vague memories of the same sort of men who delivered her from England ten years ago. The sailor carried himself with the same cocksure manner. His eyes bored into Katherine and locked on her as he made his way in and around the stacks of lumber. Dressed in denim and flannel, this sailor who looked so natural and normal on board was nothing short of a mountain, whose rolling stride reflected years spent working on pitching decks. He closed in on Katherine, who by now was starting to feel every bit as awkward and out of place as she looked.

"If what you're wanting is to be scraped off these planks by day's end, then sit right down, girl, but I suggest you head back to your shops and save us the bother." By now he towered head and shoulders above Katherine.

"I have passage on a boat for England. Is that boat Atlantic bound?"

Placing his great weathered hands on his hips, he smirked down at her. "What boat would that be?"

"That boat which you were just now working on," she said.

The sailor turned to look back at the old schooner, then back at Katherine. "The *Mariah J.*?" he asked with a grin.

"If that's her name, yes. Is she headed for England."

Just when it seemed the great man's barrel chest could get no larger, it stretched out and there burst a gale of laughter. He turned to face the ship again. "Danforth," he shouted, "the lady wants to know if the *Mariah J.'s* out for England."

Katherine heard waves of laughter from far below the cargo hatch. One by one, several laughing faces appeared over its combing.

"England, is it?" one of the sailors asked with great delight. "Well now, I suppose she might very well be, but you'd sooner find a Johnny who'd fight the Horn on Christmas Day!" He laughed as he headed back down to work. Several of the others stayed on to get a good look at this dockside rarity.

"Miss, the reason these boys are in such a hurry to off load the old girl is that they're scared to death she might just sink right here at the dock." The sailor laughed. "Now you're welcome to head her across yourself but best you let us finish our work 'fore you shove off."

"Perhaps I'll just come back when it's not as busy."

"Not as busy? What you're looking at is not as busy. Until this cargo's loaded, these ships will have stevedores crawling all over their decks. We'll work by lantern, miss, day and night. Makes no difference to us."

Searching the length of the wharf, Katherine still saw no visible signs of what she was hoping to be her deliverance. "This can't be," she mumbled to herself. "Sir..." she said as she tried to gather her wits, "I have a cargo manifest which states that I have bought passage from Chester to Plymouth England on the first available ship from the Sefton Line. I was collected not two hours ago and was told in no uncertain terms that my passage was waiting dockside in Chester, and I was to hurry at that. Do you know of any outbound ship in or out of this port?"

Her intensity was not wasted on the deckhand, whose sarcasm and wit gave way to concern for the girl's plight. He pressed his great callused fingers into his chin and slowly explored his weathered face. "Miss, I'd tell you if I knew of any one who was outbound. Best I can offer is that you march right back to that agent of yours and get your money back."

"Don't want to be unloading when the tides turns," someone hollered from the old ship. "We need your hands, mate."

The sailor shrugged apologetically and turned back to the work at hand. "I'd check the landing if I was you. Some of the bigger ships what can't clear the harbor mouth anchor out and send in their longboats for supplies. Maybe they know something."

Katherine watched as he hopped the old ship's weathered rail and started to work his way below.

"Just where would this landing be?" she shouted.

"Follow the curve of the harbor north. You can't miss the long boats." He disappeared down into the ship's hold.

"Can't miss the longboats," Katherine mused as she sat upon her trunk. By this time she was taking no notice of the activities swirling around and almost over her. "How can I find a longboat when I can't even manage to find the ship itself?"

Katherine had been staring absently down at the ground for quite some time when a familiar pair of worn leather boots came to a halt in front of her. The joy of recognition gave Katherine's spirits a boost as her eyes traveled up from the worn boots to the comforting eyes of the old shopkeeper, Dunbar. A flood of relief and embarrassment swept through her as she realized the picture that she must have presented to the old man.

"Well now, " Dunbar said, "seems as though the first leg of your journey has stalled. I was on my way to hunt down some stock when I saw you sitting here." He sat down next to the dust-covered girl. "Did you miss your ship?"

Katherine's frustration showed in her eyes. "No, I didn't miss my ship. In fact I don't even know if there truly is a ship." She turned to her old friend. "I was dropped here, almost run into the wharf several times. I have met a very nice man from that ship and have learned that if there is a ship Atlantic bound I should look for the longboats at the landing. Now I need to find out where the landing is, and what a longboat is."

"The landing's just north of here. I think that we'd best get you up towards that direction and see what we can find out about these longboats." With that Dunbar drew himself up off the trunk and set about securing a conference with the closest hand.

With a few orders and an exchange of a few small coins, Dunbar managed to accomplish what Katherine's efforts had failed to produce. She soon found herself again sitting on a bouncing flat four wheeler. This time she was wedged between her trunk and various barrels slated for delivery around town. For the second time that day she watched as Chester rolled on past her. Dunbar himself sat further forward on the cart, talking to the driver who agreed to alter his deliveries for the sake of the old shopkeeper's generosity.

"There's your landing, Miss Worthington, and if I'm not mistaken one of those longboats would be your delivery." Dunbar was pointing to where the harbor started curving to the west. Two sleek and lively longboats were riding to the harbor chop as they sat patiently tied to the stone wharf which thrust out into Chester's Atlantic entry, all oars shipped neatly into the thwarts which ran lengthwise along the narrow interior of each boat. Two men hovered by each of the boats, reflecting their ships' characters by the manner in which they were dressed and carried themselves. Two men in naval uniforms watched over the farthest longboat, while two men in worn and tattered denim and cotton jumpers were loading coils of line, tins of tar, and barrels of food into the closer longboat.

"I have some cargo here for the Sefton Line," Dunbar shouted in the general direction of the two boats. "Which one of these fine crafts would be from her now?" Katherine and the old man stood waiting for a response from either boat. Dunbar asked again, "Which comes from the Sefton Line?"

The two stooped men working the closer longboat locked eyes as they continued to load their small wooden craft. Without breaking from the stowing at hand the taller of the two shouted, "That would be us, shipmate."

"We have trade for you, sir," Dunbar said as he moved closer to the wall's edge.

A tall, gaunt and weather-crooked man slowly unfolded himself from the center of the launch. His body and leather face reflected his years of hard labor at sea. His twisted back kept him far short from rising to his full height.

"We're off the *Galatea,*" he said as he worked a small coil of tarred hemp through his hands, his eyes constantly working the horizon around him.

"Jenkins, leave it," hissed the other man in the longboat. The redheaded Jenkins shot a quick look at his mate as he placed one foot up against the rough wall. "What's your trade now?" he said to Katherine. Jenkins gave the girl a thorough going over as he continued to slowly work the hemp between his swollen and cracked fingers. Dunbar turned toward the girl and extended his hand. Katherine passed her wrinkled and worn slip of promise to her friend, who passed it on to the sailor. He slowly looked it over with great curiosity. He had had the chance to see many manifests before, but that was as far as his experiences took him. A lifetime of working the *Galatea* and many ships like her never afforded him the chance to learn how to read like the higher ranking officers around him could. Occasionally he would steal a glance in Katherine's direction. "Leave it, man," his friend shouted out as he looked toward town.

Both men had been ordered to load the supplies, nothing more. Jenkins slowly looked over the paperwork again and turned to confer with his shipmate. The man left in the longboat was putting his back into his work with great effort now, as though he were trying to build a protective barrier around him. His eyes reflected his fear. Noticing this, Katherine couldn't help but remember the same look on various stray dogs which would frequent the pantry door of Elmwood from time to time – haunted by past cruelties.

Jenkins shoved the paper back into Dunbar's hands and quickly resumed his work.

"This young lady has booked passage with your line," Dunbar said as he tried to move both girl and trunk closer to the seaman. "She has paid full passage with your shipping representative for her destination, Plymouth England. Now if you would just tell us where we could find your ship."

With nothing more formal than a simple shrug out toward the mouth of the harbor, the sailor offered that the *Galatea* lay to anchor out in the sound and that the ship's captain was due back from town soon. He and his silent partner once more set to packing the small boat in a manner intricate and professional.

"Well, this surely must be it, young lady." Dunbar smiled as he looked down on to Katherine.

For the second time that day Katherine felt her throat starting to tighten with emotion. By now she just wanted to get herself aboard and deal with the sadness of leaving her friend on her own time.

"Mr. Dunbar..." Here her voice betrayed her and started to crack. She found all that she could do was muster the strength to wrap her arms around the old man and let her hug try to express all that she couldn't.

After a few seconds, Dunbar slowly pulled back, concerned and perhaps a bit embarrassed. "You know that you're to write as soon as you land. And if you feel even the slightest bit of trouble aboard you're to tell the captain immediately. He wouldn't be in his position if he wasn't a fair and honest man."

As the two of them waited on the landing, a cold blast of air from the north spread across Chester's quiet harbor. A change was due in the New England waters, a change which would strongly announce that any and all seagoing enterprises best look toward their destination before the North Atlantic truly came to life. The two longboats which just moments ago were tugging gently at their lines were now starting to buck on the waves as they were pushed up against the granite landing. Having been witness to much worse than this, the men took little notice as they continued to load. Yet the filling autumn breeze didn't escape Katherine. Watching as the gulls above her hovered against the building breeze, she too knew that were her departure to happen any later in the season her journey home would be in doubt.

"This is no time to be kicking up a fuss," she warned the scudding clouds as they built and headed out past Draper Sound.

"No time at all."

"Weather's building and it's your backs, you've a long pull and I am not looking to fight the flood." Said a man with a deep voice behind Katherine and Dunbar.

The man who walked past the two had to be their captain, as his step and roll alone defined a man of confidence and stature, one who was capable of out-guessing the fickle moods of a building New England blow.

"It's an afternoon for breeding weather," he said. "Jenkins, are you with us or not, man?" The captain had heard the rumour that Jenkins might be jumping from the *Galatea*'s roster. He had learned the many dangerous moods and idle threats of disgruntled sailors and knew who could and should be chided into service and who should be left alone with hopes they might jump ship at the earliest opportunity. Jenkins was not a man who the captain felt offered any good life to *Galatea.* He turned to his work all right, but there was an air about the man which made one uneasy when turning his back to him. Jenkins' few moments spent off longboat with Katherine and Dunbar had not been lost on the captain, for he had seen from afar the man's twisted frame leave his work.

"Yes, sir," Jenkins said as he stood and gave the captain his undivided attention. The two locked eyes for several seconds.

"Your business is loading, mister, nothing more. Am I understood?"

Jenkins nodded slowly, showing the old man just enough respect so as not to be brought up short, but not enough to let his captain feel total allegiance.

"Once we're aboard report to the mate."

"Sir?" Jenkins asked grimly knowing full well to what the captain was referring.

"Do as I say, sailor. I assure you that you'd prefer the mate over me." The older man's eyes pushed the twisted sailor back into his work and seemed to pin him there for several minutes.

Both sailors now bent to their loading with new fervor, motivated by the scorn of their captain and threat of the mate, a man who abandoned all self-control when he handed out his discipline.

Jenkins gave a questionable grunt as he laid into his new efforts.

"Say again, sir?" the captain shouted as he cocked is head in the sailor's general direction. "I missed that, sailor. Perhaps you'd best come up here."

The old man was clearly disturbed and was not about to let this rebellion gain momentum in any direction but his. The lanky and twisted redheaded sailor made his way out of the longboat and towards his captain with an energy which betrayed his bluster of just moments ago. Whatever feelings he had about the captain and *Galatea* were now replaced by a posture of continued servitude and respect for the bull-chested man.

"If you have anything to say, sailor, say it now to my face."

The brash redheaded man tried to hold eye contact with the captain. "Captain Borland treats us fair and I've no bones about it sir."

Captain Borland's controlled fury let the man know that this was most assuredly the last time he would tolerate such attitudes. "Back to work, sailor."

The storm passed as quickly as it came up. Borland ran his hand down into the right side pocket of the vest of his dark wool suit. With the practice of a man who had made this particular maneuver thousands of times over, he pulled out his pocket watch to check the time and the status of the tide. Katherine's eyes were drawn to the great man's hands. They were thick and powerful, the likes of which she had seen on the laborers around the Hill. Prominently veined, the callused and creased hands caressed the gold watch between his fingers. Without looking up, he addressed the two who stood behind him.

"You have business with me?" he asked gently.

Katherine slowly shifted from foot to foot. Borland was a man whose distinguished and well bred features seemed to have been carved out of his face by countless gales. He had a way of looking right through one when he focused in on one's wants, seeming not to hear what one had to say, but wanting to know the need for saying it. A hopelessly broken nose betrayed what was once a chiseled and handsome face. A full head of neatly combed white hair cascaded gently down and around his ears and brushed the top edge of his starched white collar. With the thick, gray, pointed beard of a man half his age, the tall and powerfully built man positioned himself directly in front of the English girl.

He smiled. "If it's a berth you're looking for I'm afraid I'll have to turn you down. The old girl no longer makes the passenger run. But *Galatea* would be honored by your beauty for dinner the next time we anchor out."

Katherine hadn't felt bashful in quite some time. She had always been a woman of and about her own mind, yet she found that she was simply lost for words.

"I have passage, sir." she said.

"With me?" he asked in a gentle voice.

"Yes, sir, if you're from the Sefton Lines."

"At times I feel that I am the Sefton Lines." He laughed. "Perhaps you have your shipping manifest?"

Katherine handed over her crumpled piece of paper for what seemed like the hundredth time today.

Borland looked it over carefully. With habitual reflex, he stroked the cleft of his chin with a wide and flat thumbnail, leaving a neat part in his thick beard. Then he smiled and welcomed his charge with the manner and grace which he would extend to any paying passenger, steerage or first class.

"You will have to forgive me, Miss Worthington," he said, "but the *Galatea*'s not so much a passenger ship as she is cargo vessel. We haven't had the pleasure of passengers such as yourself as often as we would like."

Galatea had been one of many passenger carrying packets which made the frenetic run between New York, Boston and Europe. At one time her three towering masts powered the small 400-ton ship through the Atlantic carrying the mail and cargo of the day. Under the impatient eye of land based owners, these sturdy sailing ships were driven hard, many too hard, for their useful life spans were seldom longer than ten years. *Galatea* was one such ship which under the hands of her previous captain,

Captain Lawerence Forbes, was nearly driven under. Forbes had been a hard driver, one whose compulsion for speed and notoriety saw him force his ships beyond their designed speed, bound more for the record book than any European port. With less concern for ship and crew than fast passages, *Galatea* began to weaken and show her age far before her time. She had originally been part of Penta Line, which often boasted record runs across the Atlantic. William Sefton, one of three brothers who owned the fledging Sefton Line out of Boston, bought her from his competitor and reworked her into a slower vessel carrying nothing more than notions out of docks of Boston: rubber shoes, corn husks, sassafras and the occasionally cotton from Charleston. The infrequent paying passenger such as Katherine would provided a break in the monotony, for which Borland was always glad.

He nodded his head slightly toward Katherine. "I am Captain Phineas J. Borland and would like to officially welcome you aboard the *Galatea*. I will have a man look to your rig." With that he turned and barked sharp words toward the longboat. Jenkins hoisted Katherine's trunk up and on top of his back.

"Stow it well, sir. Settle it into the waist, away from the tar, and get a tarp on it." He turned back to face Katherine and Dunbar. "And you, sir. I'm afraid you have me at a disadvantage."

"Mahler Dunbar, of the chandlery by the same name on Aubery Street. I'm a friend of Miss Worthington's and have come to wish her well." The old man too found himself a bit in awe as most of his shop dealings were with mates and the occasional A.B. off the ships. For he was the man to see if any of these outbound sailors were in need of their boots, tin pots, panikins or blankets. It wasn't unheard of for a profit oriented owner to insist that a sailor provide his own bedding. Yet seldom did he have the chance to sell to the captains themselves. "I know your store well. I often speak of your services with the other captains. I can assure you, Mr. Dunbar, that Miss Worthington will receive all the comforts and attentions that a lady of her stature deserves."

Folding up and stowing the manifest, he once again ran his hand down into his watch pocket as he gave Dunbar a smile indicating that their conversation was over and Katherine's voyage was soon to begin. Once again he turned back to the long boat. "Secure all and prepare to get under way."

He gently reached out and offered his arm to Katherine. "Now Miss Worthington, if your farewells are all in order..."

Katherine found herself being gently guided toward her awaiting seat in the boat, which now held her trunk. She looked over her shoulder at Dunbar as she walked toward the small vessel. He too stood silent as the emotion welling up from inside threatened to fill his dry eyes with tears.

Amidst a flurry of activity, commands and shifting oars, Katherine found that she was tightly wedged between the realization that she was on her way home and the unexpected sadness that she was indeed going to miss Chester and the likes of Dunbar and all that she had called home for the past ten years.

As the fresh breeze out of the north lifted the longboat along its track, the effects of the new flood tide were beginning to be felt. Chester Harbor offered up a small but sharp chop which from time to time threw some spray in Katherine's direction. Yet the cold sting of water and wind was lost on her as she sat and watched the slowly receding Chester go about its daily business, not stopping to take notice that she was leaving. The small figure of Dunbar was slowly walking back along the waterfront, stealing an occasional glance out toward the long boat which was pulling ever further out toward the sound. In her determination to go back to England Katherine never had stopped to consider the dangers of such an effort, the fears and sadness of being totally on her own and the uncertainty of crossing the Atlantic on a boat with captain and crew whom she knew so little. She sat in the stern at the captain's feet and watched Borland as his eyes worked the two men pressing to their oars behind her. She knew that she was moving closer to the spirit and kindness among which she was determined to live once again. She was on her way home.

As she shielded herself from the building spray, Katherine

noticed a determination about Borland which she could feel from just feet away. In the man's eyes she could see that the tangle that he and the rowing deckhand had had back on the landing was still very much alive. He glared past Katherine at the sailor as the twisted man put his back into the oar which pulled through the growing chop. There was definite history between these two men and Katherine began to feel herself in the middle of it, for even though Jenkins was seated behind her, she could clearly hear his curses and threats which played under his grunts and breaths as he bent to his grating and scraping oar. Jenkins hated the man standing in the stern -- he and most of the packet rats who lived before the mast despised a better man. A simple fluke of birth drew the great delineation between the two men. Yet Jenkins was unlike most of the others in that his foolish ways of contempt, if not sheer stupidity, were far from hidden. Katherine felt his building rage press against her back as he powered the longboat through the shallow harbor entrance and out toward the awaiting *Galatea*. Her years had taught Katherine to heed and rely on her intuitions, which were warning her that she should steer well clear of the history between the two men.

CHAPTER 6

Buy food: 60 breakfasts, 60 lunches, 60 dinners, plus various juices and snacks.

Fill tanks: 40 gallons diesel.

My "to do" list had been whittled down to an almost manageable two items, one of which I was trying to put off until the very last moment. Under any circumstances I hated grocery shopping, let alone provisioning and packing for a projected 30-day ocean crossing. We had poured over *Curlew* time and time again trying foresee any possible emergency which we might run into: extra water for the tanks, survival kit to throw into the life raft if it ever came to that, a medical kit which boasted the likes of liquid Demerol, codeine and Percodan -- the makings for what would have been one hell of a halfway party a few lifetimes ago. We had tested all the frequencies of the various radios, made sure that we had plenty of propane for the ship's stove as well as an emergency sterno stove. We had insured that we had backup systems for the emergency backup systems: bilge pumps, flares, hand-held water maker, emergency tiller, extra line, cable -- so much so that I started calling the boat *Curlew-Curlew*. I had started studying NOAA's satellite pictures of the Gulf Stream to try to get an idea as to just how that powerful offshore river was running. With the predictability of New England weather, the Stream meandered up along the East Coast before it started to snake east toward England. By trying to figure out the ever changing course of its serpentine path we hoped to be able to sail along in it and take advantage of its one to four knot current which would give us a free twenty-four to ninety-six nautical miles a day. Paul had been reading the weather synopsis which, via *Curlew*'s single side band radio, the weather fax printed out daily for him. He closely watched and studied all the weather systems which rolled across the country from the west coast, through New England and out into the North Atlantic. What he was hoping not to see were low pressure systems which rolled up into New England waters via Africa, Bermuda and Hatteras. It was hurricane season and we were not counting on having a dance with the likes of one of them. The high pressure cells had been like an eastbound company of trains which would never quite stop, but slow down just enough for us to hop aboard. We were hoping to find a clear spot to jump on and carry what good weather we could. It was always a crap shoot. I'm never truly confident when trying to match wit's with Mother Nature.

Concerning *Curlew*'s mounting yard bills, we had actually postponed our departure date several times now so that we could leave with a clean financial slate. I had managed to keep the principal players at bay long enough to be assured that Jasperson paid his bill to date and even added in a tad extra for projected slip rental and various materials we bought from Fee. What he owed Barlow & Dwyer was another story, but for some reason I had faith. We were getting into the season further but we were still within a favorable window of weather trends. Madeline was staying away from us for the moment, something which had its down side as well, for she was a much enjoyed distraction. Fee was busy pulling what docks were left.

Finding her shaft and prop as straight and true as the day they were installed, *Curlew* had been thrown back into the water and at the moment she was sitting happily to a mooring, starting to swing to the slight east breeze which was beginning to spread across Chester's inner harbor. We had moved her out to one of Fee's moorings for several reasons, not the least of which being that it was cheaper for our Mr. Colin Jasperson, an owner who we were starting to learn was not unlike any other in that he had an extreme dislike for spending his money. We were waiting for the second half of our pay to be deposited, and we were assured that the check was . . . well, you know the rest of the story.

Paul and I had spent part of the cloudy morning nursing our coffee and tea at Eagle's, trying to assemble some sort of food list which would give us a variety of sustaining nutrients, and not necessarily break what little bank there was left. So far peanut butter headed the list. The food money came out of our pockets, which actually were fattened from Jasperson's pockets. Once I had finally made contact with Jasperson and again went over our financial arrangement making sure to cross every T and dot every I, I had started to feel much more relaxed about the whole trip. We hit a few bumps at the start but were all now on the same page. We were going to be paid, we just were not entirely sure at what point the money was going to come in.

"Look," Paul said. "What if we get her to Plymouth and we still haven't had the remainder of the money deposited in the boat account?"

"We sit tight with the boat and enjoy England," I said.

"The sitting part is no problem. It's the enjoying that I'm concerned about. We'll have no money to pay for dock fees, let alone food."

Paul was always the rational sort, not to be thrown by circumstances expected or otherwise. His growing concern for accounts receivable did not jibe with his usual philosophical outlook. Perhaps it was the pressure of the crossing which was starting to distract him, or perhaps it was the fact that we both knew that there could be a turn for the worse in the weather. Perhaps he was exercising controlled and logical concern for our welfare.

"We can't do anything about that now, we simply have to go on good faith."

"The pathway to Hell is paved with good faith," he said.

"Good intentions."

"Whatever." He shrugged, trying to cap the conversation but knowing that it was far from over.

We had chosen to compile our food list at Eagle's for a good and simple reason; Quint had offered to supply us with anything canned at cost. Trying to observe some decorum for our new and budding business, we felt it far beneath our station to come begging. By discussing the 180 meals well within earshot of him, we hoped that his generosity would be subtly prodded back to life. So far his generosity was playing possum.

After several tedious hours of negotiating food likes and dislikes, we finally settled on a menu which, being to both of our liking, ran the gourmet gauntlet from apples to zucchini, canned ham to canned hash and from protein bars to vitamin mix drinks. A suitable if not somewhat predictable offering, but then again, we weren't looking for any surprises. In any event, it would be Paul who would be cooking the more exotic offerings. I was happy to concede on those entrees which required more than simply boiling a pot of water.

"One final thing," Paul said as he dug into his jeans pocket. "Sweet Madeline pressed this into my hand as I walked past her this morning." He slid several sheets of stapled paper across the table to me. I immediately recognized the layout and headings of the pages and my stomach began to come to life, something it had recently started to get into a habit of doing. As I looked over the paperwork, my now churning stomach and I started to understand the cause behind my friend's mounting concern.

"What the hell's this?" I asked as I ran the numbers in front of me over and over in my mind.

"What does it look like?" Paul said soberly.

"It looks like Jasperson still owes Fee. This can't be right." I continued to do my sums. "Christ, you're kidding me. He's only paid half the bill to date. He told me that it was all taken care of."

This we didn't need. I found that once again I was beginning to doubt the sanity of this whole damned thing. What started out as a great chance for an Atlantic delivery was intent on turning into a deliverance to hell. I drew in a deep breath and tried to let it out slowly and deliberately, and at the end of it I found I had nothing to say. Whatever little offerings of optimism I looked for had quit my thought processes once I began to realize that we were very close to being back at square one.

"If this isn't paid up," I said, "we'll never get that God damn boat across the harbor let alone the fucking ocean. This really sucks. Jasperson assured me that it was taken care of."

"Evidently it was. Just not the way we wanted it to be," Paul mumbled as he dug his pocket calendar out of his wallet and began to flip through it.

We both knew what could happen if you tried to venture

offshore too late in the season. We had witnessed too many nor'easters slamming into the New England coastline with only the slightest notice. The Atlantic was starting to cool off and the days were becoming shorter. All of these facts added together were not encouraging. We were lucky that this was the first week of September and there was still plenty of good weather ahead of us, but time was running out. We were in hurricane season and to date what storm activity there had been was all down in the Gulf of Mexico. If we tried to wait out hurricane season, we would then have to contend with the winter lows which rolled out of the Canadian Maritimes and joined forces with those which were soon to start their way across from Alaska. Time was indeed running out. The good news was that *Curlew* was basically all set to go, the bad news was that what had been deposited into our boat account was just about used up.

"Look, we need this job and we're running out of time," I said. "Today's Monday, correct? We have to make the decision to leave sooner or later." Again I took a deep breath, more for my own benefit than Paul's. "So let's aim for Saturday."

Paul looked up from his calendar and chewed this over for a while. His agreement came with some reluctance. "Okay, one of us gets the boat stocked and the other gets on the horn to New Hampshire and finds the rest of the money, the rest of the yard bills, and our pay."

"As well as the money we're out on the tickets."

"As well as the money we're out on the tickets." Paul slowly tucked the calendar and the wallet back into his pocket. "You've dealt with him up to this point, best you stick with him. You think?"

I don't know what I thought. I left the corporate world because of lying Shylocks like Jasperson and within what seemed like the blink of a very jaundiced eye, here I was going toe to toe with yet one more. The decision to leave Saturday gave us five working days. Five days in which I had to get Jasperson's undivided attention and let him know in no uncertain terms that if we didn't have the money, we walked away from *Curlew*. Something which, come hell or high water, we were by no means going to do. Paul and I needed this delivery and I only hoped that Jasperson didn't realize how badly we did.

I sat for a few minutes running my tongue across the front of my teeth. I looked up at Paul. Paul looked across at me. I glanced across the diner toward Quint. He was on the phone. Once again I looked back at Paul. He was still looking at me.

"What?" I asked.

Paul gave an innocent look and slowly shook his head. "I didn't say anything."

I started to chew on the inside of my cheek. Quint was still on the phone.

I tipped back my all but empty tea mug. One more deep breath. "Fine. I'll start chasing him down today."

Again I sat, chewing on my lip, looking out the front windows onto Aubery Street. My stomach was good and sour by this time. I just wanted to get sailing. This was not the time for stress. If we could just get under sail, all of this would be slowly falling astern of us, and if any problems existed, there wouldn't be damn thing we could do about them for the next thirty days. If I couldn't get the money, more than likely *Curlew* was going to be in the firm clutches of Madeline and Paul and I would be out all sorts of money, effort and reputation.

Looking out of Eagle's steamed windows onto the weathered facades of the shops across the street, my thoughts started to wander. The changing light of fall was showing these old buildings in a true and flattering light. Time and weather had shifted clapboards ever so slightly. None ran true. The lowering angle of the sun cast deeper shadows across their witnessing faces, and one could see where countless layers of paint had built up rough and craggy surfaces. I watched as the wind lifted and carried the past summer's dust down toward the docks. Here, too, the scene playing out in front of Eagle's was reminding me that time was quickly running out. The wind had been making up from the east for a while now and where people once sat in the crisp shadows of summer, trying to get cool, now the first few leaves of fall swirled and tumbled. The shadows became softer as the sky slowly began to thicken with scudding clouds from the east.

I shortened my focus back inside Eagle's and steered it over to Quint, who was by now off the phone and back to work at the grill.

"Quint! You gonna help us with this food or what, God damn it." I shouted.

In disbelief at what I had just done, I watched as the back of his broad and powerful shoulders slowly rose up and joined the bottom of his head, his neck disappearing. I felt like I was twelve years old again and had offended my own father. You did not want the undivided attention of the man I called Dad. When my father was at odds with his immediate world, he wasn't content until he knew that the entire Barlow family's peace of mind was not only shattered, but thrown to the winds. Only then would a faint smirk spread across his face, leading him back into his study feeling very pleased with himself for upending our home yet again. The man could start a confrontation by simply walking through the room, leaving its occupants in a state of heated argument. His methods for coping with that which he failed to understand were classic and time honored, not to mention hopelessly predictable; he paced, mumbled and fumed until he achieved his desired pitch with those around him, or could set right whatever it was that was keeping his world from once again being on kilter. My father, James Henderson Barlow, was a very successful financial advisor in New York with Bradshaw, Barlow and Seamans. He had been there for thirty years, his father held the record at forty. Here his bearish behavior was truly an asset and gave him the insight and edge he needed to keep earning the private school tuition for my sister and myself plus a fair amount for his immediate fun and future reserves. We were by no means burning the stuff, but when I pressed him about our financial standings, he would let us know that today we were fine and tomorrow wasn't here yet.

My father's running argument with life was indeed one sided and deaf. When it came to ironing out all the wrinkles on which family life thrives, this was not exactly the catalyst we needed. We usually found ourselves to be mentally at arm's length from one another and really only shared hugs and concerns on Christmas and Easter, when the holidays made us far too busy to sit and talk. Although the Barlow family wasn't the sort to have camping trips to Yellowstone, we did manage to establish our own sort of off-center closeness under which ran an unshakable family loyalty. God knows we weren't crazy about each other, but that gave no one the right to run any of us into the ground. Like dogs in a pack, the Barlows could and most assuredly would protect one of our numbers from any outside aggression.

In the end life had the final smirk in its ongoing argument with the man; stress, cholesterol and attitude did what none of us ever could and silenced him at the young age of sixty-two. I never quite came to grips with that and never did understand the minister's insistence that we were all better off for knowing the man. Out of some perverse sense of loyalty or love I still carry his lucky dollar bill in my wallet, the wallet I keep in my bureau.

Up until this moment I had never quite realized just how big the man called Quint was. He slowly turned with spatula in hand and stared at me with no recognizable expression. We locked eyes for the briefest of moments.

"Well," I asked, trying not to fall off the very high horse on which I now found myself. "Are you, or are you not going to help us with the food?"

Quint leveled his stare at me. "Did I say that I would?"

"Yeah...but, ah, you hadn't mentioned it lately."

"Anybody tell you any different?" His rock like fists were supporting his full weight on the counter as he leaned over toward our booth.

"Jump in here anytime," I whispered to Paul. "Ahh, not really."

A few of the regulars at the counter were stealing the occasional glance over in my direction. The one whose support I would have liked, which right about now would have meant any of them, kept staring straight ahead.

"Look," he said with great emphasis. "I said I'd help. I'll help. Just give me your list. Nothin' I hate more than a dissatisfied customer. Except one that runs his gums." Quint turned back to matters at the grill.

"Thanks. Knew we could count on you." I turned to Paul. "Kind of close wasn't it?"

"You planning on being that smooth with Jasperson?" Paul said as he produced several sheets of fax paper from his shirt pocket. "These came in over the weather fax for the past few days." The printouts gave a full indication of the Atlantic, north and south, from New England to Ireland and as far south as the Windward and Leeward Islands. The weather guys at NOAA draw high and low pressure systems according to their most recent satellite pictures. This way one can hopefully get some sort of idea as to just what's out there weatherwise. You can get not only a current idea, but a prognosis for the next two or three days. What I was now looking at told me nothing more than what I already knew; for the moment everything out in the North Atlantic was calm. Two low pressure centers were slowly working their way across from the Pacific Northwest, but they were small and would most probably amount to very little.

"Everything looks nice and clear," I said. "I'm going to head back to the apartment and start hunting down Jasperson." I slid out from the booth. "Give me a call if anything comes up."

"We still should do some sail testing a take a closer look at what she's got," Paul said. We had already inspected *Curlew*'s sails on the dock, but Paul was right in suggesting that we take *Curlew* out for a quick sail and carefully check out each one of her sails while fully hoisted.

"Tomorrow afternoon?" I asked as I made my way to the cash register. Paul nodded a bit of a distant yes in return.

I stood before Quint's register digging through my pocket for the tea money, hoping that our earlier go-around was nothing more than one of his diversions from the skillet. Judging by the slow and methodical way he was wiping his hands on his greasy apron, it wasn't.

"Just the tea, sport?" he asked.

"Yup," I answered as naturally as I could.

He stood counting out my change for a few seconds and said without looking up, "What's all this horseshit about the food?"

"Ah, Paul's actually the one you need to talk to about that, Quint." Rain drops which began to tap on the glass next to me drew my attention once again out on the street. The easterly wind had fulfilled its promise to moisten the streets. "He'll fill you in. Rain's coming, gotta run." By now Paul was standing next to me digging for his own change.

I turned up my collar and headed out and up Aubery Street. As the new breeze from the east swirled and spun its way through the old buildings, again it carried the familiar feel and smell to it -- the beginnings of a sharp winter edge. As dull as this edge was this early in the new season, the small, cold drops of rain brought back memories of autumns past when a cup of tea, a fire, a good book, and a warm lady were all that I needed for sheer bliss. It appeared as though this year the only thing which I was going to be able to count on was the book. So far we hadn't the money for the tea, a fire on *Curlew* was the last thing I wanted to see, and the only lady in my life was Madeline, who, pretty soon, was going to start sniffing around for her money. Actually I did have one other lady who I still had to deal with, but she was no lady, she was my sister. Ellie still had no idea about my crossing the Atlantic. I was going to have to spend the rest of the day, if not week, on the phone, hunting down Jasperson and trying to get him to commit and follow through with our money. Ellie was another matter entirely. No doubt she'd find me and be more than forthcoming with her opinion about my latest venture.

CHAPTER 7

"I give up. I completely and utterly give up. You're out of your God damned mind. The *ATLANTIC*?" Ellie's support and concern was as predictable as ever. "Does Mom know?"

"Yes, Mom knows."

"You haven't told her, have you?"

"Yeah, I told her."

"Okay," she said very deliberately. "Just what did you tell her?"

I couldn't believe this, here I was a grown man and I was having to defend myself against my older sister's accusations and disapproval. This small fireball in front of me was actually starting to impugn my integrity.

"I told her that I was taking an extended delivery and would be in touch in about a month or so."

Ellie stood stone still, looking at me with abject disbelief. Actually by this point she seemed more curiously amused than anything.

"This is amazing," she said, smirking. "Here you are grown and mature man and you still have trouble with Mom."

"I do not have trouble with Mom." I really didn't. Truth be known, it was mom's eyebrows I still had trouble with. "Anyway she said that she wished me well."

"Smothered you with her usual emotional outpourings, did she?" she said sarcastically.

Of the ongoing list of differences which Ellie and I added to each time we got together, one of the things which we have always shared between us was the recognition that our mother would always barricade her concerns and worries behind her well baked crust of New England aloofness.

"She even mentioned she thought it sounded like a fine adventure."

"An adventure? More suicide if you ask me." Ellie plopped

herself down on my living room couch, rubbing her hand along the brown corduroy material as though she were expecting to find God knows what. "This couch is disgusting."

"You want some coffee or tea, kiddo?" I said over my shoulder as I headed into the kitchen. If the years had taught me anything about my sister it was that if you gave her enough rein she would eventually run herself out. Try to check those reins by arguing with her and your cause was lost.

"The Atlantic. I can't believe this," she mumbled. "How big of a boat are you going to your death on?"

"Oh, that helps a whole lot. A forty-foot sloop," I said emphasizing the words forty feet. "She's already made the crossing once and from what I've seen has many more in her."

"When is this supposed trip going to take place?" she asked as she ambled into the kitchen.

"Soon." That was about as close to the truth as I dared venture. "Pretty soon. She belongs to a guy in New Hampshire who wants to campaign her in England. We've been working on her for the past several weeks. She's down at Fee's, you should drop by."

Making room for herself, Ellie cleared one of my two kitchen chairs of various books and charts and sat at my faux wood table. She simply stared at me while I set the kettle to boil.

"Tea or coffee?" I asked gently, giving her yet more rein.

"Tea." Ellie sat firmly with her back braced against the weather wall of my kitchen. She split her attention between what lay outside my slowly fogging windows and me at the stove dealing with a boiling kettle. I was hoping that as the steam started to slowly build in one, it would start to dissipate out of the other.

"What's wrong with simply going up and down the coast? For that matter, what's wrong with getting back into video production?"

"The coastal stuff is fine, nothing wrong with that." The teapot received one spoonful of loose leaf tea for opposing counsel, one for myself and one for the bench. "It's just that Paul and I have this chance to add some mileage to the company.

Besides, it's good money. Milk?"

"I don't understand you, I really don't. You've walked away from most everything good in your life." she said

"Whoa, whoa, whoa. Is the glass half full or half empty here?" In for a penny and all that. "That's your definition. I've never walked away from anything."

"Chris, a lot of your decisions have hurt people and caused you pain."

I wondered if I had the energy or the concern to endure one of Ellie's pat and tiring sermons.

"I've been happy with my lot for the most part."

"Right, my point exactly. For the most part."

Perhaps I was wrong about Ellie's steam. This conversation was heading down a very familiar path, one that was really becoming a bit foot worn.

"I really don't want to get into this," I said, "but if it helps, I do agree with some of what you said. You're right, you don't understand me. I've tried my hand at a lot of things, for a lot of people. Where'd it get me? Divorced and broke with ulcers. What I've been doing lately is all for me and I'm a hell of a lot happier doing simply what I want to do and not necessarily what others expect of me."

"And you don't think that's pretty selfish?" she asked.

"No," I said in disbelief. "Give me one reason why that's selfish. I'm simply doing what makes me happy. Look, when I was with Carolyn I was miserable, and I made damn sure that those around me knew it, remember?" It wasn't that long ago that the discomfort and pain of my marriage was more the hair-shirt than hidden secret. After a while I found that regardless the distraction I looked for, I made sure that those closest to me felt the full burden of my unhappiness and sadness. "What I'm doing is anything but selfish. Anyway, you're not in my shoes, are you? You're judging my life as you see fit, according to your likes and dislikes, not what's best for me." My argument had definitely fallen toward the defensive side of things and I wasn't all that comfortable with it -- not now, not this close to our departure date. "Look, this is really tiring and nothing new."

"You're crossing the ocean is nothing new?" she said with a questioning look.

"No this, this whole thing, you're posturing and shit. If you came over tonight to give me a World As It Ought To Be sort of lecture, don't. There's the door and take your tea with you."

An obtrusive silence stood firmly between the two Barlow children, willfully occupying that space where one normally expects to find happy mediums.

"You're really going to do this aren't you?" she asked after a few minutes.

"Yup. Sugar?"

"Yeah." Ellie turned her face toward the window again. She used her hand to smudge away some of the moisture from the kettle in order to get a better look out on to the courtyard below and quiet town beyond. I stood at the stove looking across the small kitchen, over my sister's shoulder and beyond the wet glass. The rain had been coming down steadily for a while now and my overgrown courtyard below was looking ever more so, as the various neglected rose hip bushes hung down further with the added weight of the water. The worn, dusty bricking of this morning was starting to lose its wet shine with the fading light of the day. There was no escaping it, the scene outside my window reminded me that each day the sun would be moving further south and setting even earlier. Time was short. We still had ample time to get *Curlew* across, but time was by no means a luxury. My worry was broken by a great breath which Ellie drew in as she continued to stare out the window. I really wanted to share my concerns and worries about the crossing with her but knew that by doing so I would be feeding her passions and reasons as to why I shouldn't go. Again she drew in a deep breath and cleared her throat. She was preparing to give me her closing arguments and I'm sure that it was going to be eloquent, passionate and brutally to the point... regardless of defense's feelings.

"I guess that I'm just scared for you. I really love you, Chris, and if anything happened you..." Her eyes expressed what her words were struggling with. "I don't understand you. You have...

and had... a good shot with production here in town, yet you'd rather risk your life on the ocean. Why don't you ever do anything the easy way?" she asked as she looked back out the window. There seemed to be an unfamiliar note of resignation in her voice.

"Would that be 'easy' or 'right'?" I wondered aloud.

"You know what I mean."

"You've got to understand. I don't look at it that way, Ellie. I'm doing what makes me happiest, what I'm the best at."

"Oh please," she said sarcastically. "That's a crock. You're good at everything you do."

This support from my sister was truly foreign to my ears, unexpected if not a bit disconcerting.

"This concern and insight isn't like you," I said. "Did you get laid last night?"

Another one of her patented silences. I guess that some evidence truly isn't admissible in court.

"This just seems a hell of a risk for not that much in return," she said. "How far is it between Chester and Plymouth?"

"About 2,800 miles, as the crow flies, but we're planning on about 3,000."

"Shit."

"Look, you're coming at this all wrong. I'm not risking my life as much as adding to it, enriching it. I'm my most alive and connected when I'm on the ocean." So many times I've tried to explain and just as many times I've fallen short of getting across just what being at sea means to me. At least now I wasn't being met with the usual blank stare of disassociation. I could have delved into the simplicity of life at sea, just the wind and water to deal with, no pestering, nagging distractions like money owed and not collected, deadlines, social functions, idle talk of who's ex-mate was to be avoided and whose dinner party was a seasonal necessity. I could have told her about how I find that when I'm battling a gale or suffering a calm I'm just as fulfilled as one of Chester's finest who puts all of his energies and efforts into the ongoing dance of social obligations and deceptions aimed at country clubs, exclusive beach clubs and clubs of the fraternal order of social rank. I could have jumped into all of this but I'd known for far too long that these things which I had spent the better part of my life trying to avoid, drew Ellie like a magnet. I decided to settle for the simple explanation.

"It enriches me," I said. "Like church for some, I guess. Anyway, it's all a risk in one form or another, isn't it? Are you certain that you're going to win every case you take on? When all is said and done, are you so absolutely sure that you're going to win and be paid?"

"I may not win every case," she said "but I sure as hell am going to be paid."

She was hitting a tad too close to home on that one.

"Look, what may look like a risk from where you sit is a way of life I'm happy with." I sat across from her with the freshly brewed tea-pot and slowly poured out the two mugs. "I wouldn't dare try and do what you do for a living. Talk about risks, Christ." I blew gently across the top of my tea. "You know, hundreds of boats cross every year, some much smaller than *Curlew*. She's strong, she's made for crossings like this. I wouldn't do it if it wasn't safe. Paul most certainly wouldn't do it if it wasn't safe."

Again, Ellie turned to stare out the window as she cradled her warm mug in her hands. One of the reasons I hadn't totally written Ellie off years ago was that for every ounce of bluster and bravado which made her who she was, her seldom seen side of care and concern was every bit as strong. By her silence I imagined that she was going through a bit of a struggle with her conflicting emotions.

"She's got a single side band radio, help is a call away. Hell, I can call you at a moment's notice... from anywhere."

Ellie continued to stare out the window, past the darkening courtyard and out on to an empty Aubery Street. "It's nice to have the town back," she said absently. "It was a rough summer." She sighed. "I guess if I'd stuck at it and listened to Dad, I'd know more about what you insist on doing for a living and I wouldn't be so concerned."

My father got Ellie involved with sailing as soon as she was able to swim. She was game, she took a few stabs at it, but the time quickly came when, making her final and very dramatic departure from the docks, she pointed out to all those within earshot, as only a six-year-old Ellie Barlow could, that the water could offer her nothing more than terra firma could, and that was simply that. Yet here we sat many lifetimes later, still tip-toeing around our vast difference in lifestyles and loves. If I wasn't wrong, I think that I was beginning to see the slightest indication of regret.

"Why don't we just agree to disagree. Look, come down to the yard tomorrow. We're taking her out for some sail testing tomorrow, come out with us for a bit, we're just going to sail in the harbor. It'll give you a chance to take a look around and maybe feel better about everything."

"Maybe. How long will this whole delivery take?"

"Like I said, thirty days and at that we've built in a fudge factor for foul weather. Hopefully we're out of here by the end of the weekend."

She slowly drew her attention away from the nighttime view outside my window and turned full force toward me. "I swear to God, Chris, if anything happens to you, I'll kill you myself." She gently drew a sip from her steaming mug. "Well, I wish you great luck." She was her mother's daughter after all. "I hope you find what you're looking for. Is it good money?"

"Well, that's something that remains to be seen," I said. I started in on the whole story about Jasperson and how there was the question of the balance of what he owed us. I hit hard on the more salient facts and glossed over the parts about how little we were making and how if we didn't square things away with Fee's, Madeline would bring an abrupt end to the fledging business. Instead of telling her how tight money was at the moment, I put a whole new spin on it and allowed as to how Jasperson's potentially delinquent payments would have a ripple effect on the business and how, if accounts receivable weren't settled soon, customers down the line would feel the unfortunate effect. Actually Jasperson's account being in arrears did have a bit of a silver lining to it; by the shift of focus in Ellie's eyes I gathered that we were, for the moment, on the same page. Ellie always had a tenacious sense of right and wrong. Temper this with family love and protectiveness and you could count on her immediate involvement, invited or not. Ellie asked for all the particulars -- date of agreement, terms of delivery, Jasperson's contact numbers, money paid to date plus a list of all out-of-pocket expenses. This must have been what it was like to know that the neighborhood bully was soon to get his comeuppance from an older brother.

Tea and conversation finished, Ellie allowed as to how she had spent enough time with me and that she'd best get back to being a lawyer and get back on someone's clock. The fact that I pointed out that it was a quarter past eight in the evening didn't deter her, she referred to a caseload that could choke the proverbial horse.

"We're going to wait for the breeze to fill in and do some sail testing around one or two tomorrow. I'll count on seeing you?" I said as I walked my sister to her car, knowing full well that she wouldn't take me up on my invitation. The slight offering of rain which the day had ended on had by now filled into more of a heavy mist which was illuminated as it came down around the gas street lights which ran the course of Aubery Street. The house lights which were reflected in the wet street cast abstract borders all the way down to the town center. The dusty town of this early afternoon now looked slick and clean and so much more the snug New England village than the tourist Mecca which she aspired to be.

"Maybe. I'll let you know," Ellie said as she dug for her keys. She stopped for a second or two. "I haven't been to Fee's since I was a kid."

"I could really use your help with the Jasperson thing."

"No kidding."

A quick hug and she was off to dive headfirst into someone else's life and troubles. It was strange to look back and remember years past which had seen Ellie and me discussing matters far more trivial, at the top of our lungs. Her concern for me setting out across 3,000 miles of open Atlantic was much stronger than her concerns from years ago about who was going to sit in the front seat next to mom and who was going to languish in the back seat with the dogs, but the yelling and name-calling had long since disappeared. I guess some would say that this would be an indication of maturity and respect for a loved one's opinion. I just knew most likely the answer was to be found more in the basic fact that I was tired and, love and respect notwithstanding, simply didn't have the energy to go toe to toe with Ellie.

I had dreams that night about our Mr. Jasperson, dreams in which he was sailing *Curlew* across waters filled with coral head, waters far too shallow for what she drew. I was in a blind panic as I threw over anything that wasn't nailed down, with the hopes of lightening her load. As I threw over such things as canned goods, water jugs, extra sails, Jasperson kept an inventory, assuring me that he was going to bill our company accordingly.

Ellie never showed at Fee's, I didn't expect her to. I was happy simply knowing that she was concerned and had actually taken the time to say so.

Paul and I sailed off the mooring at 2:30 in the afternoon, leaving what problems we could behind. I had spent the morning on the phone leaving messages for Jasperson throughout the state of New Hampshire hoping that by the time I got back to my apartment, my answering machine light would be happily blinking at me, assuring me that this whole financial misunderstanding was simply that and it would be solved in short order. Paul had spent the morning making a sizable dent in our food list, and what he was able to buy was to be delivered to Fee's late this afternoon. We rewarded ourselves for our morning efforts by grabbing some sandwiches from Quint, from whom, I was overjoyed to find, Paul had managed to secure many of the canned goods. We decided to take *Curlew* for a spin around Chester harbor. We had done a dockside visual inspection of the sails, so now we wanted to run up each of her sails and take a closer look at them while under way. She had a remarkable racing inventory. We started out with a light drifter, a gossamer of a large headsail which pulled us along neatly in the first of the afternoon breeze. As we left the mooring the southwest breeze started to fill in with its usual afternoon strength. We quickly ran through the genoa inventory -- #1 light and heavy, #2, #3 and finally storm – and each set and looked as freshly cut as they had on the dock. She had a delivery headsail which was controlled by roller reefing, one that we'd hopefully find no reason to change. *Curlew* boasted not only what appeared to be a tried and true delivery main but buried way back in her sail locker up forward was a tightly folded and packed racing main built from the exotic materials of kevlar and mylar. It was a comfort to know that if it came right down to it, we had a bulletproof main which could stand up to just about whatever the Atlantic threw at it. Do to the short fetch of the harbor, we only ran up one spinnaker, a large blue and yellow symmetrical runner, one that was fairly adequate for just about anytime we were sailing with the wind well aft the beam. When she filled with a crisp snap, we rested assured here too that even her more exotic sails -- blooper, blast reacher and daisy -- were all in the best of nick. Jasperson may be a man with an obsession about spending his own money, but at some point someone had talked him into buying nothing but the best for *Curlew.* We reefed down the main into all but a handkerchief and went so far as to lock the helm down to weather while backing the storm jib, hoping to simulate just how she would heave-to in storm conditions. For the fifteen knots of air that we had she was very content to jog several degrees off the breeze, zigzagging her way up to weather. Lying happily to the breeze in Chester harbor was one test, fifty-plus knots mid-Atlantic in twenty to thirty foot seas was yet quite another, something Paul and I knew was becoming more and more of a reality with each passing day.

"Seen enough?" I asked as I pointed *Curlew*'s bow back toward Fee's docks.

"I'm impressed," he said. "I hope that that's the last time we see most of them." Paul was referring to the fact that we were looking to carry steady westerlies on our crossing, insuring that we wouldn't have to run the gamut of hoisting and dropping

Curlew's full inventory.

"We run the engine when it's under five knots and go for comfort more than speed if it blows over twenty-five," I said.

"Not to forget that the foredeck is your department," Paul said as he swung down into the companionway and headed below. "I'm going to try and catch the high seas forecast out of Nova Scotia."

There was a an edge to Paul's voice and probably one I shouldn't have been surprised to hear. He was a man who kept things to himself and didn't believe in complaining about things. "You only bitch about things if you want to change them," he would say. I agreed wholeheartedly but sometimes one simply had to let off some steam, and perhaps that was what I heard in his voice. I was sure that I was spending far too much time, awake and asleep, trying to box in Jasperson before he could financially screw us. We were both letting our worries about the crossing slip into and out of our lives at will. The trick was to keep them at bay, not allowing them to get any more of a life than they already had.

While Paul was below, I balanced out *Curlew*'s sails so that she simply glided along, leaving a small boil of water off her stern as she cut a clean and crisp path through the protected waters of the harbor. This was my favorite time of year in New England, when all distractions of the past summer and spring crawl back to where they hibernated, scrimping and saving for the next spring's invasion. It never took long for the magic of wind and water to reach down inside of me and start to calm the very core of my concerns. My decision years ago to step from the path of nagging consistencies was not without its drawbacks. Yet most of the logic behind this move was born from that unique relationship that I had always had with nature, more precisely, the ocean and her power. Lately I had spent far too much time thinking about hypothetical scenarios: what if we don't get our money from Jasperson, what if the delivery takes longer than expected and we have to pay for our flights back, what if we hit the ultimate storm and are without the proper defense.

As I tacked *Curlew* into a new slant on the wind, I felt these questions and concerns start to slip off her stern and into the small wake she left bchind. By the way her sleek bow lifted and drove into the cold water ahead of her I knew that she was as anxious to start her journey as her passengers were, and that all troubles and logistical nightmares would pale in comparison to the miles of living winds and awaiting seas ahead of us.

As we sailed closer to the harbor entrance, *Curlew* took the freshening southwest breeze in stride and asked for all lines to be snugged up as her leeward rail started to dig into the Atlantic. I balanced out her rig again, set the autopilot and climbed up to the weather side of the cockpit and settled in. Her strength in meeting the Atlantic was beginning to be shown as she started to kick back small offerings of spray which would occasionally bring my drifting mind back to the matter at hand, that of sail testing. Her headsail was sheeted in flat and looked morc thc sharp edged cleaver than the actual airfoil that it was originally designed to be. It sliced its way up to weather as *Curlew* would occasionally offer the slightest bow to the fresh blast of air which rolled in off the far reaches of the Atlantic.

"Hell, let's just leave now," Paul said from the companionway. How long he had been bracing himself there I had no idea, but judging by the peaceful and distant look in his eyes as he stared past me and off the stern, I knew that he too was managing to get a proper perspective on matters. The building breeze and sweeping seas were washing the three of us clean of everything which had temporarily blinded us to the original need and commitment to the venture. Not only was *Curlew* in balance, but I too was beginning to feel the peaceful relaxation of being in touch with that part of me which, when allowed to, let grace and peace course through my system.

As the expression goes, *Curlew* "smelt the barn" and was kicking up her heels with the great excitement of knowing that it was just over the next horizon awaiting her. The problem was that her barn lay 3,000 miles to the east and right now we needed to rein her in and head her back toward harbor. We jibed her around and let the afternoon's breezes push neatly into her outstretched sails which led the across the harbor and back to her mooring. The various mansions atop Knowles Hill looked down upon us as we sailed our way through the empty moorings.

After buttoning up *Curlew*, we started the slow row back to Fee's docks with renewed motivation for our departure. The soothing effect of the Atlantic had made its mark on Paul and me. We had said very little to each other for the past hour or so and only now, as we drew closer to land, began to come back to the reality of matters still not finished.

"I'll have all the food set by tomorrow. We should bring her alongside for loading," he said.

I only wished that I could have reported on the Jasperson situation with such finality. I nodded in agreement as I continued to pull at the oars. "I should have some news from New Hampshire by then."

As I continued to pull us toward the docks I watched a small smile spread across Paul's face as he studied something over my shoulder.

"What?" I asked as I swept the oars back to me.

He grinned. "Keep pulling.".

"What?" I asked again.

"You'll see," he said brightly.

"What the hell are you laughing at?" I asked as I pulled both oars in opposite directions, spinning the skiff on her center lines. Not fifty feet away from us, standing a good safe distance from the edge of the dock was my sister. I started to grin as he did, from sheer surprise. Ellie exhibited all the ease and grace of being on the ledge of a sky scrapper.

"What a pleasant surprise," I shouted. "Have you come for a sail after all?"

"Meet me at Eagle's," she said with a quick upward flick of her head. As she turned to her retreat, I noticed the ever present manila folders tucked up under her arm.

"Shut the door, you're letting all the flies out, damn it." Quint's workhorse of a greeting had lost humor over the years, but it had a comforting note of familiarity. At least he could be relied on.

Ellie was already waiting in an empty booth, ignoring a steaming cup of coffee in front of her and trying to scrub the residue from the maple syrup and sugar which had failed to meet their various targets. As Paul went through his usual contortions to insure that both long legs of his fit under the low-slung booth, I slid in next to my sister.

"This is really gross. I thought you left this sort of mess back in college." By now Ellie was trying to wipe the persistent stick off of her own hands, with little success. "God, all we need are empty pitchers of beer."

As Paul motioned to Quint for the usual teas for us, Ellie continues, "All right, I've done a bit of checking for you guys and it seems as though we have a new and interesting version of the proverbial good news and bad news. Let's call this one 'bad news and kinda bad news'."

Judging by the look in Paul's eyes I think that the pitchers of beer would have fit in real well about right now.

"I did some checking on your Mr. Jasperson and I came up with the following, which, as I see it, is less than good."

Another pitcher please.

After dragging out voluminous notes on yellow legal pads from her folders, Ellie proceeded to fill us in on why our employer from New Hampshire wasn't all that interested with returning my calls or making sure that checks which were in the mail had actually arrived. From what my sister was telling me, the man was far too busy for the likes of us. He was the belle of the ball, except that this belle's dance card was filled out with various appointments in bankruptcy courts. Ellie stressed the plural. It appeared as though Jasperson's fledging development companies-- Westridge Associates or Eagle Ridge, either name was fine, just depended on which company you invested in -- had appointments in court to provide and open their books for anyone who had a bone to pick.

The silence was first broken by Paul. "Shit." Even as a boy, Paul was always shy around Ellie. Truth be told, I think that he was afraid of her. She came to know him as a man of few words, even so, when called upon he always managed to cut to the meat of the situation. “Well, shit.”

“Well, yes,” said Ellie, “my feelings exactly.” She smiled at Paul. “But all is not lost. Official company letterheads commanding the respect that they do, I took a small liberty and faxed off what amounted to a play-or-pay sort of suggestion.”

“Stand in line with all the other suckers, I guess.” I reached across for the encrusted sugar dispenser. Ellie was right, I hadn’t noticed the condition of Quint’s tableware, it was reminiscent of the student union.

“I don’t remember anyone saying that the district attorney’s office needs to stand in line,” Ellie said while thumbing through the rest of the papers in her folder. “Standing in line is for, as you say, suckers. “ Finding what she was looking for, she tried to wipe a clean spot again, and placed the original of the fax which she had sent to Jasperson between Paul and me to read. Paul reached out one large mitt of a hand and slowly turned it so that it was now facing him. As he read it, his face visibly dropped three years. Reading what I could upside down, I had trouble making out the content of the fax, but there was no missing the letterhead. Ellie was right, standing in line was for suckers. Hell, if my eyes didn’t deceive me, we were the line. The heading “State’s Attorney General Office, Providence, Rhode Island” saw to that.

“Fraud?” asked Paul.

“Not really,” said Ellie.

“Fraud,” Paul said.

“Not actually. Begging,” said Ellie.

“Really?”

“Yup. A dinner with my learned colleague, Peter Roth.” My sister shifted uncomfortably. “One long, boring, insufferable, and costly dinner.”

“Good of you,” said Paul. In the all the years that I’d known these two, this was perhaps the longest conversation I had ever had the pleasure to see Paul and my sister wade through, and how nice it was to that it ended with a mutual benefit to us all.

“My office got a call right back from Jasperson’s office, what’s left of it, and they assured me that your-out-of town benefactor was going to be at Fee's late this afternoon to settle all accounts." Ellie was beaming.

I was about to ask what the contingency plan was if he, as I suspected, would be a no-show, when my sister held up her right hand as if to stop traffic. Her head was down and may lightning strike if I didn't see her start to grow inches before my eyes. Paul and I exchanged curious glances, not knowing if she was finding her coffee not to her liking and was about to add to the sticky collection on Quint's faded yellow Formica.

"Not to forget, gentlemen, I was once engaged to one Mr. Ralph Ellison, who is now chief of audit operations in the Philadelphia store of our Internal Revenue Service."

"Now that's fraud," said Paul.

"Nope, simply a casual call to a long lost friend wondering how things were in the City of Brotherly Love. I took a moment to mention to Jasperson's secretary that I was recently discussing matters with the Feds, I never made it clear as to exactly what those matters were, thank you very much."

If Paul's eyes were any brighter with admiration I think that Ellie would have felt the glow from across the table. Judging by her smile it appeared as though she did.

"So, just where does that leave us?"

"Ah. Well, if I were you I'd be down at the yard ASAP. So, any other problems?" She looked at me, then at Paul. Paul lifted his mug and started to take a long slow pull on his tea. "Any other matters in your lives which need a woman's attention."

Judging by the look of self-betrayal on her face I was sure that that didn't come out exactly as she had planned. A side-bar counselor?

Tommy McFarland's voice broke the beginnings of what I really hoped wasn't a mood.

"How are the boys?" Tommy asked.

Ellie lifted her head out of her notes and shot a glance at our councilman.

He rephrased the question. "So, how are my young friends? Ready for the crossing are we?" Tommy started to rock on his heels. "I miss being at sea, I really do." Up to this moment none of us were ever aware that Tommy had actually gone to sea. Holding up his small white right hand he separated his index finger from his thumb ever so slightly and scrutinized that tiniest of spaces as if he were relying on it to provide him with his wealth of sea stories. "This close, it was this close that I came to crewing on *Bristol Lights,* Fastnet Race of 1979."

In August of that year, as part of Cowes Race Week in England, a storm of unprecedented proportion tore through the fleet of yachts which raced the 600-mile circuit from Cowes, out around Fastnet Rock in the Irish Sea, and back. With raw and brutal fury the low pressure system devastated the fleet, allowing only eighty-five of the original 303 boats which started to finish. The storm took the lives of five men, and 136 had to be plucked from the frozen waters of the Irish Sea. In the aftermath the meteorologists referred to the storm, which produced seventy-knot winds and forty-foot waves, as simply a "bomb."

"This close," Tommy said. Politicians the world over will attach themselves to any cause or event which might add some needed depth or color to their otherwise shallow and gray souls, and our own councilman, sliding into the booth next to Paul, was no exception. Tommy's knowledge of the race was gained through magazine articles and, at best, third-hand stories. "So," he said, "do you think that the old girl's up to it."

Just what Ellie needed to hear.

"Why wouldn't she be?" she asked more of me than Tommy.

Tommy just smiled a very hollow smile and looked at both Paul and me. "Just asking. The *Skara'*s a good ship, always has been."

Did our table order an extra serving of pregnant pauses? I looked at Ellie and grinned a grin which felt pretty lopsided from where I was sitting.

"Gotta go," she said as she started to hip check me out of the booth. "I *will* talk with you later."

Watching Ellie move her small, quick frame over to Quint's cash register, as did everybody else in the coffee shop, Tommy waited until she got her change from the big man before he too announced that he must head off. "Tea's on me boys." With that he too was gone. Judging by the creeping of Paul's brows, it seemed as though we had some unfinished business between us. More to the point I think that it was actually fresh business -- the impending arrival of Colin Jasperson, and the fact that *Curlew* had once been known as *Skara Brae.* Paul looked at me for several seconds.

"What?" I asked.

"What was that about?"

"What?" I asked again.

"That *Skara* shit?"

"Old man's folly, Paul, nothing more than an old man's folly." I had no idea what the hell I had just said and hoped that it would blind Paul momentarily as well. "Well, I for one am looking forward to this evening and trust that all will be set to order and we'll be off in no time."

Paul's brows had dug in for the long haul. "I've got to do some banking," I said. "See you at the yard?"

Paul made a quick smile, nodded his head, turned up the collar on his brown canvas jacket and said, "No doubt." He made for the door.

Paul and I arrived at Fee's from opposite sides of the yard. I was hoping that our different arrival points weren't an indication of any unfinished discussions to come, that being *Curlew's* alias. Watching him cross the yard, I was reminded how, as a kid, Paul never took the straight line. It always seemed that various hidden curiosities would catch his eye, pull him off his intended course and just before he got to the point of his concern his searching eyes would spot another interest and once again he would be drawn toward the latest curiosity. All resulting in a bit of a zigzag path through and around boat yards. It was reassuring to see that he was indeed following his usual scattered path as he approached me.

What wasn't so reassuring was the short, fat, quasi *G. Q.* type with wraparound blue-tinted sunglasses who was coming up behind Paul, making a bee line for me. I didn't know if it was for our benefit or if somebody was actually on the other end of the cellular phone tucked under his chin, but the conversation he was having was clearly animated, directed all around the yard and ended abruptly with, "Look pal, I was born at night, but not last night." With that he snapped the flip phone shut and squeezed it into his hind pocket. I always thought that that was a punch line, not something that somebody would actually say.

"You Barlow or Dwyer?" the man squeaked. An awfully strained and high voice for such a mogul, I thought.

"Depends," I said as I took a moment to run inventory from the bottom of this walking pear up. Imitation Gucci shoes, complete with gold bar across the tongue. One bar was broken. No socks, gabardine slacks, an imitation Gucci belt, blue oxford cloth shirt, starched with initials monogrammed at the cuff, top two buttons unbuttoned -- actually one was missing but it did add to the ersatz Continental appeal of the situation -- wraparound blue-tinted sunglasses and what had to be hair plugs. The hand which tucked the cellular back into the hip pocket was favored with a gold ID bracelet. Years ago I had wasted many an hour listening to this type relive tales of how they won the West and what the world would be like when they were king. Their conversations always began in the same manner.

"Colin Jasperson. Now let me tell you how I see it."

Bingo.

Our Mr. Jasperson grabbed me by the arm, tried to minimize the six or seven inch deficit between our heights and started walking us both rather quickly to the sea wall. Here he sat me down, parked his foot next to me on the wall and took a long dramatic gaze across the bay. Paul followed in his usual saunter and stood facing out toward the water.

"No hidin' the fact it's late in the season, make no mistake about it. Real late indeed. She's a good boat and you come highly recommended. You got, what? Three or four weeks head of you. The sea can be an angry customer my, friends, pretty God damn angry." Here he shot his cuffs and pawed at his nose like a boxer. "Bermuda Race, 1992, *Penthasalea,* 52-foot custom sloop. Full gale howling out of the north, counterflow of the Stream out of the south. I ain't gonna bullshit, I was scared, real spot for danger, my friends." He exhaled here. "Real spot for danger. North versus South kind of thing. Not an easy one, my friends, not an easy one."

I stole a glance at Paul. A slight curl around the corners of his mouth showed that he was finding this amusing. Paul nodded his head slowly.

"North versus South," Paul whispered. "Man didn't sail on a boat, he raced in a miniseries." Pulling a scrap of paper from his tan and worn canvas pants, Paul slowly sauntered off.

Jasperson continued without missing a beat. "Rail down, dog watch, I was working the foredeck." Now he reflected as though on a long lost love. "I loved that God damn foredeck." The guy was a walking cross between Melville and Spillane. "Angry green mother of a sea took our bow in its teeth and shook that old bitch like some cockamamie dog with a wet towel. Damn near ended in the drink." here he paused for emphasis. From his back pocket his cellular started to ring. He cocked an eye towards it and continued. "Yeah, we got there all right, but no trophies for that old girl, my friends, just our sweet ass lives. Damn lucky."

Perhaps I was too distracted by this man's fat ass ringing, but I think that I missed something in the narrative; a wave over the bow and they were all lucky to have escaped with their lives?

The phone continued to breep. As though it was a child interrupting a story, Jasperson cast a warning eye toward his right cheek. "Hopped the first flight out of that burg back to the city. Six hundred miles with all that Neptune could chuck at us gave me a lotta pause to do some redesigning of the ship. Landed at Kennedy, grabbed the first thing smoking, headed into town, marched right into the design firm that drew the old gal with a new mockup of how she should have floated." He paused for emphasis. Again, his right cheek started to breep.

"God damn it!" Trying to extricate the phone from slacks a wee bit too tight, Jasperson did his own slow version of a dog chasing his own tail. "What?" he growled at it. "Hello! Can't hear you. God damn it you're breaking up. Fuck you!" He hung up, slammed the little sucker shut and once again started to slowly revolve in a circle as though this would help make back pocket larger. “Piece of shit. Where the hell was I?”

I couldn’t take it any longer. I had to stop him.

“What about the money?” I asked.

He sniffed at me. “What about the money?”

“The money to get your boat across this angry old sea of ours.”

“Where’s the problem?”

“Well, yard bills,” I said realizing that, besides prostitution, or because of it actually, we were about to begin the second oldest game going. He clearly need no explanation.

“Came down early. All paid.”

“Reimbursement for flights.”

He handed me an envelope. “Cashier’s check”

“Dollar fifty a mile times two.”

“Tell me something I don’t know. The cashiers check is made out for an extra nine large. I’d have given you a personal check but we’re in the middle of restructuring right now.”

Restructuring as in Chapter Eleven, I thought to myself. I really did love my sister.

My turn for a dramatic pause. “Lay days. If we have mechanical failure and have to pull in to Nova Scotia, Ireland, whatever. Dockage plus thirty dollars a day each.” I might as well been pitching ratings points and time slots.

He stared at me. His butt breeped. He cast an eye toward the noise and again looked back at me. This last demand of mine stalled him. When I had originally approached the man about the delivery I had intimated at this fee, but up until now had never gotten down to the actually workings of it. We were about to get knee deep in it. High noon. He seemed to take it in stride.

“What do we got, something new?” He grinned. His butt continued to ring.

“No, not new. Standard actually. I mentioned it when we first spoke.”

His butt breeped again.

“What are we talking here? Hundreds, thousands? He twitched his head and neck as though this action alone would settle the deal and stop his right cheek from interrupting him.

Where the hell is Paul? I thought as I took that moment to gaze about.

"Just contingency, probably won't even need it. 'Just in case' sort of thing."

He casually put his hand on his bulbous butt to try and soften the continuos intrusion from his fresh gabardine. He drew himself up to all of his almost height and made one final sniff. "Can't do it, my friend." He slapped the tarmac with his fake Gucci shoe. "No, sir, no can do."

I'd been here before and I hated it as much now as I did then. Now it was my turn to sniff. "Neither can we." I decided to hit him where he was the softest. "*Curlew* is going to miss a lot of good racing and photo ops at Cowes, might be some magazine covers." I handed him his envelope back, stood up and headed wherever it is one heads when one is watching a bucket of money go down the drain. I started to walk away. I knew that he was following along because I could hear his ass continuing to breep. He stopped to answer it.

"Hello?" he bellowed. "What? What? Shit, you're still breaking up. Fuck this noise!"

I don't know what I heard first, the grunt or the small splash, but it sounded as though the fat man's eyes just blinked.

"Fucking highway robbery. Draw up a contract and fax it to me," hc said as he caught up with me and continued to walk past. He was chewing the nail on his thumb.

"Better yet, give me a minute to find Paul and we'll hand over a contract right now."

Where the hell was Paul? He had the paperwork, and he was making Barlow & Dwyer look pretty God damned lame right now.

"Meet you at *Curlew* in twenty " he said as he walked past. He threw a quick nod over his shoulder toward the bay. "Get a diver and the phones yours, if you want the fucking thing." He took a few shadow punches and headed toward his boat. Not every day you get offered a cellular twelve feet under. Not everyday you meet the likes of Colin Jasperson either.

Taking full advantage of the twenty minutes I searched high

and low for my partner. Something missing is always to be found in the last place you look -- because you don't keep on looking, I guess. In this case the last place was *Curlew* herself, and with Paul came two extra bonuses. After giving up on Paul, I arrived at the boat to see not only Jasperson but two unfamiliar faces as well as the errant Paul Dwyer, all sitting around the dinette below. Paul gave me a bright nod, a little out of the ordinary, so for now I played along. I swung myself aboard and slid down the companionway.

"Mr. Jasperson and I have just finalized the lay day contract," Paul said. "I have the cashier's check and he assured me that the yard bill is paid to date." He beamed at Jasperson, who didn't look any too happy to be aboard. "The next time we all meet will be in England." He smiled at me. "Ah, Chris," he mentioned as an afterthought, "I don't believe that you've met Chance Englander and ... " Paul was at a loss, "I'm sorry...."

"Christen Bellweather," the downeaster offered.

"Yes, well, both Chance and Christian were on the delivery crew which brought *Curlew* down from Maine," Paul said. "They came back for some of their gear which they left aboard."

Both men reached out and shook hands with me, didn't actually look at me mind you, just shook with me.

This had been a very odd day to say the least. Single handidly, I lost and regained our best job to date, I had been given a $300 cellular phone which currently lay at the bottom of the Atlantic, my historically disapproving sister came to my rescue, and now my business partner of a few years and even fewer words had not only disappeared on me when I needed him most, but had suddenly become quite loquacious and was now playing at cruise director.

I nodded a brief but bewildered hello and asked if we were all finished.

"Yeah," Jasperson said as he eyed the open companionway. "We set here or what?"

Nobody spoke.

Paul stood from the dinette and shook hands with each man in turn. "It's been a pleasure and feel free to call if there are any last minute items." He looked at his watch. "Chris, we've got to run. We're going to be late for the safety seminar."

That did it. Paul had completely lost me. Just as this apparent schmoozing of his was clearly out of character, there was no safety seminar to which we were running.

I smiled back at him. "Right you are, old friend." Why not? Nothing else was normal. "Ah, Colin, we'll keep the keys, take care of *Curlew* and make you proud."

With plasticine smiles we saw all three off, locked up the boat, made sure that we had the contract and check, and headed across the yard toward Aubery Street.

"What the hell was that all about?" I said through a smile more for the two cars with New Hampshire tags which were now driving past us on their way out of town.

"Need to talk," Paul said through his own attempt at a smile. He went one better than me and managed to throw in a wave. "As in now."

CHAPTER 8

Galatea's deck rolled almost imperceptibly under Katherine's feet as she stood amid-ships, taking in all 100 feet of the old ship's neat and flush deck. The row out from Chester was without further incident or conversation, now that she found herself actually aboard one of the great ships, she found herself at a total lack for words. She stood bathed in the smells of pine, varnish, canvas and hemp which now surrounded her in the form of *Galatea.* She looked ahead to the bow of the ship and then along the length of the bleached wooden decks to her stern. All was so unfamiliar and immediate. She would later come to learn that the few small square wooden structures which were in evidence every now and again on the slanting decks were companionways which led below to the crew's quarters, to the great holds which held the cargo and to the aft quarters belonging to her captain. She would be cautioned time and again to stay well clear of the forward companionway which led below to crew's quarters. The activity in and around that structure honored no pausing foot traffic, regardless how pretty or innocent. Katherine felt awash in a tumult of foreign faces and features. Soon she would learn that as lost as she now felt, there was always a pair of eyes watching out for her. In the short row from shore, Captain Borland started to learn about the young and precious cargo which sat so rigidly in front of him, watching with great intent as each oar dipped and pulled the longboat on toward the ship. The captain was a man with the ability to glean all he needed to from people simply by being in the close proximity of them; the way they used their eyes, the manner in which they exchanged glances, how they held their body in the company of others. The young lady who was in his charge was indeed precious; she held philosophies and merit to be found out and discussed. Borland always maintained that every man was a teacher, that there was something to learn about life from every person who came before him. He also knew when a man's lessons were spent, when a man held no future promise of civility or understanding. Borland knew that Katherine held a wealth of lessons and history to be learned. No packrat was going to darken this child with surly treatment or coarse language, not aboard his vessel. It was for this reason he continued to keep Jenkins in the powerful grip of his eyes.

The activity aboard *Galatea* was reminiscent of the activity on the docks, and Katherine started to feel that same panic which met her on the docks earlier in the day. She stood back while each and every one of the ship's crew hustled about at their jobs. There was a terrific economy of purpose which belied the manner in which the great man ran his ship.

"Amberson, tend to the young lady's kit," the captain said to a man nearly half his age and twice his size. "Mr. Amberson here is our first mate. If you ever have a problem and can't locate me I'm sure that he will help you with whatever you need."

The imposing figure in the long, worn denim coat reached down and collected Katherine's trunk in one quick sweep of a massive arm. As he did he managed a polite smile, not necessarily welcoming but a learned reflex. As their smiles met, Katherine found herself drawing a small sharp unexpected breath as the eyes of the powerful dark-haired man locked onto hers. At the end of a wide jagged scar which started at the lobe of his right ear, ran under his unshaven clefted chin and up the left side of his face, lay an eye clouded over with a pale milky film, which contrasted with the gentle blue of his one good eye.

"If you'll follow me, Miss Worthington," Borland said as he proceeded toward the stern of the ship.

The mate dropped Katherine's trunk at the door of a small, white and freshly painted structure which lay twenty feet forward the aft deck where the ship's wheel was to be found. It looked no bigger than a coal bin, was slightly higher than Katherine was tall, boasted two small square ports, one on either side, and stood entirely by itself. Much like a horse box standing alone in a great field of blue. Borland arrived at the structure which couldn't have measured any larger than the small room in which Katherine used to serve the head maid her tea. The large man shouldered open the door and gestured for Katherine to go in.

"I had it built for my wife to encourage her to sail with us," he explained as Katherine stuck her head in and looked around. "I'm sure that you'll find it to your liking."

The cabin was small and singular in purpose. Hesitantly Katherine took a few tentative steps in. As she faced forward, she saw on the left hand side-- the port side, as she was later to be corrected -- a small writing desk, complete with three small drawers and a small, shallow trough which ran the length of its surface, just enough room to cradle one small pen. The ports which she saw from outside on deck were hung with gingham curtains, faded but clean. Snug against the forward bulkhead was a series of shelves with small books upon it. Curiously Katherine found a darkened and broken bird's cage made entirely out of small bamboo stalks. Any evidence of a bird was missing and judging by the fragile bamboo dowels which ran the length of it, no bird would stay captive for any amount of time. At knee level, along the entire length of the starboard side, ran a bunk which was made up with a straw mattress, a heavy tan wool blanket, a stained canvas pillow and another blanket folded at the foot. The outside lip of the bunk was raised four inches above the mattress. Katherine well remembered the purpose of such a lip; the bunk she had shared when she came west those many years ago had such a setup. Although the purpose for such a rig was obvious, in practice it was something entirely different. When the ship heeled over on to her side, Katherine's body would roll up and over the top of the narrow plank of wood, and not rest securely against it, as was the intent of the original design. This lee board looked far more substantial and offered great promise of keeping the girl securely in place while *Galatea* pushed her way east. Secured under her bunk was a porcelain set of wash bowls and pitchers of the dimensions and style with which she became so familiar with at Elmwood.

With a smile Katherine came back out onto deck and looked about. Once again her eyes became slightly lost in the maze of lines and movement which ran above her head in vertical and horizontal confusion. Respecting Katherine's privacy almost as much as proper convention, Borland took advantage of the fact that her quarters for the next 3,000 miles were empty and excused his way past Katherine.

"If you will excuse me," he said as he secured her trunk, "I have a ship to get underway and a handful of men who will be needing a little prodding."

"Yes. Perhaps I'll get organized," she said, more to herself than the captain.

Organized in this case was actually an attempt at making sense of the past twelve hours. She walked back into her quarters took another look around. She sat upon her bunk, filling her lungs to capacity with the fresh sea air as she looked out of her port. From where she was sitting she gained a front row seat, yet at a safe and manageable distance, of all that was out-side on deck, all that buzzed around her. Her eyes filled with confusion and amazement as she could hear her captain, who was not just a few minutes ago the soft-spoken, cap- tipping, grandfatherly type, now start to bark out orders. As Katherine sat there, she watched and listened with amazed fascination as the long, black-hulled ship which waited so patiently at anchor slowly became infused with energy and purpose.

"Get your men together, mate. Stow the dunnage and stand by the slack chain," Borland roared from a raised part of the ship at the stern.

This command was repeated by another voice, deeper and less formal. The pounding of feet went by not inches from Katherine's face.

"Send them aloft to cast off the yardarm gaskets."

Borland's voice seemed to be directed at Katherine, and she found herself flinching. Now his voice was aimed away from her.

"When the chain is overhauled, two-block the topsail yards and sheet them home, mister."

More shouts of the same gruff nature followed this. More feet running past her. The sound stopped and became muffled, her cabin started to reflect a slight vibration of the boots which firmly placed the weight of each man as he sprung aloft on the ratlines which ran to the top of *Galatea's* rig.

A roar of canvas fell from somewhere above Katherine's head. Even though she had two inches of yellow pine roof above her, she found that she felt a reflex to duck. Taking the courage to crane her head out of her port to insure that nobody was injured by whatever it was that fell, Katherine saw a sight above her that infused her with even more excitement. *Galatea* had started to spread her wings and was coming to life before her very eyes. A large piece of canvas hung from one of the horizontal poles above, the yardarms were holding the freshly dropped sail in place and a gathering of crew were on deck hauling on ropes which in some fashion managed to hold a fair amount of control over the sail.

"Heave short," the captain bellowed, and again a more distant voice repeated the order. "Heave short, damn you, and don't break her out until she's drawing nigh."

A small gathering of men worked feverishly at the windlass on the foredeck. By straining her neck just so, Katherine could see them all bent from the waist, pushing the capstan's long handles in a circular motion, like a wagon wheel laid on its side. Katherine surmised that one end of the wet chain was going below to a hold, a locker, while the other end held the anchor.

On deck Captain Borland surveyed the scene before him with one encompassing glance. So well he knew his ship and her workings that all fell before his gaze in a matter of seconds. Looking above and seeing that the mate had already braced, trimmed the yards to take advantage of the building breeze from the south, he shouted, "Release the gaskets and set the topsails." Again a concussion of canvas fell from its perch. "Brace your yards."

If only Bridie could see this, Katherine thought. She's being born before my very eyes.

Galatea was being held in place by the wind blowing her backward and forward at the same time. The way the captain had ordered his men to set the sails, the ones found at the stern of the ship were catching just enough of the wind to move her ahead at her anchor. The yards which supported those sails which were to be found furthest to the bow, on the foremast, were set in such a manner that they caught just enough of the same wind to slightly push her aback. Katherine heard the grunt of the men forward as they worked the windlass to bring in a bit more of the anchor chain. Her eyes followed all the standing rigging which supported the great towering masts, up to where the masts held the sails securely in place. She let her eyes wander among all the different lines, leading to different perches where the men were agilely throwing themselves across the yards to unfasten the great bolts of canvas. The masses of canvas were controlled by lines which led to their handlers below on deck. Every line and every hand served a distinct purpose. All the men acted in chorus with one another, with the ship and with the building wind. Their calls across their perches eighty, ninety, 100 feet in the air were faint and foreign, more a sailor's arcane code than actual words. At first the intensity and urgency of the movements and orders frightened Katherine. As at the docks, this was not the world from which she had just come, the world where everything was communicated by a nod or a hushed voice, the louder words being saved for chambers or long walks on seawalls.

At first her quarter's seemed claustrophobic and confining, but in the controlled and organized melee stirring about her now, the cramped area offered security and safety. Katherine started to feel that this new home of hers was going to work out just fine. The bright white paint and clean curtains gave some life to the six foot by seven foot box. As she ran her hand along the coarse tan blankets she felt the warmth and protection that they would offer for the crossing ahead of her, not simply their roughness. Even the broken bird cage gave suggestion to life that had once been there.

He may have had it built for his wife, but there's clearly only room for one, she thought. She knelt upon her bunk and again looked out of the square port directly above it.

Outside of her deckhouse the commotion continued. It seemed that the only man who wasn't running or pulling on something was the captain. He stood up by the ship's wheel, arms crossed against his swelling chest, staring forward. Katherine could see by the intensity in his eyes that something forward was demanding his full attention. He drew in a powerful breath to shout out the next command. Katherine craned her neck forward to see if she could see the object of the captain's frozen attention. The men at the windlass had stopped for the moment, the grunting had ceased. The man she had met earlier, Amberson, the first mate with the clouded eye, the one who saw to her belongings when she first boarded, was standing over one of the crew who was, like the others, still leaning on the capstan handles. Amberson began shouting, but this was a singularly directed noise and not an order for one and all to obey. The mate leaned down against a sailor who was all but hidden under the vast spread of the back of Amberson's blue coat. Again Amberson roared. There was a pointed silence of fear and horror which spread from bow to stern. It was cold and brought a choking stillness with it.

By now both Amberson and the sailor were standing erect, face to face, chest to chest. Her mind's eye swept her back to a great storm and a ship which was being torn and killed under her feet. She tasted the ink of the black night and heard again the shrieks from a ship intent on destroying itself in the teeth of the gale rather than be torn asunder on the rocks ahead. Again she was alone and being thrown against the splintering timbers of a dark and frozen hull. "There's nothing you can do young lady. Best you tend to yourself."

Captain Borland's words pulled her from this flood of a past nightmare. He was still standing on the poop deck with arms crossed, but now his stare was directed squarely at Katherine. Clearing indicating that she had no say in the matter, his gaze pushed her back into her small white deckhouse. Pulling herself back in, Katherine took the liberty to glance forward. She felt a squirm in her stomach as she now saw the object of Amberson's wrath. In their posturing, the two men had shifted slightly and Katherine clearly saw that it was the inflamed redheaded Jenkins who stood against the massive bulk under the blue coat. She didn't like the man one iota but simply knowing of him, having made some contact with him, brought her own emotions to a boil. Katherine slumped back against the head of her bunk and stared out of her port toward the land on the opposite side of Draper Sound. Her world was changing far too quickly and the burn of the familiar dream kept it spinning with horror. The brewing violence of the moment had keyed into the depths of what she had up until now thought was only a dream which tore at her during the night.

Katherine looked down across the deck to the shadows of the men at the windlass. In the shadows she could see a great arm raised high and held high above its owner's head, at the end of it was a long extension of a shaft. Both arm and club paused for a second and then swept down with terrific force and unbridled fury. She heard a sickening wet crack, a pitiful screech and then the noise of a body falling to deck, all in synchronization with the perverse shadow-play before her. Another shadow, equally as large, now sauntered into the scene. A fury of kicks was unleashed upon the body shadow on deck. Katherine lay back and covered her ears, for each time a kick found its mark, she heard the sound of a liquid retching.

"Don't break his ribs," the captain cautioned in a low, direct voice. "It will only leave us shorthanded."

Katherine pulled her knees up to her chest and shook. She was far beyond trying to make sense of what she had just witnessed. Her mind was a total void. What she had seen stripped any thought of excitement away from her. Rocking was all that she was capable of and the only thing which could reassure her that she was safe. She raised her eyes and could look out of the port on the other side of her room. Chester's harbor lay just as it had for the past day and years. Yet she found now that her definition of home had changed yet once again. Chester now offered a place of sanctuary when compared to what she was now witnessing of life aboard *Galatea.*

As she sat on her bunk, curled up against the aft bulkhead of her house, Katherine could hear the captain's commands start up once again, followed by the same repetition that she heard only moments earlier. Things had changed. They no longer fanned the excitement which she held for her trip home, now they tore at her and brought that nightmare closer to the surface. What was once a bad dream had now became visceral memory.

Forward she heard the mate holler, "Up and down!"

Aft, Captain Borland acknowledged the cry. He looked aloft once again for a brief second. His eyes swept the deck for a final time.

"Break her out!"

The remaining men at the windlass bent to their task again and hauled the anchor free of the ocean bottom 100 feet below.

Galatea gave a shudder, offered a groan. Her yards were squared and her canvas filled. Katherine felt the great surge of energy build as *Galatea's* canvas responded to the breeze. Slowly she rose and fell to the swell rolling down the sound from the Atlantic, bit by bit her great breadth of beam settled into the watery trough which supported her forward pushing mass as she concentrated on an easterly set.

Once underway new commands were issued. "All hands aft!" the distant voice shouted, followed by the anonymous shuffle of boots and bare feet going past the small port of Katherine's cabin.

"Mr. Amberson, Mr. Kemp, pick your watches," Borland said to the first and second mate. One by one each mate handpicked men whose ability they knew from previous sailings. Those men who were unfamiliar to *Galatea* were chosen not so much on physical promise, but by degree of sobriety. Katherine listened from her small deckhouse as Captain Borland gave his usual speech to the now established watches. During this ritual, Amberson went below to the fo'c'sle and performed his usual task of rummaging through the crew's quarters, looking for any knives, guns or liquor which had been smuggled aboard.

Given the sign that all contraband was found and disposed of, Borland announced, "Gentlemen we are England bound. Watches will commence at eight bells this evening. Helmsman, steer one-three-zero. Mr. Amberson I'd like to see you in my cabin."

Katherine's dream was starting to come true. She was going home.

Sometime after the wretched incident on deck, there was a knock on Katherine's door, summoning her to join the captain in his quarters for a glass of sherry and dinner. Despite Katherine's fear and repulsion from what she had witnessed earlier, she answered that she would be along shortly and started to pull herself together. Despite the horrific beginning, the sea air had its way with Katherine, it didn't take her long to realize that her immediate world had taken yet another change, this one for the better. Judging by the new sounds and smells, they were now at sea. Having made her way out of Draper Sound, past the sheltered islands into the waiting Atlantic, *Galatea* was now digging in, plowing the waters that lay between her and England. Katherine remembered the strange tilt of the deck under her feet, the jerky sideways motion which gave life to the small cabin around her. The bird cage swung with every dip and roll the ship took. She watched as the gray horizon seemed to elevate up and down outside of her starboard window.

Opening her door, Katherine now could take in the sights around her. Her eyes were drawn to the windlass, the area where the shadows had played out their macabre pantomime. Now there was no evidence of anything out of the ordinary. What she had heard and what she thought she had seen was nowhere to be found. Just aft of this was a small companionway which led directly below by means of a pitched ladder. This all seemed hauntingly familiar to Katherine and made her take a sharp breath. Judging from the activity of men going up and down this companionway ladder, they all lived below this forward deck in some arrangement. Aft of this was a deck-house very similar to her own. From the smell of it and the swirling steam and smoke, this must have been the ship's galley. Some of the men who worked on deck congregated in the lee, out of the wind, of this small white galley. All seemed to be in a silent agreement of watching and waiting for the next order. Some worked upon coils of rope, some stitched, others simply stared out at the gray void. Just aft of this was the long-boat which pulled her out from

Chester Harbor to the waiting *Galatea,* except that now it was used for storage. The long narrow boat was secured to the deck by means ropes and iron deck rings and was filled with crates of chickens, other livestock and canvassed parcels. From here her eyes ran the length of the first mast ahead of the forward deckhouse. Above her the canvas swelled. The yards from which these masses of sail hung shifted slightly, always being pushed askew a matter of inches, perhaps feet, by the various small shifts in the breezes. The forward part of the deck was glistening with spray which occasionally found its way over her sharp bows and onto the well worn wooden planking which ran the length of the ship. Far more breeze was blowing than Katherine had anticipated, and she found that instead of the sailor's axiom, "One hand for the ship, one hand for yourself," she had best practice "One hand for your skirts, one hand for yourself."

"Captain's waiting," said the boy, smirking, as he made his way aft.

Katherine's blood ran quickly. The mere mention of someone waiting kicked up her fears that there was someone waiting whom she was supposed to serve. A jumble of thoughts and emotions, Katherine followed the young boy across an open area of deck, into a heavily varnished wood and glass structure which housed the steps leading below decks. The young boy led Katherine into the captain's quarters and there she quickly found that she was the one who was to be waited on and served.

How different his quarters were from anything which she had expected to find on a boat of this size. The sides of his cabin were mahogany and satinwood, disposed in panels which lay under several layers of painstakingly applied varnish. Recessed book shelves held untold volumes, all bound in leather. In front of her was a dining table she would expect to find at Elmwood, not aboard a ship. Made from one precisely cut piece of mahogany, again, the deep red wood lay under meticulously applied layers of varnish. The table was set with silverware, linen and crystal which Elmwood would have been proud to boast. Katherine knew bees wax candles all too well, and the finest of these were lit and throwing a warm hue about the cabin.

"Every now and then a crate breaks open and some merchandise is damaged or lost," the captain said. He winked.

Captain Borland made sure that the girl was comfortable and seated well on his plush velvet couch which lay situated along the starboard side of his cabin. On the other side was a drawn curtain, its tapestry-like quality every bit in standing with the rest of the cabin. Presumably the captain's own bunk lay behind this. The brass fastenings all about Katherine were polished to perfection and even the varnished paneling above the her head held her reflection.

The captain poured them both some sherry and started to give a run down of the ship's dimensions and crew, her age and ability, and most importantly, her history and service record. Borland told the girl about the three brothers Sefton who owned the two ship line. How their first attempt at shipping some years back had failed due to their courting the trade of paying passengers, how they expanded too fast and lost ownership of all eight of their ships, how they had raised enough investments to purchase back two of their vessels, the *Sarah Minot* and the *Galatea,* and set out to try again only to have what was later to be called the War of 1812 put a stop to their undertakings. They were given a chance to get their small fleet sailing again, and would let the others chase the unpredictable passenger trade.

Trying to take it all in, Katherine found that the answers to her questions lay elsewhere. She stopped the captain short by asking why the man forward had been beaten.

Borland paused. "That's ship's business and I'm very sorry that you had to witness it," he said as he started to pour Katherine another small glass of sherry. "There can be no room for misunderstanding and I'm afraid that sailor got off to a bad start. It was wrong of him to challenge authority."

Katherine did not respond.

"If you're looking for a villain, Miss Worthington, I suggest you take your observations and suggestions to the owners. They are the ones who push us across the Atlantic the way they do.

My job is to make timely deliveries, not to make friends."

Katherine sat across from the captain. Even in the candlelight she could clearly see the years spent at sea were reflected in his face, the strain, the wind, the snow squalls and sun -- all part of the paradox which he presented to her.

"Are you well settled in?" he asked.

"Yes, thank you." she said, feeling awkward and embarrassed now that she was the one being served, and not the one serving. Trying to distract her feelings she got quickly back to the point. "No man is to be treated like an animal. No man deserves to be treated with such total disregard as those chickens I saw out on deck just now." She sipped at the sherry and felt its warmth work through her system. "You say that he was wrong? Whoever did that to him was equally wrong."

Borland took a long look at the girl. Ultimately the girl was right, her argument was well founded. He took no pleasure in the discipline as other captains did, but the law of the sea was quite simply the law. Absently he picked up a silver spoon from his place setting and began to twirl it between his fingers. He drew in a breath, then slowly exhaled.

'He who meddles in a quarrel not his own is like one who takes a passing dog by the ears,' " he said, smiling. "Look to your proverbs, Miss Worthington."

Katherine eyes lit up as she looked back at the man. " 'Surely oppression maketh a wise man mad'. Ecclesiastes."

"Touché." Seeking another tack the captain countered, "I repeat. My job is to make deliveries, not to make friends."

"But those timely deliveries are brought about by a crew which respects not only the owners but the officers as well." She took another sip. This is nice, she thought. The sherry not only warmed her, but gave her immediate and precise insight to the situation which she thought she knew. "Why, given half a chance, one of those men I saw earlier might just well make a good officer themselves some day... and perhaps not one who beats others."

Borland shook his head quickly. "The man of whom you speak, my first mate, Amberson. The man is one of the finest shipmates I've ever had the privilege to sail with."

"Because he beats people?" Katherine said determinedly.

"No, because he doesn't. As I'm sure you've gathered, that man's face is testament to the fact that he has had to fight tooth and nail in order to survive on some of the more notorious ships of our trade. These so called 'blood ships' are manned by criminals, drunkards and a class of men who have only one thing in mind, cheating the company. Thanks to Amberson, you will find none of that here. I can guarantee you, Miss Worthington, through the years he worked his way aft. First Mate Amberson has had many a bucko mate's fist raised against him, and it's for that reason that he will refrain from physical discipline until absolutely necessary."

"Or until he is given an order?"

"Or until the safety and the well being of command dictates as such."

"What I saw this morning were the actions of an animal." Katherine said as she tried to stare down the man who comfortably sat opposite her.

"This 'animal', as you refer to him, is as clever and resourceful a mate as I've ever had the privilege to sail with. Those men who can get along with him jump to his every command. Those who don't, don't last."

Perhaps the sherry made itself known in Katherine a bit too much, for the piercing blue stare from the captain's eyes saw an immediate end to the new warmth Katherine felt inside of her.

"Stupid officers make poor ships, Miss Worthington." This was all the captain needed to say to bring the conversation back round on to a even keel. Realizing the effect of his broadside, Borland started to explain. "Freight is king, Miss Worthington. If you find the time in the next few days to look about *Galatea* you will see that she is unlike most other packets which work these waters. The owners of the Sefton Line have seen to it that all passenger accommodations have been torn out to make more room for freight. A few years ago she could have carried as many as twenty paying passengers whose comfort came first, but times are changing, now we carry cargo between America and

England. I haven't the luxury of a slow passage. A captain of one of these merchant ships you see plying your waters, if they smell a gale, they can shorten sail at night for safety purposes. I carry mail as well as cargo, I have to drive my good ship hard both day and night." He chose not to mention that there was also a certain amount of pride and reputation to be taken in a fast passage, pride for both the owners and himself, but more especially reputation for *Galatea.* "Neither the wind nor the sea has time for drills."

There was a knock at the captain's door.

"Enter," he said without taking his eyes off Katherine.

The same boy who collected her at her cabin walked into the room carrying two steaming buckets with him. Katherine noticed that there was no personal exchange between the two men, simply a followed pattern which they had obviously established some time back. Borland rose, and gesturing with one of his great callused hands, invited Katherine to sit at the table. The scruffy-haired boy set about removing the contents of the buckets and placed them on fine china, which he pulled from the captain's sideboard.

So very much like Elmwood, she thought. She watched with fear, not wanting to see just what sort of dinner was brought to them by means of a bucket. As the boy unpacked the contents Katherine marveled at what came out of these unlikely vessels: two neatly wrapped, small roasted hens, a tin bowl of freshly cooked green beans which were very quickly transferred into one of the captain's silver dishes, and a larger tin filled with steaming mounds of mashed potatoes. These too were transferred into their own sterling dish. Katherine's astonishment at not only the food before her but the fact that she was now the invited guest and not the silent server was finalized by emptying the remains of her sherry in one final swallow.

"That will be all, Lewis." It was the tone and not the words which sent the boy away. "I'm sure that you will find all as you would hope for it to be," he said as he refilled her empty glass. "Enjoy this now, for the fresh food won't last forever."

Katherine had never been in the position of having

somebody serve her and at the moment she wasn't all that sure just how she felt about it.

"Take this dinner," said the captain, getting back to the point at hand. "This was a common occurrence when we shipped paying passengers such as yourself. Thinking about it now, I realize that I can't remember that last time this cabin saw company, especially as delightful as you."

Katherine smiled but was more concerned with matters at hand. Rarely if ever in the past years had she found herself in a one on one situation with anyone, especially in a situation where she had to rely on her withered left hand. Holding the knife was no problem, she had proudly learned to adjust, but now, in front of a man of such rank as the captain, her shyness quickly worked itself to the front. With silver knife wedged between her bent fingers she gently pulled the meat of the hen away from its bones, something she had done many times over, but not with such deliberation. Fearful of damaging the fine silver, she approached her meal with the gentle hands of a surgeon. How can they eat like this, she wondered, this knife must be worth more than my entire belongings.

The sight of Katherine's hand drew the captain's attention, but seeing the confidence in how she worked it endeared her all the more to him. He watched as she studiously carved the small hen in front of her. "You seemed puzzled" he said at last.

"Do I? Perhaps distracted." Katherine gazed about her with a smile. "This is so remarkably different from how I first came across the ocean. Then there must have been four hundred of us below decks."

She looked about her immediate plush surroundings, more lost in the brutal memory of the forty-day passage to America than admiring her present situation. As Katherine sat in the velvet-backed chair, leaning to *Galatea's* every roll, she fell back into the nights aboard *Pandora,* black nights of endless gales, living beneath secured hatches which allowed access to neither ocean water nor fresh air. A passage where children screamed and men and women wailed for days at a time. The passengers in steerage were forced to answer their sea sickness and daily functions below decks, where no cleansing breeze could alleviate the stench. Per British government allowance, rations were doled out once every week, enough to stave off starvation. If there was room to be found in a bunk, the long rough slatted wood beds were shelves of unplanned pine. Where the design allowed for one person to sleep, three to four ended up. The alleyways between these tiers of three were barely two feet wide and when they were not serving as living space, had to hold untold amounts of personal baggage, sea chests and private provisions which had to be crawled over were one in dire need of a chamber pot or fresh air. Many passengers escaped the hell below decks by means of death. For the almost unheard of price of three English pounds, a person could travel by ship across the great Atlantic and find new hopes and beginnings in America. The fact that Katherine was being sponsored, "treated" to this passage, overrode any concerns for stories heard of such westbound septic squalor.

Katherine paused before speaking. Collecting her thoughts she tried to keep the indignities of her earlier passage to America from creeping into her voice. "Captain Borland, have you or any of your fellow captains ever spent time in steerage? Apart from the odd saunter through, have any of you ever gotten to know life in one of those black holes?"

The captain knew all too well to what Katherine referred. He knew about the germ-laden holds where epidemics broke out as frequently as winter gales. He had hired on the mate from the *Washington,* a packet which fought the waters of the North Atlantic while cholera ran rampant through steerage, taking its fatal toll on 100 men, women and children, all bound for America. The *William Tapscott*, sixty-five deaths, the *American Union,* eighty, the *Centurian,* forty-two deaths. He had heard about the ships which offered no food from a full galley, but rather a small open range of fires on which one had to cook one's own food, which was usually sold to him by a dockside charlatan moments before sailing, for exaggerated prices. The small fire was to serve the five to six hundred members from steerage. Open to the weather and assaults from the North

Atlantic, the emigrants had to maneuver and cook between the cow stalls, pig and poultry pens, areas where disease festered and eventually erupted.

Borland tried to answer the girl but knew that his words would be hollow. "Times are changing, Miss Worthington. There is no excuse nor answer for what you and others suffered. Perhaps one day the owners of these ships will have to stand before a higher court than we on earth can convene and be held accountable. In the meantime, please know that I humbly offer whatever I can to insure your happiness here aboard *Galatea.*"

Katherine smiled and looked about. "Do all captains live so well?"

Borland seemed to take his time with that one. Looking down toward his place setting, he slowly moved his silver fork back and forth, debating. "I must say, you are a very curious young lady." He said, as he looked up at her. Making a fist, he stroked the cleft of his chin with his thumb nail. "Your straightforward questions deserve straightforward answers." Again he took his time. "I work for an unusual owner, owners actually. It is a fine match in that some say that I too am unusual. We both base our lives on hard lessons from the past. We are both oddities." He smiled at his dinner companion. "The Sefton Line realizes that when a tired old ship reaches the end of her life, there is still a lot more use for her than meets the eye. I suppose you can say that is why they keep me on as well."

Katherine continued to politely press, "And how does that make you so odd?"

He laughed. Leaning back in his chair he addressed the question with great pride and humor. "Perhaps you haven't noticed yet Miss Worthington, but I am old," he said. "One would normally find a man of my age and experience at the command of one of the larger ships with larger crew and with most definitely larger wages. Packets are mostly run by the younger captains working themselves up and through small packet fleets." Gesturing toward his surroundings he continued, "I have simply chosen to stay where I am appreciated." But the captain's years and position did not reflect comfort as much as his own personal sufferings. Borland's soul had been torn apart years ago when his wife of longstanding picked up and left him. No longer being able to face the lonely nights of howling winter gales any more, she simply moved on, new deckhouse or not. She took nothing with her but the belongings which she brought into their marriage of fifteen years. Trying to claw his way off the lee shore of misery and depression, Borland made himself available to the Sefton Lines twenty-four hours a day, 365 days a year. Borland asked only two things for his quiet acquiescence. Seeking no financial share in the ship, he would seek no percentage of her trade revenues and ask instead for a simple yearly salary. In trade for this he sought permanent command of the packet *Galatea.* Second, as long as he was worthy of that command, the owners would not tear out the deckhouse that he had built for his wife. Perhaps he would tell the young girl if she asked about his home life, about why the deckhouse was so immaculate and showed no evidence of wear. There weren't many people who would understand the pain of such a turn in one's life, yet perhaps the dinner companion sitting across from him could. No rush, after all he had perhaps a month to find out.

Borland wiped at his mouth with one of the fine linen napkins. Taking a moment to gather his thoughts, he placed his hand across his chin and again, absentmindedly ran the front of his thick thumbnail down the hidden cleft of his chin.

He returned to the original question, "Do all captains live so well?" he repeated. "Would that be on the outside or the inside?" The finery which surrounded him described so well his outer demeanor and what he had accumulated during his years at sea, but intimated at nothing of the misery he held for so long and what he had lost from his heart. "Well, I would hope not."

Katherine took time to digest what she had just learned from the man. She took a new breath, "It is my understanding that I am the only passenger?"

"In fact you are," Borland replied with a slight nod of the head. "For this crossing you will have our undivided attention."

"As did the man earlier today at the front of the boat?"

Katherine asked referring to the half dead Jenkins.

"Miss Worthington-- "

"Captain Borland?" Finding a home in the sherry, Katherine slid her crystal glass out in front of her as she had seen others do. Borland paused for a second, thought about the girl's request and figured, after all, it was she who would have to pay the piper. Again he filled the small glass halfway.

"Perhaps some explanation is in order," he said. "Several years back this country came out of a war, which for my beliefs, changed very little except the quality of sailor." The captain filled his own sherry glass halfway. "We were once a gathering of honorable men who would give their all for their ship, who found pride in working her. The war ended that, it produced a breed that is not only daring but a hard lot to boot. Given the choice, they are inclined to do little work. They have to be driven to it. Because of this, it takes a rigid mate to see to discipline. Yet you will find that once these men roll out there is as much backbone in them as any."

"Being strong and brave doesn't mean that they don't feel... or are less bright because of it."

"Agreed," the captain said quickly. "But it does mean that for the most part they have hardened and lost their respect. These men were trained to fight hard and care little for their ships... if not themselves. If a man comes to know and learn that there is always a higher source to answer to, someday his beliefs will carry him to the highest of orders."

Sherry or not, Katherine felt a familiar note to Borland's argument; hadn't this been the very core of what she was trying to convince Bridie? That there had to be a common balance of concern and respect in order for those who were to serve to be happy, to go about their jobs with a sense of purpose and respect?

"Your point rings true," she said, "but fails to tell me why a man needs to be beaten within an inch of his life in order to gain his attention."

"Aboard this vessel you will find a simple but well thought out world," he said. "Below me are three mates. The first is

Amberson. He is the man who sees that my orders are followed to the letter. If they are not, he refers the problem to the second or third. They in turn will usually make short order of the problem. They are the attitude adjusters, if you will." Borland slowly pulled his full frame from the table and went to his sideboard. From a rich mahogany box with face plaque and polished hinges to rival the condition of the silver on his dinner table, he pulled a cigar. His eyes asked of the girl if she minded his smoking one and not, as she thought, if she would join him. Bending at the waist and lighting the cigar from a candle, he said, "Amberson you have already met, Kemp you haven't. We have a ship's doctor by the name of McCaffery, carpenter we refer to as Chips, a steward, a cabin boy, twenty sailors and two cooks, one for me," he said, gesturing to the remains of the meal with a warm smile, "and one for the crew. It is all very orderly and each man's duties are very clearly spelled out. Precisely spelled out."

His brass ship's bell rang three times. From his pocket he pulled his gold watch which Katherine had so admired earlier in the day.

"Perhaps you'd understand it if I likened *Galatea* to a clock or a watch. All parts must work in perfect harmony. One part stops or slows and you can no longer rely on the workings of your timepiece."

The man is a curiosity, Katherine thought, no doubt about that. He was a walking contradiction; one moment he praised and sought after the truth of a man's higher obligation, the next he is dismissing callous treatment by comparing the human soul and effort to the workings of a clock. Yet this was a step ahead of what she left behind at Elmwood, albeit a small step.

"If a dog is beaten enough," she said, "you break the animal's spirit and he becomes listless, useless. Oh, he might answer the whistle, but he can never be expected to give the extra bit when most needed. We need to be encouraged and guided to learn, encouraged to feel our own worth. "

"Miss Worthington, you are describing the workings of a perfect world," Borland said with a smile. "Ours is far from perfect." He took a long pull on his cigar and watched the ember glow. Releasing the smoke slowly and deliberately, he said, "My men are called packet rats. Because as you will soon learn for yourself, for the most part they are just that, rats. They grew up in poverty and, under the Lord's sad gaze, poverty is where they will die. Mind you, through no fault of their own. But it's this very poverty and gutter life which first planted the seed of dishonesty and depravity, and this past war encouraged it." Borland's thoughts shifted slightly, his eyes searched, his voice softened. "For the most part they are happy with their lot..."

Katherine's eyes widened with exception.

Borland stopped her with the slight nod of his head. "Happy with their lot, not their superiors. There lies a chasm of difference and indifference between the two. Look at how they dress. Torn topcoats, Liverpool buttons, he said, referring to the single wooden peg which held most of their wind torn and tattered denim coats together. "Their shoes, nothing more than discarded boots, the tops cut off so as not to waste time putting them on when called out for watch. You talk about your dog? Miss Worthington I wouldn't want any dog of mine going aloft in such tattered and worn clothes." Borland paused to reflect on the absurdity and humor of such a situation. "These man are paid for their work. What the owners lack in generosity they make up in dependency." He took another long pull at his smoke. "Yet as soon as these men get a sniff of land, what do they run to throw their money at -- women and whiskey, not clothes, not savings, nothing to advance their position. Those that do, the very few that have the foresight to do so, usually find themselves officers before too long."

Katherine sat patiently listening to the man's words. How much she wanted to counter back that the men had to be taught self respect and helped to find the reason why they had to jump willingly to commands. She wanted to counter with these points and so many more which she had come to understand while working under the iron fist of her own mistress. She had so much to say on the subject and to her great joy, she was in the company of someone who was willing to listen. Yet what played first and foremost upon the girl's slowly spinning mind right now was to get back to her own bunk before the whole ship rolled a complete 360 degrees. The combination of cigar smoke, too much sherry and no fresh air was beginning to churn the cauldron in her stomach and if there was to be any disgrace it had best occur in the privacy of her own cabin.

The girl's pale green pallor wasn't wasted on her host. "I've kept you too long, I'm afraid," Borland said graciously. "If you'll allow me, I'll see you to your cabin?" He said as he offered his arm by her side, not out of courtesy as the girl felt, but necessity as the man knew.

While philosophies were being traded and examined in the captain's cabin, out on deck the smoky southwest breeze of earlier had continued to build to the point that all around Katherine sung out. As the wind blew through the iron tight rigging, it sounded out a hum which seemed to be in perfect unison with the ship's own internal vibration. There was a different feel to *Galatea* as she continued to set about her business and push ahead on the northwest course which Borland had set out for her. Business-like and determined were the only words the girl could come up with as she lay on her bunk still in her evening dress, her only dress. "Yes, she's a very business-like vessel now, very business like indeed" she muttered. The waves of nausea had released their grip if only for just a moment. "Tomorrow I shall look about and see just what is what." Her bravado and focus of the moment once again gave way to the extremes of earlier that evening. Katherine's cabin was lurching and the nausea was making a second assault.

"Oh no."

She leaned over her bunk trying to gain access to the porcelain bowls below. She fumbled for a moment, running a race against the roasted hens. "Oh God," she said as *Galatea* lurched and threw her from her perch. Katherine landed on the hard wooden floor with an undignified thump. Skirts askew and tossed about she won her small race with the hens and secured the porcelain bowl with only seconds to spare. Her sickness was followed by a sudden and deep sleep.

CHAPTER 9

Katherine's days aboard *Galatea* rolled by as so many of the great ocean's miles swept past the ship's keel. She and Captain Borland continued to have their passionate debates about man's rank and responsibility in the great scheme of things. She even managed to get his acquiescence on one or two of the smaller issues about which she held such rigid beliefs. But for the most part the captain and Katherine simply agreed to disagree for now. Still with her typical tenacity, Katherine was determined to see that the old man tasted a small bit of the grace and spirit which she was sailing closer to on a daily basis. In just the few days she had spent living in her new world she had managed to learn some important lessons herself. When the wind freshened or dropped, per loud and no uncertain orders from the mate, each man on watch had a specific job to tend to aloft or on the deck. Each was an important part of the workings of the ship as each link of the massive chains which raised *Galatea*'s anchors were to her security. Whether they remained on deck or were scrambling toward the top of the great tapered masts, there was organization and purpose to every command and every ensuing action. All men were expected to stand to their work without hesitation. Even the ship's cook was pressed into service, leaving his black pots to simmer as he joined several others who were already straining at a line. Unfurling the massive clouds of canvas and matching them to the wind, there was respect and concern in each sailor's actions. "This is what I'm sure of," she would say to herself, "even a ship knows when she is respected and cared for." How each man learned the purpose for the hundreds of lines she saw running aloft was a complete mystery to her, yet she knew that their purposes didn't simply disappear into the tangle of canvas, wood and hemp above her. Each one had a specific function; some lines helped to raise the massive bolts of canvas while others were connected directly to the great chains which controlled the powerful horizontal arms which supported these acres of cloth which captured the wind. These arms, these great tapered steel yards, creaked and strained at the junctions where they met the masts. They swung and rose slightly to answer each change in strength and direction of the wind, regardless how small. From the vantage point of her cabin port she could watch as *Galatea's* towering masts etch slow and lazy circles against the deep blue above. Most times during the day, with the aid of a well folded pillow, Katherine would be found resting her chin on folded hands and watching the men at work above her, setting and adjusting the sails, fashioning chaffing gear to minimize the constant friction from the ship's movements, repairing worn fittings, splicing, tarring or jumping at the latest command.

Katherine learned quickly that if the order was given to take in sail, it usually meant that a fresh breeze was building and it was best that she sought the safety of her cabin. Although Borland drove as sharp and as hard as the time schedule demanded, he was a strong practitioner of discretion being the better part of valor. Being caught with too much sail up spelled certain disaster for his charge and danger for his crew. He took pride in their abilities and their prowess. "Any fool can put a sail up," he was known to say, "but it takes a sailor to take one down." Being overpowered by a North Atlantic squall was something he did not trivialize. When his order to take in sail was sent forward, there was no hesitation in its being carried out.

From her safe vantage point, Katherine began to understand that there was a direct relationship between the amount of sail *Galatea* carried and the amount of wind she was to expect or endure. It almost became a game with Katherine; upon waking in the morning she would try to feel the angle of heel which the ship was sailing under, the amount of pitching fore and aft and the strength of wind as it blew through the rigging. Katherine was starting to develop her own sea sense. She didn't know an upper topsail from a Charlie Nobel, but she was able to make her own forecast as to the comfort of the upcoming day by watching and listening to all that was around her.

These were the days of grace, and today was going to be a

fine one, she surmised, as she watched the swollen and taut canvas above her arc and swing across the large purposeful clouds. How long had it been since she simply watched clouds roll by? Not since she was a child had she taken the time to watch as they slowly changed shape, trying to guess what they would turn into next. Forgetting the men at work above her, she noticed that even the sky wasn't to be taken for granted. Today her eye was drawn to yet a higher level of cloud, ones which seemed to be lightly painted across the ceiling of her world. "Well, hello," she muttered. "Why have I never noticed you before? You're clouds, yet you aren't."

"Mare's tails they're called, fair weather clouds," Captain Borland said as he walked up to the girl's port. "Actually nothing more than frozen water vapor."

"But they're not moving," Katherine observed

"Oh they're moving, all right," the captain said as he squinted up into the bright sky. "They're just too far away to notice. Look at the mare's tail, the direction it points, that gives you the direction the upper winds are coming from as well as a good indication of the wind's strength. These are the clouds which can give you an indication of events to come – weatherwise, that is."

"Where do those winds come from, the ones that move the mare's tails?"

Focusing his attention back down on deck, he laughed. "Barometric pressure." Knowing that he had momentarily lost the girl, he felt bad. "It's no wonder you'd notice them Miss Worthington, they march to their own drummer, they move in different directions than their friends, the cumulus which you see just below them. As the cumulus push our winds here on the surface, the mare's tails, the cirrus, influence the cumulus below them. They are arbitrarily driven by two different currents of air."

Katherine stepped towards yet another opening for her on going argument with her host. "Things such as clouds, winds, and sunsets... they don't simply happen Captain Borland. I've read where the natives of your country believe that there is a god or entity who resides in everything about us and that man should respect their powers and purposes."

Once again her dinner partner smiled and enjoyed her simplistic outlooks. "I guess it wouldn't hurt if we all took a page or two from your book once in a while, Miss Worthington."

The two of them looked up at the sky above once again, though for two different reasons.

The captain was the first to break the silence. "Now, if you'll excuse me, I have to go put into evidence some powers of my own."

She continued to watch the clouds roll over the men working at their jobs far above her, trying to place all parts of the puzzle into their proper niches, but as she was prone to do, Katherine wasn't content to leave the puzzle simply at that. There were always other parts to be hunted down and placed into the picture. Her eyes wandered back up to the mare's tails. Barometric pressure controls the steering currents? Well where did these pressures themselves come from? She looked far into the sky, into a place which she had never allowed herself to go before, a place which had been giving birth to her persistent and plaguing nightmare.

While Katherine studied the clouds and the winds, unbeknownst to her, eight or ten miles above and hundreds of miles to the southeast a new type of weather was slowly, almost imperceptibly slouching and twisting into existence. Born of pressures, temperatures and levels of moisture too far away to be recorded yet just enough to spawn life, a small whirlpool of air was intent upon growing into a severe revolving tropical storm, a great, dark, mass of fury -- something Katherine had to this point only dreamt about, something that her captain and crew seldom wanted to talk about. A perfect gathering of elements and chance began to grow a deadly cyclopean monster. Once weaned, the monster would soon learn to feed off of the warm ocean below it, gaining strength from the life-giving tropical temperatures as it arced its way westward across chain of leeward and windward islands. Finding no resistance there, and with unchecked ferocity the monster would soon learn to feed off of itself as it would turn and track northward up the Gulf Stream and explode into the North Atlantic.

CHAPTER 10

I had no idea how long I'd been tied to the chair or who bound my wrists so tight as to cause them to bleed. The pain from where the ropes tore into my flesh brought me back into the world of consciousness. The room was dark and musty and of course I heard the proverbial voices from another room. They were arguing in something that sounded like Italian. I don't know why I say that, I don't speak Italian. I tried to trace my movements of earlier that day to get some clue, some grasp on what had happened, where I was. Nothing, my mind was a void. A rat ran across my feet. It looked like he was wearing a floral print shirt and leis around his neck. Two others followed, they both had leis and were carrying cheap Japanese camcorders. The second one stopped, looked up at me and shot some footage. He had thick round glasses and a prominent overbite. Peering out from behind the viewfinder he tipped his baseball cap, said, "Obligato," put it on backwards, and left. Clearly I had been drugged.

The door burst open and I was flooded in a bath of blinding light. All I could make out was the silhouettes of the two men who walked in. I assumed they were men, in this sort of situation they usually are. They weren't. One might have been, but as my eyes got accustomed to the light I saw that she was no man, she was Brigitte Neilsen dressed in a floral print shirt with leis around her neck. She carried something in her right hand while in her left there appeared to be a small hot water bottle in the shape of Sylvester Stallone. Decidedly I had been drugged.

"What are you going to do Brigitte, lay me?"

Who asked that, I thought, as I lay pressed against the ceiling looking down onto the charade which played out before me. I was having an out-of-body experience. Bad trip.

Brigette scowled at me. "You should be so lucky." With that she hauled back with the Sylvester Stallone hot water bottle and hit me across the face with it. It broke. Hot water all over me.

"Now look what you've done," she said. She took a few seconds to survey the mess, put her hands to her face and ran from the room crying.

The other shadowy figure followed her out. As he reached the door her turned to me and said, "I'm telling."

The door slammed shut and once again I was back in the chair in darkness. Just me and the Sylvester Stallone hot water bottle. Wherever I was, I could smell tar from rolls of hemp, as well as the occasional bitter tang of salt in the air. I don't know how long I sat tied to the simple wooden chair listening to the muffled voices from the other room.

Something rang and jolted me back to my senses. It rang again. Adrenaline coursed through my system and my heart pounded in my ears. It rang again. Frantically I looked about trying to see where in this limited darkness the ringing was coming form. It rang again and again.

"Damn it, that ringing, I can't take the ringing any longer!"

It was at my feet. I kicked out. Nothing. I looked down to the other side of the chair. It rang again. It was Sylvester, Sylvester Stallone was ringing. It appeared that the hot water bottle was also a cellular phone. It continued to ring. I couldn't quite get to it. A fish was lying across the top of it. I leaned down to move the fish off of Sylvester. I suddenly realized that I was no longer tied to the chair, I had been set free. By a fish? When did that happen? Judging by the healthy condition of my wrists I was never tied in the first place. I took a look at myself. I was wearing a floral print shirt. I answered the phone.

"You didn't hear this from me, sport, but your man's check is no good and I'm taking out the chains first thing in the morning." Madeline's voice slowly pulled me from my unconscious dream world and was bringing me some focus. "Are you there?" she said.

"Give me a second," I mumbled. I looked around; no chair, no rats with floral shirts and unfortunately no Brigette Neilsen. I checked my wrists. They weren't bleeding and my watch said 2:18 "What's no good?"

"Your man's check."

"Why the hell are you calling me at this hour to tell me that?"

"I tried calling up until this evening but all I got was your machine. I hate those things."

It was true, I do hide behind the machine and therefore experience my share of hangups from people who hate those things. Only I turn it off as I roll into bed... unless I have company of course.

"Why do you leave it on if you're home?"

I was now fully awake. "That's my business. What are you doing up so late?"

"And that's my business. Here it is in a nutshell sport. After I made the deposits this morning, Kathleen called from the bank and allowed as how Mr. Colin Jasperson had insufficient funds. I called his number, I guess it was his cellular. In any event there was no ring. He was out of range, I guess."

"If you only knew," I said.

"I certainly hope that your check cleared."

"Cashier's checks usually do. Look, as far as I'm concerned I've got my money and whatever he owes you is between you guys." I knew that I was sounding rude but there wasn't much I could do about it, especially at 2:19. I trusted that Madeline understood.

"Look, I like you, Chris, and I want to see you and Paul do well, but you've got to work with me here."

I've found that sometimes in life the obvious is so often overlooked because it's so bloody obvious. You're standing in a mud puddle, a man comes by and says, "Watch out for the mud puddle." "What mud puddle?" you ask, looking all about.

"What I'm telling you is that as of eight o'clock tomorrow morning your boat *Curlew* will be chained to the dock until we get our money. That is, if she's still there." With that she hung up.

Paul and I met at the Fee's dock half an hour later. For all intents and purposes everything we needed for the crossing was already aboard *Curlew*, and what wasn't stowed could be so in a matter of hours. By no means was this the way our fledgling company wanted to start its first major job, but then again a man like Jasperson didn't get to the point in his life where he could throw $300 cellular phones in the drink by not coloring outside the lines.

Paul dug his hands deep into the pockets of his coat. "It's not stealing?" he asked.

"Nope." I said

He smirked, "Don't we need to break a bottle of champagne or something."

Curlew's engine fired right up. I kept going over my mental inventory trying to figure out what we had forgotten and why we should try to wait another day or two. We couldn't wait though, because in a few short hours *Curlew* was going to be chained to the dock. My mind was telling me that all was in our favor. Given the circumstances, the time to leave was now. My stomach was of a different opinion.

As we let her engine warm up, Paul started to stow the more obvious things in the dark -- food, charts, foul weather gear. I watched as he scurried around the cabin believing that all the hassles of the past week or so had washed past us and the moment of our three truths was at hand.

"Paul," I said, trying my best to sound nonchalant. "Seriously, what do you think, this isn't stealing is it?"

"You just said it wasn't," he said as he slowly sat on the starboard settee. "Why would it be? Jasperson had a contract with us, and he paid us. He has a sort of contract with Fee, but he hasn't paid Fee, and that's not our worry."

That's just how I saw it, but I wanted to double check. I needed some fast and dirty legal advice. "I'll be right back, keep packing." I scrambled out onto the dock and headed for the yard's phone booth. I turned up the collar of my pile jacket to try and ward off some of the chill of the night air.

The fact that it was 3:30 in the morning didn't deter my sister Ellie from allowing her thoughts on middle of the night phone calls to be aired. I tried to explain everything the best I could. With absolutely no valid defense to my credit I was ready to take my lumps which for some reason were a bit slow in coming.

With great pause and certain finality the words all but hissed out of Ellie like a balloon suddenly releasing air, "Look, its almost four a.m., I've got to be in Boston by eight. Let me throw on a coat and I'll be right down. Chris, you've come too far to stop now, leave everything to me and concentrate on the Atlantic. Hell, I might even help with the dock lines."

A soft New England mist was starting to form a sheen on the streets. I shut the door of the phone booth and tried to reassure my sister that she really didn't need to get out of bed at this hour, her word that we weren't stealing but fulfilling a contract was all that I needed. As I tucked myself further back into the phone booth I noticed that Paul and I, and now Ellie, weren't the only people awake at this ungodly hour. A tall slim figure wearing a floral print shirt was slowly approaching the phone booth. Tucked up under one arm was what to me looked like a camcorder. I stared in total disbelief. All she was missing were round thick glasses and a floral lei.

As the woman walked closer, the mist started to turn into an autumn drizzle. Trying to keep both the camera and herself dry, she made a dash straight for me and the booth.

"Coming in!" Madeline announced as she pushed her way into the cramped booth. "Tight, ain't it," she said as she surveyed the booth. It was then that she realized that I was actually on the phone and not trying to wait out the rain. "Trying to hook a date at this hour, Barlow?" she grabbed the phone from my hand. "Hi," she cooed into the receiver.

"Madeline, please let me have that." I gently tried to pry the instrument out of her hands.

"Nope." she said as she hit me on the head with the thing. "Hi! Madeline. Who's this?" she stared at me. "Well, isn't that a coincidence. I'm sort of like a sister to Chris too, I'm sorry to say."

I had the distinct feeling that Madeline had been drinking.

"Madeline, please, just let me have the --" She hit me on the head again with the phone piece. "Damn it, stop that!" I quickly put hand to scalp to check for blood. Out of the ear piece I could hear Ellie calling my name and asking about my safety.

"Ellie, I'm fine," I said over Madeline's shoulder.

"Ellie? Ellie Barrow your sister?" Madeline asked.

"The last I checked." I said rubbing my head.

"Oh," she said with a laugh and without missing a beat whacked me again. "Ellie, this is Madeline?.... from The Women's Resource Group? Yes, small world. Yup, he's right here. I'll ask him." She turned her face to me. "You planning on leaving sometime today sport?"

"Trying to," I said with my arms crossed atop my throbbing head.

"Trying to." she said to the phone. "Cool. Bye." She hung up her weapon. "She said to sit tight, she'll be right down."

The thought of Madeline and Ellie together, with me in the general vicinity, was not a pleasant thought.

I know that I should have been concerned with appearances and all, but judging by the amount of condensation on the glass of the booth, anybody who was up at this hour wouldn't see us. The rain really started to come down harder now and I have to admit that the situation did have its bright side; the harder it rained, the farther Madeline pushed her way in, and against me.

I waited out the quick squall for a few minutes or so trying to make remarkably small talk. Madeline said nothing but simply stared at me. Finally I had to ask. "Why the video camera, Madeline?" She continued to stare. Maybe I was being too obtuse. "Madeline, you have a video camera under your arm, why?"

"I've never seen the ocean," she said absently. She was beginning to notice how cold it was getting and her lightweight floral print shirt wasn't helping to keep her goose bumps at bay. "I've lived next to it all my life but have never seen it. You know what I mean, Chris."

I assured her I didn't but was willing to listen.

Her voice lowered. "Jesus it's cold."

"I suppose you'd be insulted if I offered you my coat."

"Why, Mr. Barlow, how thoughtful of you." She allowed me

to try to drape my pile jacket over her shoulders, all within a two square foot area. I was not too sure of what was going on here, but it was kind of nice.

The rain slowed its drumming atop of the phone booth and I suggested that we talk as we headed down to *Curlew*. We started to amble down to what was hopefully going to be my home for the next month.

"Now here's the deal, Barlow," she said as she slipped her arm through mine. This was stranger than rats in floral print shirts, far stranger. We stopped outside of her office. "I've never been able to get more than a few miles offshore and the way things are going I doubt if I ever will. When you reach mid-Atlantic crank off about an hour's worth of tape for me, will you? I have a feeling that there's something going on out there that I'm missing out on."

Although this request was a simple one, it seemed absolutely contrary to the sort of person I always thought Fee's bookkeeper to be.

"I didn't know that you were interested in that sort of thing," I said.

"What sort of thing would that be?"

"The ocean, nature, spirituality. That sort of thing."

"There's a lot you don't know about me," she said as she slipped her other arm through mine. We stared at each other just long enough for my heart to move up into and past my throat and settle in my ears.

"Chris!" Ellie called out.

In the past few weeks, little if anything in my life had resembled what I used to call normal. I had great hopes that as the departure date came nearer things would begin to settle down. Now that the fates were forcing our hand and our departure was in a matter of hours, not days, things were truly becoming unglued.

I started the introductions but Ellie and Madeline greeted each other like long lost friends. So far so good. Impatiently I looked down the wharf to where *Curlew* and Paul were both waiting. The eastern sky was beginning to show the slightest bit of warmth and color and I knew that it was only a matter of a few short hours before Chester awoke and whatever charm this evening had to offer would be broken.

"Can we finish this at the boat?" I suggested.

The three of us headed down the dock.

"You go up to make a phone call, you come back with two women, all at four in the morning," Paul said as I stepped aboard.

"Stranger than science. I'll try to explain later."

According to Paul, there wasn't a whole lot left to be done aboard *Curlew* which couldn't be taken care of once we were on our way. For all intents and purposes Barlow & Dwyer Deliveries was seconds away from taking its maiden voyage.

Good byes, hugs and a few tears were shared as we dropped *Curlew's* lines. Last minute requests and wishes were passed around -- check on mail, feed Paul's fish, keep bill collectors at bay.

We gathered in *Curlew's* lines, backed her out of her slip and pointed her bow east.

"Chris! Your jacket," Madeline called as she watched us start to head out of the harbor. Knowing that I had more warm gear aboard, I simply gave a smile and shrugged.

"You'll just have to come find it when you return." She smiled.

Indeed I would, I promised myself.

There was no real breeze to speak of so we motored out the sound and tried to pick up some wind once away from under the lee of Chester's cliffs. I was at the helm trying to piece together the last few hours while Paul was below checking tide tables and current strengths for Nantucket Shoals, which we were going to be skirting later that day.

Our departure schedule being as abbreviated as it was, Paul and I never had a chance to sit and compare notes about our employer's earlier visit. "What the hell was it that you needed to talk about?" I called down into the nav area.

A few seconds later Paul stuck his head out into the cockpit.

"Well, after I left you I wanted to check with Quint about the remaining food. That's when I saw Lucy and Ethel climbing aboard *Curlew.* Decided to go aboard and see if I could help with anything. It was strange, from the dock I could see below and they were going through drawers like nobody's business, but as soon as I got aboard they stopped and barely talked to me. One of them was shoving something into his pocket though."

"Anything missing?" I asked.

"Not that I could tell, except for your pile coat," he said with a smirk.

"Well, if nothing's missing..." I then marveled at what we were now doing. "Paul, we did it, we actually did it. Well... are doing it."

"We sure did it all right." he gazed at Chester's receding shoreline, "We sure did it. By the way, what's your watch say, skipper?"

I brought my left wrist up to take a look. "Four thirty-three."

"Keep reading."

"And twenty seconds."

"Keep reading," he said as he disappeared below into the cabin. "What?" I started reading quietly to myself. "Twenty-five, twenty-six, twenty-seven seconds. Ninth month, fourteenth day. Shit!"

"That's right," Paul said from below. "Shit."

The one thing we promised ourselves we wouldn't do.

"Drop the hook and wait until tomorrow?" I said.

"Oh boy," Paul said as he went back to unpacking.

I checked my watch yet again. It wasn't the time that I was so concerned about as much as that little window at the bottom of the dial which tells you the month, date, the year, and the day of the week.

Our four-week odyssey had the dubious distinction of starting out on a Friday.

The one thing we promised ourselves we wouldn't do.

CHAPTER 11

As Katherine lay asleep in her bunk, *Galatea* continued to push east through the sharp and solid seas. While she slept, oblivious to all around her, two watches of men had rolled out to the mate's commands and worked the great ship, changing or shortening sail, standing bow watch through the fogs of George's Bank, assuring that *Galatea* passed safely through the vast New England fishing fleet, or simply huddling for warmth in the lee of the deckhouses, some eyeing the girl's quarters, envying the girl her uninterrupted sleep and warmth.

Katherine's recurring dream of charging through a great storm alone on an overpowered ship had failed to release its grip on the her. In fact, now that she was on her way home under the watchful guidance of Captain Borland, it seemed as though her nightmare had gained in strength. The images which had tormented Katherine seemed to be more powerful and closer, leaving her more and more tired after her nightly bouts. Each time the sequence of events was the same except for a slight alteration; in one dream her ship was in the tropics, not the north Atlantic, in another the lone captain who stood at the rail behind her was a young man, not unlike one of the stable boys from Elmwood. Tonight's version of the nightmare was no exception. Once again Katherine found herself being thrown about in the great darkness of the ship's empty hold. As each wave lifted the ship and tossed her onto her beam ends, more and more of the planking of the hull opened to allow in the cold Atlantic. Frantically she was trying to gain a handhold on the companionway ladder which was covered in the sea moss and slime of the ages. Katherine had known this struggle before, at times she even felt as if she knew that this was nothing more than a dream and at some point she would awake from it damp with sweat and suffering a night chill.

She had no feelings of assurance tonight though, for there

was a slight change in the terror. Katherine watched in a new horror as the relentless Atlantic worked its way through the sprung planking of the hull. Instead of the usual long gray watery fingers of the North Atlantic, the pale blue flesh of rotted hands and arms from a legion of drowned souls fervently pushed their way through the bilges and up towards her legs, trying to gain a grip on her. Kicking out with all of her waning strength, the girl tried to hold firmly to the soft wooden rungs above her, but with each powerful kick her grip slipped further, lowering her toward the stench and rot which was reaching out from below. Katherine tried to scream, but nothing more than a low moan came from her clenched teeth.

Once again the ship was thrown down from a tremendous height, and the impact of the hull on the water tore Katherine's grip from the ladder and flung her against the bilge below. Blindly she tried to scramble up the twisted deck, but not before the Atlantic found its prey. The long sinuous fingers grabbed the girl's ankle and started to pull her down through the splintered hull toward the black void of the enraged sea. As each finger tightened its grip it felt as though the skin of her ankle was being torn by daggers of searing cold ice. The frozen blue flesh melded with her own and slowly started to burn itself into her. Knowing that there was no one aboard to hear her screams, she kicked and clawed with her free foot, hoping to do something, anything against the sharp killing fingers. Each time her boot made contact against the ice cold hand, she only succeeded in hurting herself more, her kicks pushing the bony fingers further into her skin. With the fury of a person possessed, she raised her free leg one final time and brought it down against soft tissue of the rotted hand.

The searing pain woke Katherine. She bolted upright in her bunk and quickly tried to gather in everything about her. As fast as the dream faded the comfort of reality crept back in and the sounds and lurches of *Galatea's* eastward progression assured the girl that all was once again safe. She was in her own bunk, with her own possessions about her, on her way back to her family. She noticed that her cotton dressing gown was, as usual, damp with the sweat, a mere inconvenience compared to the hell which her subconscious had just put her through. She could hear the great sails above her make the yardarms and masts groan. Peering out the small window she saw the occasional star through a break in the dark clouds overhead. Best of all, her ankle was nice and warm.

Still shaken, Katherine watched out of her window as the sun began to make itself known in the east. Dawn was breaking, which meant that there was now one less day until she was home again. She pulled her knees up to her chest, wrapped her blanket about her, and watched as the gray Atlantic was warmed by the sun. She listened as the mate called out for the new watch and *Galatea* was readied for the day ahead of her. She was once again nestled in her sense of peace as she thought back onto what she had just left and what she was on her way to. She laughed a bit to herself; try as she may, she couldn't will the ship to sail any faster. Yet it made her uneasy that her nightmare was about the very thing on which she was floating. But she had certainly gone through far worse, and for now was in good hands.

Katherine started her day with her usual routine. She reached to the chair across from her bunk gathered up her clothes, crawled down under her bedding and started to remove the bulky dressing gown and put on her skirt and blouse. Due to her lack of privacy aboard, she laid out her clothes on the chair beside her the night before so that she wouldn't have to get out from under the blanket to dress for the day.

Swinging her legs out from under the covers she placed her bare feet on the floor of her cabin and reached for her wool socks and boots. The salt air was keeping the wool in a growing state of dampness.

I'll soon have moss growing out of these, she thought as she crossed her left foot over her right knee. Just before she put the sock on she noticed that the skin on her foot was beginning to show the effect of the damp salt air as well, some slight flaking around reddened areas. Taking some talcum out of her kit, she sprinkled some in her sock and on the foot.

She sprinkled some talcum in her other sock, rubbed it on

her right foot, and finished dressing. *Galatea* slid down a wave just as she was placing her talc on a shelf above the small desk. With the movement of the ship, the small tin leapt off shelf and fell about her feet, spilling some of its contents on the floor and on the girl's legs. Katherine bent down to shake a thick layer of powder off of her socks.

As thick as the covering of talc was, it wasn't enough to hide the four long bruise marks around Katherine's right ankle. The marks all ended together in the shape of a palm. The horror of the nightmare coursed through her body anew as she stared at her ankle in disbelief. There was no mistaking the pattern where four long, bony fingers clamped their death grip. Quickly she looked about her small cabin. With her good right hand she rubbed frantically at the blue green bruises. Just below her shins was a bruise clearly in the shape of an index finger, followed by a long, bony middle finer and then a ring finger, all meeting in a small palm print just above her inside ankle bone.

As she all but rubbed her own skin raw, a wave of relief ran over her. The dream, she thought. I must have been grabbing my own ankle in the dream. With giddy relief she fell back on to her bunk, laughing about what her grand-father used to call having a case of the spooks. She laughed out loud again as she saw and compared the size and marks on her reddened ankle with her own hand; they were indeed one and the same. She fell back in a flood of relief and embarrassment.

"My God, girl, get a grip on yourself," she said. Taking a few moments to gather herself and her thoughts, she readied herself for the brand new day awaiting her on deck.

Reaching for the latch to her cabin door, Katherine's knees gave way under the pressing weight of her new terror, she was swept by a wave of nausea.

She sobbed as she stared with horrific understanding at her ankle.

She looked at her withered left hand with sickening betrayal. Her eyes gazed down to her right hand, which was once again methodically trying to rub away the demonic tattoo above her ankle. She realized that her own palm was on the outside of her leg, fingers pointing in. The mark from last night's dream lay in the opposite direction, palm inside, fingers pointing out, as though she had tried to mutilate herself with her left hand, a hand which hadn't been opened straight since she was three years old.

CHAPTER 12

"Wild dreams," Paul said as he wedged himself into the cockpit next to me.

After we got out from under the lee of Chester's cliff's, we had spent most of our first two days on a port tack, picking up a mild but steady northerly as we closed in on our goal, a mere 3,000 miles to the east. I had the 0400 to 0800 watch and had earlier this morning watched a second glorious and warming sunrise bring on a new day off of *Curlew's* tilted bow. All the charades and fire drills of the past few weeks not withstanding, the small sloop had clearly come into her own and was charging toward England with a bone in her teeth. We were on a bit of a shy reach which gave her quite a comfortable motion as she cleaved the cold but accommodating waters before her. From where I sat, things couldn't get a whole lot better.

Paul deftly balanced two hot mugs as he took a seat next to me on the high side of the cockpit.

"Really weird dreams," he said as he handed me my mug of tea.

"If they had anything to do with Brigitte Neilsen or camcorder toting mice, its probably best that I don't hear about them, " I said as I reached to adjust the heading on the auto pilot.

Paul looked at me closely for a few seconds. "Knock off a few minutes early. Get some rest."

Knowing that Paul was now officially on watch, I settled back sipping my hot tea, watching the gray Atlantic sweep past not a foot from where I braced my feet on the low side of the rectangular cockpit, our outdoor home for the next month or so. Not a whole lot of separation between dry and wet, I thought to myself. We were truly on a floating island and hopefully very self-sufficient. We had plenty of food, 150 gallons of water, a water maker in case that didn't see us through, 40 gallons of diesel, every navigational aid known to man, a cabin heater if it got too cool, air conditioning if it got too hot and a video tape library that had Debbie doing not only Dallas, but Dayton, Duluth and Daytona to boot. We had practically any sail for any condition and good strong jack lines to which we could hook our safety harnesses onto when we had to leave the security of the cockpit and handle sails on the foredeck. Despite all of this I seemed to gain new decisive respect for the very small barrier between the security of *Curlew* and the final certainty of mother ocean.

Taking one last 360-degree look around the horizon for any traffic, I stood, stretched the aches of the previous damp evening out of my joints, slowly worked my way down the companionway and climbed out of my foul weather gear before I slept the sleep of the dead. We hadn't any solid water aboard during the night but the extra waterproof layer added protection against the cool north breeze and gave some needed warmth. Paul and I both knew these were the days of grace and that there wouldn't be many before this gear was going to be needed for more than simply keeping out the wind. Once again it would be the only barrier between a relatively warm body and one that suffered cold seas down the neck or up the leg.

With help from the boys at NASA and any one of their wonderful twenty-four position giving satellites, I fixed our position on the chart and filled in the ship's log: 0800, course 120 magnetic, wind north fifteen to twenty knots, barometer 1008 and steady, boat speed seven to seven point five knots.

Before turning in for a few hours of needed sleep, I fixed a bowl of cereal and sat on the companionway steps looking out at the flat and powerful wake *Curlew* left in her passing. The new sun was catching the tops of the northerly chop and was giving each wave a sharp appearance. I tried to imagine what it would be like trying to walk over these seas instead of sailing across them, just as when I was a kid in school I would spend hours staring at the ceiling trying to figure what it would be like to maneuver between classes if the building were upside down.

"When I'm at sea I always have strange dreams. Epics," I said as I ate and continued to stare at the horizon behind Paul. "Played tennis on a gimbaled tennis court once. Strange part is I don't play tennis."

Remembering how he and I used to sneak onto the courts of Cooperville's stuffiest country club as kids, Paul smirked. "With or without nets?" he asked, staring ahead.

"Without."

"Not much of a sport otherwise."

"Absolutely."

"Any fool can hit a ball into a net," he said.

"But it takes an athlete to play without one. Or a racket or ball. Stoned out of his mind."

Paul was grinning at this point. "Fun days," he said.

We both took a few minutes to think back on those days of what my father referred to as "horseplay" when I was very young and "horseshit" when I was of an age that I should have known better.

"Ever wonder what's below us?" Paul asked.

"Fish."

"Besides that."

"Water. Lots and lots of water."

"Besides that."

I thought for a few minutes more. I knew what Paul was hinting at. I'm constantly awed by the vast acreage of water that covers our earth, 80 percent. So why do we call it earth, I always ask. An ever changing, totally independent and every bit as arbitrary surface which held all the strength Mother Nature would ever need to muster. All the respect and at times fear that I possessed for the ocean came simply from looking at her surface, the top few inches of what she had to offer. When I stopped to think of how much of her body lay below what we could see and what sort of ghoulish secrets she held . . . well that was when an over-stuffed chair in front of a good fire seemed the most appealing.

"We know more about the rings of Saturn," Paul said.

He and I shared the same arguments, at times passionately about our ocean's and their futures.

The wind point indicator showed that the wind had shifted a few degrees west of north. Paul leaned down to the low side of the cockpit to ease the jib a tad.

"Ever wonder what happens to someone who gets washed overboard?" he asked.

I smiled with amazement. "Where'd that come from?"

"Have you?" he asked again as he looked up to check the set of the taught and drawing sail at the front of the boat.

No, I thought, not really. Truth be told it was a subject which if allowed could keep me up at night. For a moment I imagined the horror of watching your boat sail on without you. We had both had friends who were lost at sea, but for many reasons, superstition among them, we never really talked about them much.

"This all part of you dream?" I asked as I rinsed out my cereal bowl from under a tap which supplied the galley sink with sea water.

"Yeah," he said absently as he handed me his mug. Refill?"

End of discussion. Paul Dwyer was a man not unlike that brokerage firm who, when they talked, everybody listened. The only difference was that when Paul talked, you had to listen. He wasn't a man who suffered fools easily or liked to repeat himself, and perhaps that was why he didn't become the next real estate baron of our nation's capitol. There was a city where the man was knee deep in deaf fools.

I refilled his mug from our pump thermos, and handed it to him. As there was nothing more, I was going to stumble into the small aft cabin and turn in. The dawn of the new day had charged me with a fresh energy which I was sure would last me well into the afternoon, but in the past few minutes the four hours alone on a cold night watch began to catch up with me. I stripped down to my shorts and crawled into my sleeping bag. I tried to enter a few notes in my sea journal but the combination of my down nest and the rhythmic movement of *Curlew's* easterly progress brought a quick end to that. I thought about the question Paul had raised and listened as the Atlantic whispered not an inch from my ear. I had attended the services for two friends who were lost at sea; one was swept clear from the foredeck in a gale off the Irish sea, the other simply vanished without a trace. He had been singlehanding a sailboat to France and never made port. Six weeks after he was reported overdue, a westbound container ship had found his small boat floating in the mid-Atlantic. She had clearly suffered storm damage, her bilges were filled with water and her rig had been torn from the deck. The business end of Jean's safety harness was still attached to a pad eye on deck but hauntingly there was nothing left on the torn and tattered other end. I wondered just how long he was dragged through the water before the tether finally and mercifully broke. His widow was given the ship's log and apart from the usual entries there wasn't anything to indicate that his death was anything more than a terrible accident which shook deep the roots of Chester's sailing community.

As I started to fall asleep and mix fantastical dream thoughts with reality, I started to feel like a visitor who, by the graces of something more powerful than I'd ever have the knowledge to understand, was being allowed to pass over the ocean knowing full well that all around me there were huge graceful creatures who understood the ocean better than I.

Finally I slept. The engine roared to life, pulling me from my comatose state. The batteries needed to be charged, but why on my offwatch? Looking out of the small port which I lay up against, I could see that it was the same old Atlantic and that weatherwise everything looked normal. I lay still listening as Paul tuned in the high seas weather forecast on the single side band radio. The owner of the voice, which had a Mickey Mouse type tenor to it, assured us and any other ship within a 500-mile radius that there were no gales predicted and that what we had now, fifteen to twenty knots from the northwest, was what we were going to have for the next twelve hours.

Swinging on a grab rail which ran the length of *Curlew's* ceiling, I made my way against the slant of our home and hand over hand I arrived in the forward cabin, where I plopped myself down on the starboard settee. One thing about awaking at sea, it is immediate. No time to slowly adjust to the day, wander about with cup of tea trying to figure out what lay ahead. The minute you woke up and were on your feet, you were using one hand to dress and the other to brace against the ship's movement. I loved it.

"Anything new?" I croaked to Paul, who was still up in the cockpit enjoying the in again out again Autumn sun.

"Nope." He smiled as he came below to check the charging rate on the electric panel. "Found some more of *Curlew's* checkered history." He nodded toward a small expandable file container which lay on the heavily varnished dinette. "Must have been what Jasperson's men were rooting about for, so I did some rooting of my own."

Paul and I never really had a chance to try to piece together the whole little drama of Jasperson's last minute holdout and his boys from Maine combing through the boat. The best I could figure was that the short fat man from New Hampshire was trying to stall me by water's edge while his men got what they needed off the boat. Whatever they took certainly wasn't anything of great importance, nothing from our inventory was missing. Paul and I had left it at that.

"Makes for interesting reading," Paul said as I picked up the folder. "*Curlew* has seen her share of yards between Maine and Connecticut."

As I started to read the work orders from eight different yards, I found nothing out of the ordinary: haul-outs for painting, haul-outs for replacing used zincs, haul-outs for some slight keel alteration, that sort of thing. Just the usual year-to-year maintenance.

"What?" I asked, looking at Paul.

"She's almost traveled more miles on terra firma than she has in the water," he said.

I kept reading. Paul was right in observing that she had been hauled quite a bit, but I'm afraid I seemed to be missing the point here. I checked the dates.

"Year end haul-outs. Some pre-season. What of it?"

"Not the work done, the record of it."

Not the work done, the record of it. Paul had lost me.

"The staples," he said.

I looked at the staples, I looked at the dates, I looked at the work order numbers, and not for the first time in a few days I thought back to Madeline and our early morning together and felt a bit insecure wondering what she was thinking about all of it. One thing did catch my eye. Under “Materials Used” was fiberglass wrap and resin.

“Fiberglass?” I said. “Needed supplies for routine painting?”

“Missed that one,” Paul said.

I looked at the staples again, then I looked at Paul.

“Warm.” he said.

I pulled on the staples.

He grinned, “Warmer.”

I turned each work order over.

He beamed. “Hot.”

I held the stapled corners not two inches from my eyes.

He laughed. “Red hot!”

Red hot, indeed, and blind as a bat too. For right in front of my weather-worn nose was something pretty strange. Each separate work order, all eight, had little tufts of paper in their staples, small single tufts of torn paper. Clearly there was a page missing from each set of orders. We looked at each other for a few seconds hoping that the other was going to be the one to fill in the blanks.

“What’s your take?” I asked.

“Work done that no one was supposed to know about?” Paul said as the ship’s clock chimed eight times, 12 noon. Paul started to fill in the log and plot our noon position. I stuck my head outside into the cockpit and decided that with the particular slant of the breeze and the way *Curlew* was taking the seas I could forgo the usual struggle of climbing into my foul weather gear for this watch.

“High seas forecast at 1530. Probably the same as this morning’s. Later.” Paul ducked back into the small aft cabin and climbed into his own bunk for his four hours.

Work done that no one was supposed to know about. I spent the next four hours figuring out every answer to this riddle but the right one.

CHAPTER 13

"Hunger and ease, Miss Worthington, hunger and ease."

The good captain gently pushed himself back from the empty serving plates before him. The dark brooding mahogany panels of his cabin always seemed to be illuminated by the girl's presence. Life aboard an eastbound packet offered its share of rough edges and crusty living and the old man was happy to discover that the few times he shared dinner with Katherine, the life of a sailor could be softened just a bit. The two continued to share their disagreements about discipline and order, but the ongoing debate between them did little to dampen the joy the old man got from the young girl's company. Were I ever to have had the pleasure of being a parent, he thought, I would surely want for a daughter such as Katherine Worthington. He thoroughly enjoyed her urgency and optimism. She had seen far more than her years allowed but in some areas was as innocent as a small child. Her tenacity brought the old man challenge and distraction.

"That's what the English call it, hunger and ease." He had brought up this point to counter Katherine's claim that he didn't carry enough men to work *Galatea*, that if he had more men, a larger crew, the work-load could be shared, lightened. "Their merchant ships put to sea with over sized crews, far too many men. Hunger because there is never enough food for so many hands. And ease because there isn't enough work to keep them all busy. We in these United States believe, most of us believe anyway, that the whole economy of the ship lies with the crew." Here he paused to search through his vast mental archives for something which had surfaced a while back. Finding what he was after he continued. "There is a man who writes that our species exists as it does due to the simple fact that only the fit survive, enabling each new generation with more strength. With that in mind, perhaps you'll find that it is no different than life aboard."

He rose from the table and crossed to the heavy teak lockers which ran along the starboard side of his cabin. He tapped at a barometer on the bulkhead. Opening a drawer from the beautifully grained collection of small drawers, he pulled a cigar from his humidor. As he was about to place it in his mouth he gestured with it, silently asking the girl's approval. Katherine remembered the last time he had smoked a cigar in her presence and how it had spun her stomach. But now was different, she felt secure that her sea legs had at last found a good strong hold.

She smiled. "By all means."

"Thank you." He lit the cigar and sat back to the table. "Miss Worthington, here aboard *Galatea*, that theory is boiled down to its basic of elements; the fit remain, the unfit leave, with or without a shroud of canvas sewn around them."

"But these men work around the clock," the girl said, "When do they get their time to feel, to enjoy the seas around them?"

"Enjoy?" He leaned forward onto his folded arms. "Miss Worthington, let's start at the beginning shall we? These men don't think as your landsmen do. Never have, never will." He took a slow, long pull at his cigar, gesturing about him. "This is a means of livelihood for them, not some great adventure which one reads about. These men know little of, nor are they interested in learning about your notions of the sea. Contrary to what your authors tell you, they fail to love the ocean, they hate it as the savage enemy it can be. But they respect it and all that she can do."

Judging the tight look on the girl's face to indicate disdain, Borland took another tack. "These men are not out to better themselves. Many of them were orphans bouncing from one handout to the other before they found life at sea. Either that or they were from families with too many children to support and had the door shut on them at the tender ages of nine or ten. Some have been before the mast so long they have no idea to what country they owe their allegiance. I think that you'll agree this is not the foundation to support model citizens."

Katherine sat listening about a life which had vague notes of familiarity. She had left home at a tender age, she had been thrown into an environment in which it was all but impossible to better oneself. When she allowed it, she felt some identity with these men.

"Very little is asked of them and in return they give a great deal sometimes, perhaps the only thing they can truly call their own, their lives. Yet in spite of this they are fearless aloft as well as on the beach."

"But why the cruelty?" she said.

The captain tried to tread lightly. "Because they don't pretend to be something they aren't. Miss Worthington, you know about pride, you are on your way home to what you envision will be a better life. It's your wonderful pride which is demanding more of you, demanding that you do this."

At these words Katherine flinched. The burn in her ankle had started to make itself known. Slowly she reached down to rub it. Gone was the usual warmth from bone and skin for now her fingers met ice. She stifled a small gasp. Very quickly she removed her hand and placed it in her lap.

Borland beamed at the girl with great affection. "And just as with you, these men won't go down without a fight."

Katherine tried to smile. Looking down at her folded hands for a few seconds she gathered her thoughts. "Perhaps," she said with great determination, "if they were taught more about the good things in life, the spiritual things in life, they wouldn't need such cruel discipline." She looked up at the captain. "Perhaps if they knew that there was something more powerful than any of us and that it holds our best concerns in its heart." For the first time, Katherine began to realize that this powerful entity of which she spoke was a double-edged sword. For all the fear which was beginning to rise in her, the icy grip on her ankle might as well have been around her heart.

"There isn't a man on this ship who doesn't have the strongest of awareness of God, Miss Worthington, but one thing they won't tolerate is a Bible thumper." He grinned. "Indeed I come close to the line with my readings each day. I must assure you that each one of them is keenly aware of their great debt to Providence. You won't get them to talk about it even if they could find the words, but they know what eternity lies just feet from them."

Her hand slowly shook with fear as she reached down to her ankle again. Surely she was losing her mind for it was as warm as it should be and what pain there was, was alleviated by shifting her foot beside her chair. No ice, no burn. The icy grip had released its hold on Katherine's leg, the warmth returned, her heart slowed. The dream, she thought with relief, a simple remembrance of the dream. She pulled her thoughts back to the table.

"Please don't labor yourself under any misunderstandings, Miss Worthington." the captain said. "We masters and officers belong to no high temple of the priesthood, and there is no mystery to our calling. Our job is to make timely deliveries and to honor an art which must survive intact from generation to generation."

"Art?" she asked

"The great art of sailing." he said softly.

As they continued to talk, almost imperceptibly, *Galatea* rose to a sea larger than most that she had been experiencing. With the great press of canvas that she now flew she was powerfully pushed over the swell and out through the hollow back of the large wave as the sea rolled away under her keel. As *Galatea* fell into the trough behind it she landed with a great moan and shudder. For the second time that night a surge of burning pain wrapped itself around Katherine's right ankle. She drew in a sharp and sudden breath and grabbed at it. The violence of the ship's sudden slamming and the surge of pain in her right leg spoke as one. Again fear surged through the girl's core, the reminder of her night terrors, of what she had found when she awoke several mornings ago. Her dinner conversation was a distraction, for the past hour or so she had managed to forget the shock of the marks on her leg which grew deeper every day, the terror her dream brought which came closer every night. As the icy burn gripped tighter, the tone of the whole cabin shifted; what was warm was now stifling, what was bright was too bright, the smoke from the captain's cigar was choking, nauseating. The cigar was making here feel dizzy and weak. She had always disliked the smell, she had suffered through them while at Elmwood, but never like this. The blue smoke which emanated from the end of the red glow swirled around the cabin and seemed to hang and drip from its surroundings. Borland's face contorted as each inhalation lit up the red hot ember and bathed him with a dark red light and shadow. Katherine's ankle was searing. A moist dew began to form between her breasts and slowly slid down between them. She was suddenly aware of the dampness which might begin to show on her thin blouse. All conversation stopped. There was a tremendous pressure building up around her in the cabin. She wanted to speak but it was as though the ship wouldn't let her.

Borland inhaled on his cigar again and, staring at the girl's breasts, gently blew the smoke toward her. Every muscle recoiled as she felt the smoke slowly lick at and trace the delicate curve of her neck. Blue bilious smoke and sweat painted her face. Gently she tried to hold back a grimace as her ankle continued to burn.

She looked down to the meal in front of her and then back up again to the old man. Trying not to register any alarm she finally spoke but it was somebody else's voice that she heard, far, far away. "I'm sorry... perhaps it's time for me to let you to your work." She patted her lips with her linen napkin, doing as she had seen so many ladies do while dining at the great table at Elmwood. She deliberately folded her napkin and placed it next to her china plate, each movement precise, not to alarm, nothing out of the ordinary. Inwardly she fought the power that was intent on making itself manifest, if not seizing the entire evening. She looked up at Borland again, her eyes asking if she should stay or leave. He continued to inhale on his cigar, staring at her. Where his gray blue eyes once pierced with curiosity and concern, they now bore and intruded into Kathrine's shyness. Why hadn't she seen this before? This was not her captain of moments ago. He exhaled again, and the smoke found a direct path to Katherine. Her stomach tightened threatening to violently contract and expel what was in it. Seemingly directed by the old man's thoughts, the smoke swirled around her sides and slowly drifted down to her ankle, slowly licking at her skin as it felt its way around her burns, tightening ever so slightly as it rose, past her ankle, inside of her knee. She could feel the warmth of it flow as it worked its way further up the inside of her leg. Instinctively she quickly clasped her legs together.

"Are you all right?" Borland said as he slowly drew in on his cigar and exhaled again.

Katherine's head jerked toward the sudden knocking at the captain's door.

"Enter," he bellowed without taking his eyes off the girl.

A great blast of cold and damp air preceded Amberson as he ducked through the doorway. Sweeping the small cabin free of the cigar smoke, the fresh air broke Katherine's thoughts. As though someone was bathing her neck with a cool cloth, she straightened to let the air slip down the back of her dress. The new breeze scattered the encroaching blue smoke, allowing her to breath again. She looked up to the captain, who by this time had his back to her while in muted conversation with the mate. Katherine fidgeted with her hands nervously while the two large men traded point and counterpoint. Borland issued forth a good-natured laugh, his hand on the mate's shoulder, turned and faced Katherine. The familiar and gentle eyes once again held their concern for his dinner companion.

"I'll be out shortly." He patted the blue-coated hulk of a man on the back as he shut the door after him.

"Seems that the fresh air did you wonders. I'd thought we lost you for a moment. Are you sure you're all right?"

Katherine wasn't sure exactly how she felt. What had just gone on, if anything? she thought.

"I'm fine. I guess."

Borland smiled at the girl. "Miss Worthington, I, more than most, appreciate the fact that life at sea is not for everyone, and while I am perfectly content upon my little island here, I know that there are those who..." He paused to run his hand across the pointed shape of his beard. He leaned back, causing his intricately carved teak chair to squeak its usual complaint. "How shall I say this? There are those whose reach has perhaps exceeded their own grasp a wee bit and find that fantasies of an ocean crossing and seeing new lands -- in this case old familiar lands -- are not all that they had hoped for and perhaps they have exercised the wrong decision in undertaking such an adventure." He smiled as he took a slow sip of wine from his dull pewter cup.

Here was the same gentle captain Katherine met at the landing several days ago, here was the same old man trying to find a delicate answer for her. Whatever had gone before most certainly was not of his doing, she assured herself. She had a quick flash of some of the chamber pot duties she had had to perform after one of her ladies parties at which some of the guests had to be seen to their rooms. The wine and cigar smoke, she thought, learn your lesson, girl.

"It's not that I don't appreciate the efforts you've made seeing to my comfort," Katherine said, "I guess that sometimes I am blinded by the impossible. I want to correct wrongs that I see. Occasionally I get a little overwhelmed." How could she possible explain to the gentle man at the other end of the table what had just happened, what words could she pick that wouldn't have him justly find her deluded. Her dreams were simply that, dreams and nothing more. But if she wasn't able to confide her fears in someone soon she knew that the horrors and images of the ongoing night terrors would take more and more of her conscious moments and do with her as they liked, bodily do her more harm, play with her thoughts and fill her waking hours with visions and sounds from some lowly evil place. But then again how could they? They were only dreams.

She sat looking down at her crippled left hand, again trying to find an answer to the shocking occurrence from last week. The bruises and burns on her ankle had gotten no better, in fact they were beginning to keep the girl awake at night. The pain never bothered her when she was reading, and certainly not when she was trying to envision the happiness that was waiting for her at the other end of her trip, but when she lay perfectly still and hear the song of the ocean all around her bunk, when she would feel the great power and energy of the ocean, the ankle began to throb and burn.

Since the morning she awoke with the marks on her leg, she had suffered several more nights fraught with the usual nightmare. Upon waking a wave of nausea would sweep over her as she found fresh and deeper marks on her ankle. She tried to ignore that the marks were from her useless left hand and one night resorted to going to bed wearing her gloves with hopes that she could keep from harming herself further. Upon waking she burst into tears of fright as she saw her gloves folded neatly back upon her small dresser, as though she had never taken them down.

"Do you ever fear?" she said to the captain.

"Fear what? The weather? Another man?"

"No, simply fear? Have no point of reference apart from the knowledge of dread, the knowledge that in this world of ours there exists evil and evil people?"

"The Bible teaches us that no man has room for both fear and love in one heart," Borland said cautiously.

"The Bible teaches us what we should try to obtain," she replied quietly. "In the meantime..."

"Miss Worthington, has anything I've said offended you?" the captain asked with new concern.

Were it that simple, she thought to herself . "No, Captain, just the opposite. I have a great deal to learn from you." How do you tell someone that you are beginning to fear nights because of a horrifying dream which now seems to be getting closer with every shudder of the great ship. How do you tell him what you have been doing to yourself while you sleep. You do and that's that, she said to herself. You screw up all your courage, trust that he will cast no aspersions, but listen with an open heart and advise. You simply tell.

"No, nothing you've said has offended me. There is no cause for concern." She laughed slightly to herself. None whatsoever, she thought.

Captain Borland reached for the bottle of wine and gestured slightly with it, asking if Katherine would care for a small bit more.

"Thank you, no," she said laughing as she put her hand across the top of her small cup. "I've had my share. It's just that when I was back at Elmwood, the powers that seemed to pull me to the water's edge also pulled me into making the decision about trying to gain passage back to England. And now that I'm on my way..." She took a deep breath. "And now that I'm on my way, these powers seem to be trying to pull me in a different direction." Wiping a tear with the back of her right index finger she looked straight at the captain. "I fear that I won't make it to England." The weight off of her shoulders made her more giddy than relieved. "I fear that I -- we -- will never make it across the ocean. Why?" She laughed.

Borland joined in her laughter. "Because, Miss Worthington, the Atlantic is a vast intimidating body of water than can crush us as easily as she can give us fair passage. I dare say that you are feeling a bit nervous? Ours is a very small world which makes its way slowly east, hour after hour, day after day. I think that you're spending far too much time worrying about the journey and not the destination." Borland well remembered trying to assuage his wife of these very same fears. "I see you at your port, watching the men at their work, trying to piece together the workings of *Galatea...*"

The girl blushed.

"You will them on as they scamper aloft, you put your energies into trying to keep them safe once they are working out on the yardarms. For this I am sure that they are eternally grateful, but perhaps while you are leaning at your port, you could direct some of that wonderful energy of yours and search for answers to your fears out across these great waters. If you're still enough and patient enough you will hear her speak Miss Worthington and I can assure you that you will like what she has to say."

The great ship lurched and slammed onto her beam ends again. She shuddered, rose and slammed once more. Borland looked up at the deck over his head and cocked an ear, trying to listen for an indication from the rising wind. The shouts of men's voices were heard from above.

"Lewis!" he shouted.

Galatea shuddered yet again as the young steward half fell through the captain's door.

"Get the mate!" he barked at the young boy. Standing he wiped his mouth with his napkin. "If you'll excuse me, Miss Worthington."

Katherine began to rise.

"Please, stay here. Just a quick formality."

As Katherine sat alone, she could feel a different energy, a different lunging about the ship. *Galatea* sailed to a different slant than she had moments ago, witness the new life in the sliding plates on the table in front of her. The young steward quickly began to collect the china and silver and scurry it off to wash.

"Is everything all right?" Katherine asked as she tried to keep out of his way.

"Right as rain," the young boy said and with arms loaded down disappeared out through the door and down the passageway.

As Katherine sat alone she found that for the first time she had to brace herself slightly with her foot against the solid leg of the table. It felt as though the ship were being slowly but steadily pushed over on to her side. *Galatea* would only get so far before, mustering her own strength, she would match the strength of the wind's hand and slowly right herself. Katherine's brain told her that her world was slowly beginning to revolve around her, yet her eyes told her that nothing was out of the ordinary. Unable to see *Galatea's* movement she could only sense what the ship was doing by her quickly vanishing lack of balance. A slight pressure was building around her eyes, a strange taste in her mouth. Having been this route once before knew that perhaps she best retreat to the relative safety of her own bunk and try to beat the rising nausea to sleep.

A wet and wind-blown captain came through the doorway.

"Miss Worthington, it's probably best you return to your cabin, we'll be coming into some weather soon and we might be in for a night of it."

Having no objections to the captain's suggestion, Katherine bid him good evening and all but flew past him down the small passageway, up the companionway and out on to deck, where she froze at the sight in front of her. The usual long, secure and level expanse of decking which Katherine had become accustomed to was now severely slanted down to the right, occasionally dipping her sides into the invisible roar of the ocean. The great powerful bow of *Galatea* was rising above and digging through solid black walls of water which tried to impede the ship's progress as cascades of dark green and frothy seas rolled down the deck toward her bucking stern.

Captain Borland had ridden the powerful east-flowing Gulf Stream as long as she gave him a boost in speed. Decided on a more northerly course, he sailed his ship out of the warm waters and into the colder waters of the North Atlantic, but it seemed that the meandering current had one more of its characteristic squalls to throw his way and a solid one at that.

"Helmsman! Let her run off!" he shouted above the growing tempest. As the great ship limbered down to starboard a heavy parcel of water was lifted up and over her midships and thrown at the cook's house.

"Watch for your fire!" the captain warned the cook, who was busily trying to secure the remains of what dinner had been prepared. It was not unheard of for a wave to find its way into the galley and douse the stove's fires, guaranteeing the watches, but more importantly the captain nothing but lukewarm coffee through the night. The crew scampered up the ratlines to alleviate their ship of too much canvas.

He's right, Katherine thought, just look at them, they're a whole different group now. The men took to their jobs with the pride of knowing that they were protecting their ship from getting caught with too much sail up for the strength of the building squall. None of them found any joy as the ship lurched and fell off the sharp seas, but were any harm to come to the vessel, they would know sadness and shame for letting her founder. Where Katherine would watch them ascend to heights of soaring shearwaters, now they were simply swallowed into the growing blackness of the storm. Those few whom she could see were leaning far over the yards, balancing more by their wits than anything else, clawing in the yards of canvas, hand over hand. Against the shrieking of the wind they secured the wildly flailing sail with great gaskets of ropes, rolling it into a tamed and tight cylinder of white canvas. They seemed to be coaxing, aiding *Galatea* as the ship roared into the black void. The small packet responded like the living thing she was. From what Katherine felt and now saw around her in the wild of the night squall, her ship was indeed more alive than ever before. A strong willed horse which had been spooked at the wind rustling through branches, *Galatea* now charged blindly into the night.

"Mate!" Borland bellowed. "Ease your weather sheet!"

Amberson repeated the wind-swept command toward the galley. Dropping all thoughts of creating a semblance of order for his own workspace, the cook responded with as much urgency as possible and quickly joined a small group of men working at the weather rail of *Galatea*, where he was met with a strong North Atlantic dousing.

"Don't be looking for your coffee in any of my pots," he shouted, more to himself than to the mate.

Why these men above weren't being flung off their perches and out into the dark void was more than Katherine could fathom. *Galatea* took a great lumbering roll again to starboard. Fearing more her safe deliverance to her cabin than her sea sickness of moments ago, she timed the rising of the powerful bow and dashed for her deck house and the safety of her own bunk. Slamming the door behind her and leaning against the pressure of the wind, Katherine found that, despite the weather and the strange episode she felt earlier in the evening, for the first time in many days she could once again taste the joy and energy of reaching her destination. The captain was right – she should pay attention to the destination, not the bumps in the journey. What the captain had to say had put her back on the right track. Perhaps she had been brooding about what were nothing more than scary dreams and not thinking enough about what and who was awaiting her delivery.

The burn in her ankle couldn't be explained. Some things couldn't. Perhaps she had more strength in her left hand than she knew, perhaps she was continuously scraping the bruised ankle on her bed frame as she struggled time and again with her the dream, perhaps she bruised it simply trying to get about a constantly moving deck. Perhaps it simply would never be explained. Despite the gale brewing not an inch away from her, she felt assured. She had shared her fear with a person she trusted and found an answer already. She slept.

"Captain, sir, the mate, he needs you on deck, sir."

The alarm in the young steward's voice clearly indicated that he was not accustomed to rousing his captain in the middle of the night. No sooner had the boy finished knocking on the cabin door then the captain was opening it in an acceptable state of dress, a speed trait he had learned from a lifetime of unexpected weather.

In the few seconds he had been awake, the captain's senses had surmised all that they could about the boy's panic and the state of *Galatea.* Still well pressed down to starboard, *Galatea* seemed to be riding out the remains of the earlier gale. She sailed to a steady rhythmic charge, above deck he heard no loud reports from a flogging sail, no smell of fire, and curiously enough, the usual sound of the men's voices and shouts were absent about the ship. Apart from the hissing of the Atlantic as it slid past the ship's hull and the slight groans from the working of her timbers, all was curiously silent.

"What is it, boy?" the old man asked as they both hurried up the companionway ladder.

"Hard to explain, sir. Just please, hurry."

As he ran out onto deck, the cold wet night air slapped across Borland's face, knocking away what small vestiges of sleep he might have brought with him. As his eyes adjusted to the gloom of the cold damp night around him, he found that he was faced with a strange sight. The men about him seemed frozen in place. Those who had been forward remained stationary, staring aft. The sailors who had been up the rig now held tightly as their attention was focused far below on deck. Those who remained amidships simply stood, hands in pockets, staring at the ship's starboard rail which, with every blast of air on the sails above, dipped ever closer to the black ocean. Arriving in the ship's waist, Borland looked at the small press of men, then aloft into the void of night. He turned quickly to look behind him at the stern. The helmsman working the ship's great wheel seemed to be the only movement to be found on aboard the packet. A small group of men formed a crude semi-circle around the dirty yellow glow from a ship's lantern.

In the center of the gathering was First Mate Amberson who was situated at the low starboard rail, all but hovering above it. Whatever the problem, the silent man seemed to be the center of attention. As the captain approached the gathering of men, they seemed to sense his arrival and, reluctantly parted, making a small aisle for him to walk through. Casting his shadow from the lantern across the deck, Borland arrived in the center and faced the great solid mass of the mate's back.

"Mr. Amberson, what's going on here?"

"Hard to say, sir," the mate answered as he slowly turned to meet his captain. The sight before Borland was almost as frightening as it was transfixing. He had seen the look before, but only once. When he was a boy of twelve and living before the mast of the *James Monroe*, he had watched as they pulled one of his mates from the ocean. A sudden squall and an inattentive helmsman had shaken the ships rig so violently that the old Swede, Gufstason, was thrown from his perch on the upper top gallant. A ship's boat was lowered immediately and only after a two hour search did they find their man, miraculously still alive, if just. When the Swede was hauled back aboard and laid out on deck for the ship's doctor to tend to, Borland's youthful curiosity drove him through the gathering crowd of men and right next to Gufstason's body as it lay limp on the wet deck. Vomiting out a bilious froth of seawater and phlegm, the old Swede slowly rolled his head in the young

Borland's direction and went eye to eye with the youth. Young Phineas Borland was frozen in his tracks by the haunted, raging terror in Gufstason's eyes. Judging by the reaction of the older men in back of him as they took an unconscious step away, no man aboard the *James Monroe* that night had ever witnessed the likes of what lay at their feet. He had heard about how, if a man went over and was left to float alone in the ocean for too long, he could easily lose his mind. The superstitions of the older sailors called it "possession of the deep." The more knowledgeable of the afterguard referred to it simply as the sheer terror of being left to drown while watching your ship sail over the horizon, not knowing if anybody knew you were gone.

Whatever the reasoning, Captain Borland now saw the same haunted, hunted look in the eyes of Katherine Worthington.

"As I was making my way aft to attend to the helmsman, I noticed the men all standing, staring down at her," Amberson said of the pale young girl tucked under his arm. "She was just standing here, shivering and shaking as she stared out to leeward. I called to her but she didn't budge." He lowered his voice. "Captain, she was in her night clothing, the men were all staring. Well, thinking she was near freezing to death I put my coat around her." Searching for the words, Amberson took a few seconds to try and gather his thoughts. "Captain, she wasn't shaking from the cold. She had a sweat about her."

Katherine's eyes gazed from Amberson to Borland, back to the horizon. She was speaking, but no intelligible words came forth as her thin young lips trembled. Despite the weight and warmth of the mate's heavy denim coat, Katherine started to fall into a convulsive shake. Trying to find an answer to this macabre scene before them, the two men looked at one another as the young girl's body spasmodically snapped back and forth.

"Get McCaffery," Borland demanded of his young steward, "and blankets!" Not knowing what sight he had just seen before him and at a loss for just what he was going to tell the doctor, the young boy half ran, half stumbled to the aft companionway.

Wrapping the mate's coat tightly around the girl, Borland picked Katherine up and started to carry her toward her open cabin, but as he did she cried out in pain. Her cry tore her away from wherever it was her terrified eyes had taken her. As Borland held her more tightly, Katherine screamed again, this time more a scream of terror than pain.

"Steady, girl," he whispered to her. "Steady on."

"Sir," Amberson said with alarm. "Your coat. The side of your coat, sir."

Borland looked down the length of his weathered wool coat. In the muted yellow glow of the lantern he saw that the hem of it was dark with dampness which glistened in the light.

"What in God's name..."

Dripping from the fold of the hem to the deck where his unlaced boots were firmly planted ran a series of wet dark drops, the trail leading back to the feet of the first mate.

Amberson stooped, and with his thick callused index finger swiped at one of the small dark pools by his feet.

"Blood," he said to the captain as he rubbed his thumb in circles across the top of his finger. He looked back at the girl as she pressed herself tightly against the captain's chest. Amberson could clearly see the source of the girl's pain. He gingerly approached his captain and the girl and, with some modesty, raised the blood dampened coat a few inches past her feet, exposing her right foot. Both men stared in dumbfounded curiosity as they looked upon the swollen pale blue ankle before them.

"Your knife," Borland said.

In a flash Amberson had withdrawn the large blade from its sheath and with the delicacy of a surgeon's hand started to dig at the small, choking strands of sea kelp which gripped and dug their way into the girl's ankle. Two small brown leafy strings had a tight grip, checking all blood flow. Drops of the deep red liquid were rhythmically dripping from one torn and ragged end of the weed which appeared to have been suddenly cut.

Trying to find the source of the blood, Amberson tore at the kelp. What he found just inches above again stopped both seasoned men cold; hidden under the clinging leaves of the brown membrane ran four long grooved indentations,

indentations such as fingers would make, indentations from which small rivulets of blood ran freely.

CHAPTER 14

"Hello, all stations. Hello, all stations. Hello, all stations. This is the United States Coast Guard Group North Com., United States Coast Guard Group North Com. Break."

The scratch of the computerized voice from the SSB broke the morning silence that I was thoroughly enjoying aboard *Curlew.* The weather had been behaving itself for the past twenty-four hours and the only noise to be heard was that of our good boat as she twisted and surged her way east. The hissing of Gulf Stream waters passing by *Curlew's* hull were occasionally met by the somewhat digestive sounds which gurgled from our cockpit drains as she would occasionally seat her stern fully into the warm current. We wanted to ride this extra one or two knot mid-ocean river as far as we could and in doing so would gain an extra twelve to twenty-four miles per day and stay a bit warmer due to its tropical origin and influence. There was a downside to it, though. We had spent the past few days sailing through pea soup fog. Where the warm Gulf Stream from the south meets the frigid Labrador current coming down from the north, one always find a stretch of water that has even the best of navigators chewing their pencils thinking that they had just heard a ship's engine muffled by the thick moist blanket, a large ship's engine at that.

Paul was asleep in his bunk and I had been trying to catch up on the small nagging jobs which sooner or later demand my attention. In its bag, I had dragged the storm trysail to the base of the mast and lashed it there securely. No storms had been predicted for our area of the Atlantic, but found that it was always comforting to have it right at hand if and when Mother Nature decided to sling some of her better stuff at the proverbial fan. If one of her an autumn gales did track us down, digging through an overstuffed sail locker in a wildly pitching boat was one job I wanted to avoid. The canned goods which we carried in the bilges had to have their paper labels removed, and we had to write new labels directly on the tins with a waterproof marker. Here again, if we were to be taking a sloshing of sea water down through our bilges all those paper labels would wash off and promptly clog our bilge pumps, something else I had no interest in wanting to fix while trying to ride out a force nine gale. This last job reminded me of the many accounts of circumnavigators from the 1950s, who in order to keep their eggs fresher longer would varnish or grease the shells... some things are just not that important to me.

The high seas forecast to which I had just tuned happily reported no gales for our area and none for the foreseeable future, which gave us fifty-fifty odds at best, and it was anybody's guess how far away the 'foreseeable future' was. Our weather fax recognized the chirping squeaks from the receiver earlier in the morning's broadcast and printed out a crudely drawn chart showing what pressure systems were currently doing what and to whom between the New England coast and the Irish Sea. Here again, I was happy to see that as there were no major depressions lurking about the corners. Everybody who was off-soundings was enjoying relatively fair breezes.

During the night we had passed out from under the great overhang of Nova Scotia and, judging by the change in the wave patterns, were clearly off the continental shelf. The small two-foot chop that *Curlew* had been plowing through for the last five days had been replaced by a solid foundation of a long-rolling, gray swell from the east. So wide and evenly spaced were they that *Curlew* rose to them effortlessly and slid down their gently sloping backs with even less fuss. We most certainly had been experiencing days of grace and fair breezes and were counting our every blessing.

Via the help of the High Seas Operator and AT&T, we managed to place a long distance call on our the SSB -- at five dollars a minute, thank you very much -- to Fee's yard back in Chester. Once she decided that accepting the calling charges was all in the name of safety at sea, global communications and a budding romantic interest, it did my spirits no end of good to hear Madeline's voice on the other end. To help pass cold midnight watches, Paul and I had poured over *Curlew's* incomplete yard bills time and again and failed to come up with anything remotely fitting the description of an answer as to why a page had been torn from each accounting. In the sheaves of paperwork on *Curlew*, we had also come across a Xeroxed copy of a vessel survey which had been done two years prior. We were comforted to find that even then, all of her systems were found to be in fine working order, but here too we hit a snag. Up in the right hand corner of the last page was clearly written "page 4 of 5". This last finding prompted an immediate decision to try to reach Fee to see if he could place some calls to get some answers. If something was inherently wrong with our only link between being warm and dry and freezing cold in a life raft, I wanted to know about it. Mind you, I didn't object to spending a few minutes touching base with Madeline.

"Well, it could mean something or maybe its just weird circumstances" Madeline said. "I vote for the later. Over."

"Why's that? Over"

Having to say "Over" to let the person on the other end of the speaker know that your part of the converstaion was through certainly took any of the hoped for hints at intimacy out of the radio call. The fact that all of the North Atlantic fishing fleet could also hear our call was also a bit stifling, if not totally inhibiting.

"Because sleazy is as sleazy does. Over."

Madeline was right. In any other situation we most probably would have let the whole business slide, but given the caliber of the man with whom we were dealing, the trouble we had nailing him down, Paul's coming across the two snooping lackeys from Maine and the fact that nothing else added up to what it should have, we figured that the missing pages of *Curlew's* past deserved what attention we could throw their way.

With a promise that she'd have an answer for us by week's end, I reluctantly signed off, but not before Madeline could assure me that my pile jacket was being well taken care of; she said she wore it around her house every night after she showered. Feast on that, fishermen of the North Atlantic.

Trying to find where I stowed my Walkman, I was rooting around through one of the port lockers when Paul stuck his head out through the opening to the aft cabin.

"Anything going on I should know about?" he asked, purely out of formality.

"Not much. The wind's come ahead a tad so I tightened up some." The one downside to our journey so far was the direction of the wind. Although it had been behaving itself and staying below twenty-five knots, it was slowly coming around and filling in from the east. According to the pilot charts and rule of thumb, we were supposed to carry westerlies all the way across and have a nice smooth go of it. The fact that the breeze now started to move ahead to the east meant that we had to tighten up the sails some and that *Curlew* heeled a bit and took on more of a slant. I checked the starboard lockers for the Walkman.

"Weather?" he asked, rubbing his eyes with the heels of his hands.

"Got a fax from Portsmouth earlier and the audio broadcast supports it. More of the same, a few low pressure systems up north which will hopefully stay up there, nothing behind them pushing them our way. Seen my Walkman?"

To try to make our best time, Paul and I opted to take the Great Circle route, the straightest shot across to England. We decided not to go south to avoid the gales of the farther northern reaches of the Atlantic. Although this was the season that storms were born ad infinitum north of us and common sense said to head further south, we didn't want to be too far south in case a straggler of a hurricane decided it didn't want to miss out on the end of the fleeting season.

"Seems to be a weak high just above us that's kicking them further north," I said. "Maybe that's the reason for the wind coming ahead. Maybe I didn't pack it."

"Any news from the yard?" he asked dropping down onto the port settee.

"Not really," I said as nonchalantly as I could. "We've got an hour on them now. I was going to try later. Unless you wanted to."

"Nope, that's your department." Paul tried to adjust his eyes to the brightness of the morning. We had been riding the elusive wave of an Indian summer ever since we poked our way into the east-flowing Gulf Stream, and for the most part had been treated to our share of wonderful autumn sun.

As we had about 2,200 more miles to go, I thought it best not to inquire as to what he meant by "your department", but continued rooting for something I think that I remembered seeing on my kitchen sink about 800 miles ago. I smiled back at him. "I brought the heavy weather main up on to deck. Just a precaution, and I stored the last of the canned food in the bilges, might have mixed up a label or two, but then that's all the fun of it, isn't it?"

Paul sat staring at his feet for a while as I gave up my search, sat at the nav table and pored over one of *Curlew*'s many books on navigation. The first one that I grabbed was on celestial navigation, an art form that I had at one point almost mastered but then very quickly forgot. I felt a bit sheepish sitting there reading about Greenwich hour angles and local hour angles when right in front of me was a small box with an LCD readout that gave me instantaneous updates as to exactly where I was in the world. Even in my best days, reducing a sun sight took about half an hour, then I had to wait another four or five hours to do it again and hope that the two lines of position would cross and show me where I was. Now all one had to do was push the button and read out the latitude and longitude that the small computer spilled forth. There is a downside to all this wonderful technology, though. I had been told that this GPS's computer was only accurate to 100 yards. As long as there's a hair to split...

"Weird, weird dreams," Paul said as he continued to stare at his feet.

"That's what you said the other day," I said as I continued to read and absorb more guilt.

"Every one of them. "

"You wearing a patch?" I asked, knowing that the anti seasickness patches which you put behind your ear could make for some pretty wild sleeps.

"No, this is the real thing."

Paul had never been a man of many words, but what he started to tell me about, the images and feelings which he struggled and tossed with as he slept in his bunk, was nothing short of remarkable. Given the circumstances, the fact that all of his dreams dealt with the ocean was not so surprising. What was surprising, if not very concerning was the fact that they all dealt with the bottom of the ocean and what was to be found down there. No pirate's chest overflowing with jewels here, no dancing crab or singing mermaid either. What Paul started to describe to me was a close second to Heironymus Bosch's Vision of Hell. He described a horrific and vivid picture of the horrors which have kept men whistling in the dark as they walked past graveyards for years. Bodies which had been brutally swept from decks, walking and wailing among the rot and decay of ages past. Phantasmal ghouls lying in wait, aching to tear into the of warm and fresh flesh of men gone overboard. Drowning victims who, since the moment their lungs choked full with water, had been held in the icy cold death grip of all the evils that exist just inches under the water, unseen by the casual passerby.

"Wild, huh?" Paul said with a look in his eye which I hadn't seen since our days of shenanigans and punishments.

"To say the least," I said as I looked back to the aft cabin, knowing that I was shortly to go off watch. I wasn't so sure if I wanted to try to sleep back there. Couldn't exactly look under these beds. "Unless you need me for anything I'm going to call it quits for a bit."

"Nope. Sleep well."

We both laughed at this one.

Happily, my dreams were more of the usual type: driving a shoe through downtown Chester and cooking at a church picnic in the nude with nobody noticing.

The sound of Madeline's voice squawking its way from the speaker of the SSB awoke me with confusion, joy and curiosity. Dream or reality? Paul was at the navigation station listening intently to the SSB's speaker, writing and taking notes with his right hand. He stuck his left back into our small cabin, snapped his fingers several times with great force and hastily waved me out of my bunk.

Clad in my boxers and socks, I swung out of my bunk, ducked my head, lurched through the small aft doorway and dropped myself onto the port settee, assuming the exact posture that Paul had not two minutes ago. Judging by how many times the ship's clock rang, I was three hours and fifty eight minutes off. Couldn't be, I thought to myself. My watch agreed.

"All the same thing, all the same job," Madeline said.

"You're sure?" Paul asked as he looked at me.

"To the letter. What're your thoughts?"

"Don't know. Have to talk it over with Chris, I guess. Take a look for ourselves." Paul grinned at me. "Thanks for the help, Madeline. Got someone here who wants to say hi." Paul handed me the mike and decided now was a good time to check things out on deck.

Madeline and I talked, mostly about the weather. She said that Paul would fill me in and that everyone was asking after *Curlew's* progress and that she was thinking about me and was greatly looking forward to my coming to retrieve my fleece jacket, although she had grown quite accustomed to it. At five dollars a minute and a three minute minimum, small talk was not cheap talk and we left it that we'd be in touch when we made a decision -- about what I didn't know, but I was keen on finding out.

I threw on some pants and a jacket and went out on deck to find Paul out on the bow checking the tension of the headstay.

"Safety harness," I shouted. Paul and I had made a pact that when one of us was out on deck alone he would always wear his harness regardless the weather, especially if the other was off watch asleep. If one of us was to go over while the other slept the likelihood of the boat turning around to come back and get him was fairly slim.

Since coming on deck I noticed that the wind had picked up noticeably and we were taking the occasional lump of spray over the starboard bow. The sails were full and pulling well, perhaps just on the edge of too much up. With this new increase we found that unless we raised our voices, our words were falling a bit short of the mark. Paul worked his way back to the cockpit where I was eyeing the sail combination.

"Has the breeze filled in or is this temporary?"

"Don't know. Give it five." Five minutes to see if the rise in velocity was here to stay or simply an isolated increase trying to work its way west.

"So what did I miss?" I asked, leaning back under the canvas dodger to stay dry. Technically it was still Paul's watch and if anyone was to get wet it stood to reason it should have been him.

He began to spell it all out. He heard our name on a ship's traffic list out of Portsmouth and checking in he found that we were to call Fee's. What he learned from Madeline was not good news; we were sailing damaged goods. Seemed that sometime back, *Curlew* must have suffered a good solid contact with the bottom for she suffered damage to her stern tube, the area where the driveshaft from the engine passes through the hull of the boat. Nothing remarkable in itself, except for the fact that she had been in and out of eight yards up and down the eastern seaboard trying to get the situation fixed. In what we were learning was typical fashion, Jasperson had floated bad checks at six of the eight yards. The original damage had been patched up with no great fuss, but shortly after that the damaged area started to weep an excess of water. Jasperson then went to another yard, because the original yard was obviously not going to start any new work until they were paid for the original job. The second yard tried to do what the first couldn't and so on and so forth down the line until the eighth. Each yard manager or foreman had told Madeline that the man was too cheap to have the boat hauled and properly fixed, but instead opted for a quick fiberglass wrap, a sort of band- aid against the Atlantic. To date we had experienced relatively benign weather, at least for the North Atlantic. What concerned us was the fact that were we to meet up with a good blow, the size and spacing of the waves generated by a storm could possibly make *Curlew* "hobby horse", twist and torque, which would put undue pressure on the fiberglass which held the tube in place. Part of our watch schedule was to check the bilges every few hours and for the most part they had been found dry. The small amounts of seawater which had accumulated there was normal for to the slight drip one expected at the stuffing box, the actual collar through which the driveshaft runs.

"I guess we should take a look," I said. This was a job which was best done by the both of us and didn't necessarily fall to one person's watch or the other.

Directly under our feet in the cockpit was an aluminum hatch which gave immediate access to the engine room, an area on a sailboat not know for its surplus working space. One didn't necessarily climb down into this room but more hung upside down as one did from monkey bars.

With the blood rushing to my head and my head banging on the block of the engine with every new wave, I twisted my body around a thankfully cold diesel and shone the flashlight back into the recess of the area. I could see that indeed several wraps of fresh fiberglass had been added to the stern tube, but no more. This was something which neither Paul nor I had thought to look at when we originally checked over the boat but perhaps should have. But we weren't buying the thing, only trying to deliver it. I tried to see if there was any working, any movement as *Curlew* rose and fell with each new swell. Everything except my body from the waist up stayed exactly where it was supposed to.

"Clean," I said as my eyes bulged from the added blood pressure, "and dry."

It took a minute to wrench myself up from out of the pit and as I sat in the cockpit catching my breath I tried to figure out just what becomes of one's agility and stamina when it deserts you overnight.

"Jesus," I panted. "Here, take a look." I handed Paul the flashlight.

"Nah, it's okay. Your word's good enough for me."

Suitable revenge for not being able to stay dry under the dodger, I guess. We adjusted the autopilot to take the new seas in a more comfortable direction and went below to regroup and start an early dinner.

"You know," I said while heating up some stew at the stove, "there's some sort of perverse theory at work here. The more we try to help *Curlew*, the more this job dumps on us." I stirred the stew over the flame. "Christ, getting across is going to be the easy part."

"Well," Paul said, "she was dry when we got her and she's dry now. You know yards, each one says that the previous one did a lousy job and then tries to sell you a bill of goods."

"But why try to hide it from us?"

"Maybe he was trying to hide it from a prospective buyer."

"Why the goons from Maine going through the files?"

"Maybe the buyer's in England?"

"Maybe," I said.

We ate our meal and discussed every possible scenario. We both agreed that it was something which we should monitor. Seeing as *Curlew* came from the design board of a naval architect commissioned to deliver speed, her bilges were inadequately deep. She was capable of holding perhaps ten gallons of errant seawater and not the forty of fifty one should expect. We had both raced boats of similar configuration and felt confident that, worse coming to worse, this too was nothing we couldn't handle. At least that was the position we took with each other.

Separately and quietly we both fully understood the dire implications on which our mutual decision rested; if we were to fall from the Atlantic's good graces and suffer a full gale, it would be doubtful that *Curlew's* stern tube could take the torturous pounding.

CHAPTER 15

For several days eight-year-old Roland LaChristien had been watching with curiosity and concern as the tropic birds around his stone feeder became fewer and fewer. Each morning the bright eyed boy would gather up Ke-bok, the small well loved toy donkey his father had fashioned for him out of palm leaves, and put him in his canvas bag and head down toward the docks.

Roland was only four years old when his father brought the small toy animal home. "I think that the little donkey's lonely and needs a friend," he said as he presented his son with what was to turn out to be the boy's companion, confidant and, at times, comrade in arms.

Roland would scamper barefoot from his family's small hut, down the rugged hill and rummage through the pickings he found around the docks of English Harbor, looking for what small scraps of bread he could find for the birds hovering around the feeder back on the hill. Those sailors and merchants who did take notice of the small brown skinned boy never gave him a second thought. It was 1866, not a year of vast wealth on the small tropical island of Antigua. There was a change of fortune in the air of the Caribbean for blacks, but these things took time. If out of nothing but pure habit, the various native children were still wont to grab at the odd crust here and there. Roland LaChristien's mission was not as these Englishmen thought, though, for if the resourcefulness of his mother's love provided the boy with anything, it was most certainly a full stomach and lack of want.

Making his daily rounds through and behind the inns, pubs, sail lofts and shipwright's buildings, the small toy donkey Ke-bok and the only child of the LaChristien family would gather what crumbs they could and tuck them away into his canvas pouch tied around his small brown waist. After saying hello to Miss Epivey, who was on her way to the laundry, and his Uncle

Carsan who helped the sailors seize and parcel the running rigging which had been brought in from the English fleet at anchor in the harbor, he and his small toy beast of burden would defy the blast of the morning's heat and take what scraps they found back up the hill to his birds. With feet toughened and callused beyond those of a normal eight-year-old boy, Roland scrambled back up the circuitous dirt road, back to the small stone feeding platform which he and his father had built on the boy's fifth birthday. Cut into the side of the green volcanic hill behind their shack, Roland had made a small effort of a sanctuary for some of the more daring of the tropical birds of the island, a place where they could feed or find relief from the brutal Caribbean sun. Each morning scores of small colorful birds would dart around and through the rough undergrowth as they waited to see what Roland had found for them today. As the boy approached his feeder, the still and choked vegetation on the hill would slowly become alive with the flutter of birds hidden just inches from their rugged brush cover. Yet this morning the usual count of birds was down, as it had been the hot, bright morning before and the morning before that.

"Flying to the northeast side of the island, child," said his father, whose own father had been a slave purchased to work the sugar fields. It was thirty-one years earlier that the powerful and now "enlightened" empire of Great Britain gave to her slaves everywhere, freedom which ultimately allowed the likes of young Roland the freedom to wander the yards of English Harbor and watch as the great commanders of the Leeward Islands stood to their business. Although he and his family were no longer indentured to any man, Roland knew that the refinement and status which these captains and their magnificent ships displayed was never to be approached, only watched from a side quay. Roland sat by the deserted feeder, looking for answers in the green rugged hills around him.

"The cat, she's gone too," he said to his father. "Maybe she's getting to them and hiding from me."

Roland's fascination with the island's bird population had been a curiosity to both his parents. There were times when as an infant wrapped to his mother's back, his infant chirpings and coos seemed to keep a constant flurry of island color around both of them.

"Two birds today. Two birds." He scratched out a small corral for his donkey. "Why only two, Papa?"

"Why anything child?" His father laughed, for the disappearance of a handful of birds and a somewhat domesticated cat was not what was demanding Albert LaChristian's attention at the moment. He stepped a few paces away from his son and turned his black weathered face toward the east, where the bright tropical sun had already started to burn its path across the dusty sky. For several nights now he had watched as the moon had begun to exhibit the slow but steady formation of a corona, a halo of moisture, as it worked its way across the night sky far above the tiny lush island. Just a few days ago Albert saw that even the sun had begun to exhibit its own ethereal ring.

"Go down to the market, child, gather your mother," Albert said as the boy brushed at yesterday's crumbs on his small feeding platform.

Roland didn't do as his father asked but instead sat at his feeder and beamed as he watched a figure wrapped in an island print with a large straw basket of neatly wrapped parcels atop her head move up the path.

"No need to gather no one," Said the tall strong black woman as she came into the tidy back compound of her family's hut. "I can smell it from down there. I smell it in the wind."

In one swift movement, the young boy's mother shifted the heavy weight from her head down to the ground. The large sigh she let out as she straightened up and brushed at her faded pink and blue print dress was more for the benefit of her two men standing idly by than anything else. She wiped a small bead of sweat from her upper lip.

"You may smell it but I know this you've never seen," Albert said as he nodded at up the morning sun. "Look at the sun, woman. Never before have I seen two rings."

The burning white orb above them was now boasting two

brilliant white coronas. They had both heard the tales and been warned by the elders, who told of a year in which double angel's halos were seen for two days before the coming of great winds and rains, but such talk had only been the folly of old men. Tall tales from years gone by.

The woman looked up into the sky, shielding her eyes. She drew in air between her clenched teeth. "Two," she whispered.

The LaChristien family sat silently as they had so many times before, looking down onto English Harbor from their vantage on the side of their hill. From here they would watch the comings and goings of the English fleet below them, the ship's of war, the trading vessels.

Taking his wife by the hand, the two climbed the small rise behind their shack and watched as Roland, oblivious to his parent's concerns, scampered on ahead of them. From the small rill above them they could see past the sharp volcanic hills of their island, out toward the east. Many times when the sun was too hot to work under or the small family needed a simple distraction, they would come to this spot where they could watch and wonder from where their family was uprooted those few generations ago. But today there was no imagining as the three inconsequential figures stood in the middle of it all. What they saw before them was all too real and immediate.

"In the name of what's holy," she mumbled to herself.

The high wispy clouds overhead led in rapid succession to the far horizon, where an ink black wall of rolling weather stretched from horizon to horizon, brooding and stalking. Without taking her eyes off the scene and in a reflex made from both love and fear, Pontie LaChristien slowly reached out and took her husband's hand.

"Roland's birds have all left. Gone to the other side of the island," Albert said to confirm what lay before them.

"Cat's gone too," Roland said. Gently the young boy took Ke-bok out of his canvas pouch and placed him among some sun-burned sea grass at his feet. He studied the gathering of small stone chips around him, picked one that suited his purpose, showed it to his donkey companion for final approval before he threw the it aimlessly out toward the Caribbean.

Pontie watched as the small stone bounced down the sheer cliff and onto a rock strewn beach. "The sea's as flat as glass. No wind," she said in a hushed tone.

"All the airs been eaten by that," Albert said indicating the black mass. "We take what time we have to save what we can and tell the others."

Looking down below them into the harbor, it seemed as though bad news was indeed traveling fast, for those boats which weren't already underway were hastily preparing for immediate departure. Longboats were being frantically rowed out from the great stone quays to their awaiting ships, crews busily readied their vessels to sail out to the impending storm rather than suffer her fury in the congested harbor. Shopkeepers were busily fashioning protection across their windows. Knowing that very little else other than their stone buildings could survive the impending blow, families took to the shelter of the hills to wait it out.

The explosion hit Antigua as the new day was first casting its purple and green hue across the Caribbean sky. It was impersonal, it was sudden and it was total. The once lush green hills were denuded with as much power as indifference; where trees and one-room homes once stood now there was only wet brown mud. In the far end of the harbor two wooden masts stood askew marking where their 100-ton hull had been torn and crushed. Fifty feet inland, nestled up against the base of a palm, rested a child's straw donkey.

Like several other family names, LaChristien was stricken from the island's list of inhabitants. There was no malice in the devastation, there was no premeditation, Antigua simply stood in the way. Fueled by its own energies and determination, the hurricane brushed land with callous indifference and then swept back into the Gulf Stream, where it rode the northeast current. Flexing her great back with pride, the waters of the North Atlantic readied themselves as the storm tore at the ocean to the south.

Eight hundred nautical miles to the north east, the Dead

Ones intensified their nightly games of charade with a terrified young woman and drifted into a great gelatinous concentration which lay directly in the path of *Galatea* and her precious cargo. There they awaited their mother ocean's latest charge of wind, rain and wrath. Heeding the pleadings and cries of its insistent child, the great ocean would indulge her denizens. She heard the pleadings and conjured up a wet and screaming counterclockwise spiral of demonic proportions. Once the destruction began and her winds tore *Galatea*'s flesh from her wooden bones, the ocean would let the rotted and lost souls of her Dead Ones fight among themselves for the remains. Or she would simply take the vessel, lives and all, and command it to her dark and frozen hells. No decisions had to be made, no destructive plans, for the ship and its company had already been chosen. The storm was simply the executioner.

CHAPTER 16

"As long as I have a rag to show the wind, Mister, this packet will keep sailing east."

"Sir, it's only a precaution."

"Take nothing off her, mister, she can stand it. Now turn out your watch." Captain Borland dismissed his first mate back outside into the building winds.

Since dawn, First Mate Amberson had been watching the ragged southern sky as it seamlessly changed from dark purple to green, maroon to red, dirty yellow to pewter. The man who was born in the bowels of New York's Hell's Kitchen felt the hairs on the back of his neck thicken as the steady pressure of humid tropical wind started to build against *Galatea's* already drum tight canvas. Her timbers and spars creaked in loose unison as she heeled deeply onto her port side, slicing across the top of the perpetual dark and cold which stirred thousands of feet below her keel. Normally at this time of year one could expect to be pushed along by the dry and colder component of air which rolled in from the northwest. Now instead, warm and moist tropic pressure was being pumped out of the south, an unexpected and, for mid October, an untrustworthy point on the compass. There was a hidden edge to the thick and damp wind, a razor sharp edge which had the ability to cut with unchecked ferocity, separating man from his basic civility. With the uncommon sea sense which stood by and ultimately delivered him from the physical rigors of living before the mast to his present position of second in charge of *Galatea*, Amberson had felt the edge all day. He knew that as great as the potential was for a substantial blow out of the south, there was equally as much potential for trouble from those who worked on deck and in the rig of his ship. Funny, he thought, he and the second mate, Kemp, had been whistling for a change of breeze, but not necessarily a change of this nature.

The past few days *Galatea* had found herself fresh out of air. She all but wallowed in her own wake. At times she carved slow, fat, lazy circles in the very waters she should have been decisively plowing aside, a situation which the captain didn't need remind the first mate was far less than acceptable. At one point he noticed that the garbage which the cook had thrown over the day before was not five feet from where it sat in the water twenty-four hours later. Amusingly he thought that if he could at least sink some of it, the captain wouldn't be constantly reminded of their lack of progress. Trying to coax speed from their ship, the past forty eight hours saw the two men send their respective watches aloft with as much sail as their ship could fly, trying to make up for the absent prevailing winds. *Galatea* had all of her sail set to the top of her royal yards, all to no avail. The loud explosions from the limp canvas above kept all on edge as the sails threatened to shred themselves as they slapped into their masts at every roll of the ship. The men knew that for each minute the wind didn't fill in and move their charge along, *Galatea* would be that much later getting into Plymouth, where she would deliver not only her cargo but bitter disappointment to her awaiting merchants.

When the winds did fill in at last, Amberson would have rested far easier had he seen them come from a different direction and carrying less weight. Even the lowliest of greenhorns could tell you that early October was no time to be getting a full press of tropical air out of the south.

There were no hard and fast rules found in a book to fall back on, just as there was no dead certain way to sail the ship. It was one thing to suffer through the lack of sufficient wind as they had for the past while, yet as he now looked aloft at the over-pressed rig above him, he knew that it was quite another to keep the old girl over-canvassed and pushed beyond her limits. Regardless what Amberson felt, he knew that the final word wasn't his and that it had to come down from the captain, in whose hands the responsibility of ship and her crew ultimately fell. Amberson was at a loss as to why, for the better part of the day now, Captain Borland seemed not to heed the morbid colors of the lowering sky and the steady build of the moist southern air. It was between watches, after a foredeck conversation with Kemp, that Amberson felt he should take his concerns to his captain. For the past few days the wind had been fluky, at times leaving the surface of the gray Atlantic waters with an uncharacteristic flat and glassy swell from the south. *Galatea* hadn't been keeping a steady course, and what easting she made was trivial, far from something to be admired. Although calms on the ocean test the limits of most men's patience, the new building breeze should have alleviated that. But what the mate felt in the air this day told him that it wouldn't, if anything it would add to the already stirring cauldron. There was an uneasy feeling aboard the ship, something devoid of form as well as familiarity. For no reason other than sheer instinct, Amberson found that he was looking over his shoulder every few minutes.

It was the cook who first brought it to Amberson's attention. The old black man from the islands usually kept to himself, joined in when he was needed, made do with what he was given, and more times than not had a smile or a kind word. But since dawn the weathered, quiet man with the musical patter in his voice had shown Amberson a different side. When going to the galley and seeking a cup of coffee, Amberson was met by a man deaf and distant as he frantically worked at the small beads of condensation which built up on the bulkheads. Only after the mate had had to ask the old man for a second and third time for coffee did the cook turn and acknowledge him. Paying no heed to the request for coffee, and with no trace of humor or recognition, the cook expounded on the fact that the air was too wet for cooking, too wet for sailing, too wet for living. He bitterly complained how his knees were giving him trouble. Using the same words that his father and his father before him used, he told the mate about his "miseries," the "grinding ache" which kept him from bending to the lower racks in his soot blackened ovens. Although he would be loathe to admit it, Amberson was concerned for the health of the men on his watch and most times he knew how much stock to put into their complaints. It wasn't until the black cook adamantly pulled up a pant leg to show the visibly swollen joint which made up his dusty black knee that the mate put any credence in what the man was complaining about.

"You'll see, you'll see," the cook said as he rolled his pant leg back down. "When de miseries come means no good for any man. Too much water in de air, soon we'll be having too much wind."

Amberson was used to the ramblings of island lore, and most any other morning he would have paid little heed to the old man, but this morning the back of his neck told him to listen.

"Most times dees ovens keep my walls dry," the cook said, "but looky hear." He reached across the mate's shoulder and took a quick wipe of the bulkhead with his long black fingers. He simply held his black hand in front of Amberson's face, letting the damp sheen on his wrinkled palm speak for itself.

With a subtle twitch, the mate pursed his lips. "Let me know when all this water in the air starts to raise hell with your oven," he said sarcastically, trying not to let his concern register with the old cook. "Report to Chips, he'll give you something for your knees."

"What I need for my knees he ain't got," the cook snapped as he took a filthy rag and started to wipe down his small galley. "A tree is what I need. My knees would be just fine were I had a tree to lie underneath."

Amberson ducked his large bulky frame through the doorway to the galley and back out onto deck. The air was thick and heavy, and small drops of dew had begun to add weight to his worn cotton shirt. The mate had been at sea long enough to recognize what the weight on his cotton shirt meant. He took a minute to look about and gather in his thoughts; *Galatea* was continuing to make good progress eastward, and occasionally the building breeze picked up plumes of spray from her bow wave and tossed them across the ship's slanted decks. The wind was a steady twenty to twenty-five knots across the mastheads. Above him a handful of men worked at the never ending business of ship maintenance.

Everything was normal, yet he was having a hard time

dismissing thoughts that they were anything but.

Now that there was a fresh breeze to push the packet along, Katherine had come out of her cabin and stood on the high side of *Galatea's* starboard deck, staring out at the source of the wind. The new breeze was making her soft brown hair thicker and unruly, as she was trying to wrestle a scarf over it. Despite his distraction, the mate stopped to talk a bit, "exchange a few pleasantries," as the girl put it.

Katherine took her eyes off the horizon and turned with a smile to the broad-backed man "No need to be helping me carry my meals from the galley anymore, Mr. Amberson, for I think at long last I've found my sea legs." .

"Only a matter of time and patience," he said. He chanced to look down at her firm grasp on the ship's rail and was quite amazed that after two weeks at sea and several chance encounters he had never noticed that the young woman had a claw for a left hand. In a world fraught with dangers that was not remarkable into itself, but the manner in which this twisted and stunted hand seemed to hold her against the rail was quite remarkable; as with the ship's own grappling hooks, the fingers of the withered hand were bent over the rail and secured the rest of her firmly in place. Feeling the unfamiliar sensation of awkwardness and embarrassment, Amberson realized that perhaps the few seconds that he had stared at the hand were a few seconds too many. Somewhat distractedly the mate looked up into the towering sails above him and then back down to the southern horizon. He too found himself focusing on the distant dark band on the horizon.

"How many more days would your guess be?" Katherine asked as she rested her back against the waist-high wooden rail which ran the length of *Galatea's* decks.

"Oh," he said laughing, "I'd never want to guess at that. Not long perhaps."

"I must say the sky certainly was impressive this morning, Mr. Amberson. I can't recall ever seeing so many colors in one sunrise. I'm afraid my weather lessons with the captain haven't covered a display from nature such as that." She turned back to the rail and took in the vast and empty expanse of ocean in front of her. "We arc so small and insignificant in all this water."

The mate gave a sardonic grin at the girl's awe, his own having long since been buried beneath years of scrvice. "And you're only looking at the surface of it."

Katherine gestured with her head toward the south. "What are we looking at there?" she asked, indicating the distant black wall.

"More clouds," he said, "Just not as pretty." The girl's question had snapped him back from her world of fresh and new observation and to the moment at hand. He nodded. "If you'll excuse me..."

A man of habit, Amberson realized that he still had not had his normal mug of coffee at dawn and with his usual pragmatism decided to resign himself to the fact. Noticing a scupper choked with Sargasso weed from the occasional bouts with the Gulf Stream currents of a few days back, he walked down the pitching deck to kick the green lump out through the small deck level door. He watched as a small grouping of his men huddled in the lee of their fo'c'sle, not as much hiding from the wind or a restless mate's eye, but trying to keep their ragged clothes out of the damp press of new air. As though he were looking for something which was late in arriving, he gazed up at *Galatea's* rig yet again, and once more back down to the horizon.

Amberson watched as his men traded silent quips with one another. For the first time that morning he noticed that the water and air were devoid of sea birds -- shearwaters, Mother Carey's chickens, none of their usual antics were to be found nor their cries heard. Wondering about their curious absence, he again found himself drawn to the low black line on the southern horizon. The captain may pay it no heed, he thought, but I'll be damned if I'll let her get caught with too much canvas, not on my watch anyway. Some decision was better than none. It would be no secret from the captain if Amberson ordered sail struck, especially if there was no cause for the action other than a gut feeling, but certainly other measures could be taken.

"Riggins, Winslow, Hayes. Ready a jack line."

The men were slow to rise to the odd command, too slow in the mate's eyes.

"Now!"

Rigging a jack line, a stout length of tarred hemp which ran the length of the middle deck at waist level, was usually reserved for full gales, when the ship had too much of the sea running across her waist to allow for safe passage by foot. The old saw, "one hand for the ship, one hand for yourself," never rang more true than when you had to cross slick decks which had a continuous river washing across them. Rigging such a line was a quick and simple task which certainly three men were capable of, yet Amberson knew it was what the order inferred that would ultimately bring about the groans of discontent. A packet was a fast, wet ship with a fine bow, which could power and slice its way into and out of the back of any wave the ocean chose to throw her way. Yet during heavier weather the fact that the butt of her bowsprit, the horizontal mast which flew the ship's headsails off the front of the boat, passed into the crew's quarters in the fo'c'sle, guaranteed quantities of seawater would ship into the very area that the crew wanted most to be kept dry. One inopportune wave would keep their bedding and clothes in a state of constant dampness and mildew for the rest of the crossing. This is what kept the mate's men just this side of an irritable state of caution, for any heavy weather over the horizon meant untold dampness would be added to their already meager lives. Fo'c'sle living was dark, smoky and crowded at best. Add to this an uninvited sea and Amberson knew that orders had to be given with measured weight. Preparing a jack line was a tip-off to these men that some wet and uncomfortable conditions were to be expected.

Slowly the three men and sauntered to the line locker, not out of any disrespect for Amberson's order but more for dread of what they thought was to come. Amberson recognized their postures and chose to cut any word short before it could spread to the rest of his watch and the second mate's off watch as well. He felt it start to well up inside of him.

"Damn you, Hayes, are you deaf?" he demanded of the

youngest of the three.

"No, sir, just that a jack line means weather," the boy said as he picked up his step.

"You let me decide what a jack line means and what it doesn't boy." The mate moved up to the small group as they ambled along. "Nobody said any word about weather, now did they?" He stood face to face with the young boy, who was easily half his size.

"No, sir," he said, terrified of the man with one pale white eye.

Amberson's face remained inches from the boy's, threatening to explode any moment. "Then ready the damn thing!"

The mate's brutal beating of Jenkins was not wasted on the three men. They moved on with new purpose.

Amberson's lack of patience and emotional distance from his men gnawed at him for a few minutes. He was not a man who believed that all things foul ran downhill; simply because the captain had taken a bite out of him earlier didn't necessarily mean that he had to go and find someone lesser to take his own bite out of. He took an off white piece of what used to be a handkerchief from his coat pocket and mopped at the back of his neck. He folded it over and did it again.

The heavy tropic winds continued to push at his ship, yet all Amberson could feel was the oppressive sticky heat. He couldn't breathe, it was as though all the oxygen had been sucked out of the air. His captain's demeanor earlier in the day was as far out of the ordinary as his own. Maybe Borland was feeling the pressure of the impossible time schedule which the Brothers Sefton had hung on *Galatea.* But, both men knew what possibilities lay beyond the horizon to the south.

CHAPTER 17

An explosion rained splinters of wood and metal down upon *Galatea's* decks as her terrified crew dove for what cover they could find in the ink black void of the night. A second electrical concussion tore at the mizzenmast's iron backstay, sending a ghostly blue glow down the length of the great cable, illuminating the stern of the ship. The men who stood watch gazed in stunned silence as they slowly recovered from the concussions. Around them all was silent and still. *Galatea* had been hit but they didn't know the extent of the damage. Cautiously they climbed into the rig to assess the situation. Another shearing arc of lightning found its target, exploding the thick cable of the backstay. With each new explosion *Galatea* was violently rocked from stem to stern. Without having to be called out, the ship's off watch poured from the fo'c'sle into the black of the night only to be momentarily blinded and turned back by the electrical forces which toyed with *Galatea.* Milling about trying to make sense of the destruction, men started to rig a preventer for the dismembered mizzenmast, trying to secure it momentarily. Ripping through the dark night air, another lightning bolt tore at her superstructure, turning freshly painted wood into deathly projectiles. No wind, no rain, just deadly silence and darkness between the sporadic bolts of destruction. First Mate Amberson had experienced electric storms before, but this was far from old hat. The mate sent a man aft for the captain, but the storm sent another volley, blasting the sailor from the deck with one of its hot splinters of electricity, dead before he hit the water.

Within the first few seconds, Captain Borland was already on deck. Knocked off his feet by yet another salvo, the old man's piercing steel blue eyes were blinded as a lightning bolt tore through the ship's galley, scattering iron, red hot coals and human flesh across the still decks before him.

No orders could be given, for there were no orders to combat the energies unleashed.

The captain lay on deck, gasping for an answer. Frantically he rubbed at his useless eyes, trying to gain at least a modicum of vision. He shook his head violently. *Galatea* was struck again, but who? He should try to save his ship and her company, but from what? She's under attack, he thought, but from where? Something else was wrong, dreadfully wrong, a wisp of burning tar drifted past his nose; the intense heat of the strikes was burning the tar off the ship's rigging. In the dark a man's small and helpless voice cried out. Above him the upper and lower topsail yards grated and rasped as they now dangerously swung loosely. Splitting the black silence, a scorching javelin of raw energy struck, the deck of his boat flashed with a brilliant explosion of raw and pale blue light, and the old man was thrown back into the side of the companionway house. Around him men ran wildly, far above him steel yards swung uncontrollably. An ice pick was being pressed down into his ears. His hands shot up to the sides of his head where they found small rivers of moisture running from his now deaf ears. Tasting the liquid he immediately knew it to be blood. Men were running madly, trying to douse the growing flames with buckets, but Borland heard not so much as a footstep and failed to see the massive effort by his ship's company. The proud skipper rolled helplessly about the deck, trying to stand but falling to his knees again, using the deckhouse to claw his way to his feet and face the attack, only to tumble over sideways. Devoid of his two senses, his equilibrium had vanished. Captain Phineas J. Borland lay helpless on deck as the sickly pantomime of his ship's destruction raged about him.

Men scrambled to the mates' commands. *Galatea* was slowly becoming a derelict before their eyes, but from what? Chaos was born out of the unknowing; there was nothing to save her from; no wind, no rain, no mountainous seas threatened to drive her under. The great ocean was calm, peaceful, and the winds had been nothing but steady. Borland had been right in keeping as much rig as the old girl could muster, there was no reason to shorten sail then just as there was none now. *Galatea* was pinned down by a blanket of explosive electricity. How could someone fight what they couldn't see?

Silence. Then again the black of night was torn in half by a white hot strike from above, and another explosion raked at the ship's deck. In the brilliant light of the explosion, small pockets of fog were seen to be hovering just above the menacing waters. Slowly slouching and twisting their way toward the ship, these pockets of carrion stench were approaching their prey.

During the silence between each assault, Kemp tried to gather damage reports while Amberson was tending to a man who had landed at his feet. The one leg of the sailor's pants was on fire. Quickly the mate withdrew his knife and cut the burning canvas, but it was the man's leg that was burning. Kemp found his way next to Amberson as the larger man was wrapping his denim jacket around the man's burning flesh. Quickly both men recoiled in revulsion as the carrion pockets of fog started to drift aboard.

"My God, do you smell that?" he said.

A sound jerked Amberson's head around to the south, a noise which his brain told him he shouldn't be hearing a thousand miles from land, but one which his ears insisted that he did hear. Steam being released, a fire, a furnace, the roar of a furnace from the brickyards. But this was small, far off in the distance. Grabbing at the ships' rail, he stood to his feet and looked toward the horizon from which the noise came. Both men watched as the dark band on the southern horizon, which had been watching and waiting on *Galatea's* every move for the past 24 hours, began to come to life. Charged with electricity, the hideous bank began to revolve slowly and grow before their eyes. The undulating mass was gaining sufficient life and proportion to dwarf the electrical onslaught. The cloud bank grew into a towering black wall. There was no mistaking its purpose. Large rolling cylinders of black cloud gave birth to a sulfuric breeze which whipped and tore at the great ocean's surface, whipping it into a frenzy of spume and spray. Not being intent on black, the clouds now glowed with dark purple, blood red, towering high above as they grew in height and strength. Flashes of electricity coursed through the layered mass. First and second mate stared in morbid disbelief as the faint distant roar of a killing wind grew louder.

"Christ almighty," Amberson said. "Strike every God damn piece of rag we have."

"All hands, all hands aloft!" Kemp shouted. Both terrified watches turned out to an order that was unfamiliar and confusing. "Strike anything that flies, cut it away if you have to."

The terrified and confused men scrambled up the ratlines, trying to figure out the procedure for an order which they had never heard before.

"Helmsman, run off!"

"From what, sir?" the bewildered boy asked as he looked about the ship in terror and confusion. "From what?"

The storm threw two more rounds of electricity in rapid succession, silhouetting the macabre dance onboard *Galatea.*

Before the men could get the sails on the foremast safely secured or at the very least cut away, the great storm, acting in concert with her sister ocean, summoned a wave of deathly power and violently slammed *Galatea* down sideways on to her beam ends. The packet shuddered to a stop as ten sailors were whipped from their perches high in the rigging out into the black waters. Just under the surface the awaiting Dead Ones clambered and fought for possession of the sailor's bodies and souls in a frenzy. Hoping to end their purgatory, the Dead Ones tried to invade the drowning men's bodies and wait to be pulled back on deck, ending their timeless wanderings below and allowing them back into the world of the living.

Galatea slowly shook off the assault and began to right herself against the tempest. Timed with great precision and in delicate unison, the growing roar of the wind announced its arrival with sister ocean's mighty seas. The second stage of the attack hit.

Where only seconds before the ship sat to light, indifferent breezes, she was now suddenly being torn by hurricane forces. Those men who miraculously remained aloft wrapped their arms and legs tightly around anything solid, but no human strength was capable of withstanding the wind. When the ship was hit by the blast, some men flew out horizontally, screaming as they were fed to the Dead Ones below. Others had their clothes torn off of them like so much rotten paper before they gave up their grips and fell into the ocean. As though she were intent on trying to pluck her charges out of the water, *Galatea* acquiesced to the building press on her rig and lay down on the surface of the boiling cauldron, burying the remains of her yardarms in the wet blackness. There she remained, pinned helplessly by the force of the tempest. Everything loose flew across the lengths of her now vertical decks far into the depths below. Easing back to regain more strength, the wind abated slightly, allowing the ship to lift her head out of the wet and try to regain her breath, if only for a second.

Again it hit. The wind shrieked through what was left of the snapped rigging, sounding the death keen for the great ship.

Amberson's mind was lost in a maze of horror and confusion. Where was the captain? To no avail, he called out for the man. The great winds played with the mate's terror and concern as they tore the words out of his mouth no sooner than he had hollered them. He tried calling for the captain again, but over the tortured screeching of the wind and the explosions of bursting sails no sound could carry.

The third stage of the fury hit. The great ocean started to present a display of her own. Out of ambling swells, mountains of black water began to build and charge at the ship, seemingly from ever direction. *Galatea* quickly rose up a sheer vertical cliff which formed in front her, only to fall turning and twisting into a trough forty feet below. What was left of her mainmast snapped and fell forward, shattering the fo'c'sle in a thundering mass of wood and hemp. Black mountains cascading with phosphorus wet avalanches rose up and crashed down upon the weakened wooden decks below.

Buried under an onslaught of water, Amberson tried to fight the assault and started to crawl aft, trying to make his way to help secure the wheel. A towering wall of menacing green rose behind the stern of the wallowing vessel and collapsed, dropping thousands of tons of water on to the back of the ship. Readying himself for the assault, Amberson wrapped his arms and legs tightly around a piece of shattered and burnt topmast which lay in front of him. The weight flattened him into the deck, threatening to split it at any moment. Swirling in an ungodly mass of water and fury he was lifted and thrown, battered into the bulwarks below him, bodily compromising the wood which made up his ship's hull. Water cascaded over him as he tried to hold off unconsciousness. Gasping for air, he violently shook his head. He was alive and at least for now he remained on deck, too large to be squeezed out the scuppers which allowed the angry sea to flow back to her own element and re-gather strength. As he once again tried to crawl toward the wheel, a sharp pain tore at his side, limiting his movement. Again he had to climb over the remains of *Galatea's* once proud rig, which now lay scattered about him in a maze of splinters and foam. Bracing against the violent lurching sea, he tried to roll over a splintered keg which was half encased in the young English woman's deckhouse. Up until now he had reacted only with adrenaline, trying to stay one step ahead of the attack. Good Christ, the girl, he thought to himself, what in God's name has become of her. He felt the ship lift from under him. *Galatea* was raised up sideways and again thrown down on to her beam ends. Seeing the opportunity, the ocean swept across the ship's rail and tried to tear Amberson away. Amberson lost his grip on the barrel and fell from a now vertical deck. He landed against and held on firmly to the splintered stump of a mast which stood just forward of where he had been laying. His feet dangling in the air, he screamed out as the pain in his side scorched through his body. The raw wind tore at the wave tops and filled the air with a clinging and suffocating spume. Amberson found that he couldn't breathe. Slowly, once again *Galatea* shook off the onslaught and rose to an even keel. A brief respite. Motivated by the anger of failure, another solid black wall of Atlantic swept across the flexing decks, Amberson was torn from the mast and pushed along in the torrent.

Again the searing pain tore at the mate's side as he came to rest not three feet from where the sea had deposited him before. He began to feel a nauseating warmth in the side of his chest, trying to roll over he screamed out in pain as the yellow and red stub of an exposed and broken rib caught on a coil of some running rigging which lay under him. Don't pass out, damn you, he swore to himself, keep alive, man. Out of the darkness a screaming wall of green water crashed onto deck and charged at the mate as he tried to regain his footing. In the horrific wind his world swirled about him. Among the confusion of rope, canvas and wood he could hear the cries and calls from fellow shipmates who hadn't yet been taken by the ocean. At least I'm not alone, he thought to himself, but that was little consolation. No ship, no man could survive the onslaught he was now facing.

The storm reached a new level of violence; the brutal strength of the hurricane pressed *Galatea* down into grasping troughs of water. Backed by the wind, sheets of rain blinded the mate as he once again tried to make his way aft. As he crawled on his left side across a deck which ran with several feet of water, Amberson's hands stumbled against a long still taught, rough length of line. For some perverse reason the jack line had survived the onslaught and ironically was still serving its purpose. Hand over hand he pulled himself forward against the swirling waters. With luck he might be able to wedge himself against the elevation of the aft deck, secure in a partial lee. From there he could gather his thoughts for just a moment and try to get a handle on the storm. Another violent explosion bathed the ship in a white hot light, illuminating the shattered masts, shredded canvas and the menacing ocean which boxed in the ship. He rested against the white deckhouse which so many years ago was promised to his captain's wife, he laughed at the irony of it. Perhaps now it was a mausoleum. If he was still alive, and from what he could hear over the wind and sea others were as well, then there was a chance that the young woman might be too. He laughed morosely to himself. Then what, row her to shore?

Laying on his side, he tried to force the small white cabin

door open. Inside a sea chest had exploded and spewed its contents across the liquid flooring of what was once the young woman's cabin. Amberson pressed his great mass against the door until the pain screamed out in his ears. He bit his tongue to counter the searing from the exposed raw rib as it was twisted and bent by the gripping muscles on which he used to depend, muscles which now thwarted his efforts. The driving walls of rain and ocean made it all but impossible to breathe. Spitting out of seawater and blood, he gave the one final push. In the blue light of a lightning flash, Amberson thought he saw the girl on her bed. Green water swept past him on its way to capturing some other soul, enough water to clear his vision, now he clearly saw the young woman in front of him. She was on her bunk, her knees curled to her chest, half crying and half singing a child's lullaby. Rocking herself, her eyes wide, she tried to comprehend the unholyness of everything around her.

"Miss," he called out. "Miss, look at me."

The wind grabbed the mate's words as soon as he released them. The pain from his lungs threw the man down onto his back. His sudden and violent movement registered with the girl. Her attention slowly moved in the direction of her partially opened door. The great hulk of a man lay as limp as a doll, and blood seeped out from under his shirt. She began to rise to help the man, but *Galatea* was lifted and thrown from a tremendous height into a trough, slamming Katherine back against the bulkhead of her cabin. As the packet landed on her side, a wall of water pounded against the side of the small deckhouse. Huddling in terror, the girl felt the flex of the thin wood paneling against her back. A muffled explosion at her door jerked Katherine's head around. She braced her feet against the lee board of her bunk. Her small cabin became awash in a seething mass of green froth.

As *Galatea* rolled back to port, the hands of the Atlantic released their grip and ran back out onto deck. Amberson looked about in bewilderment as one moment he was laying on deck and now was curled in the splintered wreckage of Katherine's small writing desk. Dumbfounded, he and the girl stared at one another.

"Are you all right?" he hollered. The searing pain in his side robbed him of air.

Katherine nodded tentatively. Amberson looked about trying to assess the situation and gauge just how much longer the small wooden cabin could withstand the storm.

"Best we sit tight," he said. "Too much for the ship." He knew that he should be reassuring her that all would be well and that *Galatea* could hold her own against anything the elements threw at her, but what she was now facing of this earth, nor was it heaven sent.

Her fear locking her into place, Katherine sat curled, staring at the spot where Amberson lay in a jumbled heap. With great deliberation, she slowly spoke. "It's me, it's me they want."

Trying to speak, the man cautiously drew a breath, the pain from his side stabbed at his efforts. He clawed at the air in front of him and moaned. From where she sat, Katherine quickly searched the man's fallen body with her eyes, trying to see how she could alleviate his pain. Her eyes stopped at the yellow bone which protruded from his bloodied shirt. A flood of repulsion and nausea swept through her. Telegraphing the movements of panicked lungs, the splinter of yellow bone took small stabbing jabs at the air.

Lightning struck again, followed by an earsplitting thunderclap, and *Galatea's* last mast was reduced to splinters. Amberson and Katherine listened to the distant shrieks as the wooden projectiles found their targets.

With no more capacity for shock, the girl began to cry to herself. Again she started to assume the tucked posture in which Amberson first saw her.

"Stay with me now, girl." He winced as he spoke. "We need you here."

Katherine almost laughed. Here? she thought. Anywhere but here. She breathed deeply, deliberately. Focus on the mate, she demanded of herself.

As they sat staring about, wondering from what direction the next assault would come, it began to happen. At first Amberson dismissed it to the ship's rise on another wave, but this was different. *Galatea* climbed with a steady, deliberate movement. For the first time since the attack began it felt as though she were drawing up to brace against the hurricane, to try to press on through it. Although awash, her decks were finally level enough for the fortunate few who scrambled about and seeking shelter. As she continued to rise, pride coursed through Amberson's body, momentarily checking the pain.

Seeing the look in his eyes, the optimism in his raised eye brows, Katherine began to release her grip on the wood slats of her bunk. *Galatea* was even keeled now and was perhaps beginning to hold her own. A giddy feeling spread through Katherine. Amberson's eyes started to narrow, he looked about quickly. *Galatea* was still rising, but far beyond her limits. Amberson knew this action was nothing of her doing.

Galatea was lifted to great heights on the back of a hollow wave and then catapulted through the air. Freefalling for several seconds, the 110-foot ship landed against the stone hard waters of the Atlantic with shattering finality. The tiny white deckhouse was ripped from its secure platform and reduced to just so much more Atlantic flotsam.

From the ice cold depths of their watery purgatory, the Dead Ones swarmed and awaited to attach themselves to the girl. Clawing to be the taker of Katherine's soul, they clamored among one another, knowing that of anybody she would be plucked from the ocean and dragged back on deck. Ravenously they searched the waters for her. Above them *Galatea* lay wallowing, her deck awash in a maze of humans, hemp and canvas; from the gaping mouths of her shattered hatches barrels and wooden packing chests started to gain their own lives and floated out of the flooded holds.

Katherine's limp body came to rest against the stump of the great ship's wheel. The waters rolled her body back and forth across the deck. She could hear the familiar screams and cries from the great depths of the ocean getting closer. Her nightmares were no longer distant, they were immediate and on board. All about her was chaos and tortured sounds. Yet there was a difference, this ship was not being torn apart, it was hell bent on deliverance. Keeping a firm grasp on the wooden rail, Katherine held tightly as the ship charged at great speeds through the night. Suddenly, as if hitting an invisible stone wall, the ship slammed to a halt, violently throwing the girl to the water washed deck. All about her the storm raged but the ship had stopped moving. Gripped by invisible forces *Galatea* groaned and twisted as she was held in check, waves washing past and under her with no intent to cause damage. Wind screamed through the rig, but left no destruction in its wake. The dream *Galatea* sat peacefully secured while the nightmare tempest raged about her.

Katherine started to stand. As she got to her knees, a screeching wail sounded out of the darkness and she was pulled back down onto deck. Something gripped her ankle. She tried to jerk her foot away, and more screams of rage filled the air about her. Looking down to her foot she tried to see the cause of the searing pain but was jerked backward across the deck. Again the girl tried to pull free but all about her screams of defiance and rage shattered the night. Violently she was dragged across the wood on her stomach and slammed against the bulwark of the deck as it came to a sudden stop. Again she tried to reach down to her right ankle. As she did, a wave of nausea swept over her. She cried out in horror as her hands met the ice cold wrapping of dark green seaweed which held her leg. The weed ran from her ankle, across a small bit of deck and out a scupper into the ocean. Trying to pull Katherine's leg out to the ocean through the ship's scupper, the weed tore and ripped at the girl's skin. In frenzied panic Katherine tore at the weed, freeing her ankle from its grasp, yet what lay under the weed made her world freeze about her. Digging into her bruised ankle in the same manner it had done dream after dream, was a long white-blue hand, fingers laced around her flesh, yellow fingernails spiking into her skin. Katherine's ankle seared with pain as the hand tried to drag her through the scupper and into the deep. The Dead Ones sought to hasten the great ocean's delivery of the girl. Katherine's right leg was fully extended out the small scupper, but her hip joint kept her in place. Sitting up, she raised her left leg, placed it firmly against the bulwark and pushed herself away from the sinewy hand which was so intent on dragging her into the depths. *Galatea* violently lurched back to life, tossing her backward, slamming her head on the deck as it did.

A rough thick hand reached out of the darkness, felt her face and then lifted her head above the swirling water about her.

Slowly the assault on her senses began to pull her back into the destruction of the night. A loud voice, too loud cried out against the fury of the storm.

"My God, you're alive."

The sky above her exploded into blinding light and lit the ship's decks from above. The bolt of lightning illuminated the captain's salt and blood encrusted beard. Katherine saw the look of unknowing terror which had spread across his face. The deafening concussion of the thunder shocked her fully awake as she looked at the crumpled man who held her so securely.

"Try to sit up," he hollered.

Katherine could see that something was wrong. He pulled her back against the face of the raised aft deck where he had managed to keep out of the storm. Here Katherine felt a small sense of security as the tempest roared over them.

With her holds filled with water, *Galatea's* hulk groaned in protest as it rose almost vertically in the air. Another black hand of water gripped and twisted her high into the black night. As the ship fell from the great height, the captain grasped onto Katherine. Throwing the two of them forward, *Galatea* slammed violently against the Atlantic.

"Will she sink?" Katherine cried to the old man. He simply stared about at the hulk which was once his ship. "Is she sinking?" she shouted.

Even if the captain could hear her words, his attention was far from her worries. In a horrible world unbalanced by lack of sight and sound, Captain Borland continued to look about in the dark. Although he couldn't hear or see it coming, he felt it -- a sailor's one true fear personified. Every bit of sea sense in the man told him it was near, yet his ears were deaf and eyes blind to the approaching rage of the sheer vertical cliff of angry ocean which now stood the length of the ship.

"It's God's balance," he shouted out, trying to comfort the girl he held her tightly. "We're in God's hands now."

From forces far from godly, the final blow was delivered. Thousands of tons of water coalesced into a monstrous wave. The wall of water bodily lifted the packet and simply threw her. As she landed, long white spuming fingers of the Atlantic grasped *Galatea's* hull and rolled her onto her side. Slowly, hundreds of tons of ship were pushed under and the painted green undersides of her hull began to show. A barnacle encrusted keel began to present itself to the terror of the night. Turned turtle, *Galatea* hung in balance for a few final seconds as all vestiges of hope and life were swept clear of her upside down decks. The wash from the ship-killing wave pushed her along through the water at breakneck speeds. Coming to rest, the 110-foot ship struggled for a final gasp. In a dying reflex, the weight of her lead keel encouraged her to complete her arc and roll back upright. It was over.

Devastated by a night of unholy wrath, the gray dawn gave witness to the remains of a wallowing hulk. So sudden and precise had the attack been that the ship had no chance to mount a defense let alone secure herself and her charges for the duration. About the packet lay a death wreath of canvas, timbers, splintered boxes of eastbound cargo, and bodies. Her decks now barely three feet above the water *Galatea's* shattered hull lay burdened by cargo holds filled and anchored by cold water. No storm, no fury, apart from the remaining confused seas, no evidence of the night's apocalypse remained.

The occasional timber would groan and snap, echoing in the still of the morning. Below her silent decks, no off watch slept. The new inhabitants of her submerged holds started to venture in and investigate their new surroundings. All manner of sea life floated and swam about in the confines of a hull soon to be leaving the cold of the morning air, on its way to a future of rot and decay thousands of feet below. Just skirting beneath the slowly sinking hull, the larger, unseen marine creatures of the deep glided back and forth effortlessly, waiting for more of the lifeless remains of those who once worked the decks of the ship. The continuation of the food cycle; life above surrenders to death, death provides sustenance and life for those who live below, who in turn are hunted and killed for the benefit of those who live above.

Obliging no one, the great storm and ocean moved on, transforming themselves into accommodating breezes and seas. A promise to her Dead Ones had been made and then forgotten. In her wrath she insured that there were no survivors to be hauled back onto deck. Far beneath the surface, into the darkness where no light could find them, the Dead Ones writhed in the agony of their plight. Seeking deliverance they had taken and invaded the bodies which were thrown to them, but to no avail, none were plucked back onto the ship's deck to safety. Surely the girl would have been plucked from the water, such precious cargo she was. The fight for possession, the tearing at the shrouds of her spirit, the long awaited deliverance by a body so young and promising as hers, all for naught. There was no deliverance to be gained from any of the fallen. No sailors were left to try and pluck their comrades out of the sea. The Dead Ones had clawed at her and for one brief moment one of their numbers had seeped into her body, but there was to be no rescue of the girl, no one left on deck to give her the breath of life. A drowned and wasted vehicle, Katherine's body was vacated, left to rot and decay as small jaws and sharp pincers began to systematically tear at the flesh which was once alive with hope, spirit and love.

Katherine's spirit floated aimlessly, trapped in the great currents of the Atlantic, watching as what was once her body became so many strips of torn flesh. It was repulsive but she was now indifferent to it. She felt the press of the frozen elements about her as she began to gather the rules of her new incarnation. Timeless, hopeless wanderings, devoid of sound or sight. Souls wandered in mute and frozen desperation, awaiting deliverance. Entombed in the frozen black purgatory with thousands of other drifting and rotting souls, Katherine was not to see England, nor find that spirit of love and hope which she sought.

In timely fashion and with small personal concern it would be posted around the docks of Plymouth that the Packet *Galatea* was overdue and missing, presumably all hands lost at sea. Far from the quays of the harbor, beyond city center, across the Tamar and into the rolling green fields of Salt Ash, hushed word quickly spread that the Worthington family had suffered another tragic loss.

Across the resting waters of the Atlantic, insurance companies would struggle with bottom lines and settlements with angered merchants, while the Brothers Sefton looked toward their remaining ships to pick up the slack left by their own loss. Through personal telling of those who never shipped out with the man, the sailing reputation of Captain Phineas J. Borland, master of the *Galatea,* would grow by leaps and bounds. And while winter winds pushed at the doors of New England's wooden seaport homes, men who had ridden it out in safety on shore would relive again and again the great storm 1860. Ensconced before a tavern fire, they would regale one another with such phrases as "ship killer," "devil's own" and "not a trace," all the while failing to comprehend the strength of such words.

And several thousand miles out into the reach, hundreds of fathoms in the gray Atlantic, the ice cold grip of perpetual night held the pained and tortured soul of a young English woman who had become yet another lost and wandering Dead One.

CHAPTER 18

I'm not ashamed to admit that cooking was never my forte. When I was married I avoided it like the plague, my college meals were always taken at the cafeteria and the sight of men working a back yard barbecue has always left me cold if not curious. Our meals aboard *Curlew* were by and large prepared by Paul. He understood this. Just as I understood that in a blow, I was the one to go forward and work a pitching foredeck. Yet despite this neat arrangement, from time to time my guilt and I would announce, "Tonight, dinner is on me."

Cooking on a small boat is akin to being locked in a small closet while somebody outside tries to roll the rest of the house down a very rocky hill. It's a challenge, but not impossible. As I stood leaning against the waist high bulkhead which separated the galley area from the salon, I gazed down upon the attempts of the past hour and a half which lay around my feet on the ship's sole. Offered about lay the remains of two meals which had gone south, north, east and west. The first attempt at dinner, tuna casserole, which for reasons beyond my comprehension had evolved into tuna soup, fell victim to a wave we sailed up, over and down. *Curlew's* waterline length wasn't long enough to power us through some of the larger Atlantic swells, so like a small duck she would ride up the front and down the back, all at a respectable seven knots. The result of this sprightly action was that the bottom of any well secured pot on the stove would suddenly and quite unexpectedly drop out from under its ingredients, and then move ahead at seven knots just enough to insure that the ingredients came back down shy of their original launching pad. The evening's second attempt was a rice and meat combination. Using the wrong foot pedal to pump water into the pot, which no longer had the tuna soup in it, I mistakenly boiled the rice in seawater instead of fresh water, resulting in a sort second rate seafood risotto. I would have to make a note to

Jasperson that the two pedals were installed entirely too close together for true cooking convenience.

As I tried to cool down an anger born of culinary frustration and Paul tried to work up an appetite for what was basically a pretty terrible meal now sitting before us, we pushed our dinner of beanies-and-weenies around our plates.

Between us on the dinette was the latest weather fax from NOAA. A low pressure system was slowly filling in west of us and as far as we could see, the isobars were widely spaced. This all indicated that we were to expect winds out of the south but nothing to be concerned about.

"Well," he said as he ran his tongue around between his cheeks and gums, "looks like it's going to move north, but we're going to get it."

"Give us a good push. Broad reach from the south." Without asking I picked up Paul's half finished dinner plate and wedging myself into the small galley area, began to wash up the remains of the insult.

We had sailed about 1,000 miles so far, and considering the time of year, all was going remarkably smoothly. No unexpected surprises from *Curlew* just as there were no unexpected surprises from the weather. She had been proving herself very capable on all points of sail and only once did I have to venture forward in the dark of night. Being set too far south by an easterly breeze, we had had to tack her over to starboard, when the headsail caught on an exposed tip of a cotter pin. The miracles of sticky back cloth being what they were, I took a small piece of this adhesive sail cloth forward, dropped the sail, cleaned the tear with alcohol and applied the patch. After feeding the luff tape back into its track, I climbed back to the cockpit and with a jib halyard that was led aft, as were all the other halyards, raised the sail back up to its full drawing height. All in a span of fifteen minutes, all an easy job for one person and all with the minimal of fuss. As I had sat in the cockpit with Paul asleep below, I thought about how drastically travel across the Atlantic had changed in the past 100 years or so. What would have been a job for at least three men that would have taken around an hour was handled by one so quickly that *Curlew* almost never lost speed. Remarkable.

Having finished with cooking duty, I suited up in foul weather and woollies, brewed a quick cup of tea, and headed out on deck for the remains of my watch. Two men taking a small boat across a large ocean can make for crowded and cramped quarters, and that in itself could make for flared tempers and heated debates. That is, if they were ever to see one another. Shortly after we left Chester and fell into our watches, it became quite apparent that once we got to Plymouth, Paul and I would have to go to some pub and over a beer tell each other how our crossings went. Apart from meals, we never really saw one another. While I worked and navigated, he slept. While he worked and navigated and cooked, I slept. Such schedule would have helped my marriage to no end.

"Give a shout," Paul said as he climbed in the aft cabin for his four hours of sleep. We were always on call for one another if needed, but given *Curlew's* easy sail plan, there really was no need. I tucked myself up under the dodger and started to sip at my tea.

The beginnings of a solid cloud covering had rolled in earlier in the evening blanketing the efforts of the bright white wedge of moon which had so far been keeping us company at night. Above no stars were to be seen, and we had long since stopped seeing welcoming lights on shore. In fact there wasn't much of anything to be seen in the pitch black of night through which we were sailing. A small gimbaled oil lamp which hung against the forward bulkhead below cast a warm yellow light throughout the cabin, some of which seeped out into the cockpit, adding some needed cheer to a fairly gloomy night.

The Atlantic is a remarkable place to visit. Because there are none of the shore side distractions of buildings, trees, people, and cars, your sense of isolation can be overwhelming, if you let it be. Or you can fully embrace your alien surroundings and ask to be part of the moment-to-moment miracles of the sea. When the sun goes down the ocean really begins to strut her stuff. Out of nowhere, dolphins streak at, under and around the boat, leaving bright paths of phosphorus light behind them as they do. Like so many crisscrossed torpedoes, they carve brilliant pale green lightshows out of the black of the ocean. Behind the boat a small boil of bright green water trails as the stern hisses on ahead. From horizon to horizon, above you is a firmament so bright and active that one doesn't have to wait more than a few seconds for meteors, shooting stars, satellites, comets, Martians or Venutians to send shiny white traces across the heavens.

Not that it is strictly a visual treat. The sounds that Mother Nature supplies her ocean with are, quite appropriately, not of this world: the whistle and whine of the wind as it passes around the wire shrouds and stays, the calling of night birds which fly invisibly around the masthead in the dark, the wet bursting of blowholes large and small as her underwater mammals rise to the surface seeking needed air. Laying in one's bunk, the high-pitched squeaking of dolphins can be heard plainly through the wood, or in our case fiberglass, which makes up and describes your small world. Out there the problems which face a person are immediate; either it once worked and no longer works, or it never really worked but shows great promise of someday working again. No phones, no bills, no uninvited neighbors, except for the dolphins and whales, who, as far as I'm concerned, have a standing invitation to come and visit anytime they want. If the wind is too strong, you do something about it; if the equipment breaks, you do something about it; and if you find yourself as I now did, feeling very small and vulnerable, you do something about it by trying to figure out where you fit into the great magnificent scheme of things. As long as you're content with a rung pretty far down on the ladder of significance, the ocean is a wonderfully unambiguous place to be.

What wasn't very unambiguous was the dull thump and slight rise to *Curlew* which had just shaken me out of the night's revelry. As I looked about a bit wide eyed in the dark, I grabbed for the cockpit torch and shined it aft into our wake.

"Was that you?" Paul asked as he stuck his head out of the companionway.

"Be a pretty neat trick if it was," I said. "Feels like we hit something."

By playing the strong beam of the searchlight across the waters I could see that there was nothing trailing behind us, nor was there anything to leeward. Sailing east in the darkness we looked about long enough to ease our concerns.

Paul stood in the companionway looking out into the black of the night. "Scary stuff," he said. "Always been afraid of sailing into a half-submerged container at night, just floating out there with its sharp metal edges." He pressed the heels of his palms against his eyes and gently rubbed them in slow circles. "More tired than I thought. Once I get that picture in my mind I can't release it." He laughed as he looked up at me. "Call me if you need me. Night."

Now two of us were thinking about these shipping containers which floated just under the surface. Large container ships which haul modern day cargo back and forth across the oceans of the world fall victim to storms as readily as anyone else, with the usual result being that a container, a large forty-by-eight-foot steel box, may be washed from its secure perch on deck and into the ocean. It's estimated that in just one calendar year alone perhaps 1000 of these containers fall off the decks of their storm tossed ships. Many boats report having struck an unknown object floating just below the surface. When wood or fiberglass meets sharp thick metal at seven to ten knots, it's usually the former that gives way and via a twelve inch hole the ocean floods in very obligingly. Soon thereafter captain and crew find themselves in a life raft and their boat on the way to the bottom. These containers are a hazard to navigation but a fact of life as well, a fact of life that I would have preferred Paul had kept to himself. Now lurking behind every dark wave I saw a container just floating, gnashing its teeth, waiting for the likes of *Curlew.* My overactive imagination had to be quelled. I went below to root around for my Walkman and tapes. While there I made the usual log entries on the hour. Wind was fifteen to twenty knots out of the SSE, barometer was steady, course was 050 degrees not where we wanted to go but in the general direction. Battery banks looked good, we had plenty of amps. I flipped on the bilge pump and was a bit surprised to hear the pump suck up some water. *Curlew's* bilges were very shallow and water that did find its way into them was almost immediately sucked up by the automatic pump and discharged overboard. For some reason there appeared to be a bit more water than usual in them, most probably due to the occasional wave we took over the bow during the last twenty-four hours. Indicating that it was dry, the pump cycled and I flipped the switch back into the automatic position. I made a note in the log, grabbed my Walkman, and went back out onto watch.

It took a few seconds for my eyes to adjust to the darkness and when they did, I found that they still hadn't. As the moon hadn't made its nightly appearance yet, and ahead of us it was too dark to see anything except the hand in front of your face. I blinked my eyes a couple of times and then just waited for my pupils to dilate. Judging by what I now saw in front of me, those old eyes of mine had dilated quite some time ago and the reason I couldn't see the low thin line of the horizon in front of us was because there was no horizon, for the same reason that the sky above was only half filled with stars. Silhouetted by the multitude of heavenly pin holes which normally ran from horizon to horizon lay the profile of a large, unlit ship, not 100 yards ahead.

"Jesus Christ Almighty," I whispered. For fear of performing a pretty pathetic and definitely unnoticed T-bone on the starboard side of a ship almost ten times larger than us, I had to tack *Curlew* away immediately. I threw off the leeward jib sheet, yanked the mainsheet out of the jaws of the traveler, prepared to dump the weather running backstay and turned the wheel to port. It didn't move more than half an inch. Checking the break to make sure it was off, I tried to turn it again. Nothing. I tried to turn it down to starboard, but it still wouldn't budge. For reasons which could be many, *Curlew* was not answering her helm. Something was keeping the wheel from turning the rudder and until it did, we had a problem ahead of us, a 300-foot problem. I was going to have to have *Curlew* tack herself. We were starting to lose boat speed. I scrambled to bring in the jib, the main and tighten up the backstay. I was just about to holler out for Paul when I saw him sitting next to me in the cockpit.

"Where the hell'd you come from?" I asked.

"You didn't hear them, just then?" he asked calmly. "Jesus, Chris, you could have hit them."

"Hear what?" It sounded as if he didn't notice the small problem we had on our hands. I climbed back up onto the high side of the cockpit.

"The whales." Paul looked about for a second or two. "It was like they were screaming." He looked about casually. "You must have sailed right through them."

With everything I had I pulled at the wheel again. "Going to be a lot of screaming if she doesn't come about soon." I pulled in the opposite direction. "Or fall off."

By this time the ship was not fifty yards from us and the absence of any deck or navigation lights told me it was stopped in the water, so I couldn't count on her moving out of the way. She was close enough now to see that we weren't at total right angles to one another. Her bow was a bit closer to us than her stern, although it was still in the neighborhood of perpendicular. If I managed to let *Curlew* run off and sail down to leeward, who's to say that I would be able to reverse course enough to clear the ship's massive bow? I had to take the shorter angle and try to tack her. Either way there was clearly no time to think about it.

"Shit." I quickly reached for the main and jib sheets. This God damn boat's not going to sink, I thought to myself, not on my watch. I needed to balance the sails, get *Curlew* sailing without the help of the rudder. Having accomplished this, I could haul the main in tight and by throwing her out of balance, give her too much weather helm, causing her to round up and tack herself. The hitch in this whole theory was that in order to make this happen I had to gather a lot more speed, speed which headed me straight for the ship. Judging by the speedo, it wasn't going to happen. Because I had momentarily freed the sheets and lost all the air in the sails, *Curlew* had lost quite a bit of speed. She was making three knots through the water, not enough to tack. I nursed her along, and slowly it began to climb. Four... four point two... four point three... four point seven... four point three knots.

"God Damn it!" I stole a quick glance at Paul, who was still looking about a bit vacantly. "Jump in here anytime, my friend." Pushing Paul aside I looked at the wind instrument, we had ten knots of breeze and it was dropping fast. The ship was creating a huge wind block and we were clearly sailing into its lee.

With each passing second we were getting closer to the ship. For some very unexplainable reason, Paul was no part of the solution. He sat and looked about curiously.

We now had five knots of speed over the bottom. In front of us the ship was a huge towering wall of black, blanking out all but the stars directly above us. We were close enough that I could see the glow of her red navigation lights in her unmanned bridge. We weren't twenty yards from her now. Not only could I hear but I could feel the throbbing of her engines inside my stomach.

Thinking maybe something would happen if we could use the engine and throw it into reverse I half pushed Paul and bellowed, "Get below and start the engine!"

Slowly and methodically he responded and went below, not to start the engine but to climb back into his bunk. We were down to eight knots of air and the boat speed had dropped to four point five. I looked back up at our bow. I could have thrown a dry sponge at the ship and hit it with no problem. Now or never.

Not knowing if it would work, I quickly hauled in the main, all but twisting it into a U shape. *Curlew* answered far sooner than I had expected and began to head up. With the momentum of her four and a half knots she painfully rounded up into the swell, sat there head to wind for a second or two and then, sailing a course parallel to the massive side of the ship, gently headed onto a course a little west of due north. There wasn't twenty feet between us and the black structure which loomed eighty feet straight up. Around the ship's waterline there was a pale green glow of phosphorus as it was pushed along the rough course of barnacles. Great rust streaks ran down her sides. Including the two hurricanes, this had been far closer and far more terrifying than anything I had ever sailed through.

I had not had sufficient time to prepare the boat below, so when *Curlew* tacked over, all matter of things that lived on what was once the low side, found themselves on the high side, only to have gravity invite them back down to the low side. This included Paul. Once again his head appeared in the companionway, he was apparently back to normal. "What the hell are you doing?" he asked with some alarm.

Words absolutely failed me. We stared at one another for what seemed to be minutes. I was shocked to find the measure of my fear; when I tried to speak I couldn't for fear of crying, such was the lump in my throat. I tried to gather my thoughts and my senses around me. I had never been gripped by such immediate and all consuming terror.

"Wow. You see that?" Paul casually asked, looking off our stern at the ship which was now becoming smaller and smaller.

Finding I still couldn't speak, I simply nodded, trying not to cry from fear.

Paul sat at the companionway and looked about in total innocence. "Christ, I've been having some weird dreams."

Right now I was none too crazy about my reality. For a moment the thought of miraculous timing ran through my head; what if it had taken me a minute longer to find my Walkman, or if the batteries had needed changing. Made the floating container look like child's play.

Waiting a moment or two, I decided to test my legs and tried to stand. Underneath my gear I was soaking wet. I was sitting in a puddle of sweat. Trying to clear the lump from my throat, I coughed a couple of times.

Paul looked about below. "Chris, it's a shit house down here. What've you been doing?"

Slowly *Curlew* began to sail head to wind.

With a combination of disbelief and betrayal I watched as our stainless wheel was now turning freely by itself. I grabbed it and settled down onto a steady course.

Again we looked at each other for a few seconds.

"What's wrong? You're sweating like a horse."

"I think we need to talk," I said.

As if none of the previous moments were anything out of the ordinary, Paul then announced that there were still a few more hours left in my watch, he was going to turn back in and try to get some more sleep.

As I tried to settle back underneath the dodger, I began to run through the events which had now left me in a state of near exhaustion. Looking about I realized that sometime during our near miss, the cloud cover had slightly broken up and allowed the moon and stars to add wonderfully welcome, if not momentarily, illumination to the sea around us. Tops of waves were cast with the moon's white light, allowing me to see some definition of the water we were passing through. The way the moon's reflection played across *Curlew's* deck cast strange and fantastic pale blue shadows. The wind had dropped sufficiently since the incident and as I gazed about, for once it was a comfort to see that the ocean's surface had settled down into a soft reflective sheen. We were now ghosting along, *Curlew's* hull hissing through the gentle swell which rose and fell before us. So bright were the stars now that, looking down to leeward, I could see their rippled reflections on the surface of the flexing dark Atlantic. As though they were hundreds of sets of eyes staring out at me from the great depths, they blinked and shifted, holding *Curlew's* easterly progress in their gaze. Erasing the scene before me, a large cloud cover passed in front of the moon once again. Quickly all about me fell into the black void of the Atlantic night.

Out of the darkness came a sudden explosion of ocean, a dolphin jumping. I was amazed that I still had any adrenaline left. I leaned back under the dodger and chuckled at the state of my raw nerves. Yet as I did I noticed that something was indeed strange. I stood and looked out into the darkness. Double-checking, I looked above me at the solid cloud cover -- no moon, no stars. Yet there they were in the water all about me, hundreds of small piercing lights which seemed to focus on and follow our track. What before looked like reflections of the stars above now appeared to be energies from below. Whether it was glowing phosphorus, small sea creatures or simple adrenaline depletion, I had the sickening feeling that *Curlew* was not alone and was being watched.

It was time to close up shop. Quickly I went below, slid the hatch cover shut and fired up the radar and spent the rest of my watch with eyes glued to the circular rings on the green screen watching for traffic, trying not to think that anything was watching us.

"I have no recollection of that. Are you sure I said 'screaming whales'?"

After our previous night's close-encounter-of-the-worst-kind, Paul and I had gone over every inch of the suspect steering gear. The only area we hadn't checked was the actual rudder itself and it was for this reason that I was now rigging a safety harness around Paul for his descent into the Atlantic. I had won the coin toss, so Paul had to don the wet suit and go over the side. Had I lost I would have insisted best two out of three, or five out of seven. I really hated swimming around in water that was three miles deep; all sorts of unseen things can nibble away at your toes, not to mention your courage.

"No doubt about it, you were actually pissed that I sailed through them."

Paul zipped up the front of the suit and then just stared at his feet for a bit. Out of respect for our friendship, I gently approached the subject of Paul's lack of response to the emergency. We had several thousand more miles to sail and an all-out screaming match filled with accusations and permanent vows would have seen an end to our future.

"I don't know what to tell you. Sorry I let you down."

"It's over. Now let's do the same with you."

The day was by no means conducive to going over the side, but as far as the Atlantic goes, it was about the best we were going to get. Besides this really wasn't a problem which could be put on the back burner. Since last night we had had no further problem with the steering gear but that didn't mean that the problem was behind us. A good-sized swell was making up from the south. A small chop of a foot or two ran across that, and the wind was out of the south, about five to ten knots. To hold her as steady as possible, we decided to heave to. So that *Curlew's* bow would be pushed down to leeward we had dropped the main and backed the jib. In order to counter this movement we turned the still working wheel all the way to port so that she would try to sail back up to weather. Basically she was slowly jogging in place. We had tied a spare halyard to the safety harness Paul was wearing. As he lowered himself over the side, I fed out the line.

"Did you do like Ulysses?" I asked just as he entered the water.

"What's that?"

"Did you do what Ulysses did, put wax in your ears? In case you hear the siren's song."

"He was lashed on deck, where it was warm."

I refused to feel guilty over a coin toss.

Rigged with only a snorkel, fins and mask, Paul quickly dove under *Curlew's* dancing hull, for hanging about the waterline of a boat which was bobbing along freely was inviting a smack on the head. *Curlew* had about a knot or two of speed, seemingly not much from where I sat but enough to drag him slowly through the water. Coming up to the surface every twenty seconds or so to get air, he would roll onto his back like an otter and try to keep his snorkel above sea level. Looking up at me he'd shrug his shoulders, indicating that so far all looked fine. Trying to keep a solid connection between us, I slowly played the line in and out. Winning the coin toss had afforded me the chance to sit high and dry and keep watch for sharks or traffic. I wasn't too worried about the ships, and sharks were pretty rare this far out, but I was trolling with live bait. We were all alone in a big and potentially hostile world. By sailing across the Atlantic, Paul and I were keeping it pretty close to the edge and I wouldn't have wanted it any other way. I am not a man intrigued by complex situations and the basic level of life which one faced out here was about as far as I wished to get involved.

I cursed the fact that I wasn't born a painter, for the day which was developing around us was remarkable. The deep blue of the cloud-specked sky above us was a smooth mirror image of the deep blue of the ocean and her fledgling whitecaps.

Trying to figure out repair scenarios for anything which Paul might find, I sat on the combing of the cockpit and watched the line as it snaked down into the cold depths. A burst of water from Paul's snorkel shot out in front of me.

"Duthing, absolutely duthing." Paul said nasally through the dive mask. "Dot a scratch." He spit out some seawater as he bobbed about. "Deed more slack." He spit again.

"Give her a good shake?" I asked.

"Yeah." A small wave broke over his head. "Gonna check again" Putting the snorkel back in his mouth, he took couple of breaths and dove under again.

Watching him submerge, I let his descent pull the line freely through my hand. I found myself taking stock of the friendship which Paul and I had shared for more years than I cared to count. By no means were we in touch and connected all that time, but in a world fraught with ambiguities and early obsolescence, it was a gift to know that a friendship such as ours could be established, go on hiatus for fifteen years and then start up again without missing a beat. Had I lost the coin toss of this morning there were very few others to whom I would entrust my safety. I found myself thinking how much better I would have felt were Paul and I connected by a thicker half-inch line and not the quarter-inch line that we were presently using. I was still angry about last night but it was trivial compared to my concern for his safety. Apart from when we were kids, we never really had spent any prolonged time together, certainly not in these quarters as tight as this. It was all an adjustment. I had to regard Paul's dreams as simply that, dreams. Nothing to be concerned about and something which could be resolved between him and a shrink.

Behind me an unexpected geyser of ocean and air found Paul quickly rising to the surface from under it. Frantically he pushed his mask atop his head. "Tell me you didn't hear that shit."

All bets were off. I quickly pulled the line in.

"Christ almighty!" He was swimming around the back of the bobbing stern and timed his ascent up the swim ladder with the rise and fall of *Curlew's* transom. There were no surplus motions. "I'm outta here."

My system wasn't ready for any more surprises after last night.

"Frigging cold." Paul shivered as he climbed back up the swim ladder into the cockpit. "You didn't hear it, did you?."

"Paul, I didn't hear a thing."

"God damn. Tell me I'm dreaming again," he mumbled. Paul looked up at me, gave a small snort and pulled at his nose. "Ah boy..."

"What?"

"I guess it's the dream. Sounded like whales or something screaming." From either the cold or the fright, he shivered. "Jesus. We got any brandy?" he asked as he headed below. Needless to say I was right on his heels. *Curlew* could tend to herself for a while.

"Paul, I didn't hear a thing, but you did, twice now. Talk to me."

Paul busied himself with a towel, rubbing at his wet hair. I gave him a few seconds.

I laughed . "I don't remember your hair having that much gray in it when you went over the side."

"This is weirder than science," he said. Rooting through the small booze locker he came up with a bottle of B&B, and knowing that our very absent owner would insist, lurched for it. He tore at the seal, twisted the cork put the bottle to his blue lips and slammed back a very indelicate shot. Again he shivered. "That, my friend, was no dream. It was loud, it was powerful, and I was right in the middle of it."

Taking a final shot, he winced, blew some fire and with no uncertainty slammed the cork back into the jug. It appeared that he was ready to discuss the screams that he had now heard twice. He described it as the cry one would imagine a whale would make were it to be hit by a fast moving and sharp keel.

I clung to what adrenaline I had left from the previous night's encounter. I wasn't willing to jump right into the swamp of fear along whose banks Paul now seemed to be gingerly walking.

"Whale songs?" I knew that it was a stupid thing to say as soon as I asked it.

Paul shook his head. "Humpies are your only singers. Rare around here. Far-fetched, but maybe."

Occasionally the humpback population of the Atlantic has been known to sing their haunting melodies in northern latitudes, but they tend to sing closer to their breeding grounds off of Bermuda, not this far north.

"No this wasn't humpbacks." Taking a slow deep breath, Paul found a new energy. "Okay, ready for this? I'll tell you what it was. Put on your bell bottoms and love beads, 'cause this is right out of the '60s, man, coming to you straight from the Generation of Love." This was vintage Paul. He tucked himself in behind the dinette. Elbows on table, he ran his fingers through wet hair. "For lack of any better description, what I heard sounded like echoes from centuries past." He folded his arms in front of him and stared down at the table. "Echoes of pain from whales long dead. Chris, this had depth, you know, like a sense of history."

I didn't know, but I had to say something, anything. "It doesn't seem like -- "

"And it wasn't just one, it was like a chorus, a chorus of pain and agony." From under his thick eyebrows he gave me a bit of a sheepish look, as if checking to see if I was with him on all of this.

"Your point being?" I asked sarcastically.

"My point being... God, I don't know."

There was no mistaking that Paul was genuinely shaken by what he had heard down there. I wasn't exactly sure just what he was talking about but it sounded as though when he was in the water checking the rudder post he had had some sort of repeat episode of his dream.

"Well, as the little girl said, things are getting curiouser and curiouser." I really didn't know what to say.

Paul reached for the towel and with his mind clearly

somewhere else started to rub slowly at his hair some more.

"Take a break," I said. "I'm going back up to get us underway."

Arriving on deck I found *Curlew* still hove-to and sitting very patiently to her sail combination. Nice to know that if we got hit with any tough weather she could take care of herself. After hoisting the main, bringing the jib over to the starboard side and getting us back us on course, I clambered up to the small pitching foredeck and found a comfortable place to sit and think.

We had come to a bit of a crossroads here. Since that day I first heard Colin Jasperson's voice on my answering machine things were anything but normal; an absent owner, a boat with a hidden history of work, our company's maiden transatlantic voyage beginning in darkness and on a Friday, strange dreams, schizophrenic gear which worked, didn't work, then worked again, and now screaming whales. Paul was not a man who fell into flights of imagination easily, and as far as I knew he didn't believe in a world full of flying saucers, leprechauns or Ouija boards, yet from where I was sitting it appeared as though we were beginning to find ourselves in just such a place. There was no question that a schedule such as the one we were keeping was bound to take its toll. Four hours of semi-sleep, four hours of work. It wasn't anything out of the ordinary but perhaps the pressures of trying to get away from Chester had taken more of our reserves than I had realized.

I looked back the length of the boat. *Curlew* was happy with the new sail combination and to have her freedom again. She was definitely starting to kick up her heels for England. Jib and main worked in perfect unison with one another, one giving her her needed lift, the other her power. The bold white expanse of sail cloth which made up our mainsail gently pumped each time she rose and fell, the belly of the sail pumping in and out, appearing to take in great full lungs of air as she charged ahead. No two ways about it, *Curlew* was a powerhouse of a boat. It was uncanny how you could feel the energy in her decks increase with each new change in wind velocity. She transferred this energy down to her waterline, which was pushing the Atlantic aside as one would if walking through a field of tall wheat. It was hard not to be anthropomorphic about the whole thing, but when you put your life into the hands of a collection of canvas, wood, wire and fiberglass it's hard not to start developing a trust, a definite like, if not the beginnings of a love. Like a good field dog, all she really wanted to do was please. I took hope that she too wasn't crazy about all this hopping back and forth through the looking glass.

I looked down at my watch. It was noon. Across the lurching deck I made my way aft and double checked the autopilot. So far it was minding its manners. I guess that I was starting to run out of steam for I was beginning to regard the thing as the one, if not the only, voice of reason aboard *Curlew* right now.

"Grab some rest, my watch," Paul said quietly from below.

As I went down to join him I took a final look at the behaving wheel. Just one of those things, I thought, just one of those crazy things.

Just as up on the foredeck, below I found that there was a most definite a new air about our little ship, one of serious intent and deep contemplation.

Paul was slowly stirring a freshly opened can of soup. Again his thoughts were far, far away.

I made my log entries and started to call it a day for the next four hours. "You still worried about it? Want to check it again?"

"Huh? No, I was just thinking. I'm sure it was a one-time deal."

Not really realizing how tired I was I all but fell into my bunk. At that moment a mother's womb couldn't have offered any more security than the comfort of my sleeping bag.

"Chris?"

"Make it quick."

"Supposing it wasn't whales. What if it was something else."

"Like what?" I really wanted to sleep but the tone of Paul's questions wouldn't let go.

"I don't know, just that... maybe … I mean how could it have been whales?"

"I have no idea. Later."

Curlew gently lifted and moved me forward ever closer to England. Above my head on deck the autopilot chirped away as it kept us on a true course. It's a shame the damn thing never sees what a good job it does, I thought, maybe better that it didn't. Who knows what was waiting for us up the road.

There are no rules in the Atlantic or any ocean for that matter. Man hasn't lived out here for thousands of years as he has on land. Here he hasn't explored, settled, cleared, built and muted the original voice of the ocean. She won't let him, that I know. Out here man never has, and never will have a hold, not that he wouldn't die trying.

As each new moment becomes old, all the rules and definitions of the neighborhood change. Nobody says, "Oh yeah, I sailed past that wave a few years ago." Every day and every minute she changes, taking her history with her, never to repeat or tell it twice in the same manner. Each new crossing, each new day spent at sea is by anyone's definition a virginal experience. Because of this we have nothing to which to compare our individual experiences -- new day, new breeze, new never-before-seen wave, new history. For all intents and purposes we and our little ship are the first explorers. Men have been sailing these waters for thousands of years, but they leave no road signs, no graffiti, no "Kilroy was here." When it comes to unexplained happenings and curious events, all bets are off, all rules of the game dropped. No squeaky doors to blame it on out here, no obvious answer to put your concerns at ease, no easily found deductions. How could it have been whales? Don't know. Out here, wanting to find an answer, wanting to get to the bottom of things, brings on a whole new connotation.

Falling off into sleep I realized that I'd never know the one precise reason which would explain why *Curlew* failed to answer her helm, any more than I could explain why Paul thought that he had heard whales screaming. It really didn't matter. We had a small boat to deliver across a big ocean and we were going to need all the rest we could get. Out here sleep was a precious commodity and I had already frittered away far too much of it. If

Dwyer/Barlow was going to stake its claim in the competitive world of yacht deliveries it was going to have to do it with or without screaming whales.

For the sake of my dwindling sanity, I prayed for the latter.

CHAPTER 19

"Oh, man, I hate this part."

As Paul was climbing into his foul weather gear, he was watching over my shoulder as E.T. lay dying by the stream. I had recently come off my 1200-1600 hours watch and was feeling very smug that for the next four hours I was going to be the one sitting below surrounded by the comforts of the diesel heat and he was going to be the one who got to sit outside in the North Atlantic downpour. I had decided to sacrifice my four hours of sleep and check out *Curlew's* video library if only so I would be able to say that, yeah, I watched a movie in the middle of the Atlantic. After rummaging through all of Jasperson's titles for a while I decided that *E.T.* was about the only one that wouldn't get me to thinking about how long it was going to be until I got a chance to pick up where I left off with Madeline, or didn't give me a real good case of the willies. Watching a National Geographic documentary on great storms wasn't quite the distraction I was looking for, nor for that matter was watching as the four convict girl's from hell spread their joy across the Midwest. So, small benign and loving creatures from outer space it was. Elliot had been searching for E.T. for the last few minutes and seeing that little extra terrestrial lying by the creek bed in the rain always tore me up.

"Save me some hot water," Paul said. "Later." He climbed up the companionway stairs, slid back the hatch cover and pushed his large foul-weather-geared body out into the cockpit.

During the night we had seen front associated lightning on the horizon and after a few end runs and broken field running, we managed to sail *Curlew* around most of the major activity, but avoiding the rains was another thing. We had been tracking the depression which was south of us and as expected it arrived to the west of us, more or less on schedule. The ensuing southerly winds put us on a great track for England, but we'd been in steady rain since its arrival. Great volumes of tropical air were being pumped up from down south, which made for remarkably heavy rains. On several occasions the ocean acquiesced and simply laid down under the weight of the downpour.

Paul and I had both settled into our watch schedules by now and we found that as our bodies acclimated to the abbreviated days, we were finding more energy to deal with the surroundings. Sailing shorthanded like we were had its obvious downsides, but when you compared it to carrying superfluous crew and their superfluous amount of noise and idiosyncrasies, I found it much better to do a little more work for a lot more peace. So far there hadn't been any more trouble with the steering gear and we were happy to find that *Curlew* was performing as advertised. Only as they can in the Atlantic, squalls and wind shifts came and went, but our small ship eased us through every tack and sail adjustment with the grace and strength for which she was designed.

In a few more days we were to be crossing the halfway mark. Although we hadn't the chance to sit and figure out an appropriate celebration yet, both Paul and I knew it was going to be a moment marked more by a crease in the chart than anything else.

"Checked the bilge?" Paul hollered down from the cockpit.

We had been noticing a small yet significant increase in the water which was finding its way into the boat, but after checking the stern tube and rudder post we assured ourselves that there was really noting to be concerned about. The fact that *Curlew* had a bit of a hidden history was something which we found hard to dismiss, but for now there was no point in fixing something that was clearly not broken. Double-checking the automatic function on the pump, I went to the electrical panel and flipped the switch. As hoped for it cycled dry.

"It's fine," I said. "I heard it pump out just as... just as..." What's wrong with this picture, I asked myself. Like one of those drawings they give you when you're a kid and among a kennel of dogs you have to find the one with three legs, I looked at the LCD numbers and dials which made up *Curlew's* navigation area in front of me. Something was amiss.

"You what?"

"Give me a minute," I said. I looked back at the panel again. Something odd had caught my eye, yet all in front of me now looked normal. The wind was south to south-west, fifteen knots apparent. Boat speed was a very healthy eight knots. Water temperature was fifty-eight degrees Fahrenheit. Plenty of amps in the batteries. Fuel fine. Holding tanks were thankfully empty. Water, fine.

"What?" Judging by he increase in the drumming on the cabin roof above my head, a new rain squall was arriving and Paul was having trouble hearing me.

"Nothing," I said somewhat absently. I was still looking over the readouts trying to figure out what I hadn't seen. Nothing. Whatever. "Bilge is fine, pumped a small amount this morning, no big thing."

"Probably the rain. I could use a mug of coffee," Paul hollered against the building rain.

I looked out the small port just above my head and saw that the latest squall was upon us. The waters were once again falling as the rain was coming down in sheets. And right behind it was the wind. *Curlew* heeled deeper over to port as the increase in pressure against her sails made her dig her rails a bit deeper into the Atlantic.

"Need any help up there?"

"Gonna give it five," Paul said.

So fickle are the Atlantic winds that at times it's more like day sailing on a lake. Simply because the wind shifts or builds in speed doesn't mean that the change is for real and that it's going to stick around. Wait five minutes and you could save yourself a whole lot of work.

Dealing with the new angle of heel, I got up off the nav settee to slide myself down to the galley area and damned if it didn't happened again. Just as I turned my back on them, something in the nav readouts caught my eye. It was an abnormal number which was there and then it wasn't. In the split second it took to focus back on the panel and run my eyes around it, everything looked normal. It was like one of those bad Saturday morning cartoons; every time I turned my back, the worm came out of the apple.

"How's that coffee?"

"On the back burner," I mumbled.

"How's that?" Paul asked as he slid back the hatch and poked his head below.

"Coffee's great. Now I'm the one who's losing his mind."

He laughed "Whale's singing four-part-harmony?"

"You seen any strange readings on the cockpit instruments?"

"No, just the usual. Pouring like hell though."

Bracing for any unexpected waves, I leaned against the galley sink and braced one foot up against the top of the small locker which was under the gimbaled stove. I struck a match and, timing it to the swing of the gas burners, I lit the stove. I knew full well that whatever it was that had caught my eye was right now, because I had my back to it, blinking away madly tring to get my attention. The worm taunting from the big red apple. Making more out of it than I'm sure was needed I whispered to Paul, "Don't be real obvious here, but when you get the chance, slowly look over at the nav instruments and tell me what you see."

Rearranging himself under the dodger, Paul took off his sou'wester hat, pulled a towel out of a pocket, mopped at his rain-spattered face and humored me.

"Wind, eighteen knots. Boat speed, seven five, seven six. Depth... now that's funny."

Bingo.

I was glad to hear that Paul was having a hard time committing to what he saw.

"Depth reads... depth reads..." He continued to stare for a few seconds, wiped at his eyes again and then leaned back out into the cockpit to check the instruments there against what we now had in the nav area. "No shit."

Paul laughed and read off the numbers from both displays. "Screwy stuff... sixty feet of water and closing... fifty-five feet...

nothing... fifty-two, fifty-two... fifty."

I had a few minutes until the water boiled so I pulled myself back up to the high side of the boat and wedged myself into the small seat in front of the nav panel. There it was, the number which moments earlier had been flirting with my sanity. Had we been anywhere else but mid-ocean I would have been extremely concerned. According to this small modern electronic miracle we were now sailing in forty-eight feet of water. Knowing that the answer laid not with me but most probably behind the panel, I slid back the small barrel bolts and lowered it down on its hinges. Mentally scratching my head for a few minutes, I checked fuses, connections, splices, grounds and leads. When in doubt, wiggle the wiring, which I did. Each time I performed one of these tests, Paul's observations from the repeater readout in the cockpit confirmed mine below; the readings didn't change, they told us we were now in forty feet of water. I lifted a floorboard to access the area where the transducer is situated in the hull. I traced the cable which goes from the transducer in the hull to the back of the instrument. Here again, nothing was suspect, not that continuous shallow readings would indicate that there was a problem with the cable. Getting down on all fours, I put my ear next to the transducer and was happy to hear the rhythmic clicks indicating that it too was healthy.

I buttoned everything back up and shrugged. "Weird, something to keep an eye on I guess. At least we have a few weeks to try and figure it out."

"Would've been better to have the thing turned off," Paul said as he buttoned up tighter against the rain.

He had a good point. Why it was on in the first place was strange but I guess our habits of sailing in coastal waters for the past summer had gotten the better of us.

"Whatever." I turned it off.

I got Paul his needed coffee. To help *Curlew* against the building breeze, Paul had tucked another reef in the main and I once again wedged myself between canvas cushions and watched as E.T. pointed to Elliot's chest and told him that he'd be "right here." Looking back toward the nav area I felt confident in leaving our small glitch alone for the next fourteen days and deal with it when we were closer to the coast. That was on the outside; my insides were telling me to flip the switch one more time and make sure that I had seen what I saw. I'm sorry to say that I listened to it. Both the main readout and the repeater in the cockpit said that we were now sailing in twenty feet of water.

Paul stuck his head below and laughed. "What happens when we run aground?"

"Get out and push. Mind if I turn it back off?"

"Pull the fuse on it as well."

I figured that it could have been a lot worse. If this glitch made up the small percentage of normal wear and tear which one experiences, we were not so bad off. That's what I told myself in any event.

The ship's clock chimed five times.

"It's 6:30, if you don't need anything I'm flaking out for a bit. Give me a call if you need me."

Bundled up against the driving rain, Paul raised his hand and gave me a small benediction of approval.

I climbed into my bunk, which was now on the high side of the boat. I listened as the rain hit the deck above me. Like being in a small cabin in the woods but only a tad bumpier. The chattering of the autopilot above me had by this time become a comforting sound, almost a third entity aboard *Curlew* to which we actually deferred at times, though I'm happy to say that we didn't go as far as some do and actually name the damn thing.

I was feeling every bit my father's son as I lay there stewing about the problem with the depth sounder. There really wasn't a problem. Delicate electronics have a habit of going on the fritz when constantly exposed to moist and at times downright soaking wet sea air. I worried and worked the situation to every extreme without coming up with a logical answer for the errant readings. Sleep wasn't long in having its way with me and I left it all far behind.

While traveling through the air between bunk and floor, my first thought was that I had grossly overslept and that after repeated attempts to wake me, Paul actually had to drag me out of my deep sleep. When I landed on the cabin sole my next thought was that I had been a bit too energetic in my dreams and had actually managed to toss myself out of bed. Not for a moment did it occur to me that the reason I now lay on the floor was because we had run aground with enough force that I had been bodily ejected from my bunk. Yet for the past ten minutes that was what Paul had been trying to tell me.

"I have no idea. You tell me." he said somewhat incredulously. "You tell me how we can run aground in the middle of the God damned ocean."

The rain continued to pour down around us as we both stood in the cockpit staring out into the darkness. Oddly the wind had died and we now found ourselves totally becalmed. The hissing of fresh water hitting salt was the only sound to be heard. Even with the lack of wind *Curlew* should have been standing straight up and down, she should have had some active motion to her. Yet she now lay at a severe angle on her side, occasionally bumping against what sure felt like the bottom to me. Searching for an answer as to why we were no longer moving, and afraid that I might actually see one, I cautiously played the beam of my flashlight out across the water. The white shaft of light cut through the sheets of rain, giving me no indication as to the cause of our predicament.

The incomprehensible was happening to us. *Curlew* had violently come to a stop and was no longer moving. She had come to rest upon something very large and solid.

"Gotta be a whale," I said as I pulled my foul weather gear around me tighter. "Couldn't be anything but."

"Look at the depth gauges."

By both accounts, the LCD readouts were telling us that we were in four feet of water... in the middle of the Atlantic.

Dumbfounded, we walked the perimeter of *Curlew's* decks looking over the side and down into the ocean, hoping to find some small hint as to an explanation. With each step that I took, I braced for the worst. Small gentle waves lapped at *Curlew's* hull as she remained firmly rooted in place. From what we could see there was no whale, just as there was no justifiable reason for our situation. Against the steady downpour, the slatting of the limp sails was the only sound to be heard. Each time *Curlew* moved, the sails would roll with a snap which echoed out into the black night around us.

"Let's get the sails down before they tear. Start the engine." I jumped back down into the cockpit to release the halyards.

"That's the other problem," Paul hollered against the torrent.

I stared at Paul in disbelief. "What other problem?"

"Starter's not getting any juice. We started to lose the breeze about an hour ago so I went to crank her up. Nothing, solenoids not even kicking. I was just about to check the amps when..." He laughed. "When we ran aground."

"When we ran aground," I mumbled to myself. God almighty, this couldn't be happening. "Look, we hit a whale and killed the fucker and it's jammed onto our keel and there's no breeze so that's why we're not moving. We are not aground." We both stared at the LCD readouts as they continued to contradict me. "This is nuts," I said as I looked about. I wiped the rain from my face. "All right, we're going to do this the old-fashioned way. We'll see just how much water we're in."

I opened a cockpit locker and pulled out a spare halyard. Leaning down into the companionway, I reached around to one of the galley lockers and pulled out a can of soup. Tying the line around the can with one end, I secured the bitter end to a deck cleat. Making two separate coils, I gave the whole mess a good heave off into the darkness. The sinking can took all 100 feet of the line as it snaked its way toward a bottom thousands of feet below us.

Paul dug down into the lazerette and came up with the boat hook. Twisting the tubes and extending them he lay down on the deck, leaned out through the lifelines and jammed the pole down into the water. He then went to the lowest part of the starboard deck and did it again. "Nothing," he said.

A slight swell from the south pushed at *Curlew's* hull. We both reached out and held tightly as she lurched forward a few feet. What we heard was not a pleasant sound, her fiberglass hull grinding on what sounded like rocks.

"Fine, now we're on the rocks. What the fuck is going on here?"

"Only one way to find out." Paul had dug into the lazerette and was already out of his gear and halfway into his wet suit. So heavy was the rain now that it was hard to breathe without getting a mouth full of water.

Keeping my head down, I pulled my hood far out over my face and yelled, "Are you nuts?"

With a sickening groan *Curlew* lurched again.

"I don't give a shit if we're sitting on a sub Chris, she's grinding on something and it's not soft."

I was having trouble trying to apply logic and common sense to the situation, which clearly defied both. Yet there we were leaning to starboard, and *Curlew's* hull was clearly starting to take a beating.

"Look, there're other ways of doing this, you don't need to go over."

Paul continued to dress.

"I think that we should wait until first light," I said.

From deep inside *Curlew* another groan and raw scraping resounded through her hull.

"We may not be here by first light."

Paul was making absolute sense, but I was concerned for his safety and every fiber in me refused to see his logic. By now he was sitting in the cockpit putting on his fins.

"I'm not exactly looking forward to going over, Chris, but we've gotta do something."

"Okay, how about this? We each get one end of a line, throw the loop of it over the bow and walk it back to the stern."

"Proving what?"

"Jesus, I don't know. Maybe if we're on the bottom it'd snag."

Curlew lurched again, sending a torrent of rain water down her starboard side.

Paul rigged the swim ladder over the transom. “If we were on soundings in the Caribbean and this happened, what would you do.”

He was right. If we ran up onto some uncharted reef in the islands I’d be over in a minute to try to asses the damage. It was apples and oranges, though, we weren’t in sparkling clear blue seventy degree water, we were in the mid-Atlantic, in the black of night and in the pouring rain, all factors which clearly added up to Paul’s staying aboard.

I reached for the port shroud as *Curlew* settled down even further to starboard. Paul and I locked eyes for a few seconds.

For the second time in as many days I found myself rigging up a harness and tether for Paul’s descent into the Atlantic. Neither of us had any idea of what he was going over the side to find, but we did know that *Curlew* was not designed to be dragged across what sounded like rocks or coral without eventually suffering irreparable damage.

“You don’t have to do this,” I said. “If it comes right down to it, we’ve got a life raft.”

“Just keep the line taught.” Paul climbed over the stern and started down the swim ladder. He paused for a second to adjust and prepare his mask. As he did we both gave a pathetic nervous laugh.

“I’ll have some hot coffee on your return.”

He didn’t answer but the look in his eyes made my throat tighten. The man was truly scared. With eyes wide he very deliberately climbed down the steps into the black water.

Trying to stall or give him a chance to reassess, I suggested that we flip a coin.

“This one’s on me,” he said. Around his wrist was looped an underwater flashlight which he now adjusted in his hand and turned on.

I wanted to give him some encouragement but found that I was at a complete loss for words.

“Don’t stick around for anything,” I said. “Take a look and get the hell out of there.”

Again *Curlew* shifted and dragged her hull forward a few

feet. The sickening screech echoed throughout the boat. Second thoughts began to take over.

"Paul, forget it. Until we know where to begin let's just wait until first light."

The rain continued to pour down and left small explosions of water where it hit the ocean. The line running out of my hands told me that Paul hadn't heard what I said and was now on his way to investigate the bottom.

I tried to follow his descent but could only see a foot or so of the line as it snaked its way down into the cloudy green water. Occasionally I could see the pale green sweep of his light.

Very gently *Curlew* was lifted and then dropped again onto what felt like rocks. From deep in her hull I heard a small snap as once again fiberglass and lead rasped its way across something solid and apparently very ragged. Bottom or not, my thoughts now were to try to keep Paul from getting caught under her hull as she continued to shift.

Holding securely to the shrouds, I leaned over *Curlew's* port side. The line attached to Paul's harness led straight into the depths. I recoiled suddenly as the surface and the rain in the air about me was illuminated by a blue white glow. Seconds later the thunder followed. Enough was simply enough. Trying to tell him that time was up, I gave a strong pull on Paul's safety tether. Two great minds sharing the same thought and all that, I saw Paul's snorkel break the surface. He pushed his mask up onto his forehead. He was actually laughing.

"Far as I can tell, the bottom's right where it's supposed to be, three thousand feet down."

"Then what the hell did we hit?"

"Nothing." Paul spat out some ocean as he treaded water.

"Then why are we on our ear?" I hollered over the downpour.

"We're not, not from where I sit. She's floating level."

"What the hell are you talking about?"

"Chris, I was just under her keel, she's floating free."

I looked at the very obvious scene around me. We were clearly aground and lying on our side. "You're crazy. She is not floating level."

Things were so far out of reason at this point that I too found that I had to laugh. Standing on a slanted deck in a torrential rain, listening to the sickening grating of fiberglass on rock, it didn't take much to tell that we had hit something, come to a stop and now were being impeded by it. Yet from the water, Paul was telling me that all was fine. I started to haul him in. "Time to come back through the looking glass Alice."

"Just want to check the rudder."

"Paul …"

Where Paul treaded water only seconds before, the ocean now swirled around over his head. As the line made its way aft, I looked for any indication of Paul's movement around *Curlew's* waterline. I jumped again as another bolt of lightning struck the surface perhaps a mile away. Getting down on my knees I leaned out over the lifelines, hoping to get a glimpse of my partner. As I watched the rain pour off of my rain hood and land on the surface, the water began to take on the strange dimension I had first noticed a few nights back. Before me I could clearly see the reflections of what seemed to be the stars. I became transfixed as I now realized that these lights weren't randomly scattered but clearly came in pairs, pulsating pairs coming from all directions, slowly converging on *Curlew's* hull. They seemed to meet along her waterline and then ran aft in Paul's direction. Making my way to the stern, I tugged at Paul's tether for all I was worth. Dumbfounded I watched as the groupings of lights arrived at the stern and started to swarm into a pulsating and deep cylindrical shape which extended down into the area where Paul was diving. Every fiber in my body told me that Paul had to get out of the water immediately. Not concerned about what I was doing to his shoulders, again I tugged with everything I had.

With a violent explosion the line was ripped back through my hands with such force that the speed of it tore my flesh. Quickly I took a few wraps around one of our cockpit winches. Another lightning bolt coursed through the night, illuminating everything for 100 yards. On the surface of the ocean I saw pockets of low-lying fog which were slowly moving in on

Curlew. As they swirled around me, the air became thick with a carrion scent, and I instinctively covered my mouth. The fog enshrouded every surface of *Curlew*, all but entombing her in its grotesque odor.

I put a handle in the winch and furiously started to grind the tether in. A sudden and powerful back force snapped the handle out of my hand and stung my wrist into numbness. As *Curlew* lurched again there was a new sound to be heard and not one that I was particularly pleased to acknowledge. From the great massive depths which supposedly lay beneath us I began to hear the sound that had pulled at Paul a few nights earlier. Trying to separate the soft screams from the steady downpour, I found that they built from below, vibrating the surface.

I took another wrap of Paul's tether around the winch and frantically wound it in again. With all my strength I gave a final powerful turn on the winch handle. My feet went from under me as I found that now there was simply no resistance on the drum. Taking a second to catch my breath and footing, I stood back and watched in horror as the handle snapped back and flew out of the socket where it sat securely not a second earlier. With the impossible sound of grating metal and twisting fiberglass, I stood in fixed fascination as the winch was slowly being pulled from the secure mount where it had been glassed into the deck. My eyes refused to believe what they saw. The winch was built to withstand thousands of pounds of pressure. A strength which I couldn't fathom was ripping out my only means of getting Paul back aboard.

Out of the fog an explosion of tortured, horrific sounds came from *Curlew's* stern. The screeching grew to nauseating proportions. I covered my ears with my hands and turned my body away from the sounds. I bent double and ended up on the cockpit sole trying to shield myself against that which I couldn't see. I was firmly in the grips of something which had absolutely no explanation yet total control.

Curlew lurched violently, this time backwards. Slowly, as though she had been pulled off a ledge, she straightened out and once again floated evenly on her lines.

And there it ended. In the blink of an eye, everything had changed, yet everything remained the same. *Curlew* was no longer on her ear, but was now standing straight up and down. The tortured screaming had stopped, the stench of carrion was gone and the red tint of the glowing depth gauge was again reading "1,000 +." The test alarm for the oil pressure in the engine was ringing, indicating that the key was turned on but not engaged. A feeling deep in the pit of my stomach was telling me that for the first time that night, we were in serious trouble. Trying to fight the building tunnel vision, I realized that my only sense of reality was still trailing off the stern, under the water. Hand over hand I continued to reel in Paul's tether. The faster that it came in the more nauseous I became; there was no movement on the end of it, simply dead weight.

Above the partial moon began to make itself known, casting its hue across what was left of the storm clouds as they scudded by overhead. The small pockets of mist were retreating and dissipating. The ringing of the engine alarm resounded across the water. My eyes were riveted to the ocean's surface. I stood glued to the deck. As I came toward the end of Paul's harness, a dark red mass slowly became visible through the water, a hulk of foul weather gear. Slowly the rest of Paul's lifeless body came to the surface. He was floating on his back. I watched with sickening disbelief as his trademark well groomed hair swirled around and over his face like so much seaweed. What I saw before me gave rise to no thoughts of rescue, mouth to mouth, or hot soup to warm a cold body. I had no sense of anything except death. Paul's mouth was ever so slightly opening and closing with each passing wave. The seawater made its way in and out of the lifeless opening with marked indifference. The webbing of his safety harness was twisted and frayed. I would have given anything short of and perhaps including my own life to have awoken from this nightmare, but the building breeze told me otherwise. I wasn't dreaming.

"You fucker… you God damned mother fucker!" I screamed at him. I found myself furious with Paul. He didn't need to take the second dive.

I hollered his name several times, but to no avail. The pale blue of his skin assured me that he wasn't going to answer. I began to shake, my whole being began to shake, for the first time in many years I fell into an uncontrollable fit of tears. I sat on deck alone, truly alone. The soft bumping on the transom nagged at me. I was going to have to do something with Paul's body. I leaned over the stern to try to figure out what was to be done. Paul was now floating on his stomach. Once more I tugged at his tether, and the combination of my strength and a wave pushing underneath his body quickly rolled Paul back in my direction. Bathed by the faint illumination of the moon, Paul's still open eyes settled on me as though I were the cause of his demise. I stumbled backward, tripping over the tangle of lines which lay about the cockpit. Half-kicking and half-falling, I landed hard against the companionway opening.

The pressure and fear of the growing isolation was beginning to numb not only my body but my mind as well. I crawled aft, continuously searching the horizon, for what I had no idea. My eyes refused to accept the facts that I was now alone and Paul was dead. A wave of grief slammed my body into awareness that the ocean had claimed another passerby, one who dared to cross her vast watery plains. Grief followed my nausea and rage. Not caring where *Curlew* wanted to take me or what further plans she and Mother Ocean had for me, I watched the water pass by *Curlew's* hull, taking me further and further away from any sense of sanity. With a determined effort I winched what remained of Paul back onto deck.

And there we were, there we sat. My closest and oldest friend dead for reasons I couldn't begin to understand.

The practicality of the situation began to make itself known. After digging through the sail locker for something suitable, I wrapped the cold form of the man I once knew with a sail and secured his hulk securely across the small stern deck. For reasons obvious this situation would be temporary at best, for we had hundreds of more miles to go.

I slowly began to gain an idea of what was to happen but was lost as to why it had to happened. I went over the scenario again and again. I played out every possible explanation as to what had happened and what I was hoping to find. Spending my first night alone at sea was as macabre as it was devastating. Voices which were never there and shadows cast from the moon created characters who strolled and dodged their way down *Curlew's* damp decks. My fatigue began to raise its voice and my mind answered its call. For one brief second, my friend Paul sat beside me in the dark, grinning at the close call he'd just had. The spray of a tossed wave dissipated the sight and my hopes. Night and grief took their toll. As sleep overtook me, I rolled back and forth lazily on the aft deck, not caring if I was strapped in or not. Paul was dead and at this point the option of living was not one with which I was necessarily concerned.

CHAPTER 20

Curlew's roll awoke me, reminding me that it was all true. I prayed that it was quick and painless and that, as so many who had nearly drowned have said before, a wave of serenity and peace swept over my friend.

Judging by the sun I had slept the better part of the day away. *Curlew* lay in a shambles all about me. At some point I had dropped all her sails. Lines and gear lay about my feet in a maze of confusion, and the auto helm slowly rolled back and forth below my feet, mocking my fear and grief. Paul's shrouded body lay where it had all through the long night.

From below the static and screech of the SSB reminded me that calls had to be made and that my grief had to be shared. Paul's death had to be announced and whatever authorities needed to be advised had to learn the facts. Family members had to be notified and I had to make some sort of sense out of the past few days. Going over the facts again and again I realized that the incidents which led up to this moment were bordering on fantastical. I had to begin somewhere.

The high seas operator caught Madeline at home. Saying that it was good to hear her voice was an understatement; trying to break the tragic news was nothing short of impossible.

"Chris, tell me, what's the problem? Are you guys getting along okay?"

I wouldn't mind having a good go-around with Paul right about now, I thought to myself.

"No. I mean… oh Christ, Madeline, things are bad, really fucking bad."

"Chris?" The concern in her voice told me that my specific choice of words was an illegal offense in the eyes and ears of the FCC. One can get slapped with a hefty fine for use of any of the seven deadly words which are never to be uttered across the airwaves. I laughed.

"Let the fuckers come and get me." I said back.

"Chris, what's going on?

"Paul's dead," I said, still laughing, double absurdity. My announcement on the airwaves took its toll on Madeline, and it drove the reality further home for me. After several seconds she came back.

"What?"

"Paul is dead."

"How?"

What could I say? What words could I possibly find to explain? "He's gone. Swept over. I couldn't get him aboard in time" It was all so small and hollow.

"There haven't been any storms," she whispered. "What happened?"

That was the moment Madeline became more than just a friend. In spite of all her boisterous pretenses, despite all her tough facades, her true voice came out of the radio, speaking reams and volumes of support, love and compassion for the both of us -- one dead, one not knowing up from down. At that moment I felt wrapped securely in the woman's arms, across several thousand raw and open sea miles. Then it all fell apart. I hadn't cried with such uncontrolled fury since I was a child. It was perverse knowing that a small radio speaker was my only source of comfort and support.

"It's a mess. Nothing makes sense. Paul heard whales screaming, we almost collided with a container ship, *Curlew* wouldn't answer the helm. Nothing has been right since we left." My thoughts were jumbled and exaggerated but at least there was someone to talk to. "Madeline…"

"Listen, right now only one thing counts. Are you okay?"

"Yeah."

Madeline's voice was registering with me but at that moment I felt that I was anywhere but in the middle of the Atlantic. Slowly but doggedly, I was being gripped by a sense of tremendous doubt tempered with waning self confidence. I was scared and wanted to go home.

"I really don't know if I can take this. Paul's harness should have been checked, Paul should have been checked. This fucking boat has no cause to be out here. We rushed the whole God damned program…" It started to flood now and how disconcerting it was to not hear someone's energies, breath, coming back through the speaker at me. "God, I don't even know if you're still there."

"Chris, get rest. This isn't anything you can't handle. You and I are going to do this by the books, step by logical step." At this point Madeline's voice was that of an angel who was sent to pump faith and strength into a vessel going nowhere. "Step by step, Chris. Now listen to me, this is going to seem pretty hard, but you've got to do something for me."

"Step by step. What?"

"Do you still have the video camera I gave you?"

The least of my concerns. "Yeah, somewhere."

"Good. Get some food in your stomach, some rest and then start talking."

"To who?" I asked.

"Chris, you're going back to the world of TV. To the camera. Document everything, every little converstaion you and Paul had, every odd occurrence, no matter how trivial. Get it all down on tape.

I didn't like the direction this was heading. "Look, I've got to figure out what happened myself before I do anything with any camera. I'll write it up the best I can and get it all down on paper."

"Chris, say it to the camera, everything. You know as well as I do that there has to be an inquiry."

"He drowned, pure and simple."

"Chris, cover your ass, get it down while it's all still fresh, while you have some calm weather. Get shots of the wheel, show where it happened on the chart, anything, just cover your ass."

"Madeline, this call is costing a fortune and it's not getting me anywhere. I'll try to get an operator tomorrow and let you know what's happening. Just know that I'm fine and somehow this will all shake out… " I knew that any boat on this frequency anywhere in the world could hear our conversation. "It's best you keep this to yourself for a day or so. Give me some time to figure it out."

"Just get it on tape," she said. And as much as I wanted to cling to her every word, her every breath, we both signed off.

Madeline was right about a couple of things. A meal and some sleep were in order and it took what emotional strength I had left to keep myself below decks and tend to my own needs for a while. Paul was gone. There was absolutely nothing I could do about it. I had no options. I was more than halfway to England and turning around now was out of the question. I had to get the boat across and deal with Paul's death when I could. I had to get forecasts, *Curlew* had to get underway again, I needed food in my stomach. Once this was all taken care of, only then I could think about some sort of sleep schedule. For now I had to take care of *Curlew* so that she in turn could take care of me. If it was at all possible, I'd have to put Paul's death on hold, a haunting thought if there ever was one.

CHAPTER 21

The cry had gone out in the dark, cold void. They amassed their energies to devour and inhabit the freshly fallen flesh. The Dead Ones had been following and calling out to the two men on the small boat for days, hoping to gain a foothold toward an ascent back into the world from which they had fallen.

With their collective energies, they had lured the new man into their cold, silent world. Once in their element, he had quickly fallen to their strengths. Vying and lunging for his body, each of the Dead Ones fought to gain hold of his form with hopes that another living one would come and rescue the drowning man.

When the young woman herself had fallen, she had been tortured with the forced energies and entries of the Dead Ones, only none of her own kind came back for her. She and the entire crew of *Galatea* all sank to their frozen deaths. First the more powerful, the larger and the older of the evil ones raped her spirit, forcing themselves into her, caring little about the fresh horror with which she was struggling. Soon it became apparent that she had been left to drift, nobody was coming to her rescue, she would not deliver them. Slowly the weaker ones took their turn in the invasion of her vessel. Wracked and spasmodically jerked by the attacks, she was tossed as though in the jaws of a great denizen of the deep. No ship, no man was coming back. The great ship's keel slowly sank into the depths, then began its own demise. She wasn't alone in suffering this. Shipmates and new friends alike were falling prey to the evil and dark thrusting of the Dead Ones. Finally she too was left to drift with the underwater rivers, awaiting her own chance to be released.

The years passed. Katherine learned that if she were to get home she would have to fight for her soul's deliverance. Any time a new body fell from deck Katherine would swarm along with the rest, but time and again she would be beaten aside. This time was different. The hundred or so years had seen her gain in strength and resolve. Now there was a fresh determination which she knew when she was alive. Katherine desperately and savagely fought her way through the seething mass of Dead Ones, into the darkest of the fray, down against the freshly fallen flesh of the sailor. She had heard them calling and enticing him for days, they had all followed the slick shape of the small hull as it made its way across their waters. She too had kept vigil.

Now the girl felt that it was her turn and nothing was going to keep her from gaining her own spot in this latest drowned mortal. Savagely she fought as the other Dead Ones gouged and ripped their way toward their own hoped for deliverance. Katherine was not to be denied. Charged with hopes and dreams not delivered she reached down into the depths of her demonic strength and sunk her teeth-like energies into the still soft and firm flesh of the man trailing by a tether behind the small boat. For all she was worth she held and screeched at any other Dead One who dared come close. As the memories and hope of where she had come from and where she was fighting so to get to coursed through her, she gained inch by inch until he was hers. Katherine had fought and had won. With the lone grayness of her once shining soul, she held firmly to her prize. Yet as she saw and felt the Dead Ones slowly acquiesce, she realized that something was entirely wrong, the man was slowly sinking away from where he had come. The small rounded hull of the sailboat was floating higher and higher away from them. Katherine and Paul were now drifting in the wrong direction. The Atlantic's dark currents were slowly pulling them farther and farther away. And then the body reached the end of its tether. Then an unseen power began bringing Katherine and her charge back to the surface. It was in the hands of fate now. Katherine had spent all of her strength trying to get the man, and now deliverance was on its own agenda. Slowly they drifted back to the surface where for the first time in many lifetimes Katherine saw one as alive and active as she had once been. The clothes were different, the vessel was unrecognizable, but the life form was familiar and promising. Slowly and cumbersomely Katherine's spirit and Paul's body were dragged up out of the deep haunts of a world of cold terror. From inside of her new body, Katherine's spirit could once again feel the cold dry air play about the new flesh which she now inhabited. She could hear the sounds of the world above for the first time in a long time.

Through the dead man's eyes she watched as the other man lifted and groaned, screamed and cried as he tried to bring the remains back aboard the small, unfamiliar ship. She was now on deck, lying among a maze of ropes and objects unfamiliar. This new ship was nothing like her *Galatea* which fell from under her, it was a ship with only one man aboard. As she stared out of the dead man's eyes she knew that if the next process were to be successful, it had to happen soon. No measures were being taken to try and bring her dead host back to life. The tall blond man just sat and cried as he covered his face with his hands.

"God Damn it… Paul!" the living one screamed into the dead man's eyes.

Katherine was rocked by waves of conflicting emotions: hope, joy, sadness, and fear. She wanted to reach out to this devastated man and comfort him, but any strength which she had brought along with her from the depths now had to be used precisely. She knew that she had only one chance at it. The Dead Ones were falling away, back to the world of cold death and decay, and nothing was going to keep Katherine from staying above. This man who was called Paul was never to go back into the water. She had one more chance and it had to work.

CHAPTER 22

I can't say that I had become used to the fact that the dead body on the stern was once my best friend, but the dull ache of denial had served its purpose and given me the strength to get *Curlew* closer to her destination. I knew that something had to be done with Paul. Time was running out and I didn't want the memory of my friend to be saddened further by the hideous effects of time and nature. Sooner or later all things no longer living pass back to whence they came -- ashes to ashes, dust to dust. But some of the biological processes which they had to go through weren't what I wanted for Paul. I had decided that tonight, under the care and concern of a bright moon, I would have to say goodbye to my friend and let him depart in a way which he would have wanted.

The day was given over to a through checking of *Curlew*'s systems. The past few days had been anything if not extraordinary. We had lost our steering, gained it back, run aground and then were floated free, whales had screamed and my friend was no longer. I had been told about a leaking stern tube and at one point before the recent nightmare began, I had heard a definite and resounding crack from below the waterline. The chances of my going over the side to check were slim. Several times I had spoken with Madeline, and as per her suggestion I tried to put down on video tape as much as I could. I had set the camera up below, wedged against the saloon table, and squeezed myself in behind the nav area. I found that once I began to talk, the facts, as unbelievable as they were, spewed forth in no particular or logical order. What I had to say to the uncaring lens seemed as though it were a bizarre and macabre lost chapter out of Alice In Wonderland. Madeline was my only link to reality at this point and I found that she was working herself deeper and deeper into my daily wants and needs. The comfort of her voice coming from the SSB speaker eased any cares and worries which had managed to gain an upper hand. She was not only my link to reality, she allowed me to bypass the macabre scene around me and get in touch with reserves I knew existed but for which I never dared search. Madeline was showing me a side of her I never knew existed. At her urging and coaxing I came to grips with Paul's immediate needs. She was gentle in her suggestion that the time had come for a proper burial, a soft and caring suggestion which sent me into a flood of inconsolable tears. She gave me the strength not only to face this task but once again to take full responsibility for the fate and delivery of *Curlew*.

"There is no other person who he would have wanted to do this," she said. "This is the way he would have wanted it."

"I know, but it feels like a second death for him." I didn't want to see Paul's body start to suffer the disgraces of time, but sliding him over the side was something I wasn't able to face.

"You won't be alone, you know. I'm here. The power of what draws you out there in the first place is all around you."

"I know. That's what scares me. For the first time in my life I'm beginning to wonder about the motivations of the sea. I don't feel at home here anymore. Babe, it feels like I'm crashing a party."

"It's the same as it's always been, Chris. The sea shows mercy only when she wants to. You know your place there."

Madeline and I hadn't a chance to get to know one another before the night of the departure. Through the years we had traded the odd and pointed quip back and forth, but never did we find the chance to sit and compare philosophies and concerns. The woman who was on the other side of this tenuous radio connection was someone who had become very meaningful to me, someone whom I was growing more and more anxious to see again.

"I guess. Just talk to me, tell me about Chester's problems, tell me about yard expenses, tell me anything, just get me back on track here."

"Everything's as you left it. Ellie has stuck her head in a couple of times, and I've assured her that all continues to go well. I've left messages all over New England with Jasperson but so far no answer."

"I've got the feeling that he was hoping that his beloved *Curlew* would actually sink out here."

"The thought did cross my mind. I didn't have the nerve to check and see if he'd taken out any extra insurance on the boat."

As far-fetched as it sounded, there had to be some answer to my client's seeming lack of responsibility in helping to assure a safe delivery. Stranger things had happened.

"I'm going to take care of things tonight. Maybe with any luck another ten days and I'll be in Plymouth. With any luck."

I started to think about the situation and what long reaching problems could arise from it. Somebody somewhere was bound to hear the topic of our discussions and a dead body was not to be trifled with, especially seeing as I was the only witness. I could have called the Coast Guard then and there but it would have been a tricky situation trying to explain all the oddities which surrounded Paul's drowning. I figured that until I could make some sense out of the whole scenario, it was best to keep it all to ourselves.

" Look, let's continue to keep this low until I get in, okay?"

"Don't you think that it should be reported?"

"Absolutely, but the whole thing is so nuts I think that unless the authorities hear something that makes sense, they'd best not hear about it at all." A justifiable wave of paranoia swept over me as I thought about the fact that at that particular moment every radio for thousands of miles was tuned into my particular frequency. I wanted to end the whole converstaion and go hide in my bunk, not to mention the arms of the woman I was missing.

"Look, you have to promise me that no matter what, after tonight we're not to talk about it until England. None of this happened. Too many ears."

Madeline didn't seem to share my concerns but I did get her to agree that to make no mention of Paul's death.

"Just worry about yourself." After several seconds she came back in a slightly different tone. "Chris? Just one final thing?"

"Yeah?"

“What time are you going to do it?”

“I really hadn’t given it any thought. Any suggestions?”

“No, but I want to do it with you.”

“Synchronize watches sort of thing?”

“Ah, yeah.”

This woman was wonderful. Although her energies and concern were weeks away from me she had found a way to be next to me when I was going to need her the most, when I returned Paul’s body to the Atlantic. It had been years since I allowed myself to feel the warm rush of relief and compassion. How remarkable it was coming from a two inch by two inch speaker.

“Nothing would make me happier.” For the first time in days I actually felt up about something. I thought for a minute. “I’ll do it at one o’clock this morning, eleven your time. Set your watch to a WWV time tick, get a hold of a short-wave or single side band and we’ll both have the precise time from Greenwich.”

“Eleven o’clock. Are you going to… ah… read anything?”

I really hadn’t thought much about this. I took a deep breath. “No… just talk to him I guess.”

“Whatever you do I’m sure it will be wonderful. Know that I’m next to you. I guess we should go.”

God how I hated for her to leave me. Once the radio was turned off it would be like a massive vault door slamming me back into my fears and solitude.

“Yeah. I’ll call tomorrow.” We signed off in the usual manner and once again I was shaken by my paranoia; although it’s illegal to listen in on SSB conversations, somebody somewhere was getting an earful. I was amazed that nobody ever called back wondering what I was doing with a dead body who was once named Paul.

After getting off the radio with Madeline I felt a difference in my attitude for the first time since I saw Paul’s body surface. I felt that somehow everything was going to be all right and although many unanswerable questions were going to have to be stabbed at, I was going to come out of this with some modicum of sanity left. I wish that I could have felt that same optimism about my dead friend. Throughout our history together, Paul and I had from time to time discussed our own theories of God, the hereafter, angels, reincarnation, and simply the void of death, just as we had tried to figure out the reason for being here in the first place, all to no avail. Theories flew, assumptions were made and beliefs were stood by, but never did we define our own true belief with unerring confidence. Paul was an unbeliever. He held firmly to the theory that this shot at life was all that we had, that there was no ultimate grace or spirit which guided us and then brought us to our final reward. I, on the other hand, had my spiritual roots firmly planted in my strong Protestant upbringing and believed that there was solace to be found in the fact that we weren't alone in our struggles. It always came down to the same thing. I would ask him what he thought gave the ocean her strength, or what caused the sun to come up, or simply what was behind the life force of a budding flower. My friend would counter with his usual and pat response; there was no divine plan, there was no ultimate grace or spirit and that even if he were to concede and agree that there was, then what was behind wars, murders and starvation? If there was a divine spirit guiding us, why, when given a chance, would man sink to the lowest common denominator. We were on our own to tend for ourselves, he would say, and that was that. We both stood firm knowing that we were never going to need to put any of these thoughts into actual practice; we were never going to die. Tonight that was all to change. Paul would experience or already was experiencing firsthand that which we and millions of others had for centuries only guessed at or hoped for. That would be tonight, now was now and I made myself get grounded enough to give *Curlew* her promised once over.

We had been enjoying a fair and steady breeze out of the north and judging from the forecasts which I could gather, a stationary high was just west of us and the next few days were supposed to be more of the same. I got a fix from our GPS, updated my D.R., and plotted our position for the day. Using the dividers I noted that, were all to go well, we had just a little over a thousand miles to go. Since this last talk with Madeline I truly felt as though I could do it and promised myself that each day would have to stand alone. I couldn't afford to think about the total one thousand miles but had to concentrate on 150 miles at a shot. I just had to get through tonight.

Having made the rounds on deck, and trying not to think too much about the shrouded corpse on the stern, I assured myself that everything was fine for today. The lowering sun brought a slight chill with it and I headed below and started to think about dinner. Pausing in the companionway, I took stock of my plight and again found some strength in the fact that, through some very perverse circumstances, my best friend's departure was being left to my care. All about me the orange flames of the setting sun reflected off the wisps of clouds as they scudded overhead. The tips of the waves caught and threw back sparkling orange glints as great ocean flexed her broad shoulders. Another time, another day, I thought. For now I simply seek permission to cross, just as I seek permission to resign my friend into your care. Please, I begged as I stared out into the vastness of her arms, please take care of him.

Once again I found that day's end was bringing about a flood of sadness with it. My eyes filled as I started to talk aloud to anybody who would listen. "I didn't ask for this," I said, "I didn't make any brash claims, I only wanted to be out here where I love it. You've taken my friend. I can't argue with you, your power is so much greater than mine, but I can ask you. Please don't let this man suffer, please welcome him into your heart, let your own take care of him and love him. Maybe he's already gone." I looked at the lump of sail cloth. "But all I know is that after tonight he will truly be gone from my sight and I ask that you love him as I have."

Lighting a few lanterns against the dark of the Atlantic, I set about getting some soup on the stove. The burners rocked back and forth to the timing of the ocean's swells. I placed the contents on low. A long hollow silence followed as I watched the vegetables slop back and forth in their broth. Only the sound of the bilge pump cycling reminded me that I had one more item to check before I could lay down and catch a few minutes of rest.

Back out into the dark of the young night, I unscrewed the hatch cover in the cockpit sole and removed it to expose the engine, transmission and shaft. Shortly before we left Chester I bought a miner's type flashlight arraignment which you could wear as a headband. The small light at your forehead could free up both hands to work. Never did I think that I would not have an extra set of hands aboard. Playing the light out into the darkness, I focused the beam, and lying on my stomach on the cockpit sole, I slowly leaned down into the manhole, legs staying out on deck. I swung freely with *Curlew's* progress. How much louder the ocean was now that my head was only inches from where it passed beneath the hull. The space of the engine area amplified each slap of a wave as though it were the inside of a bass drum. The sounds from the constant chattering of the autohelm were bouncing all about the small dark area. Hanging there upside down as I was I could hear the occasional chirps from dolphins as they came from over the horizon to surf our bow wave. I was amazed that despite how much my entire life had changed in the past few days, everything else was absolutely the same. Perhaps the dolphins knew of my loss, I believed that the Atlantic definitely did, but judging by their seeming indifference, they cared little.

By turning my head, I aimed the beam of the light down onto the still shaft and ran my hand all along and under it. Feeling the small amount of expected moisture, I presumed that all was fine. What light there was from the moon played about the engine and its frame as *Curlew* bobbed and weaved her way east. My senses had become sharpened in the past few days, or perhaps I was simply exhausted, for never before had I felt so much a part of the world around me. I turned off the light strapped to my forehead. The sun's reflection off of the moon's surface gave me enough light to see without it.

We must have had a bowfull of dolphins by now for the squeaking which came up through the hull were almost deafening. I braced myself atop the engine and slowly and deliberately spun down out of the cockpit manhole and wedged myself down aft of the metal frame. A whole new world of sensations were opened to me here. As though my eyes had seen enough for one lifetime, I found my ears became more and more attuned to the world. Every few seconds a sharp and sudden crack only inches away announced the arrival of a new wave. It felt and sounded as though I were sitting on an underground river, for the sensation and sound of the water rushing past the hull surged through me. I don't remember when I first became aware of it, but the dolphins' calls had slowly turned into something which I had heard once before but couldn't place. The squeals were becoming long and drawn out and began to overlap one another, almost as though they were crying. Another sharp report inches from my ears made me grasp for a breath as the whole small compartment became charged with something with which I was very uncomfortable. I began to feel as though *Curlew* and I were being pulled along just a little faster than we were a few moments ago. The pale blue of the moon's shadow played about my body as I crouched there. Shadows came and went and the most mundane of engine parts began to take on fantastic shapes and characteristics. My back felt the heavy press of gravity as *Curlew* lurched to her starboard side. Some cold spray found its way down into my small cramped area. I was tired and the combination of strange sensations were beginning to get to me. Enough was enough, it was time to get out.

Suddenly my stomach lurched, not from my small boat's movement but from what I heard. Far, far away, over the horizon in the dark reaches of the cold black ocean, I heard the beginnings of what sounded like a whale's scream. I refused to believe that this was happening. Regardless how cold my blood was running, I knew that I was over-tired and badly needed rest.

With energy just this side of being frantic, I started to twist my legs under my body, and grabbing at each side of the cockpit above me I started to pull myself out of my tomb. Suddenly the whole compartment was bathed in total blackness, my hands released their grip and I fell back against the cold hull. My head jerked up to see what had become of my illuminating moon. As though someone had thrown a blanket across the opening, the ambient sound of the ocean in my ears was muffled and shut off, and a final blackness surrounded me.

I lay back against the inside of the cold damp hull and recoiled in horrific disbelief. It was now much closer and more immediate. Inches from my ears I heard what was unmistakably a whale's scream, followed by another. Tortured and pathetic screams echoed all through my dark hole. Another wave shook *Curlew's* hull. Another scream. Above me something slammed against the deck.

"Jesus Christ!" I shouted as I struggled against the night.

It sounded as though something were being dragged through sand not three inches above my head.

My nerves were shot. I lay curled in a tight ball. I had lost any grip which I had previously fooled myself into thinking I had. I had no more strength. From above me I could feel it now, I was being watched. Trying to resist, trying to will all of it away, I lost the battle of the nerves. I glanced up toward the hatch opening.

With a prosaic politeness the black form in the darkness said, "Your soup is burning."

I passed out.

CHAPTER 23

"Welcome back to the land of the living."

I stared in total and abject disbelief.

"Thought we'd lost you for a minute."

My eyes slowly moved about in fascinated horror. As they say down south, I didn't know whether to shit or wind my watch. I was aboard *Curlew,* I was lying on the starboard settee and my name was Chris Barlow. Those three facts were the sum total of all that I knew.

"Think you can get some of this soup down? The other batch was pretty burned so I put on some more. Hope cream of mushroom is okay."

In any other place, any other circumstance, any other lifetime I would have to recognize that the man speaking those words and cooking my soup was none other than Paul Dwyer, but obviously that wasn't a fact that I could rely upon right now so I figured that it was best to not try to make sense out of any of this. I would sit back and watch it unfold like a bad movie gone bad.

Paul returned to work at the stove. "You okay?"

"Am I okay?" Where was I to begin? Not wanting to bring any undue alarm to the situation I answered slowly and deliberately. "I'm fine. And yourself?"

"Never felt better." he said.

Well, isn't that spiffy, I thought.

"Chris, you're acting weird," Paul said as he placed the mug of soup down on the dinette in front of me. "Here, try some of this."

Why not, why the hell not, I thought to myself as I sat up and faced the dinette. Trying not to take my eyes off of Paul my right hand blindly groped around the small teak table for a spoon.

"I took a peek at the chart and from my reckoning we have a little less than a thousand miles to go. Pretty excited about that, I can tell you."

Now, for some reason, I didn't want to look at Paul at all. This was obviously a bad dream which was going to get out of control any minute, and I didn't want to see my friend's face turn into whatever it was that my subconscious was going to turn it into. "Yup, about a thousand more." I stared down at the table and drank my soup. It was bound to happen. The past week had clearly taken its toll on me and my dreams were starting to reflect the horror which I had been through.

"Getting you out of that small compartment was no easy task, I checked your head and there don't seem to be any bumps. What in God's name were you doing down there in the first place?"

"Checking the stuffing box," I said, not looking up.

"The stuffing box," Paul said as though speaking from a faraway dream. "And this stuffing box is fine?"

"Yeah, the stuffing box is just fine." My reactions to the whole seen were strange and varied. Under the circumstances I managed to forgive myself. I wanted to look at Paul, I didn't want to look at him, I wanted to get up and run, I wanted to stay put and get my brain to settle, I wanted to get up and hug him, I wanted to get as far away from that boat as fast as possible. I bolted down my soup. "I think I'd like to lie down for a bit."

"By all means. I'll wake you in four hours and see how you're feeling."

"By all means," I said.

Swinging myself against the lurching of our small ship, I made my way back to my bunk and pulled my sleeping bag over my head. If I had ever wanted sleep to knit the raveled sleeve of care, it was now. My dead friend Paul was not two feet away from me nattering around the galley acting as though he didn't have a care in the world and not like a man freshly drowned. Fantastical thoughts slowly pulled me back into the land of the unconscious. Dreams abounded in my mind, yet none more surreal and fantastical as the one I was now living.

From time to time I awoke, only to turn over in my sleeping bag and listen to the shuffling of Paul's feet out on deck. I had to deal with this somehow. Perhaps a good rest would give me the strength to find the answer.

We both sat in the cockpit watching the sun set over our shoulders.

"You have no recollection of any of this?" I asked.

"None. But it sounds pretty damn intriguing, I can tell you that."

"The whale's screaming, running aground, drowning?"

"No, sorry." Paul smiled.

"Well, then we have a lot to talk about, you and me." I looked down at the cockpit sole and got a brief flash of optimism, optimism that I was going to be able to convince my friend that he was dead. The joy of Paul's return was clearly missing.

"What about that?" I asked as I kicked at the still damp sail which up to a short time ago was wrapped around this man's corpse.

Paul kicked at it as well, then turned and smiled. "What about it?"

I just didn't have the strength to look into his eyes. I was terrified what I was going to find. I knew that I wasn't the crazy one here and that everything that I remembered had actually happened. I knew as surely as I was watching the sun set that my friend had come back from the dead, I knew that we were now discussing something that was an absolute impossibility, and as surreal as it all appeared to be I had to get across to my friend that something unexplainable did indeed happen.

"Paul, look, what I'm about to tell you is going to sound really nuts and I'm asking you from the bottom of my heart to simply listen and see if any of it feels familiar, if any small part of it rings a bell." While I went into an elaborate account of the past few days, Paul gave me his undivided attention. Occasionally I would notice the beginnings of a smirk on his face, and I would then slow down in the telling of the tale, trying to warn him with my eyes and the inflection of my voice that I must finish and that his was to simply sit and listen and believe if at all possible. When I was through he just sat, staring out to sea.

"Paul, every word of this can be backed up. You have to trust me, this happened. For lack of a better explanation, you drowned."

Paul's silence indicated that indeed his mind was turning and that something I had said had registered. After several moments he turned to me and spoke.

"I'm really beat. If you've no objections, I'm going to take my fours hours now."

"Best that you do."

And with that, my friend who had just come back from the dead went below to sleep. I was scared as to what the night was going to bring. I had absolutely no frame of reference here and had to admit to myself that it was possible that I was the one in trouble. My mind knew no limits and held no rational boundaries; perhaps it was I who drowned. Nothing, absolutely nothing made any sense anymore. I had to believe in what I saw and not what I thought I saw. I had to trust that the sun would come up tomorrow, that I was proceeding east to England in a boat named *Curlew.* I had to believe that maybe I was by myself, maybe not, and that God was still in his heaven. I felt as though I was on very thin ice. I headed below hoping that the SSB held the answer.

In a minute I was patched through to Madeline. "Please, don't ask," I said, "just tell me what our conversations of the past few days have been about."

"What do you mean what they've been about," Madeline replied. "You, Paul."

"Specifically, what about Paul?"

"Well, what you guys are going through out there, the delivery."

God, get to the point, I thought, tell me what I have to hear. For fear that I was the crazy one, I wasn't going to tip my hand by putting words in her mouth.

"And that would be what?"

"Chris, what's the matter, is everything okay?"

"That's what I'm hoping to find out. Again, what has the

topic of our conversations been?"

"You and Paul and the trip."

Madeline was obviously holding fast to our pact not to discuss Paul's death over the airwaves, and as much as I admired her honesty, this was no time to be stalwart and true.

"Listen, I know what we said, but trust me, this is really important. Did the words drowning, or death get used in the same sentence as Paul's name?"

"I heard that!" Paul hollered from his bunk only seconds after I keyed the mike to answer Madeline.

"Thank you, thank you very much," I said to no one in particular.

There was no mistaking the appropriate alarm in Madeline's voice. "Chris, what's going on out there?"

This might be my way out. Perhaps I was becoming a bit paranoid about the whole thing, but I felt that were I to proudly boast over the airwaves that Paul was indeed alive, somebody out there in a position of authority might break in wanting to know why I thought he was dead in the first place.

"What? Did you hear something?" I asked.

"No, just concerned. Is everything fine, any new problems?"

"No, just a few little wrinkles in what has otherwise been a perfectly delightful crossing. So, what you are telling me is what exactly?"

"What I'm telling you is that I can't wait to see you again. You've been gone too long."

Both sides of my head were being squeezed. I had what I knew to be a dead man in the aft cabin and my only means of any possible explanation to the matter was playing by the rules and doing exactly as I had instructed her. Madeline was not about to corroborate my story of Paul's death and perhaps it was best that she didn't. When the facts were going to be presented I wanted them all to be in order and with absolutely no trace of any foul play. As it stood now, trying to explain to authorities via the airwaves that my friend of twenty-five years drowned because he was over the side checking out why we had run aground in the middle of the Atlantic was going to be hard to do, not to mention screaming whales and steering systems which were there and then not there and then there again. All of this was predicated on the fact that Paul had indeed actually drowned and that the man who was sleeping in the aft cabin was nothing more than a hitchhiker I had picked up along the way. I was once again beginning to come unraveled. I decided to seize the moment and get bold.

"I really think that I need to have you meet me in Plymouth. Ask Fee for the time off."

It took her too long to answer.

"Time off or not, I'll be there. I'm tired of chaining boats to docks."

To say that my spirits soared would be a massive understatement. "Are you serious?"

"You just tend to what you have to and let me get busy on this. Chris, this has been rough on everyone. I miss you. I promise you, when you land at the dock I'll be there to catch your line."

And with that we signed off.

"Is everything fine back home?" Paul asked from his bunk.

I had spent so much time dealing with Paul's death that every time he spoke completely unnerved me. "Just peachy." I said. "Just hunkey-funkey-dorey-peachy."

CHAPTER 24

According to the satellites orbiting above our heads, we only had another 180 miles to go before we were to get our first sight of land, the Scilly Isles, a small outcropping of islands off the southwest tip of England, off of Land's End itself.

The past five days aboard *Curlew* had been pretty straightforward and, dare I say, normal. Paul and I gingerly stepped around the great big white elephant which sat so prominently in the middle of the boat; I still maintained that he had drowned and that I was currently closing the English coast with an apparition. I wasn't entirely convinced that Paul wasn't going to disappear at any minute. His actions on the other hand, were in complete contrast. He acted as though nothing, absolutely nothing was out of the ordinary.

Madeline and I had talked a few more times on the radio and at five dollars a minute, the charges for our budding long distance love affair were going to be second only to my psychiatrist's bill. As many times as I went over the list of events in my mind, it always came out the same, yet regardless what I felt or what I remembered, the fact that Paul Dwyer was walking about our small boat was the only truth I needed to know. The nightmare seemed as though it happened months ago and in someone else's life, clearly not mine. I had been basking in denial for the past week and now that we were all but smelling the fresh green hills of the English countryside, the need for an explanation came knocking at my door.

Despite the strange company, *Curlew* was doing what she did best. We were quickly closing in on the English Channel and things had once again become a bit hectic aboard our small boat; daily we were picking up more and more shipping, which made our watches at night a bit more hectic. Container ships hundreds of feet long began to pass to the north and south of us. Coming in from or heading out into the North Atlantic, these massive floating city blocks of steel went blindly about their business. We had to start keeping our eyes open not only for fishing nets but for the small and usually unlit boats which set or trailed them astern. A middle of the night entanglement with an all but invisible net hanging just under the water's surface was not anything I was going to be able to deal with. All I needed was for one of us to have to go over the side to free the net from our prop or keel.

The beauty of nights with nothing but wall to wall stars and vast reaches of uninterrupted ocean had come to a close and once again our VHF radio had come back to life with chatter and talk from the comings and goings of local traffic, both English and French. Ship to ship, land bases calling their fishing fleets or the occasional small child trying out his latest prank on the airwaves.

Several days after the incident I began to notice that the bilge pump had been cycling more often and for longer spells. My concerns were backed up by an increase in the amount of water that was weeping its way out from under the stern tube. Upon closer inspection, I found that the glass wrapping around the shaft had to be getting weaker as the usual drip every ten seconds which was to be found coming off the shaft itself was now in the neighborhood of two to three drips a second. In order to give our batteries the charge they needed to give us enough electricity to get us through the day, it was necessary to run the engine for at least half an hour daily. To date we had only needed to actually use the engine for propulsion once or twice, so I felt pretty secure that the stresses which were being placed on the stern tube were minimal at best. I wasn't really happy about the fact that sooner or later the shaft was going to have to turn and heavy pressure would have to be placed on the supporting fiberglass around it. Were damage to happen to the shaft area it would be quite a large opening quite deep in the water, and trying to stem the resulting flood would be futile.

I sat in the cockpit staring at the beginnings of the English Channel and across the waters toward France, wondering what I was going to have to face or come to terms with once we were back on terra firma. Knowing that we had perhaps two more days was very bittersweet. The peace and inner stillness which one finds at sea was going to be shattered by having to find our way into a new and strange harbor, once again honoring channel markers and rights of way, locating the marina where we were to leave *Curlew*, clear customs and immigration, fill out health forms, secure funds in English pounds, and lastly -- and this one depended on whether Paul was here to stay or not -- perhaps give testimony at an inquest. Yet despite all of this, the anticipation of walking on solid ground again was something I couldn't overlook, as was a full eight hours sleep, a queen-sized bed, an hour long hot shower and seeing the woman whom I left back in Chester. I had to keep myself from starting to count the miles.

Autumn had stayed with us across the Atlantic, and for each day the sun continued to set a little earlier and lower, allowing the cool and damp air of the ocean quicker access to my bones. From my seat in the cockpit, I leaned below and yanked my heavy sweater from the nav bench.

"Very exciting, isn't it?" Paul asked as he wedged himself in beside me.

"What's that?" I asked as I slid the heavily oiled wool over my head. After almost four weeks at sea I was beginning to tire of my own smell.

"Being back in England and all."

We sat for a few more minutes thinking about what lay just over the horizon north and south of us. What Paul said finally registered with me.

"What did you say?"

"That it's was great to get back to England."

The feeling that my head was being squeezed in a vice was beginning to return. "You're excited to get back to England, is that what you said?"

"Yes," he said as he stared at me with a "what of it" expression. "I'm very excited to get back to England."

"Paul, if you remember back, one of the reasons that we took this trip was that you'd never been to England."

He didn't answer.

"Remember, we were in the final stages of debating about

the whole thing when you said that you had never been and I said that this would be a great chance to see the English countryside, or whatever it was that I thought would be cool for you to see." I was giving the whole incident far more attention and energy than it would normally have merited, but I had a lot hanging in the balance on this one and if I was ever going to gain a foothold on my life now was the time. "We were going back and forth about the decision to take the job and when I found out that you had never actually been here I said, 'That's it, we're doing it.' Remember that?"

As though he were trying to hear some distant tune, Paul's concentration was cast out across the water.

"Tell me when you've been to England," I said.

He turned to me and gave me a look I had seen only one other time, when his limp body was floating in the water at the end of his tether. The shock of his gaze ran from my heart to my toes. There was anger in Paul's eyes. "I was born here." After a few seconds he whispered, "I was born here." And with that he got up and went below.

I had to laugh, because right at that time if I had started to cry I don't think that I would have stopped. I knew that I wasn't going crazy, but clearly I was beginning to lose my mind. I took a quick inventory: we had run aground, Paul had drowned, we floated free, Paul came back to life. And now, despite the fact that one of the main reasons we took this job was the fact that Paul had never been to England, he just got through telling me that not only had he been there before but he was born there. I was being torn in two. On first blush there is absolutely nothing wrong with not knowing a fact about a friend, just as there is nothing wrong about forgetting conversations, but add this last fact up with the other events of our crossing and I'd have to say that once again, things were starting to fall apart. I found that I couldn't leave him alone. I followed Paul down into the main salon.

"You're saying that you were born in England?"

"Exactly."

"How old were you when you came to the U.S.?"

"Fifteen."

I had to sit down. Paul and I had met and began to play together as children when we were nine and ten years old. By the time his family moved away from Cooperville he was sixteen, and now he was telling me that he moved to the U.S. from England when he was fifteen. We had one maybe two more days and I simply didn't know if I was going too make it. I had to keep busy, I had to keep my mind away from the complexities which flew all around me. It seemed that at every turn something else was becoming unfastened and falling into the category of that which couldn't be explained.

The ship's clock struck eight bells. It was four in the afternoon and soon night was going to be falling. I felt about as comfortable with this fact as I did when I thought that my best friend lay dead on the stern. Just moments ago I was excited, exhilarated about making land-fall. Now I was resisting the upcoming night and held great fear for what it might bring. There was no hiding the fact that this last conversation raised great alarm with me and that I was reacting in a way that wasn't going to help anything, but once again it came down to Paul or me. Was he dead or alive, was I crazy or sane.

"Chris, it's eight bells. Why don't you flake out for a bit and I'll take the next watch."

Did I notice an air of condescension about my partner or was he simply relieving me?

One, maybe two more days.

"Chris, there's all sorts of water sloshing around in here. I'm not really sure what to do."

The little sleep that I had gotten wasn't enough, there's only so much that one nervous system can take. Although it sounded as though Paul's words were layered under several gallons of syrup, they found their mark and tore me from my sleep. I opened my eyes to find the boat in total darkness. Grabbing my flashlight from my sleeping bag, I quickly swung my feet over the leeboard of the bunk, only to hear them land on the cabin sole with a very distressing splash. I also noticed that *Curlew* was sailing very heavily on her ear, an indication that we were getting quite a strong breeze and perhaps had too much sail up. Funny thing was, I had absolutely no panic in my system left for this latest calamity. The ocean was clearly where it shouldn't have been and it needed to get back out to where it belonged, easy as that. No thoughts of sinking, no worries of collision, just the plain and simple fact that it was now wet were it should have been dry. I worked my way into the main cabin and flipped on a light.

"Well isn't this lovely," I said. Looking every bit the stranger in a strange land, Paul was standing in the middle of the main cabin with a complete lack of expression on his face. "Surprised to see that you're still here."

"Meaning?" he said

"Nothing. Have you checked the bilge pump?" I sat at the nav station and started checking the breakers behind the panel. None had tripped. "The bilge pump. Have you checked it?"

"No. Not really."

No, not really, I thought to myself as I tore up a floorboard. Like the guy whose car breaks down and the first thing he does is lift the hood, I didn't know what I'd expect to find, perhaps a note telling me the problem, cause and needed repair. I was pleased to see that I did have some semblance of an emergency reflex. The trip had clearly taken its toll and at that point I really didn't care about *Curlew's* future. We had a life raft aboard and by now must have been within twenty miles of the English coastline. The breeze was starting to freshen out of the northeast and if my recollections were correct, we were soon to face a flood tide, which was going to make for some very choppy seas, exactly what *Curlew* and her suspect stern tube didn't need.

"Start working the manual pump, I'll check the electric one."

Paul's reactions to this whole mess were anything but predictable. I was talking to someone I didn't know. He continued to star at me wide eyed.

I spelled it out deliberately and precisely. "Get the handle and start working the hand pump!"

A small helpless simile spread across his broad face, his eyes started to search the cabin for something. Seeing what they wanted he calmly walked past me and went straight up the companionway and out into the dark. Whatever.

"It's these damn shallow bilges," I yelled up to him. Moving the companionway stairs away from for the hatch, I exposed the front of the engine and, resting on the cabin sole in front of it, extended my arm down into the bilge area. Following the greasy rubber hose to its end I groped at the strainer and found exactly what I was hoping to find. Actually I would have been very happy had I not had the occasion to find anything at all. The strainer which sits in the deepest part of the bilge had done its job, perhaps a bit too well. Wrapped around it was the usual assortment of dirt, silt, and grease. The true culprit was a bit less forthcoming. I found a piece of material had been sucked up into it, successfully blocking anything from going past it, including seawater. Hand over hand I pulled the black hose out into the open and immediately started to dismantle the whole sticky mess.

"Plugged," I hollered up to Paul. Knowing that it was the cause of the problem and not the actual problem itself, I reached further past the engine front and started to feel for the belt on the small motor which was our bilge pump. The tips of my fingers immediately had the answer burned into them. The pump was still red hot, clearly telling me that she had burned out and not too long ago.

Paul still hadn't made any motions toward the manual pump. I stuck my head out the hatch. "Didn't you hear the motor cycling?" I asked. "Paul?"

With his back to me, Paul stood in the darkness, his hulk silhouetted against the night sky. Slowly he turned to me. From underneath his foul weather hood a small smile spread across his face, yet this was no smile of joy but more one of fear and acquiescence. His jaw was firmly set, but in his eyes I saw the sadness of a man feeling tremendous grief.

"Paul, talk to me. What's going on?"

"Not again. Not again." he said.

"What? What 'not again'?"

"I'm going to go home. This will not happen again."

“Paul, we’re both going to go home.”

He simply turned from me and continued to start up to the north.

“Paul…” I really should have been getting used to this by now, but I found that I stood in shock. The coldness playing about my feet reminded me of the problem at hand. I had no idea if the water was still rising or if what was sloshing around the cabin sole was simply a build up in too shallow bilges. I had to make a choice, Paul or the water. Paul could wait, the ocean couldn’t. For now I had to assume that I was with a complete stranger. I took a deep breath. “Paul, I promise you, you’re going to go home. Just give me a hand here.” I had to get him to start pumping while I, once again, pulled the manhole cover in the cockpit and checked the stern tube. We had a backup hand pump fitting in the aft end of the cockpit and I felt that it was probably best if Paul, whatever condition he was in, started working it from there. That way he could continue to keep an eye on the thin sliver of English coastline which was bordering us to the north. I pulled a handle for the pump out from behind a settee cushion.

Curlew was starting to buck into building head seas by this time and, the violent motion caused Paul to hold on to the weather lifeline with his right hand. “Here,” I said. “Start by putting this in the small hole in the plate by your feet… catch.”

I tossed the small metal shaft out toward his left. As I stood there, totally dumbfounded I found that once again, I couldn’t believe my eyes. Paul stood frozen in place as he watched the handle to the pump simply fly by his left side, out over the lifeline and into the English Channel. My mouth shot open for a very loud exclamation but absolutely nothing came out. The man who had sailed more than twenty thousand miles offshore, the man who had spent most of his earlier life living on boats, the very same man who had taught safety seminars to junior sailing classes made no effort to catch the handle but instead simply watched as our one means of getting the water out of the boat flew overboard. I guess that the expression on my face spoke volumes as immediately Paul’s body slumped into a posture of great apology.

"What in God's name...."

He slowly and remorsefully held up his left hand. Judging by the sudden and forceful pressure which was rapidly building in my chest and around my eyes, I knew that my world of reality was once again on its way out. He said nothing, he simply held it out for my inspection.

"What?" I said. "What are you showing me?" By the light of the main cabin flooding out into the night, I could see Paul's face begin to redden, his eyes were starting to fill. He was having a great difficulty speaking. Rising above the emotion building in his throat he tried to offer an explanation bordering on apology.

"It's my hand. But I can balance things on it," he said.

"I'm sure you can." I said softly. I knew the answer to my next question as soon as I asked it. "Any recollection of where the spare handles for the bilge pump are stowed?"

Paul continued to stare at me. My friend appeared to be in a state of great distress and humiliation. Yet until I found out the exact cause of the water aboard I couldn't stop to deal and cope, to coddle, to put any rational or plausible explanation into things. My thinking was anything but linear. Again I found that I truly didn't know if I was alive or dead, sane or certifiably nuts. The cabin full of water gave me something to focus on. "I'm sure you can," I muttered as I once again dropped to my knees to assess the situation. Our electric motor for the bilge pump was burned out, our handle for the manual pump just reached the bottom of the Channel and I really didn't have time to look for the spares.

Judging by the steep and sharp faces of current-against-wind waves which *Curlew* was starting to slam into, I imagined that her hull was beginning to flex quite a bit. We had a very strong current with us which gave us quite a good push toward our destination, which was all fine and good. What wasn't so fine and good was the fact that I could only imagine the amount of twisting and torquing her hull was undergoing. I had no idea how much more movement she could take around her stern tube without opening it up further. Desperate times called for scanty measures.

The engine aboard *Curlew* was a fresh water cooled diesel surrounded by a raw water jacket. Basically it used the coldness of the seawater to cool down the engine. A hose which was attached to a seacock in the hull sucked in the cold water from the sea, circulated around the fresh water pipes in the engine and then returned it to the sea via the exhaust. It was the intake hose which my hands were probing around for at that particular moment. To make sure that this intake never sucked up air instead of water, the manufacture placed it as far down into the bilge as possible. Lying on the sole with my arm extended down into the sump, the rising water was beginning to chill me to the bone. Finding the thru-hull, I closed the seacock, loosened the two hose clamps and pulled the heavy rubber tubing off. So far so good. What I had to do next didn't make me real happy, but as usual, appeared to be my only option. If I were to start up the engine I could hopefully get the intake hose to start sucking the water out of the bilge. Firing up the engine in a seaway such as we were in posed two problems. First, due to the excessive amount of time that *Curlew* was spending on her ear I was afraid that the engine wasn't going to be able to pump its oil around the needed parts, and no pumping meant no engine. Second, I was afraid that putting more pressure on the shaft would in turn put more pressure on the fiberglass around the stern tube, which, if my luck was continuing, was the cause of our problem. There really wasn't any choice in the matter. I fired up the engine and was happy to see that the hose immediately started to suck up the invading water.

"Keep an eye out." I hollered out to Paul. What Paul would do if he saw that we were on closing course with another boat was anybody's guess.

A fresh blast of air rolling down the Channel put *Curlew* further over on her ear. As I rolled down against the foot of the nav bench, my spirits were lifted as I saw how quickly the water in the bilge was being sucked out. That, I guess, was the good side to shallow bilges -- quick to fill, quick to empty. I shut down the engine, climbed back out into the cockpit and once again removed the manhole cover. I swung myself down into a position of hanging over the shaft, where I saw exactly what I didn't want to see. All around the area where the shaft exited the hull, the water was weeping in fairly quickly, at a rate that five days ago would have been alarming, but was now only a pain in the ass. We would obviously have to run the engine several more times before we made landfall, but how much more pounding the fiberglass could take was not something I had any inclination to guess at.

By now our bow was digging into dark green head seas and the resulting waves rolled aft across the deck before splitting around the cabin house roof. Bright patches of phosphorescence lit up the side decks as the water found its way back out into the sea. Paul continued to stand firmly planted on the weather rail. He was absolutely impervious to the conditions around him. The wind had blown back his hood. The spray which was being kicked up had plastered his hair down across his face. Occasionally with the back of his left hand, he would swipe at his eyes, trying to keep the salt from obscuring his view of the English coast. Nothing could have moved him from his spot. I climbed out of the engine compartment and started to head below. I had to brace my foot against the low side of the cockpit combing as the wind was beginning to overpower us. Suddenly I too found that I froze if not for just a minute. I was experiencing a sensation which I had been without for the past four weeks. All about me in the dark of the night the smells of England played about my senses. The aroma of freshly cut fields, the bittersweet tang of newly turned earth, occasionally a whiff of exhaust from a tractor or a car -- it was as though part of me was beginning to wake up and once awake was assured by old and familiar senses that something somewhere was as it should have been. A dousing of Channel water found its way over the dodger and onto the back of my neck and pulled me back to matters at hand.

"That was it," I said as I stood there. "The damn glass around the shaft has weakened." Looking at the night lit wind instruments I tried to get an indication of the intent of the new breeze. We clearly had too much sail up and with each new blast *Curlew's* teak port rail was pushed further under water.

“We should dump some of this canvas, we’re overpowered,” I shouted against the wind.

I didn’t expect Paul to be with me on this one. I don’t know where I expected him to be but had given up on getting any help from here on in. I found myself starting to get furious with him. He had completely removed himself from his surroundings and not only was leaving the safe deliverance of *Curlew* entirely up to me but was scaring the shit out of me to boot. My anger had me look at the events in an entirely different and very disturbing manner. I was starting to doubt my own role in the nightmare. Quickly I ran through it all again but now thought perhaps I was the villain, I was the scary one; Paul had indeed gone over the side where he had gotten into trouble. Yet for reasons totally alien to me, I must have panicked and dragged him out expecting him to be dead. I must have simply assumed that he had drowned and that was that. I was exhausted from the watch schedule and the pressures from the other unexplained problems. Perhaps Paul had suffered trauma while he was under, perhaps he had stopped breathing and had a small stroke, perhaps that would explain his claim of his useless left hand, I had no idea. But for now, that was the only plausible answer. I could settle for this; Paul never was dead in the first place, I panicked and I snapped, easy as that. I could buy into this theory for another day, maybe two. Until then though I had to deal with matters at hand. The wind gauge read that we now had thirty knots sustained. We needed to shorten sail. I wound in what I could of the headsail and tucked a reef in the main. *Curlew* didn’t lose any appreciable speed, but was riding the large chop far easier, less strain on her hull and rig. It was hard to work the boat and not let my fury rage at Paul. The sense of isolation which one normally feels during a passage of this type was now being brought to the forefront. I found myself becoming more and more angry as he stood his vigil on the weather rail searching for whatever it was that he needed.

“Jump in here anytime,” I said as I worked the boat.

Paul continued to stare out. *Curlew* bucked and once again I could see him favor his left hand as he tried to steady himself on the lifelines. I wound a bit more of the headsail in. Leaning out over the low side of the cockpit I trained my flashlight up and down the length of our jib, checking to see that she had enough power.

"I think we should hash this out, my friend."

"And what would that be?" he said.

"Good, you're still with me. Well, let's talk about that hand of your for starters." I didn't know if Paul's new disconectedness was the result of his almost drowning or if he was simply trying to get out of work. "What's with it? You were able to use it yesterday, it wasn't useless then."

"I can assure you that it was. When will we be in?"

"Soon, maybe."

He turned back toward the north and watched as the silhouette of England's hills started to make themselves more visible on the night's horizon.

"It's been so long," he said with growing excitement. "I'm about to pop."

"That's it. That's fucking it! Look, pal, you tell me what's going on and you tell me now. For the past week I haven't known if you're dead or alive. I've been sailing with a stranger. You haven't lifted a God damned finger around here, you're not the least bit concerned about what happened back there and I'll be God damned if I'm going to play this fucking game of yours any longer."

None of this seemed to be reaching Paul. Bracing my foot against the wheel stanchion I reached up and pulled Paul down onto the cockpit seat. He slammed hard against the wet teak, harder than I had anticipated but hard enough that I got his undivided attention.

"Talk to me!"

Paul's eyes dressed me up and down. "You are the very last person I would have expected this from. You, who claims to be my friend." He looked down at his left hand. "I told you that I could balance things on it, I could pull my share, but you're just like the rest. I didn't ask for this." Paul was filled with such sadness and rage. "Why don't you understand? What small matter does it make how a person looks, what they come into this world with. If we can't see the good and love in one another than we're no better off than those men are back there. You treat a man, me, like an animal and that's what you're going to get in return."

I had no idea what he was talking about or going through, but my stomach told me that now was no time to try and drag him back into some level of reality. "Paul, I'm sorry about things. I'm lost here and I need your help. I'm scared for you and for me. Let's just get *Curlew* in the docks and work this out when we have less distractions around us." The truth of the matter was that I was rocked down to my toes by Paul's tirade. His eyes and words spoke with such conviction that I feared to venture any farther. "Let's just get *Curlew* to the docks, okay?"

Again Paul stood, took his watch at the weather rail and searched the horizon. He took a few deep breaths and turned back to me. "I don't think that they know I'm coming."

I went below and got a GPS fix. Plotting our position I was happy to see that during the past hour or so, we had been pushed along nicely by the current, so much so that I felt it was safe to bear off and make a straight run for Plymouth Harbor. It was my hope that we could fetch her in one tack, and I was counting on the in-flooding tide to give us some extra northerly tracking. I was also hoping that we could get this whole episode over with as soon as possible, get the good ship *Curlew* and her crew tied securely to a dock. I was drained both physically and emotionally. Whatever Paul was going through, he needed attention, and I had no idea where to start.

I eased the sheets out and brought our charge off the wind. Immediately the pounding stopped and she was very happy riding up and over the sides of what the Channel now had to throw at us. Balancing her out I went below and plotted our final course. Twenty-nine more miles to sail. We had a healthy seven knots over the bottom and the northerly set was going to stand us well. As hard as it was to believe, this was the final leg. I called the night crew at the yard and advised them that we were going to be in around daybreak. As I talked I found that I was standing next to this person who was Chris Barlow; I was listening very intently to my VHF conversation with the yard and was in total disbelief that I was actually making arrangements to dock our small boat in England. The crossing was over, we had delivered as promised, had a few minor wrinkles to iron out, but aside from a slightly psychotic episode, we had quite a nice time of it. After twenty-eight days at sea we were just hours away from our destination. I pulled back the sleeve of my foul weather jacket and looked at my watch. The sun wasn't due to come up for another two hours but there was absolutely no way my body and mind were going to let me lie down for a brief nap. The adrenaline was coursing through my system, I couldn't sit for even a minute. Even Paul had a smile plastered to his face. Holding firmly to the weather lifeline he turned and beamed at me and in the dark of his eyes I finally began to see some recognition of the Paul of old. I had to believe that that the joy which was pouring out from under his monobrow was genuine and that he felt the same sense of accomplishment as I. Regardless his motivations, he too was a happy man. For the remaining stretch of sailing I rummaged through the boat finding such things as passports, instructions for entry procedures into England, contact numbers and the location of the yard where we were to dock *Curlew*.

Sailing further in toward the harbour, we started to feel the effect of the lee of the land. The northerly began to ease somewhat and the sharp green seas of just moments ago started to lie down. I found that my excitement of arrival was completely overriding any sense of patience I could muster. Throwing caution to the winds I started the engine, struck the sails and put her in gear. My sense of relief and accomplishment was suddenly thrown into overdrive. I found myself hollering in excitement.

The breeze was now off of our starboard beam. We entered Plymouth Harbor with the confidence and appearance of having just been out for a day sail. *Curlew* had stopped her bucking and now with the shaft turning full bore, I hadn't taken to the pump for the past few hours and could only imagine the water which was beginning to collect in the bilges. As we rounded the massive breakwater which keeps an unruly Channel out of a peaceful harbor, I felt like the great man who after sailing the six hundred miles in a Fastnet race of years ago in a damaged and severely leaking boat, uttered the famous words as he crossed the finish line in first place. Lighting a cigar he stood tall and gave the final order: "We won, boys. Let her sink" Due to all the pent-up frustration, rage and bewilderment, nothing would have made me happier. As I turned to talk to Paul, he quickly brushed past me and headed below.

"I'll need some help with the lines," I said.

No answer, not that I was expecting there to be one.

Rounding the inner breakwater I brought the boat around to starboard and entered what I hope was our marina. Looking for a place to land her at the dock reserved for "HMS Customs and Immigration" I gently glided Curlew towards an open space. I reveled in sights and sounds which I had only weeks ago been all to happy to go without for the rest of my days. Plymouth was just beginning to wake up and you could hear the low distant rumble of a city starting her chores. Trucks and busses, construction sights gearing up, day shifts replacing night. Up until then I hadn't realized just how much I had missed the sounds and smells of everyday life ashore, but at that moment I wouldn't have wanted to be anywhere else, except for fifteen feet ahead of me. Standing in the misty light of an English dawn and looking as though the morning dew had been delicately and purposefully placed in her blond hair, stood a woman who not only had talked me through a living nightmare but for the past 3,000 miles had held my heart with tender and loving care. Madeline had done as she had promised. There she stood. My pile jacket was tucked securely around her body, her arms outstretched in anticipation of catching either some dock lines or perhaps me. Try as I might, I couldn't find an appropriate snappy comment to break the silence. Even if I was as clever as I had always hoped to be and found just the right words to do the whole scene justice, I doubt very much if I could have spoken. Thank God she was who she was.

"I believe that this jacket belongs to you?" she said.

Very cautiously and deliberately I steered *Curlew* slowly into the waiting slip.

"Depends. Might have to take it off and check the name tag."

"Well, I would but tell you the truth after I got the call from the yard this morning I was in such a hurry to get down here," She pulled her collar out and looked down inside of the jacket. "I can't remember if I'm wearing anything under it or not."

Seconds later Madeline and I broke the first of many of England's laws, disregarding all rules about no one making contact with freshly arrived foreigners, boats and their crew. I climbed down off of *Curlew* and, wobbly legs notwithstanding, reached out and pulled Madeline into my arms. As we slowly rocked back and forth, nothing was said. Here was a woman who I had met only briefly, admired from afar, made contact with only moments before I was to sail across a major ocean and then subsequently, over the airwaves, started to get feelings for. I knew that her hair was going to smell as it should, like memories of home. Pressed tightly against each other as we were, her body made itself known through the multiple layers of clothing, I became a bit embarrassed that mine too was awkwardly beginning to make itself known.

"God, I was worried." She pulled herself back from my arms and looked into my face. Her grin couldn't have been any bigger than mine. "I swear, I turn my back for a minute…"

We both scurried about the dock setting *Curlew's* line and adjusting fenders.

"Dock office?" I asked.

"Up the ramp and to the left. I already contacted Customs and Immigrations." She pulled back to look about. "If I were you I'd get my 'Q' flag up, skipper."

I looked up at the starboard spreader and sure enough in all the excitement I'd forgotten to fly that small patch of yellow cloth which announced to the authorities that I had freshly entered their country and was requesting clearance.

"And you are aware that there will be no fraternizing with the locals while ashore awaiting clearance."

"None whatsoever," I said hopping back aboard.

"Are you okay with all of this?"

"Absolutely. I couldn't be finer."

Madeline reached out a gently touched my leg. "Chris, I am so sorry about Paul… how did the rest of the trip go?"

My stomach lurched. "Get ready for a shock." I said sheepishly. Just jump right in, I told myself, don't hold back, step right up and take your best god damn shot 'cause there ain't noway, nohow you're going to be able to prepare her for this one. "Well, maybe he'd best answer this one for himself."

Madeline's face was devoid of all expression.

"Let me call him up here."

She stood on the dock staring at me. I imagine that right about now I was starting to grow two heads, for that was the look I was receiving from her.

"Give me just a minute here," I said with a wink. "This won't be pretty." I headed below decks.

"I'm sure it won't," she muttered to herself.

"Paul, I'm going to need you topside for a bit," I said, climbing down into the main cabin. I noticed that for reasons all of his own, Paul had chosen that particular moment to retire to his bunk. "Customs will be here any minute." No reaction. "Paul, sorry to bother you, but we have to deal with Customs."

From the main salon I could see him curled up in his bunk. I pushed the small folding wooded door to the aft cabin aside. Reaching over I gave him a good shake. "Paul?" I realized that the pile of clothes which I was shaking wasn't going to wake up and answer me. I quickly turned around. The main cabin was as empty as it was seconds ago. I went forward through the head and into the sail locker. No Paul.

"Shit." Again I went aft. I tore his clothing and mattress off his bunk. No Paul.

I breathed a sigh of relief as I heard some chatter and laughter from outside on the docks. Through the hull I could hear that outside on the dock Madeline was now talking to who I thought was Paul and despite her calm and gentle tone, I was willing to bet that she had a head full of hornets. I started to laugh, a real good healthy laugh, not one of those "I'm so scared

I don't know what else to do" laughs, but a solid "Who gives a shit" laugh.

I climbed back out the companionway and into the cockpit. "Surprised, huh?" I asked with a grin.

"Understand that you had a bit of a crossing." said one of Her Majesty's Customs officers. He stepped aboard.

My eyes ran the length of the docks. Shit. No Paul. Just a man who represented those who were in the position to decide if I was sane, crazy, guilty of neglect, or perhaps even manslaughter. "Well, yes. No! Well, actually not."

The officer went below, sat at the dinette, looked about, sniffed and then opened his briefcase. He proceeded to take out forms, official stamps, pens and ledgers. "How many aboard?"

This was truly rich. I pursed my lips, blew some steam through them, and thought to myself, Might as well cart me off now, either way I'm screwed. If I lied and said one, then, if and when Paul returned, we were going to have a hell of a mess to straighten, if Paul was for real. Now, if I said that there were two aboard, well then, where's the second man? As awkward as it was going to be, I think that the second of these two unacceptable scenarios stood me more of a chance to keep my fat out of the fire.

"How many aboard? Two, yes, just the two of us."

"Well, that must have been quite a sail," he said as he started shuffling through his papers.

"You have no idea."

"Passports."

"Yes, here's mine and… " With arms and feet of lead I reached into the drawer which held all of the ships' papers. Where the hell was Paul? "And this would be his."

The man from Customs looked about the cabin. "Right. And just where would he be?"

"Ah, I'm not quite sure right now. I'm really not quite sure. I told him to stay put, but as you can see he isn't here." I offered with a pathetic smile as I too looked about.

The man who now held my immediate and far reaching future in his hands continued to look down and write. "Any weapons, plants, vegetables, animals, currency over five thousand dollars? And for what purpose is your visit?" He looked up.

"Ah, no, no, no, no, no and to drop *Curlew* off for her owner." I slid my papers across the table to him. "And then leave for home."

He shuffled through my papers, gave me a look as though he wanted to know where it was that I had hidden the twenty kilos of heroin, and continued to fill out the forms. Finally, with a flourish and a wave he stamped what was in need of stamping, folded what was once too long for his briefcase and packed everything away. He took his briefcase off the table and placed a business card in its place. "Right. This is all bit out of the ordinary, but if you could have Mr. Dwyer report to our offices as soon as he returns I would be most grateful. Enjoy your stay, Mr. Barlow. We are located two blocks east of town center. Tell Mr. Dwyer to ask for either myself or the officer of the day."

Madeline and I watched as the man who could have ended my life walked back up the ramp toward the marina office. It wasn't over yet. It felt as though Madeline and I were about to have our first misunderstanding. I could feel the heat from her stare of incredulity. I didn't dare make eye contact with her.

"I know what I told you, but Paul is not dead," I said still through a false smile as I watched the customs man walk away.

"Think we're going to need some breakfast and tea." Madeline stepped aboard and proceeded below. Looking about the cabin she took it all in, opened some ports for fresh air, started to tidy up but had a change of heart. "If Paul's not dead, where is he?"

And with that I started to go through the entire crossing, mile by mile. I omitted nothing, I spared no emotion in the telling of a story even I was having trouble believing. Throughout it all Madeline remained stoic, asked a few basic questions and produced a wonderful breakfast out of thin air.

"If what you say is true, we most definitely have a problem," she said. Pushing the dishes away to the other side of the dinette, she started to map things out for me. What she said made pure and logical sense. She pointed out that there was no indication that Paul was or had been aboard for the past few days. She had to assume that he was dead, as I had told her for two days that he had drowned. Remembering the grief and concern she heard during our talks over the airwaves, she could accept nothing except that Paul was indeed dead. And until I could prove otherwise, she had to believe that Paul had drowned and that I, very rightly so, was not only having some trouble dealing with it but was most probably exhausted and in major grief and denial.

I really had trouble keeping my temper and wits about me. How I wanted to pop, and rant and rave about how I asked for none of this, and why would I lie about something as dire as my best friend's death, and why would I put myself in jeopardy with the English authorities and lie to them as well. Despite every ounce of what was left of my mental fiber imploring me to do otherwise, I stood firm and resolute and told her that I knew it was impossible to understand, but none of it ever happened. None of it. Paul was alive and in terrible mental straits and I honestly had no idea where it was he nipped off to but I was not going to sleep until I found him.

Madeline sat quietly for several moments. She turned and rubbed my back with her hand. "Chris, I'm not doubting you, it's just that…." Abruptly she changed gears. "Chris, did you do as I asked?"

"Which was?"

"The tape, did you video tape any of what happened out there?"

My stomach fell through the floor for the umpteenth time in as many days. I had sat down in front of the camera and spilled my guts about Paul's drowning, yet since he had arrived back on the boat, I had never thought about playing it back.

"Yeah, I did." I was not ready to face that tape.

I reached in our electronic drawer and pulled out a set of red and white patch cords. "Video-out, audio-out," I said as I handed Madeline the ends to plug into the small yellow camera. I pulled the television out from its mount and started to hook up my own video-in and audio-in. It felt as though I was signing my own death warrant. Taking my time at getting things hooked up, I ran through the scenario of events in my mind over and over again. One possible but not very plausible explanation did come to mind: hallucinations. The annals of shorthanded sailing are filled with stories of singlehanded skippers seeing and hearing things which weren't necessarily there. In the 1960s, seeking relief from several days of being slammed by a typhoon, a French sailor took great pains to maneuver his small boat into a tropical atoll where he dropped his anchor and slept for two days. Upon awaking he went out onto deck to find his boat floating in the middle of the Pacific, anchor chain hanging straight up and down. Apparently there was no atoll at all, his subconscious had conjured one up so that he could get the needed sleep his conscious mind was keeping him from getting. Joshua Slocum, the first man to sail around the world singlehanded, took to his bunk with a raging fever only after a sailor from Columbus' flag ship the *Pinta* relieved him at the helm and assured him that he would man the boat while Slocum slept. By no means was I placing myself in the company of such noted adventurers, but I was starting to think that if the video tape showed what I thought was on it, mine was going to be a hallucination for the ages.

After securing the cables and placing a freshly charged battery in the camera, I pushed the small gray power button. The camera whirred to life as it automatically loaded the tape. I sat down on the starboard settee next to Madeleine as the television screen in front of us began to flicker with the verdict. I leaned forward, elbows on my knees, chin in upturned palms, not knowing if I was going to be afraid or relieved at what I was about to see.

It started.

"What you're looking at is the remains of my best friend, Paul Dwyer." A saddened and detached voice narrated the shaky scene. Laying amidships on the stern, wrapped in a sail, was a body. As the camera slowly panned the length of the corpse, it came to rest on Paul's bare feet, sticking out from the end of the hastily wrapped cloth. Judging by the pale blue color of the two objects, Paul was dead.

"Jesus Christ," I said. Madeline's hand rested on the back of my neck, fingers slowly massaging what were beyond exhausted muscles. I just turned and looked at her, speechless.

"Chris, it's okay," she said, rubbing my neck. "It's completely understandable. You're exhausted. He was your best friend. Now we know what we're dealing with."

I looked back at the screen. This time the scene was below in the main cabin, recording each carefully chosen word which was being spoken to the camera by a person I couldn't recognize. It was my voice that I was hearing, but the worn and haggard man who was speaking the words was someone I didn't know.

"My God, do I look that bad?"

Madeline ran her hand under my chin and held it firmly as one would do to reassure a disturbed child. "Chris, you need rest. We can deal with this later."

"It's like my brains being split in two. I know what I saw, and then I know what I saw. God, Madeline, I don't know what to believe anymore." While I kept looking at the screen and listening to the retelling of the death of my dearest friend, Madeline got up and started to slowly comb through some lockers. An anger of previously before unfelt dimensions began to well up inside of me. "He was here. I don't give a shit what this tape is saying, he was here!" I knew that I couldn't argue with the video tape, just as I couldn't argue with Madeline telling me that yes we did indeed have those gut-wrenching radio conversations for several days, but I knew what I knew. For the past week I wasn't sailing alone, I was sailing in the company of one Paul Dwyer. "Listen to me, he was here, he was a completely different Paul than when he went into the water, but he was here."

I was talking to Madeline's back while she was fixing something at the galley. She turned to me with a sheepish grin on her face and a tall plastic tumbler in her hands. In the sink behind her sat a freshly opened bottle of Jasperson's vodka, down by at least a quarter.

"I knew if I looked hard enough I'd find some. And the seal

wasn't even cracked so I guess we can rule that out."

"What's this, hemlock? Am I that crazy?"

"Just the opposite. You're wonderful, wonderful man. An exhausted man, but a wonderful man. Now drink it."

"What is it?" I asked as I took the tumbler from her hands.

"Good for what ails you. Now knock it back."

I did.

As I remember the fire started in my throat and lit a path like so much Napalm being shot through my system. It must have been shortly after my toes caught fire that I decided to strip out of my clothes, but why Madeline was also out of hers was a complete mystery. I would never have guessed that two people could fit in my small bunk but nonetheless, there we were. How unusually wonderful it was to be lying in my bunk on an even keel. In the dark *Curlew* rested very patiently in her slip. How very civilized things now appeared as I propped myself up on one elbow, not having to brace myself against any further assaults from the Atlantic. Yet all that paled by comparison to the beauty who lay curled up against my side.

"Hi." Madeline said through half-opened eyes. "You okay?"

"Yeah, I guess." Looking around I found that I was at a loss. "Ah, yeah. You okay?"

"Peachy."

I looked down. Our nudity was glaringly obvious. "Okay then. I miss anything?"

Madeline slowly worked her soft knee between mine. "You mean did I take advantage of you?"

My two legs were now the two outside halves of a Madeline thigh sandwich. "Yeah, I guess."

"Nope," Pulling in closer to me she started to kiss my chest, a sensation which I hadn't known in far too long, and most definitely not during the past month. "But that was then… now is now."

I felt a slight flush of embarresment as my body started to react purely independently of my brain.

"Why Mr. Barlow," she said softly with mock surprise.

"Why, Miss… " I gave a nervous laugh. "Madeline, I don't

know your last name."

Slowly the angel who was curled up in my arms began to release herself and started kissing her way down to the cause of my concern. "Shut up."

As far as I could figure out, we missed two dinners, two midnight snacks, and one breakfast, none of which could have made heaven any more heavenly.

CHAPTER 25

"Bloody stupid, that's what they are!" The passing horses of the hunt had thrown enough mud onto Derick Smeeton's wool walking pants to soak through the coarse material in a matter of seconds. Try as he might the tall fastidious man couldn't coax the wet Cornish earth from the cloth. "Honestly, Sam, there ought to be a law."

The small tarmac road which Samantha Southworth and her fiancé were hiking on had suffered the ravages of another round of the summer traffic. With typical English reserve, the town council took their time in addressing the fact that many off the small hedgerow-bordered lanes which laced throughout the countryside of Saltash were in a state of disrepair. Pockmarked by potholes several inches deep, the recent autumn rains had made swamps of the roads. If a horse's hoof managed to hit one just right and a hiker's timing was just wrong, the ensuing result would most predictably be along the lines of what the lanky young man was now dealing with.

"Bloody farmers!" With red cheeks ablaze, the displaced visitor from London threw the epithet to nowhere in particular. "Wouldn't last a day in a real city, I can tell you."

"Such a baby. Let me see." Setting her canvas camera bag aside she bent down, and like a mother tried to address a situation which echoed more class distinction than soiled clothing. Samantha examined the mess which the helpless man was making only worse. "No damage done, let's go."

"Sam…"

"It adds character. Now they don't look as though they're straight from your tailor's press."

"Ruined is what they are." Derick sniffed. "Simply ruined."

Paying no heed to the man's usual histrionics, Samantha continued walking down the lane toward the glen which she had been trying to picture ever since she last saw it. She never had a problem remembering the colors. If anything, they had lived and grown inside of her mind, becoming louder and more vibrant with each passing day. So many times she would try to get the images onto canvas and give life to the memory which lived in her mind's eye. A few weeks ago she knew that the time had come. No longer satisfied with near misses, she had done the seemingly impossible and talked her fiancé of two years into leaving the secure confines of a Knightsbridge existence and take a week's holiday at the coast. In the past few months, things had been bumpy and a bit distant between the two and Sam was hoping that away from the distractions of London they could get themselves back on track. The young girl's aunt had a small cottage near the seaside town and had said that her favorite niece was most welcome to make use of it. The cottage was primarily used as a getaway for the London based aunt and her paramour of long-standing and for the most part sat empty.

"Let somebody else watch your computer screen for a bit, you need to get some country air," Sam had said. Protesting that he could get all the country air he needed not forty-five minutes away, he held fast the idea that the financial team of Collins, Leavitt & Chesterwick would know if one of their minions went missing. Fact is nobody knew the last time that Messrs. Collins, Leavitt or Collins ever saw the trading room. One would be hard-pressed to find somebody who even knew if any of the three founding fathers were still alive. Finally entrusting the market trading to the others who where trying to claw their way from obscurity to relevance, Derick Smeeton acquiesced to the persistence of his betrothed..

"Oh, do hurry. I don't want to lose my light," she said, continuing down the lane. "I'll meet you there."

Trying to keep up with the girl's pace, Derick followed at a growing distance.

"You seem to have me confused with someone who actually knows his way about this grotty little town," he muttered to no one in particular.

Samantha had driven a hard bargain. No week in Plymouth, no introductions to her father's solicitor firm. Covington & Buhl represented some of the more successful financiers on the continent and the mere mention of career making portfolios was enough to make him weak at the knees. The first class reservations on the train out of Paddington had helped to soften the deal, yet Sam felt that if his attitude didn't change, what was to be a long tedious week would be made brutally short. But then he might as well have kissed away his meal ticket for getting out from behind the work station which he shared with so many other keen young men. And now this.

"Perfectly good pair of handmade Italians," he muttered as he tried to scrape the droppings of a passing horse from his shoe.

Smirking at the sight, Sam called back, "You look as though you're doing a one-legged moonwalk." Laughing, she quickened her pace. "Do hurry."

Watching as his fiancée's well fitting pair of hiking shorts made their way down the lane Derick had to admit to himself that despite the more obvious inconveniences, things could be far worse. Samantha was everything his family had hoped for and she managed to fill quite a few of the young man's needs as well. Never had a flannel shirt tied at the waist complemented a pair of canvas shorts so well.

"Oh please do hurry, Derick… this is it." She was pacing back and forth in front of an opening in the thick undergrowth. Last summer while on holiday with her cousin Thomasin, Samantha had come across what the locals had referred to as The Black House, a crumbling stone foundation existing from a time no one could quite pinpoint. The surrounding forest had claimed the two remaining sides of the intimate remains of the stone house, but when the entrapping vines had taken a hold, or why whoever had lived their had decided to give up their fight against the encroaching forest, was not known. The usual lore claimed that the area was haunted, but the more practical knew it as a spot where the occasional young men would gathered to drink and wax poetic about what they would do to certain girls if they were only bold enough to bring them along. That was all secondary to what Samantha and Thomasin had felt though. Both on holiday from the city, the girls needed a place to unwind, to take in the country and discover nature. Stealthily an autumn gale had taken the short run up from the Channel and dropped on the girls with unexpected ferocity. Laughing and dashing from the country lane into the woods, they found respite from the warm driving rains among the crumbling walls of the long dead homestead. The boisterous winds shouldered their way through the dark forest, scattering the freshly laid carpet of leaves. Taking refuge against the one remaining wall, Samantha and her younger cousin Thomasin braced their backs against the cold and perpetually damp stone work as they watched the wind-driven rain showers coursing horizontally over their heads. Being stuck there just long enough to make an adventure but not so long as not to appreciate the storm-clearing rainbows, Samantha's attention was riveted by the light forms and shadows from the lowering winter sun as it played through the trees around the foundation. The muted colors of the dying fall foliage were warmed and accentuated by the slanted afternoon rays. Standing up and walking about the ruins, Samantha cursed the fact that she had left her paints in her flat in London. Framing the whole scene was the horizontal border of red brambles which marked the serpentine hedgerows just up from the stonework's.

Samantha had promised herself that she would be back to try to photograph what had been so brilliantly displayed before her. She knew that the light would never last as long as she needed to paint it, but if she was able to capture on film the subtleties of beauty which played all about her, she would have all winter to work on it.

"What is it?" Derick asked as he arrived where the girl stood.

"It's in there. Oh, this is brilliant, you're going to love it." She started headlong into the deep undergrowth.

"What? In there? Sam, it's all muck and mire."

"Then take your shoes off and quite your wingeing."

Taking a few moments to digest the suggestion Derick felt if far better to ruin his hand-made Italian shoes than step on something which might slide between his toes and perhaps rise up and kill him. "Fine." He followed the young woman.

It actually wasn't as bad as he thought it would be. The carpeted forest floor was firm. Hopping over the remains of a fallen stone wall, Derick had to admit to himself that despite the inconvenience of not having proper hiking attire, what Samantha was leading him toward wasn't without its charm.

"Here. Stand right here," she said from the center of the once strong house. What stones remained in place had obviously been placed with precision, enough to still stand erect against the ensuing weight of nature. "Tell me you can't feel it."

There was an air of dignity which lived in the remains, a gentle air of peace. He found himself smiling.

"Look at the light Derick, it's almost as though it's being played off of a ball of mirrors. Like in a dance hall."

While Samantha set about trying to capture on film exactly what she would want to commit to canvas, her fiancé aimlessly shuffled his feet through the layers of long dropped leaves.

"Yes, remarkable," he said absently "How much longer?" He shot his arm out from his thick tweed jacket and checked his watch.

"How much longer what?" Lowering her camera from her eyes she fully focused on Derick who was now seemingly lost in his own admiration. "Do you need to be somewhere? Derick, just look about you. This is beautiful."

"What?"

"This. Everything.".

"Yes, right. Well, it feels very nice, I suppose."

"Well, yes, compared to a computer bank and the to-ing and fro-ing of workaday London I would expect it would."

"Perhaps." He watched Samantha as she was looking for her shots. Allowing himself to relax and perhaps take in some of the ancient country around him, he did manage to see the rusting leaves of autumn. He watched as Samantha scurried about the area. Setting himself down on a damp bed of moss he leaned his back against a jumbled offering of fallen logs and bathed in the warmth of the lowering sun. The young man began to notice the sensuous form and figure of the young woman in front of him.

"What?" she asked with a smile.

"Nothing."

"Nothing," she said, "Judging by the look on your face it certainly is something. You look as though you've swallowed the canary."

"Do I? It's just that you're so busy trying to capture the light you can't see that you're part of it." The energies from The Black House had found their mark on the smiling young man. "You're just so lovely."

"Why I thank you, sir." She blushed.

"In fact," he said trying to sound like one of the farmers he had not long ago held in disdain, "I wouldn't mind snapping the elastic on your knickers, I wouldn't."

With mouth agape and eyes flashing, Samantha stared in disbelief at what she thought was an overture from her well starched fiancé.

"Steady on," she said, smirking.

Throwing all caution to the winds, Derick rose to his full height and slowly approached her. "Perhaps your pictures can wait." He slowly removed her camera from around her neck, right hand slowly brushing against her breasts.

"Derick!" she laughed. "This isn't... well, you've never... not that I'm complaining, mind you."

He started to kiss her neck, slow kisses.

The need to capture that certain light fell by the wayside as the two slowly lowered to the forest floor. Wrapping her arms around him, Samantha leaned back onto the damp bedding and drew him on top of her. "I just knew that this trip was going to do you wonders," she said as he began to unbutton her flannel shirt.

Samantha and Derick heard the oddly dressed man before they saw him. Sounding like a large animal charging headstrong through the broken limbs and twigs of the forest undergrowth, he stumbled around the side of the foundation. He was dressed in a suit of red, wore gray rubber boots and appeared not to have shaved in the past few weeks.

The two lovers froze where they lay, not knowing if this red apparition was ghost, a homeless wanderer or a mass murderer.

Falling onto his side, the man rolled against the remains of the foundation and slowly, hand over hand, began to pull himself up. Wet brown leaves were plastered against the red suit. He started to make a noise.

"My God," Samantha whispered.

"Shh, he doesn't see us."

Very deliberately the man ran his hands across the smooth stones of what was left of the wall. He started to whimper as he slowly walked along the face of crumbling structure.

"What in God's name is he doing?" Samantha whispered.

"Have no idea, but it doesn't appear as though he's in the mood to kill anyone right now."

The man's whimpers gave way to gentle sobs which were soon overtaken by rolls of laughter and tears. The man threw his head back with glee and sank down onto his knees. He appeared to be reaching out and hugging the thin air. Half laughing, half crying, the man dressed in red fell onto his back, hugging his chest with great sobs of delight.

"I think we best leave him on his own," Derick whispered as he tried to slowly rise to his feet.

Grabbing his pant leg and trying to pull him back down to the soft damp earth Samantha clearly felt otherwise. "Discretion being the better party of valor and all that."

"He who fights and runs away?" Derick pleaded.

Going nowhere for now, the two tried to take shelter behind what broken gray limbs and shrubbery they could. Dropping his arms beside his body, the man in red lay on his back on the leaf-covered forest floor, slowly twisting his body from side to side. His great joy of moments earlier was erased by struggle and conflict. Arching his back, he writhed in silent pain, kicking out with his feet to propel himself across the forest floor. As though he were no longer capable of standing, let alone walking, the strange man in red was tryng to move on his back like a snake. Flailing out and grabbing desperately at dead and exposed roots he was slowly dragging himself toward the slick embankment which he had earlier walked down.

"God, look at his face." Samantha grabbed onto Derick's

coarse tweed jacket. "He looks like he's having a heart attack!"

Just then the man arched his back violently and once again reached out with stiff arms, only now his grasp was extended toward the blue sky above. With what appeared to be a final breath he screamed, "No!"

Cringing, the two recoiled in horrific fright.

"I can't say as my heart's up to this." Derick once again tried to stand for an quick departure and once again he was pulled back down to the forest floor by his fiancee.

"Look," she said, pointing toward the man.

What the lank Englishman saw was enough to cement him in place. "Good God, Sam, he's an epileptic!"

What the two now watched was as macabre as terrifying. The strange man's head was suddenly and violently thrown from left to right, a froth of pink and yellow discharge was pouring from his mouth and nose. Violently he clawed at the air above him. Mixed with the putrid mucous which foamed about his mouth were deep and pitiful eruptions of raw sound. His guttural howls seemed rooted in fear, a fear which was slowly being quelled by dying energies.

Samantha crossed the few yards between her spot of safety and landed at the man's side. The man was clearly dying if not already dead.

"Derick get over here!"

"Sam, don't touch him."

"Get over here," she said, but her fiancé sat frozen in place, staring with repulsion at the man in front of him, a repulsion which the young girl was far too involved in. "Now, damn it!"

Landing by her side and looking down at the man in red, Derick found that he had to very deliberately fight wave after wave of nausea. The man's face was slowly turning blue. Samantha tried to wipe away some of the yellow foam which was slowly snaking out of the man's nose.

"Good Christ, look at this," she said as she noticed his ears, which began to trickle small rivulets of blood. "I've got to clear his nasal passages. Stick your finger in his mouth and see if he's swallowed his tongue." Derick stared at her for several seconds, again not registering her request. "Derick, check his mouth."

The tall Englishman began to stand.

"Check his mouth, Derick," she said.

"No, really, this is too much. The man is obviously dead. Leave him Sam"

"As far as I can tell he is not dead and if you don't get down here and help me he most likely will be dead. Now help me."

Torn between his repulsion at the man's oncoming death and his own want to help Samantha, the lanky investment advisor continued to backpedal toward the road. "He's dead now. Leave him, Sam, and that's an order damn it."

Samantha turned slowly toward her fiancé. "Your order?"

"Yes, now leave him and stop playing at nurse. You could catch a disease or something."

"Piss off." She once again turned her attention to the man on the ground.

"Sam!"

"At least go and call for help. Can you do that?"

The Englishman dug far into his inside pocket and produced an flip-top cellular.

"You told me you left that in London?"

"Well, even so. You wouldn't be getting your help now, would you?"

"Bloody wanker," the girl mumbled as she quickly removed her coat and tried to give the dying man some warmth. Stripping off his red outer coat she realized for the first time that it was a garment far from home. "This is rain gear," she said, tugging at the stiff fabric, "and rain pants. Where in God's name did you come from?" Trying to get his wet gear off with one hand she attempted to administer to his needs with the other. "Oh, god," she said, noticing that the yellow mucus was now turning pink. "What is wrong with you?"

Again the man retched great amounts of mucus.

"Derick… call for help!" she hollered out. Hearing no answer she took a quick glance behind her. Derick Smeeton was nowhere to be found. "I should have known." She turned her attention back to the man in her arms. "You won't die. That I promise you, you will not die. Just don't ask me how I can promise." She again tried to free some of the mucus from his throat. "I haven't lied to you yet have I?"

In an unconscious stupor the man retched once again.

"Well, now, that's your opinion, isn't it."

CHAPTER 26

"Samantha Southworth?"

The young women looked up from her magazine to the sister dressed in her muted hospital blues. For the past three hours Samantha had been reading the same boring account of Hollywood's Academy Awards. As much as she hated hospitals and their crowded and contagious waiting rooms, she felt obligated to stay. Apart from a nametag in his red foul weather gear and a crumpled work order for a "Yacht *Curlew*" in a pocket, the dying man gave no clues as to who he was or where he had come from. Perhaps when he awoke, if he awoke. Samantha had ridden in the ambulance and with what information she could provide had admitted the stranger to the emergency room.

"Yes?"

"Doctor will see you now. If you'll follow me?"

Walking behind the sister, Samantha passed along through shining white halls where people either dying or coming back to life lay behind closed white curtains. This was not how she had intended to spend her day and judging by her fiancé's pitiful reactions to the emergency she was starting to feel that it was not with him that she was wishing to spend her life. That could wait, yet the biter tang of disappointment and cold truth was still in her mouth.

She was led into a small dark cubbyhole hole of an office where behind a cluttered and undersized desk sat a tired man.

"I apologize for the mess. Do sit down," the doctor said.

Squinting in the dark, Samantha found a stiff-backed wooden chair to the side of the desk. Before she sat down she removed a small stack of brown and white journals and raised them up with a questioning look.

"Ah, yes, sorry." The old man half rose from his torn leather chair. He took the stack and placed it on yet another stack.

"Well, we seem to have a mystery here which we hope you can shed some light on." He started to fold back the pages of a medical chart. He took a pair of tortoise shell glasses from the chest pocket of his doctor's smock. "His name is Paul Dwyer and as far as we can tell he must live on or around a boat named *Curlew.* This boat seems to be from the States." Being careful not to dislodge a broken temple from a thick wrapping of tape, he gingerly removed his glasses and looked at the girl. "Does any of this sound familiar?"

Samantha slowly shook her head.

"I'm afraid I'm blind as a bat. Really should get them fixed," the man said as he delicately slid his reading glasses back onto his thin face. Taking several seconds to glance at Paul's chart he continued. "You say that you found him in the woods?"

"That's right."

"Out past Ellison Lane?"

"Yes."

"And how far would you say that was from the water?"

"I haven't the foggiest. I'm here on holiday, I'm afraid I don't know the area very well."

Removing his glasses with great care, the man neatly folded them up and slid them back into his pocket. Her eyes having adjusted to the light she could now see that the doctor was actually a young man, perhaps in his early thirties. It was the exhaustion and fatigue which painted the age around his inquisitive eyes.

He pursed his lips. "I won't bore you with all the mumbo jumbo but I will tell you what we have. Judging from the results of the various routine tests as well as the x-rays, you seem to have been an angel sent by heaven."

"Meaning?" Samantha asked, somewhat confused.

"Meaning you saved his life."

"From what?"

He smiled. "From drowning."

"From what?"

"It appears as though had you not come along when you did, your man would have drowned."

"Drowned? In what? There wasn't any water."

"Well, yes," the doctor admitted, "but nonetheless here we are." He held an X-ray up to the desk light. "This white area represents pockets of water. We ran all the standard tests. He was in shock, he was suffering from hypothermia. He fits the profile completely." He held up a handful of paperwork. "The tests don't lie. If you hadn't have come across him he would most assuredly have drowned."

"Drowned. In the middle of the forest." With a short burst of laughter, Samantha dismissed the implausible situation. "How is he now?"

"He's stable. He's being monitored and for now we'll observe him closely for the next four to six hours. If things look fine after that he'll be discharged."

"To where?"

"Well that's where we thought you might help us. My rather obvious guess is that he must be off a boat and judging by what we found in his pocket I'd say that it was U.S. in registry. Plymouth has only a handful of boatyards. We can turn this over to the authorities but we wanted to consult you first."

Samantha thought as she sat there. She still had Derick to deal with. If he wasn't willing to help her with the man's life he most assuredly wasn't going to be interested in finding out where the stranger belonged.

"I have some obligations here in town. I don't know. As I said, I'm not familiar with the area and am only here on holiday." Samantha only hoped all of this didn't sound as weak and as lame to the young doctor as it did to her.

A beeping from the man's coat pocket announced that he was being paged elsewhere in the hospital, and out of blind reflex he reached into his pocket, withdrew the small black unit and passed a quick glance at the rectangular screen.

"Well, either way he will most probably be discharged tomorrow morning. It would save me and I would imagine him as well untold paperwork and inconvenience if we didn't have to notify the authorities." He stood from behind his desk, quickly grabbed a piece of paper from the clutter and jotted down some numbers. He handed it to the girl. "This first one is the number for the hospital."

"And the second?" she asked while walking back out into the harsh light of the hallway.

"That's for our government offices in Plymouth."

His beeper paged him again. The young doctor started off down the hall, onto his next emergency, his next patch job, his next family conference. "That's where you'll find immigrations, at Government Centre in town. They know of all the arrivals and departures on foreign vessels into and out Plymouth Harbor."

"You're assuming an awful lot, aren't you?" she asked to his disappearing back. Through the comings and goings of the hospital hallway he shouted back over his shoulder. "Miss Southworth, you saved the man's life. I'd expect that you'd want to see that he was delivered home safely. Good day."

Samantha watched as the man disappeared into the maze of medical confusion.

"Oh, absolutely. Just like a lost kitten I get to keep him," she said to no one in particular. She flipped the piece of paper back and forth between her fingers. She hadn't noticed before but the front of her flannel shirt was stained with a pink and yellow foam. "Lovely, simply lovely."

Finding her way back out thorough the labyrinth of halls, Samantha arrived back where she had come from hours earlier. Stepping outside she was hit with a stiff cold wind laden with ocean moisture. The deeply angular shadows of the fading autumn day pressed in around her as she started the search for a cab. Turning her wool collar up against the breeze she realized that she never got her jacket back. She still had Derick to deal with. Not wanting to be involved or being too squeamish to help the dying man was one thing, deserting her in the woods was another. I guess I should be thankful that he called the emergency in, she thought. Yes, on a phone which he swore up and down that he would leave in London. Derick's small and unresponsive behavior had spoken volumes to the girl. The man waiting back at the cottage would have some explaining to do, but that all seemed secondary to Samantha right now. She could not care less if he were waiting for her or not. The events of the day were sorting themselves out and surprisingly she found her concern for Derick at the bottom of the pile. The black rectangular shape of an English cab pulled up in front of the hospital entrance. Samantha reached for the door and got in.

"Where to miss?" the driver asked.

"Across the bridge. Three Chimneys Lane."

"Us'll be right," he said and started the meter.

Sinking into the deep back seat Samantha continued to play with the piece of paper with the phone numbers.

"You know where the government buildings are?" she asked.

"Cross town."

Taking one last look back toward the hospital she couldn't help but feel akin to the man lying under observation. Whether he'd ever be aware of it, they had shared a hauntingly emotional afternoon together and at that particular moment neither of them had any real place to go. "Oh, hell," she said. "In for a penny and all that."

"What's that, miss?" he asked, looking at her in the rearview mirror.

"Nothing." It wouldn't take more than a few minutes and she was in no particular rush to be anywhere. "Driver, change of plans. Take me to the Government Centre."

What can it hurt, she thought. He was probably nothing more than your run of the mill ax murderer wanted by Scotland Yard, the CIA and Interpol.

Inside I was beaming. The shoe was very slowly being taken off the wrong foot and about to be placed smack dab on the foot where it rightly belonged. Madeline's face was as blank as it could be and I was enjoying every moment.

"You know that feeling that's in your head right now?" I said. "Like your brains are going to spin right out of your ears and take off for points unknown?" My question was dripping with a complete and well deserved coating of I-told-you-so and for the first time in I don't know how long I felt vindicated, justified. Now it was someone else's turn to play the befuddled clown. "Well get used to it because that's what I've been living for the past few weeks."

We had gotten the call at the bed and breakfast where we had been enjoying a prolonged version of both. Per her orders, I needed and took a sabbatical from *Curlew* and all that she reminded me of. I had handed the yard her keys, instructed them to do an inspection on the suspect stern tube and to fax Mr. Colin Jasperson with the particulars, in either English pounds or good old green backs, their choice.

Madeline and I had had long conversations about Paul and his demise and for reasons politic I falsely started to acquiesce to her insistence that he had indeed drowned. In an very unspoken sense, we had agreed to disagree, or at least I had. Madeline was convinced that she was scoring major points and she was, but not about Paul. After receiving the call from the yard her face had registered a very nonplussed expression, which I was comforted to see that she was still sporting. The voice on the other end had assured Madeline that Paul Dwyer was now recovering in St. Paul's emergency room and he appeared to be making a full recovery.

"That look on your face is reserved for after you've seen the ghost," I said.

Madeline's body slid against mine as the cab driver dove into the fray in the traffic roundabout. The fact that he was exceeding the speed limit, any speed limit, wasn't so much of a concern as the fact that he was entering the circle from the wrong direction, at least for we Americans.

"Just don't look," I said to Madeline. "It's a whole lot easier that way."

Grimacing with each rolling turn she said, "Well it can't be that Paul Dwyer, our Paul Dwyer."

"And why not?"

"Because he's dead."

"Not according to some."

"Well," she said, which is what some folks say when the feel the corner pressing up against their back. "We'll see now won't we?"

"Oh indeed we shall." I said.

At the admitting entrance to St. Paul's, I hastily paid and over-tipped the taxi driver and all but raced Madeline for the front desk. Behind automated glass doors a security guard and receptionist were discussing the ramifications of their hospital's new addition, an addition which was going to streamline the admission and release procedures. Madeline and I waited patiently while these two drew their predictions to and end. Perhaps streamlining should have started at the grass roots level.

"Yes?" The woman smiled from behind her desk.

"We're here to see Paul Dwyer." I couldn't help but beam at Madeline.

Looking up from her computer screen, Midge smiled. "Mr. Dwyer would be in room twenty-one in the Huntington Wing. Just follow the red line to the lifts and go to the second floor."

A walking race is what is was. Madeline and I wasted no time following the red line through the serpentine maze of corridors, past hospital gurneys laden with mounds of white bedding, under which patients were recuperating or waiting to recuperate. We passed along side nurse's stations where well read and well paid doctors looked down their pointed noses through half-framed spectacles at charts and said, "Hmm," and "Yes, yes, right, right." We slid around yellow signs warning that the floor was still wet and to watch your step. I pressed the button for the second floor, looked down and smiled at Madeleine. Perhaps she was right, perhaps it wasn't our Paul Dwyer, but judging from the description which she was given over the phone, the odds were pretty good in my favor.

The elevator came to a heavy stop at the second floor, and as the doors opened I found that my sense of vindication was slowly being overtaken by a sense of urgency. Up until now I had been basking only in the thought that finally, after all this time, I was going to be proven right, that feeling was taking a back seat to a sense of joy and hope that the next Paul Dwyer I was soon to see was going to be mine.

Exiting the elevator we stood in the middle of the hallway, which looked just like the other hallways – white, narrow and occupied. Madeline looked one direction while I looked the other.

"I think it's this way," she said. Madeline's motherly concern told me that my sense of anticipation was leaking out. So much was riding on what we were to see, let alone my own sanity. Taking me by the hand, she started leading me down to the brightly lit corridor to the right. I found that we were both counting the room numbers aloud.

"Looks like it's at the far end," she said, dragging me after her.

Pulling up short in front of room number 21, we both paused.

"You ready for this?" she asked.

"The question is, are you?" I said with false bravado.

She nodded. "Let's go meet Mr. Paul Dwyer then."

And with that we walked into a semi-private hospital room.

"My God," Madeline said.

"My words exactly!" I laughed. "My God damned words exactly! I knew it, I God damn knew it!"

Nothing, absolutely nothing could have proven a sweeter sight than what lay before me tucked snugly in his hospital bed. Forget the intimidation of the monitors, tubes and wires. Never mind the fact that Madeline had spent the better part of the past three days convincing me that I had to deal with Paul's death. Video tapes? Forget about them, they obviously failed to grasp the truth of the matter and simply lied to us. Three feet in front of me was a sight which could not have been sweeter. Paul Dwyer was very much alive and well and judging by the devilish glint in his eye had a few things to share.

"My, my, my," I said. "Mr. Dwyer I presume. Long time no see."

Paul grinned his world famous tight-lipped grin and beamed at me. His eyes slowly moved over to look at Madeline and then looked back upon me. Quickly he did a double-take and once again looked at Madeline. His monobrow arched in curiosity. I think that if he had had the strength he would have rubbed his eyes, shaken his head and taken another good long look at her. Releasing a big sigh, he once again focused on me. The three of us simply stood there, all dumbfounded for their own reasons. As though I expected to find an answer there I looked down at Paul's chart. The only consolation I found was Paul's name, which oddly enough reassured me that when I looked back up I was going to see my friend in bed, alive.

Madeline looked at me and exhaled. "Well..." She was every bit as flabbergasted as I was, though for different reasons; she thought that he was dead but he was obviously very much alive, while I knew that he was alive and had been about to throw in the towel and agree that he was dead. I was delighted to see that he was indeed still alive, and that I wasn't crazy as England's very own King George. As for Paul, he just kept silent and continued to beam at us from the comfort of his narrow bed.

After what seemed more like minutes than seconds it was Paul who actually broke the silence.

"Well, anybody seen anything of a great white whale?"

Compared to that question, all of Winston Churchill, Patrick Henry and Neil Armstrong's spoken words combined fell to nothing more than pithy observations.

Where could we begin. There was a big white elephant standing between the three of us and somebody had to approach it. I was at a loss for words.

"You two look as though you're ready to announce your engagement." Madeline observed.

"Oh, I'd marry him in a heartbeat beat if he asked me," I said, "but he's just too undependable. Now you see him, now you don't, now you see him again." After pulling up a chair for Madeline, I propped myself at the foot of his bed and stretched my legs down toward his head. We stared at each other.

"So?" I said "What's up?"

And with that Paul started an accounting of a dream so remarkable that because I had been there to see a great deal of it, I found my blood running cold once again.

"I don't know, Chris. It's as though I went to sleep. It's like I was watching myself from below the surface of the water... sort of like an out of body experience, but I was following, under the boat."

Whatever it was that Paul was trying to tell us was not easy for him. The memories of what he had gone through provided a visceral reaction. His eyes became hard, searching wildly about the room they tried to find just the right words. He spoke of voices which had called and coerced from beneath *Curlew's* hull, voices which had spoken to him a few days before the whales had started to scream.

"I never told you about any of this. If I couldn't explain it to myself, how could I expect you to understand?" Here he paused to gather his thoughts. "Chris, I saw things, sights… Jesus, the dead." He closed his eyes. "They were all around us. Oh, God." Unconsciously Paul began to rub at his hand, the left one which up until now he had insisted was useless.

"Forget about it for now." I said.

He looked at me. "Do you know what it's like to feel like bait? As though there were a legion of fish out there who were all vying for my body, all wanting a piece of my flesh. They don't die, you know. They wait, just like they do on land. She was the only one who had the strength and determination to bite and stay on the hook." Paul raised his good right hand to his face to hide a sudden burst of tears and grief. "Fuck, what's happening to me?"

Madeline slid toward the side of his bed and started to stroke his jet black hair.

"Paul, whatever happened, it's over. You have to know that it's over."

"Oh, Christ, maybe… maybe. Ah, look..." He was doing his best to suck up the pain and confusion which was tearing at him. "I guess I need to sleep or something." Reaching down to his bedside he pressed the nurse's call button on his intercom cable. We continued to reassure him that it was still early days yet and that once his body became settled from whatever hell he had gone through he would gain a better grip and understanding of his predicament. After a cursory check of his vital signs, the arriving nurse felt it best to call an early end to visiting hours and let him get his rest.

I stopped to get a quick cup of tea from the hospital cafeteria. Madeline and I sat quietly looking about at the small groups of doctors.

"What do you make of all that?" I asked.

"Right now I'm not too sure what to make of anything."

I sipped at my tea. What a wonderful country; even in the fast food lanes of institutional lunch rooms they are civilized enough to offer Earl Grey.

"That's the first time in two weeks I've heard anything like sense come from his mouth, and he still wasn't all here, right?"

"Perhaps he was under too long. I don't know. I'm sure the doctors have some information."

I couldn't help but laugh. "Strange, ain't it? Try being offshore with that."

We continued to sit and separately digest what we had experienced. As the moments went by I was feeling more and more relief, simply because Paul was alive. Madeline, however, was feeling the pressure of the unexplained. As we sat and tried to reassemble the parts, a soft, lyrical, voice broke our silence.

"I'm sorry to interrupt, but I was told that you were Paul's friends." Samantha Southworth switched a bouquet of flowers into her left hand. "I was told that perhaps you might have some questions."

Introductions were made, more tea was ordered and the lovely brunette in the heavy blue sweater filled us in on her part in this on-going curiosity. The comely Miss Southworth, laden with one of the most beautiful bouquets of fresh-cut flowers I had seen, at least in the past month, told us the circumstances in which she and her soon-to-be ex-fiancé had found my friend.

"It's as I told the doctors. As odd as it may sound, he appeared as though he had just been pulled out of the ocean and was exuberant about it. He wasn't really conscious but was clearly on some agenda."

"Well, you truly were an angel," Madeline said. She gave me

a quick look. "We obviously are very thankful for you being where you were when you were. I'm only sorry that your friend wasn't there for you when you needed him."

"Oh, no worries there. Derick is a complete prig. He showed me his true colors, whatever shade of yellow that might be." Samantha poked her nose through her original air of formality and started to relax. "When I get back to London he most certainly will be hearing from me."

"We don't have much to offer." Madeline looked at me and laughed. "In fact we have all but officially run out of money and as far as I can tell have absolutely no way to pay for any of this," she said as she gestured about her, "but we'd be honored to have you come and dine aboard the good yacht *Curlew* as our guest this evening, providing you have no other plans."

"I'm so sorry, but I have to be back in London early tomorrow morning. I was simply going to drop these off to your friend and be on my way to the rail station."

"Well, another time I guess," said Madeline. "Maybe someday we'll find ourselves in London."

After a grateful exchange of hugs, phone numbers and addresses, we headed back to our small B&B while Paul's savior hailed a taxi for the station. Madeline and I were truly down to our last few pennies here and decided to walk the five miles or so back to our lodgings and move aboard *Curlew*.

Once back aboard it wasn't long before we were in my bunk, wrapped in each others arms finding comfort and love as we started to brainstorm about our immediate future… like tomorrow. Thanks to Madeline and her behind the scene efforts, we had several days until our flight back to the States and at this point we were none too sure if it was going to be a party of two or three.

"I don't want to leave until the doctors give Paul a clean bill of health," I said. After all we had been through there was no way that I was going to abandon my friend and leave him in the care of doctors I didn't know, no matter how competent they might have been.

"Well, what if they don't release him?"

"Then we stay, I stay, anyway."

"How? What are you planning on doing for money?" Madeline rested her beautiful head in the soft crook of my neck. The gentle pressure of her warm breath against my skin made rational thinking very difficult.

"Well, I'm getting to that," I said, "You see, all we have to do is actually get some."

"Well," she said, "that's a terrific plan, a real crackerjack of a plan. While you're at it, get some for me. Not too much mind you, just enough to eat."

"I can always call Ellie."

"Have your big sister bail you out? Don't mention my name."

"Credit cards?"

"Mine's maxed. Last minute tickets aren't cheap, you know."

I remembered that I was presently between credit cards. "Well, any suggestions?" I slowly rolled her closer to me. "What would you have me do?" I slid my leg between hers.

"Do just what you're doing Skipper. Keep on doing just what you're doing. Today we're fine and everything's peachy."

"And tomorrow's not here yet," I mumbled to myself. "All's kind of well that ends kind of well."

Madeline reached up with her hand and gently pulled me down to her.

"I am never going to let you play out of the yard again."

After a while Madeline and I fell asleep locked in our new love, a sleep so sound and sudden that we didn't hear the dock manager slip aboard and deliver the freshly arrived fax.

"You want a laugh? Read this." I said as sat on the corner of Paul's hospital bed.

My friend had made a drastic change for the better during the night and from a physical point of view was clearly out of the woods. Mentally though he still had memories of being in that over- grown forest, flailing about the crumbled foundation where he was found. He hadn't gained any recollection of the past few weeks but was able to describe the area where he was found to a

T. Earlier in the morning I had had a quick conference with his attending doctors and we had all agreed that he would be much happier back in his own bed and that there really was no cause for him to stay in hospital. "We'll need to see him once or twice in the next week or so, but that's simply precaution. Your friend has been through a lot and perhaps has written a new chapter for himself in the texts, but he's fine to leave."

All of this was good news, very good news. What wasn't good news was that his own bed was 3,000 miles to the west, we hadn't any money to stick around and his clean bill of health came only from the physician. The psychiatrist had a slightly differing opinion. It was his determination that Paul needed to get his feet firmly back onto some relatively safe mental plane, and as long as his mind was filled with the horrific images and events of the past few weeks, it would be best for him to meet with him some more over the next month. We both agreed in principle and asked the doctors to start to arrange for his release.

The fact that we weren't entirely free to make our flights back wasn't exactly what we wanted to hear at that moment. Actually we were looking for something more along the lines of a clean bill of health. It was because of this I felt that the fax from Jasperson would lighten the moment.

"Oh, right." Paul beamed as he read it. "Bloody cheeky."

"You've been here too long. 'Bloody cheeky'?"

He stopped reading and briefly looked up. "What?"

"You said 'bloody cheeky'. You're beginning to sound like one of them."

"Did I?" Paul continued to read as he very consciously tried to tuck his left hand under the covers. I agreed with the doctors. Paul still had a few wrinkles to work out and it was best that we hang around until then.

Our very absent owner faxed us that he was going to hold us personally responsible for the "extreme damage" which the yard found around the stern tube, damage which would most probably cost several thousand dollars to correct. What brought the biggest smile to Paul's face was the phrase Bristol fashion, as in "... when Curlew left Pachico's yard she was in Bristol fashion."

An outdated and telling phrase which meant best of the best.

"Bristol fashion?" Paul threw his head back and laughed. "What the hell has he been reading? I love it, Bristol fashion. Abaft, ye mateys, stand by to swab the conigular bolts. Bristol fashion," he mumbled again. "Did you fax him back?"

"Yeah, I told him to come and get us." I handed Paul a copy of my reply. With that we started the procedure to get Paul back out on to the street and back to the vessel in question. He scheduled an appointment with the psychiatrist who had been working his case and promised that he'd be in the man's office promptly at 4 p.m. in two days.

"And how are you going to manage this?" I asked as we started to head back toward *Curlew*.

"The same way I'm managing to pay for the hospital visit. I'm not, I'm letting the Queen pick up the tab. National Health." The fact that Paul wasn't an English citizen didn't faze him in the least. He was determined to either place his hospital costs in the hands of the English government or tie it up with his own U.S. insurance for years.

"A rep from the business department came in to see me last night. She was very accommodating. She said she'd try to submit it to National Health and if that failed she'd flood my insurance company with paperwork."

We were still debating the issue when we arrived back aboard. Madeline had spent most of the day alone and judging by what lay before us she had wasted not a moment. For all intents and purposes, the good yacht *Curlew* looked as though she were ready for her long winter's nap. Running gear was stripped off of her decks and stowed below, all deck hardware had been pulled, lubed and tucked away in boxes sealed with tape. Two large boxes with signed receipts sat on either settee. Packed carefully and very professionally in these sat *Curlew's* electronics. The receipts taped to the front were to assure one and all that the yard now held responsibility for them. Forward her sail locker was stuffed to the gills and threatening to overflow with blue sail bags. The food that was left was stowed in a few boxes which sat out in the cockpit beside our own personal duffels. Madeline had worked wonders, for *Curlew* showed no visible signs of having just made an ocean crossing. She was ready for the travel lift's straps. Even her shrouds were loosened to help facilitate a quick and clean removal of the mast.

"Jesus," I whistled as I looked about. "This is remarkable."

"Quite," said Paul. He didn't look entirely happy to be back aboard. His eyes slowly searched throughout the boat as thought they were trying to find an answer for a question which they didn't even know they had.

"Well, I guess we'll make our flight after all," I said. "And you won't be having any heart-to-hearts with your shrinks."

"I don't know about that," Madeline said as she taped up a final box. "Here, we'll need this." I took the box from her and placed it next to our duffels in the cockpit. "Actually you're wrong on both accounts."

"Meaning?"

"Well, we don't have to worry about flights or missing doctor's appointments."

Curlew gently dipped to her starboard lines and I heard footsteps overhead. Our eyes followed the deck above our heads.

"Nope don't have to worry 'bout a thing."

A pair of lovely legs descended down the companionway. I watched as Paul's face registered a slight blush of recognition and surprise at our visitor.

"Hi there, haven't packed the kettle yet, tea?" Madeline said. I looked at Madeline with the old familiar curiosity.

"I called Sam for a little advice last night, between the two of us we came up with quite a plan."

"Yes, that would be nice, thank you. By the way, you were right. Received this late last night." She handed Madeline a piece of thermal paper on which one usually finds a fax. With that, she headed in the direction of Paul and made herself comfortable on the settee.

"Paul," I said, "meet your angel from heaven."

"You look wonderful," she said referring to Paul's recuperative powers

“Ah, you too,” Paul said. It was good to see that Paul’s experience didn’t leave him with any character disorders. His boyish charm was fully intact and not wasted on Miss Southworth.

“Why thank you,” she said blushing.

The awkward silence was broken by Madeline. “Why that son of a bitch,” she said as she read from the fax. “That lousy son of a bitch.”

“Who?” I said.

“I knew it. I damn well knew it.” Madeline was truly angry.

“What?” Paul and I said simultaneously.

Madeline slowly lowered the paper. Her eyes held pure contempt. “Jasperson,” she said. “I can’t believe this shit. Read this.”

Paul reached across my chest and grabbed the paper out of Madeline’s hand. After scanning it quickly his mood changed as abruptly as Madeline’s had. He stared at me.

“I can’t take much more mystery,” I said. “Somebody fill me in.”

“Seems we were set up pal, if all had gone according to plan you and I probably wouldn’t be here right now.”

I quickly snatched the paper from Paul’s hands. It was from Ellie’s firm back home. As I was reading, Paul started to fill Samantha in.

“It appears as though shortly before our departure,” he said “our owner had taken out triple hull insurance on *Curlew* as though he was not expecting her to make the crossing. He was planning on her sinking,” he said staring at me. “Chris’ sister Ellie has uncovered a wealth of information for us.”

I picked up where Paul left off and read bits and pieces from the fax, “Against the advise of several yards, *Curlew* should never have been put back into the water, let alone sailed across the Atlantic. According to Ellie, he had been warned by three yard managers.” I continued to read, “This not being bad enough, he picked up a ton of insurance on her, in the off chance that she sunk.”

“In this case, the off chance means the hoped for and very

likely chance." Madeline said.

The four of us stood and stared dumfounded. "How do you want to handle this?" Paul said.

I thought for a minute. If I knew my sister, not only was Colin Jasperson getting his affairs in order for an upcoming I. R. S. audit from hell, he was most probably getting ready to meet with various inter-state zoning boards, banking commissions and insurance investigators. There really wasn't much one could do seeing as no crime was committed, but if there was anybody out there who knew how to ruin someone's day, it was my wonderful and very protective little sister Ellie.

"We don't, I'm sure all is being taken care of for us. Now," I said clearing my throat, "back to matters at hand."

Another long pause, this time it was broken my Samantha. "Yes, well, Mad told me your situation and I love a challenge. I rang up my aunt and as long as I was willing to vouch for the three of you, she offered the use of her cottage until things settled out a bit more." Sam stole a very concerned and protective glance at Paul.

I really wasn't sure just what to say. Was I to be glad for their efforts or did this just add more confusion to a scenario which didn't have a whole lot of strength left to it. "That's great, we have a place to stay for the night. Thank you." I was still confused. Why did Jasperson not care if we went down with his ship? And now why was this woman back in Plymouth? She lived in London and she told us she had obligations there. "I'm afraid I have to be a bit blunt and rude here, but why are you still in Plymouth? I thought that your vacation was over."

"Well, it was, until Mad called. Besides, after what I had to deal with back in London, or rather who I had to deal with, I needed to get away.""

"Look, Paul has to stick around for a bit," Madeline said.

I started to say something but was cut short.

"I know that you guys are above all of this, but the fact of the matter is that he went through quite an ordeal. Look at his eyes, he needs some more time to piece things together."

I looked over at Paul, who still held a bit of a blush about his cheeks. I've known him for the better part of my life and I was quite surprised to see the look Madeline was talking about. Except she was wrong, it wasn't vacant, it was focused and direct and locked firmly on to our new friend Sam.

"This is all great, but we have no money remember?"

"Sam to the rescue again." Madeline nodded to Sam.

Sam took her cue and told us that at that very moment her aunt and paramour were doing something spontaneously for the first time in their staid English lives; they were packing their bags for a sudden chance to travel to the States. Sam had sold them our tickets. How they were going to travel under our names didn't seem to bother anyone at the moment. Sam assured all that her aunt was very securely plugged into the workings of Plymouth, and I guessed that this included those who worked behind desks in travel agencies.

"So what you're trying to tell us is that we not only have a place to stay, but some money on which to live as well?" Paul asked as he pushed aside a box and sat on the level settee.

"That's exactly what I'm telling you."

"Well, here we are." He smiled. "Fat, dumb and happy tourists."

"Precisely," said Sam. "And as such you are going to need a guide to show you all the wonderful sights of Southern England."

"As well as western, northern and eastern?" Paul asked from behind a soft smile.

"Time allowing," she said, sitting beside him.

"That seems to be one thing that I do have." Paul turned to me and exhibited some of the old Paul who had been missing for far too long. "Well, I say we get settled in auntie's cottage, pop some popcorn, and then watch some of the video tape that Chris shot of the crossing. You did shoot some video?" he asked.

I turned to Madeline.

Madeline looked down at her feet and scratched at her cheek. "Yes, somewhere there is video, but to tell you the truth, in the rush I've forgotten exactly which box it's packed away in. Now the way I see it we have two options here…"

And with that Madeline, Fee Pachico's right-hand woman, the lady who had only gotten me through one of the most horrendous and completely unexplainable events of my life, the woman who was becoming as much a part of my heart as the sea, started in on Paul, convincing him that we should distance ourselves from *Curlew* and the ocean for a bit and, with the help of Miss Southworth, we should immediately and thoroughly start to immerse ourselves in our new English lives.

There were no arguments from *Curlew's* happy but bedraggled crew.

Six statute miles to the south, as the crow flies, across green and rolling Cornish hills crosshatched by silvered hedgerows, rests the spirit of a young woman who, after having left a home of love and kindness, persevered against human debasement and beings unholy and once again found her way back. The crumbling ruins of a vine choked stone foundation transcended through time and housed the family Katherine Worthington fought so desperately to reclaim. Her vehicle was as ungainly as it was foreign, her delivery was as steadfast as it was focused. For all the years she struggled, the young English woman knew that, unlike our temporary forms, the spirit of family and love cannot be displaced.

After one hundred and sixty years and 3,000 miles, the Worthington family was once again whole. They sat in reunion gazing out across the Cornish hills which had changed so little in that time.

Out past the confines of Plymouth Harbor, past the imposing efforts of a modern day breakwater, down the English Channel and out into the night-black cold canyons of the deep, the great ocean stirs and waits, watches and cajoles. She rests for now, knowing that all those who muster the arrogance and dare to work her waters and reap her denizens know in the very midnight of their soul that she is only biding her time, waiting to welcome those who seek to challenge the reach.

ABOUT THE AUTHOR

Sprague Theobald's writing history includes two years as staff writer for the Showtime Network, five years as special features writer for an NBC affiliate where he received several national and international awards, not the least of which being his "Emmy". As a freelancer he's been published in The New York Times, and Horsdale & Shubart out of Canada. He brings to "The Reach" an intimate knowledge of the ocean in that he was a professional sailor and has amassed approximately 30,000 off-shore miles. He's raced for The America's Cup, as well as the Two Handed Trans-Atlantic Race from England to the U.S.